WITHOUT THE MOON

WITHOUT THE MOON

ACT ONE

LARISSA C. MOYER

LCM

Without the Moon
Copyright © 2024 by Larissa C. Moyer
All rights reserved.

No part of this publication may be reproduced, distributed, or transmitted in any form or by any means, including photocopying, recording, or other electronic or mechanical methods, without prior written permission of the author, except in the case of brief quotations embodied in critical reviews and certain other noncommercial uses permitted by copyright law.

All references to historical events, real people, or real places are used fictitiously. Names, characters, and places are all products of the author's imagination. Any resemblance to actual persons, living or dead, events or localities is entirely coincidental.

ISBN: 978-1-6653-0963-9 – Paperback
eISBN: 978-1-6653-0964-6 – eBook

These ISBNs are the property of BookLogix for the express purpose of sales and distribution of this title. The content of this book is the property of the copyright holder only. BookLogix does not hold any ownership of the content of this book and is not liable in any way for the materials contained within. The views and opinions expressed in this book are the property of the Author/Copyright holder, and do not necessarily reflect those of BookLogix.

Cover Designer: Anto Marr

First printing edition 2024

0 9 2 3 2 4

AUTHOR'S NOTE

Dear Reader,

Typically, I save this fun for the end of the book, but with my venture into new, darker territory, I feel a need to touch base before we dive in.

I've referenced Act One of *Without the Moon* as my "bridge" to dark romance, and while I do believe that to be true—even when we cross the bridge and cozy up in the shade below—it is likely some readers will still find it to be "too light" and some will find it "too dark."

When I tell you I've agonized over how to properly categorize this book—I truly have.

The darkness of Act One is not in the romantic relationship between the MCs, and I want to make sure that expectation is set. *Without the Moon* was originally supposed to be one book—whoops!—but now it is the first book in a series that will get progressively darker and darker.

Which is why I've decided to categorize this as dark romance. And Act One is by no means a "light" book, it just might be a different "dark" than you're used to reading. It is a trauma exploration and the nature of that alone can be highly triggering, so please make sure you've read the warnings available on my website and Instagram page.

The only specific warning I'll mention here is the sizable section after Chapter 46. I have written a summarized version of this scene for sensitive readers and it is available on my website.

However, if you feel safe to do so, I strongly encourage you to read the scene, as I believe it helps the reader feel the full emotional impact of the story. But if you choose to read the summary, please come back and continue to the Epilogue!

Either way, thank you for reading. I hope you enjoy Act One of *Without the Moon*.

Till the end,

To anyone who has ever hoped for better—found it,
lost it—and then summoned the courage to keep on driving.

"Do not go gentle into that good night."
—Dylan Thomas

To be haunted will be an awfully fucked adventure.

That's not the line, but it's the truth. *My* truth.

J. M. Barrie lived in a time before disclaimers. The tale of *Peter Pan* gives zero warning that if you *do* grow up, if you *do* pass that age we've deemed "adulthood," you'll learn that the world is a darker, *far* more fucked up place than you ever thought imaginable.

This is your warning. Stay in Neverland, kids.

I huff, but there's no humor—remembering now that in the stage show of *Peter Pan*, Captain Hook is usually played by the same actor who plays the kids' dad, so, pretty sure *that's* saying something.

Some people are probably lucky enough to not learn the world's dark realities *weeks* after they've graduated high school. Some people are lucky enough that they might only *ever* know about it through the safety of their television screen. Cautionary tales. Stories. The newest true-crime obsession.

But not me.

And unlike *Peter Pan*, I'm not being promised the adventure of death. I'm being forced to live *knowing* treacherous things exist.

Not in the shadows, not at night. The true darkness, the really sinister shit finds you in life's most unsuspecting moments, ripping away any semblance of belonging and comfort, shredding it to pieces, and then blowing it back out like confetti to poison the air.

And the haunting begins . . .

My chin dips and my eyes scrunch closed.

I have years *of existing ahead of me and . . .*

I don't think I can do it.

Not after this.

My eyes reopen as the plucked melody of the chimes to my music box slowly come to a stop, and the quiet stillness of the night threatens to break through my skin. The cuts and punctures around my wrist pulse, wrapped in bandages, and my fists tighten.

The edges of my vision are framed with the rest of my bedroom, dusted with the dim light from the lamp on my nightstand.

Focusing back on the music box, I see the paper I woke up with in my pocket yesterday morning sitting at the iron ballerina's feet. A weightless death sentence.

I visualize the words, but I can never make it past:

> Dear Pip,
> I'm leaving

White hot fury blinds me, and my throat rumbles, my glare deepening at the box.

How fucking dare him.

After what happened, after everything we've been through in our lives—

A deep breath pulls through my nose, trying to tame the anger shooting through my veins.

There's no denying it. It's *his* handwriting. I found it when I *somehow* woke up back in my bed yesterday morning. My wounds on my wrists were cleaned and wrapped, the horror from the night before still stabbing through me. The memory of the way he looked at me—*the last look . . .*

Dark hazel eyes, bloodshot. Broken. Repulsed.

I wince.

I can't think about that.

It's softening the anger—*twisting* it to despair. And the rage is what I need.

"Rage. Rage against the dying of the light."

A steady breath lifts my chest at the thought of Gram's voice, reciting her favorite Dylan Thomas poem. She said it in nearly every distressing *life moment.* Her affirmation to *carry on.*

My eyes move to my bedroom door, knowing she's asleep just across the hall.

I have to keep going. For her.

If nothing else, I have to carry on—*rage*—for the woman who holds the specks of debris that make up my heart.

But I won't be the same. The person that existed before, a vital part of her is missing, and a hollowing sensation carves deep into my chest—*deep, deep inside.*

That's where I'll keep it all, I think. I can't name what it is, but

I feel it—a place hidden even deeper than my heart—untouched and unseen by anyone.

I'll keep it all in here. The despair, the devastation, the anger, the gut-wrenching heartbreak that I'm too afraid to fully feel—*our memories. Anything* that threatens to break me while I'm still broken—I push it down into that deep place.

But before I tuck away the event that tore my life apart, the one that inspired my best friend—*my boyfriend*—to leave, I study it one last time.

As my memory blips and stutters to find the disturbing images, my shoulders tighten along with my throat as the sight comes into focus.

Me, him. The Man. The view.

But I'm not floating above us—not watching.

I'm the goddamn walls. I'm the floor. I hold the *whole scene* and keep it all in the walls of my arms.

It's fucking mine.

I'll keep it for years to come.

I'll examine it like a snow globe. Shake it up, once, twice—however many times a day. I'll watch the way the flurries swirl and fall. Admiring the pretty distraction and chaos until the snow finally drops. The swirly patterns will dissipate, and *this* scene will remain.

And as its keeper, I'll guard it in my walls, hold it tight to my chest, deep inside. And one day, after this necessary pause—*when I'm less fragile*—I'll take it all fucking back.

"MOTHERFU—" My curse is cut off as the car behind me lays on their horn—which is fair, seeing as I just crossed over four lanes of traffic on the jam-packed 101.

The commotion on the freeway is even louder with the car's top down, and it mixes with the big-band sounds of "Sell Out" by Reel Big Fish as it blares it through my speakers.

Karma strikes immediately, though, as I pull off the exit ramp and see a long line of cars at a dead stop.

Goddamn LA traffic. It's unpredictability and my poor time management have conspired to *fuck me* once again.

With my foot on the brake, I lift my chin, trying to look over the line of cars—seeing if it's an accident or just a random cluster-fuck—but I can't see anything past the red light at the end of the ramp.

I pick up my phone and tap out a quick message to Jackson, letting him know I'll probably be late . . . *er.* I'm already twenty minutes behind, and a groan escapes at the lecture that inevitably awaits me.

Ugh. And then there's the dislodging of the stick up his ass before he holds it like a baton while he reprimands me.

Usually I don't have a good excuse. But today's different. I knew it would be a hard day and I just . . . lost track of time.

I went back and forth about calling out, but I think the distraction will be good. And the money, of course.

My nose twitches through my inhale as the smells of Hollywood resettle in my senses.

After spending the majority of the day over in Venice, the varying scents of the city are more noticeable. I had gotten used to it, I guess, in my year of living out here but . . . I forgot how much I loved the smell of the ocean at home.

I sigh, pulling my eyes back in front of me—willing the traffic to *fucking move.*

It's torture. I could probably park my sweet little blue Cabrio right here and walk to the club faster than this.

My fuse is wearing thin. After spending the day in my own personal pity party, I just want to get through my shift. If I make enough money, I even promised myself that I could continue the party back at my apartment later with a solo bottle of sad-girl champagne.

My chest jumps as my phone buzzes, bringing me back to now, and I look down at the screen.

Jackson: Get here in 10
or I'm giving your spot to Cherry.

My mouth flattens.
Asshole.

And who the fuck is Cherry?

Stupid club names.

The Window is LA's most exclusive burlesque club. An institution for the upper echelon of Hollywood society where anonymity is required.

They claim the strict use of our club names is to protect our privacy from patrons, but I have a feeling it's mostly for the benefit of our famous and incredibly wealthy guests.

Either way, given my stellar ability to space out, it makes it all the more difficult to remember everyone's stupid names.

The stoplight finally turns green and relief lifts my chest. The Window is only a block away—but my heart suddenly drops.

The song changes. A few familiar, heart-wrenching, acoustic chords play through the speakers.

It's the song I never listen to.

The one I thought I had deleted.

My hand fumbles for my phone to switch it. *Not today.*

Not today. Not today. Not today.

My thumb trembles, finally managing to unlock the phone and stop the music. I breathe in, still not pushing the gas as my hands grip the steering wheel.

"You're okay, Paigey May."

Fuck. My eyes slam shut as a line of people pass by me in the left lane, yelling a variety of *"fuck yous,"* but I don't care—well, I *can't* care. All of my energy is going into breathing through the unexpected attack.

Please, stop. This day already sucks so fucking much.

I have no idea who I'm talking to in my head. But I aim the message at my heart, taking a series of practiced breaths.

After a moment, when I'm more calm, when the song fades, I let the voice resurface. *"You're okay, my girl."*

I'm okay, I tell myself, nodding. I open my eyes just as my foot abruptly taps on the gas, jerking the car forward and lurching my body with it. My seatbelt does its job, though, and then my pressure on the gas evens out.

Another deep breath. The breeze whips around me with my moderate speed, as I finally pull off the ramp and onto the street, the sky is a heavy set of pinks and oranges, with just a blip of yellow peeking over the mountains.

The Hollywood sign is illuminated in the distance, and I huff a small laugh. It always kind of reminded me of getting your name tattooed on your forehead.

Continuing to focus on my breathing, my heart rate begins to calm, and I mindlessly start to hum the first song that comes to mind.

"Daydream Believer" by The Monkees.

One of Gram's favorites.

My mind floats to all the times I'd hear the song sneaking its way through the walls while she was washing dishes. Or the countless times I'd hear her humming the chorus out in the back-yard while she tended to her garden.

The corners of my mouth tilt as I start to sing it—using her lyrics, of course. She always switched, "Sleepy Jean," to "Paigey May."

Her voice follows mine until my singing trails off just as I pull into the public parking lot south of the club. It costs five bucks, but whatever.

Only in LA do you have to pay for parking to go to work.

Maybe that's not true. But the parking laws are so fucking crazy here, that I'd rather not mess around and get a ticket or towed. And I like that it's not a far walk from the club since I'm typically not leaving until one or two in the morning.

Before I even park, I'm pressing the button on my dashboard to put the top back on the car.

She's an old 2002 Cabrio convertible and whenever I utilize the top-down feature, I feel a little bit like the asshole making an eighty-year-old woman stand up to give me a hug.

Once I hear the top lock in place, I grab my keys and bag, lock up my girl, then start quickly in the direction of the club.

After practically sprinting the last five hundred feet, I make it to the big brick building on the corner, but continue around to the back and I put in my code, 2496, on the keypad beside the door.

As soon as it turns green, I pull the door. Glancing down at my phone, I see it's been eight minutes since Jackson texted me.

I walk over to the tablet on the wall by the bathrooms and put in the same code—waiting for the green check to appear that says *IN* before I smirk.

Made it.

The building is huge. There's five different showrooms—the Saloon, Drawing Room, Great Hall, the Library, and then there's the Veranda upstairs for VIP events. I guess the check-in tablet is a way for management to know who's here and who's not.

I'm hereee, Jackson.

I snicker breathlessly to myself, before dropping my bag on my usual vanity seat, taking a second to catch my breath, still winded from my little bout of cardio.

"Hey, Blue," a girl . . . *Fuck. What the hell is her name again?* Is *that* Cherry?

I give her a quick, "Hey," back, but leave it at that. Clearly, I'm late, so I don't exactly have time to chat and it will save me the awkwardness of having to ask her name.

Not that I make a habit of getting to know anyone here, anyway.

Thanks to the club-names rule, Rio is the only person who even *knows* my real name—to everyone here, I'm known simply as Blue.

Real original given that my hair is blue. But I picked the name before the hair color.

Naturally blond, I started dyeing it about a year ago, and it's kind of fascinating the way the color takes to my hair. The first few days it's always a bit Smurf-ish, and after a month or so, it fades to an icy silver with a light blue hue.

I like it. It's weird.

I strip all of my clothes off, but do a quick peek around to see how many people are still in here. The doors open in ten minutes, so other than a couple of dancers still stretching by the doorway, the room is empty.

Quickly, I slide my wristbands and bracelets off, revealing the silvery-pink, puckered flesh around my wrists, and then replace them with the thick lace wrist cuffs Rio made me to go with my costume.

She's made me a few colors to go with different corsets. It's been an unspoken kindness she's done without ever mentioning it to me or asking questions—something I greatly appreciate.

My waist cinches as I tighten my plum-colored corset, giving my petite frame a slight hourglass effect. I pause on lacing it up once I reach my tits—I like to give them till the last possible minute to breathe.

Twisting my hips, I lift my barely-covered backside to give it a quick check, and my lips tilt into a smirk.

If I do nothing else in this life.

Rio's been working with me on new tricks and, thanks to most of them being of the *upside-down variety*, my once-flat ass is really starting to become something.

Without sitting down, I start in on my makeup. The big bulbed vanity lights give my pupils that little ring in the center, and I line my eyelids with some purple liner, making the blue in my eyes a nice blend between my corset and my hair.

Shaking out the icy blue strands, I use some spray to lift it up just a bit, but I'm a big fan of the bedhead look so I mostly leave it alone.

I flex my arms and dip one of my makeup brushes in some glitter, using it to outline the light definition in my arms—another thing that's gotten stronger thanks to my extra work with Rio. I mean, it's no heavy-weight champ bicep, but there's some faint lines of muscle.

And now it's become a preshow ritual.

Outlining my strength.

And Buffy knows, I'll need it tonight.

I pick up the tube of my darker lipstick, almost a cabernet color, and paint my lips real quick, then step back.

Bam.

Got it done.

I rub my lips together, like I'm mentally rubbing my snark into Jackson—who is nowhere to be seen—but that's to be expected.

I give him a lot of shit, but the guy works like a machine. I think he's ex-military or something, and it shows.

After one more look in the mirror, I pull down my corset, only to shove it back up, pushing my tits into little half-moon mounds on my chest, and then lace it up the rest of the way.

Checking the clock on the wall, I see that I have exactly *negative* minutes to warm up, and I groan, doing what minimal stretching I'm able to do as I start out the doorway and head out into the back hallway.

Performers use the smaller, back hallways during operating hours. It lends itself to the guest experience to not see us unless we're in place and ready to provide the *escapism* The Window promises.

My heart ticks up as I pass a few other performers, but I keep my head down and breathe through it.

For someone who is perpetually late, I cling hard to my habits. Getting ready, warm ups, driving routes. The small rituals that help me to keep track—to not forget shit.

Not warming up is going to cost me. Literally.

As I reach the door, I hear Simon making the announcement through the walls.

"Greetings, Eager Spectators," he teases through the sound system, and a loud applause roars. "Welcome to The Window— whether you're looking out or looking in, there's always a view."

Fuck. This is going to suck. But today was always going to suck.

CHAPTER 2
LINC

Bad ideas.

I don't indulge in them often—well, not physically, anyway—but here I am . . .

Sometimes it all just becomes too much—living in the walls of my fuckin' head.

A prisoner pacing the floors, out of space for tick marks on the concrete wall of his cell . . .

And *that's* when it happens.

Just below my skin starts to tingle, my heart takes flight, and the leash to my awareness frays.

The prisoner becomes a passenger.

Go, go, go.

Dangerous, bad ideas.

The trespassing kind. Just after midnight in a house with no electricity, no running water, no people. Like a thief that didn't understand the assignment.

But I knew the house would be empty. I wouldn't have come

if I expected anyone to be here. The bad ideas haven't toppled over into completely reckless.

Yet.

Standing in the darkness of an old, distantly familiar, abandoned kitchen feels slightly contradictory to that sentiment—but before I have time to think about it too much, my phone buzzes in my pocket.

I let it go. I happen to know that the only person who could possibly be calling me carries the risk of reason—and I don't *want* reason. I'm too amped up, and trying to *reason* with me right now, runs the risk of shoving *bad* into *reckless*.

So I'm hiding. And looking. Breathing. My lungs *kind of* contract, and through the dust, the haze . . .

Lemon, lavender . . . the smallest hint of Irish breakfast tea.

God, I've missed this house.

Darlene passed away a year ago. I wasn't there.

The last time I'd seen her—*the last time I was in this house—* was seven years ago. And I wish *so badly* I could remember what we talked about that day.

A fuzzy image flickers through my mind, but as soon as I blink it's gone.

My cheeks puff through a heavy sigh. Memories are weird for me. Like right now. I can feel my muscles relaxing, my heart evening out for the first time in what feels like hours—*maybe even all day*—but no specific memory comes to me.

It's still dark.

My feet inch me forward, knowing that another two steps will land me—

Bump.

The smallest *screech* pushes against the linoleum floor, and my mouth ticks up at the corner as a wave passes through me. The warmth of familiarity.

There are no silhouettes of my former life dancing around in the shadowscapes of the furniture. No echoing, ongoing, creepy laughter.

But there's *something*.

And I can *feel it*. Even in the dark. The house transcends this time tonight. I can *feel* the happiness, the warmth—my chest even tickles with the *feeling* of laughter, but it's like it fizzles out before it even makes its way to my throat.

My eyes adjust to the dark with the help of the small bit of moonlight spilling in from the archway leading out to the living room, and my eyes catch on a few mugs in front of me on the table.

My hip drags along the round perimeter of the table so that I'm standing in the soft muted light, scrutinizing the mugs when I suddenly see . . .

My mug. The one I'd used whenever I came over. It's dark, but I remember it's a forest green color—and I can faintly make out the simple design of two little peaks.

"It kind of looks like an M . . . " I said, holding up the mug.

"For Mmm-orrow," she said, holding the 'mmm' sound a little longer as she said my last name.

My smile grew, saying, "Or Mmm-ichaels," back to her the same way, nudging her shoulder.

It's a mountain, I think with a chuckle. We got it camping in Big Sur—should have been the first giveaway. Reaching for the mug, I pick it up, but my eyes widen.

I nearly drop it, but my hand snaps out, and I regain my hold, keeping my eyes locked on what shook me to begin with—*two oversized labels that look like old-school, No. 2 pencils.*

What the fuck?

Years of wear and tear have bent the edges, frayed the paper. One has my name, the other has hers. But the longer I stare at them, the torn edges slowly brighten and straighten, almost like sunlight's creeping over them . . .

The noise of the busy classroom tunneled as I stared at the big, pencil-shaped name tag, taped to the desk in front of me.

First day of first grade, and everyone was already going to know my stupid name.

Maybe my teacher would make me a new one.

"Linc-on," I heard a voice say just a couple feet away, pulling my eyes up. A girl with golden hair, wild and long, stood across from me and giggled.

Stupid, stupid, name.

"When you're sleeping, you should have people call you Linc-off." It took me a second to understand what she meant, but once I did, I laughed.

So did she. And the sound tickled my belly.

"I like your shirt," she said, and my smile stretched. I didn't need to look down at my Batman shirt to know how awesome it was, but . . .

"You like Batman?" I finally asked.

Dad said that was a boy thing.

She shrugged. "He's my friend Ellis's favorite, but I like the Bat signal."

My face scrunched. It's what was on my shirt, but out of all the things someone could like about Batman . . . I couldn't help but ask, "Why?"

She pulled her lips into her mouth and rocked on her heels, then shrugged again and said, "Just think it's a cool way to ask for help."

My shoulders felt less tight. I liked that answer. She was nice.

I finally looked at her pencil name tag, tracing the letters on my thigh with my finger.

P-A-I-G-E.

"Paige," she said. "Like in a book."

I liked books. My breath stuttered in my chest.

"Do you wanna arm wrestle for the window seat?" she chirped.

I blinked back at her. Arm wrestle?

That wouldn't be fair. She . . . she was a girl.

"My dad said girls don't got any arm strength," I told her.

A couple weeks ago when I was helping my dad collect firewood for him and his friends, I'd asked him why Momma wasn't doing it with us, and he'd said—it was 'cause girls got no arm strength.

Paige's eyebrows pinched. She looked angry. "Nuh-uh. Ever seen Buffy the Vampire Slayer?"

I shook my head. Those were all new words—except "vampire."

And I didn't mean to make her mad. I just didn't want to hurt her. She was really pretty, and she smelled like lemonade.

Her eyes were so pretty. The same color as Neptune in my book about the planets, and they twinkled like there were stars around them. I had never seen eyes that blue. As soon as I noticed them, I couldn't look away—it was like she'd captured my face, and I suddenly found myself wondering . . .

Was my new friend a vampire?!

Even as my eyes snap open with a gasp—cutting off the memory—*her eyes* linger in my mind, slowly shifting, darkening—filling with anguish.

No.

It all happens fast and slow. My jaw clenches just as her spine-numbing scream rings between my ears. I plow through the dark—back through the kitchen and into the mudroom—practically flinging myself out the back door.

Holy fuck.

I'm bent at the waist as my chest heaves, blinking through the spots in my vision. Curling my fists in search of oxygen. I gasp again when I realize I'm still holding the mug.

Looking down at it, I'm still not able to see it well—just like the memories.

Dark. It's all just so fucking dark.

My hand shakes with a violent urge to smash the mug. A deep, digging desire to release *some* of the explosive panic that pushed me through the door. The panic itself plateaued, but the tremors—my heart pulsing through every part of my body—tells me this episode isn't over.

I look for anything I can throw my fist into, but even through the surge of adrenaline, I find it in me to tighten the reins.

Do not hit a fucking thing *in this house.*

Do not.

My breath hisses through my teeth. Arms tightening, I look down and see my knuckles turning white under my tattoos. The mug rattles in my shaking fist before I suddenly throw it into the darkness—into the overgrown mess of the backyard.

No.

The second it's airborne, I regret it.

No, no, no.

My eyes follow it the best they can through the abyss, and my body flinches, waiting for the sound of it shattering.

My ears strain against the silence—*save for the rock concert from the bugs*—but I . . . I don't hear it.

Ah, fuck. Did I throw it into someone else's yard?

I'm not actually expecting to find it, but my feet move on their own accord, down the few steps and into the mini-rainforest.

It used to be an oasis back here.

I shake my head. No more memories right now. Moving is helping to reroute the memory. It's still there, but the images are pushing through my mind at a less violent current.

I breathe through my nose and out my mouth. Pulling out my phone, I push through the weeds—some of which reach as high as my hip—and I turn on the flashlight.

A spotlight appears on the ground, illuminating the dry, dead plants, leaves, the dirt—there used to be flowers. *Life.*

My eyes clamp shut, and I stop moving as the thrumming energy threatens to come rushing back.

It's a-fucking-lot. To be here again. To see it like this. Part of me wonders if the house feels the same way about me. Like the dust and ghosts are joining together and throwing a depressing arm around my shoulder, asking, *"What happened to us?"*

I push out a heavy sigh, still searching the ground.

You need to leave.

My head nods, absently agreeing with whatever dazed part of my brain is giving the order.

And I will. I'll go. I just want to . . . find the mug.

I didn't *hear* it break.

Suddenly, I reach the big tree in the back corner of the yard and pull my phone up, shining the light upward.

My heart trips at the sight, just a second, before the whooshing in my ears eases up. *One, two, three . . .*

Lemons. So many lemons.

It's still here.

Reaching up, I pick one off the branch closest to me, holding it just below my nose, and the earthy, zesty scent feels like the first clean breath I've taken in years.

Seven years and a single lemon ago.

I pick another, then another . . .

The tree is still here.

Another and another. I pick until I can't carry anymore.

With both of my arms full, I start back toward the fence, carefully stepping through the dark. Even through the weeds, the route is still the same.

I don't miss a step, navigating my way back to the fence, but I stop to take one more look.

The dark yard is overgrown. The house is empty.

God, I miss her.

The squeeze in my chest lifts when I see the small porch. The door. The *open door.*

Maybe next time I need to . . . *go*—I'll come back here. At least as long as the house is empty.

Maybe I'll make it past the kitchen.

Maybe not. But I'll come back.

For the mug.

For the lemons.

CHAPTER 3
PAIGE

There isn't enough glitter in the world to give me the strength I need to get through this night.

Having spent the day in heavy emotional ruin—I'm realizing now, I've made a mistake. *Surprise, surprise.*

I shouldn't have come in tonight, and I knew it. I *knew* it was a mistake, and I did it anyway.

Why?

It seems to be a sweet little habit I've adopted—*challenging* my own intuition. Maybe when you've experienced the scummy bottom of humanity's floor, there's just this reckless seed that plants in the cracks of your brain.

Though, I think part of me just wonders if the *predictable thing* will happen. And usually it does.

Like now. I'm working in the Saloon, and there are only three poles built into the bar—which means I *should* be making a *shit ton* of money.

But since my head is *not* here, I'm flailing through my tricks.

My body isn't stretched or warmed for the way I need to bend and climb—*to entertain.*

My arms physically shake as I work to lower myself back to the bar counter, with what *should be* an easy corkscrew spin—but with the back of my calves hooked around the pole, my knees land with an uneven *thud,* and my face scrunches.

"You okay, sweetheart?" I hear a man's voice that I don't recognize lift over the music, and my teeth clench.

Great.

I take a second, continuing to sit on my knees. My chin stays tilted down toward the bar, curtaining my eyes behind the blue strands of my hair, while my hand still holds the pole at my side.

I imagine the sight as a contrasting art piece—instead of a happy boy hugging his arm around his best friend, it's a sad stripper hugging her pole. Light and warm meets shadowy and dark.

Sounds like something he *would think of . . .* the thought slips into my brain so unexpectedly, I gasp.

Oh, fuck no. I cannot deal with both of my life's tragedies swirling and twirling together like spaghetti fucking hellfire.

No.

Finally, my eyes peer up, surprised to see a man looking at me, curiously. *Right,* someone asked if I was okay.

I put all my energy into tilting my lips in a smirk, but it still might look like a scowl because he shuffles off.

Wait! No. Money . . .

Dammit.

I pop up to my feet, but even now I can feel the soreness

setting into my tightened muscles. Out of the corner of my eye, I see Jackson weaving through the crowd.

The guy may be pushing fifty, but he's built like a mountain. His biceps are the size of my thighs and then some, and his buzzed salt and pepper head towers over the *enthusiastic* men that decided to wear top hats tonight.

The Window is . . . *theatrical* if nothing else. And as it turns out, rich people get bored easily, so they've started promoting different themed nights.

Tonight is *Gentleman's Night.* My eyes suppress the urge to roll at my own reminder.

I start to move, but it's jagged and I wince.

You came here. Make some fucking money.

I grab onto the pole and start walking around it slowly, building some momentum, but I attempt to keep my focus by watching Jackson as he heads toward a guy in a dark jacket and jeans.

Ooo. I bet he's getting kicked out for not adhering to the *dress code.*

Honestly, I'm surprised the guy made it past the door. All the guards wear black T-shirts and black jeans—but that's as casual as it gets here.

Stacking my hands, one on top of the other, over my head, I grab the pole and do a quick fan kick, earning me whistles as some bills are thrown at my feet. I drop my lower half over, kicking my leg out into an allusion to scoop them up, flinching when my inner thigh pulls.

Ow! I might as well have just done a full fucking split, cold turkey.

But I manage to hide it and keep moving. If I stop now, it'll hurt worse when I try to move again. I tighten my thighs and start to walk around the pole once more. Building momentum. *Watching.*

If I was the kind of girl who still noticed things about men, I'd say the guy Jackson is in fact kicking out is pretty cute. His hair is too light though. It needs to be darker, closer to black. The brown eyes need some green, a little gold . . .

Focus.

Jackson and another guard move the guy along, and I let my eyes fall to the men surrounding the bar area, ordering drinks, and I take a breath.

My legs are already aching, my shoulders sore. My head is caught somewhere between this room and the moon.

Closing my eyes, I do some *cheap* moves, swaying my hips, rolling my neck, and rustling my hair.

Summon the energy of desire. Want.

"Fucking gorgeous," I hear some guy call out below me and my eyebrows flinch.

Just make some money.

My mind starts to manipulate the empty words from below to a raspier voice. Heady, even.

Keeping my eyes closed, I let the noise in the room fall away, even the music, and it's enough to find . . . *him.*

In my mind, anyway.

A bad idea, but I think that's my thing today.

And . . . *I need him.*

Imagining his eyes on me, my chest lifts.

The hazel pools of his gaze would glisten as they watched me from below the bar. Just him.

His eyebrow would lift in that quietly confident way that made my heart skip a beat.

My heart stutters and I gain energy with my movement. I use it to start climbing the pole, fighting through the pain in my shoulders as I reach halfway up.

I lock my thighs around the cool steel, then let my upper half drop backward, hanging upside down.

It's sloppy—and I can *feel it* as the pole smashes between my shoulder blades. A whimper threatens to escape, but I bite my bottom lip and screw my eyes shut.

Breathe. Focus.

Him. I imagine him right at eye-level with me. His face right in front of mine. A dark lock of his wavy hair would fall over his brow as he chuckled, his chin tilting at my upside-down state.

The imaginary sound tickles through me as I think about the sexy smirk he would give me.

I hear his voice, rumble, "*Fucking gorgeous,*" and a warmth spreads through me, my core tightening.

I use every bit of strength I have to move.

"*Keep going, Pip.*"

Using the momentum from lifting my upper-half, I quickly grab the pole with both hands and hook my ankle around it, twisting to give myself some power before I kick both of my legs out and sustain it.

It earns me a roar from the crowd below. I'm using the right muscles, but they're *not ready* and I feel a sharp pinch somewhere in my back.

Still, I don't stop.

I use his eyes. Him.

The sad stripper and her pole. *Dancing for her other ghost.*

As soon as I push through the door to the staff hallway, my *Bambi* legs wobble into full effect.

I lean—well, *fall*—into the wall just outside the door, then twist, so that my back presses up against it, helping to keep me upright.

The cool surface of the smoothed concrete practically sizzles on my hot skin, my muscles still pulsing.

I tilt my neck back and forth. *God, ow.* My shoulders feel like they've permanently merged with my fucking neck.

Ugh. My chin drops. I want to slide down to the floor, but I don't think I'll be able to get back up.

Suddenly, a pair of slender, dark feet are in front of me. I can tell by the black ballet flats that they belong to Rio and my eyes flinch.

I peer up. Even with my heels on, she's a few inches taller than me. Her caramel color eyes are lit with admonishment, making the fine lines in her dark brown skin just slightly more visible.

My eyes blink, taking in the variety of bright colors she's wearing. A sage colored kimono with big fuschia hoop earrings and intricate purple and black braids woven through her hair tied up in a bun.

She stares at me, not angry but expectant, and I sigh.

"Sorry," I sign, genuinely. A sign I know well.

Rio is deaf, but she was also the prima ballerina of some ballet company in San Francisco until they made her retire at the ripe old age of twenty-six.

I've watched some videos of her performances online. She's fucking incredible. Her inability to hear gives her such a unique connection to music and movement—it's beautiful. Even when she's just walking around, you can see that she moves to this internal rhythm. A commanding presence.

I don't know how old she is—midforties maybe? Not that it matters. She can still dance circles around any one of us. But her standards are also incredibly high.

She sighs, signing, "That was dangerous. You could have really hurt yourself."

Damn her. I didn't even *see* her out there.

I don't even have time to sign my case before she's invading my space—twisting me around, and I yelp as she uses her voice to tell me, "Stand up straight."

I listen without a second thought. Never have I ever met someone with such an even display of drill sergeant and momma bear energy.

She presses between my shoulder blades, and I wince.

"Mhm," she drawls, and I feel her sass slither between my ears as she holds the front of my shoulder and gently pulls my arm back, forcing another flinch from me. *Dammit.*

My knees continue to shake, and she turns me back toward her. She signs something, but I'm too busy trying not to fall to the ground to catch it.

I bend my right hand and tap my fingertips to my left palm, signing, "Again," asking her to repeat the signs.

As with everything in my life, I'm a work-in-progress with my ASL skills. Gram taught us some when we were little—she'd trace letters on our backs, and we'd spell them back to her using the ASL alphabet. Gram and I even picked it back up after she had her stroke six years ago.

But signing conversationally is a whole other ballgame. Luckily, Rio's a good teacher, and she's patient with my spacey ass.

I watch carefully as she signs again, slower.

Rio can and does use her voice, but I know she prefers signing. The only other person I've seen her do it with is Jackson, and it makes me feel . . . something resembling the idea of special. So I really try.

And I gather she's telling me she wants me to come in early tomorrow to test the injuries.

Fuck. She's going to pull me.

"I'll be fine," I sign quickly, pinching the imaginary penny between my shoulder blades, straightening my back. But really, it just feels like I'm being *stabbed* in the back.

Rio grimaces, signing, "We'll see. Be here at five, sharp." It's an order, but her eyes hold a warmth that soothes some of the ache in every part of my body. With a parting pat on my shoulder, she continues past me, gliding away like a goddamn angel as she walks down to one of the rehearsal studios at the end of the hallway.

As soon as she's out of sight, I let my body slump, but a muscle between my shoulders spasms, and I hiss through my teeth.

Fuck. I can't afford to lose more money. Tonight was a bust. And tomorrow night I'm in the Drawing Room—the highest roller room aside from the Veranda.

After a few breaths, I start to hobble my way back in the direction of the dressing room. Halfway down the hallway, I have enough sense to take off the heels.

Dumbass.

My arches scream as I walk—the thin material of my thigh-high stockings my only barrier between my feet and the floor.

Which does look pretty clean, for such heavy foot traffic through show hours.

But I don't care. Suddenly, I'm exhausted.

Just get back to the apartment. Go to sleep. At least tomorrow won't be today.

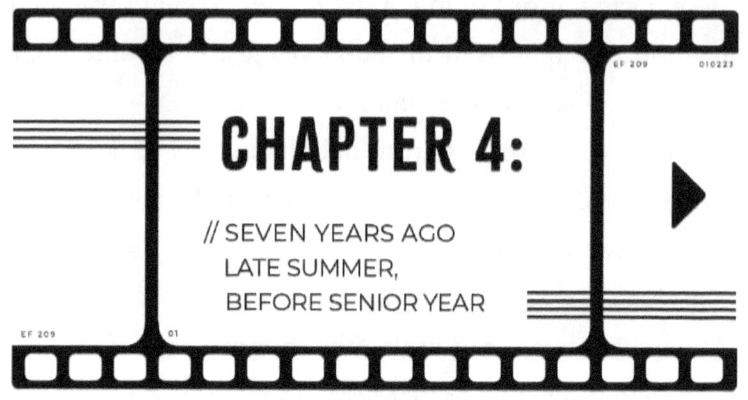

PAIGE

The familiar sound of Janis Joplin singing, "Come on," filtered through my bedroom walls and my mouth pinched at the corner as I slid my feet into my slippers.

Guess Gram is up.

I pushed through my door and continued down the hall, passing the olive-green walls covered with pictures of Gram and my grandpa in all the places they had traveled.

Sea caves in Iceland, a cabin in the Smoky Mountains.

And then there were pictures of my parents on their adventures. One that unfortunately took them from me when I was only three years old in the way of a tragic boat accident.

But then there was Gram.

Her singing was only getting louder, along with the music, just as I hit the extra creaky stair at the foot of the steps and made my way into the kitchen.

Thick waves of long, dove-gray hair were swaying as Gram stood by the coffee pot, wearing her signature, oversized beige cardigan and some pajama pants that had YOLO all over them. She was *loving fucking life*—and I breathed a small laugh.

It caught her attention, and she spun around. "Hey, Paigey May. Want some coffee?"

I smiled, nodding through a yawn, as I slid into a chair at the small round table.

"What mug ya want?" she asked over her shoulder, going to the shelf with our favorite collection. It was a ritual Gram had instilled in me. Choosing your mug sets your tone for the day.

I pointed to the copper-colored bell mug, and Gram's denim blue eyes narrowed back at me. "You always pick the one that takes the whole damn pot to fill."

I snorted a laugh. It was true. It was a big-ass mug, but I shook my head, yawning again as I said, "Just fill it up halfway. Linc's coming by in a bit. We're shooting today."

"Ooo!" she all but barked and my shoulders jumped. "My sweet Lincleton." Her face shifted to that of a nosy dog smelling its favorite treat. "I've said it once, I'll say it again, you really oughta' let that boy touch a tit. *At least* one of 'em."

"Gram!" I scoffed, my face scrunching. "Jesus, I—" I shook my head and stared back at her.

What was one to say when one's grandmother dropped a tit bomb pre-coffee?

She shrugged and then slid the mug toward me, her eyes widening with faux-innocence before she turned back to the fridge and pulled out the milk.

I leaned back, watching her *pretend* to mind her own business but secretly analyzing—*wondering.*

Darlene Hansen—*Gram*—claimed to be a "*highly intuitive person.*" But really, she was just fucking nosy.

"*Tomato, tomato,*" she'd say. But she'd say the word the exact same way, twice, infuriating me.

"So, is that why you're not over at Queenie's this morning? Got a hot date—" A sharp inhale inflated my chest as my eyebrows lifted, giving her a leveling expression.

Mind your business, woman.

"Right. Shooting." She put too much emphasis on the *shoo* part of the word, before giving me a half-hearted finger gun.

My blank stare was enough for her to pull her lips into her mouth—either that or she *intuited* that this was not something I was willing to talk about.

The tension stacking in my neck halted as she went back to humming along with the music, preparing her coffee.

Why was I so sensitive to this shit lately? It's not like people hadn't speculated about Linc and me for years.

Shaking my head, I reassured myself, *it was just a hormone hiccup.*

I had known Linc since we were six, and we'd managed to bob and weave around our respective puberty bullshit thus far. Though, the year my tits came in was a tough one for him—so maybe it was just *my turn.*

I was just . . . *highly* aware of my best friend's seemingly overnight and *very real* transition into manhood.

A jaw line that had squared up a bit. Noticed *that* at a very inopportune time last spring during a voice recital. And since he was filming it, there's undeniable evidence that I kept looking over at him.

Ugh. My brain wanted to pop—*so embarrassing.*

But then, a few days ago when we were shooting in the woods—I kept getting distracted any time Linc's newly cut biceps would bulge, the muscles bunching any time he moved a piece of equipment.

I gawked like the creepy dude in a fucking car wash scene.

A small noise from the back of my throat rumbled as Gram said, "Ooo, you feelin' okay? Your cheeks are red . . ."

My eyes pulled up, squinting over the brim of my mug. She knew I felt fine.

Just a hormone hiccup, I reminded myself again.

Gram turned down the music, then slid into the chair across from me. "So, the shoot today—is this the movie where you're playing some kind of woodland nymph?"

I stared back at her, blinking.

But it did nothing to help my confusion.

What the hell is she talking about?

She must have noticed because eventually she took a sip of her coffee and shrugged. "I don't know. You came home in a *see-through* white dress with dirt all over you last week."

I snort through my nose, shaking my head. "Oh my God. First of all, I was wearing a bodysuit underneath, and two, no. I'm not playing a slutty fairy," I laughed again and after it passed, I told her, "I'm playing the moon."

"Right, right," she says. "But you are not a moon."

"Are you calling me a slutty fairy?" I shot back, giggling.

Gram joined, and once our laughter settled, I sighed. "No, it's for that film festival in San Diego in a few months—the one Mr. Harris got Linc into? Some hoity-toity, rich-as-fuck organization is giving the winner money to fund their next film project. It'd be a big deal, so . . . we're trying to get it all shot as quickly as possible. Linc thinks he'll need a lot of time to edit, but Mr. Harris said he'd help him."

Gram nodded, murmuring, "Talented boy," then smiled. "And he already has his muse."

Before I had time to shoot her another glare, the back door in the mudroom off the kitchen opened, and a familiar voice called out, "Morning!"

Linc walked through the archway at the same time I heard the pitter-patter of quick little steps behind him.

"Paigey!" All fifty-three pounds of Maisie Morrow came barreling into me just as I quickly put my mug on the table to return the hug.

"Hey, babe," I clasped my hand on the back of her head and hugged her a bit tighter. She was so damn cute, a mini-Christine with almond-colored eyes and a dainty little nose—whereas Linc's hazel eyes and almost-black hair were features from their dad.

I knew the resemblance bothered him, but . . . I liked his face.

"Paigey, guess what?" Maisie's light brown pig-tail braids bounced up as her big brown eyes lit with excitement—but I got distracted by the slow, stealthy movement beside me as Linc slyly tried to hand Gram a bag of . . . *peanut butter cups?!*

"Duuude," I whined at Linc, a partial-scold, then looked at

Gram. "I'm pretty sure those aren't on the approved food list from Dr. Weiner."

Gram snorted a laugh. "I mean, if he wanted me to take him seriously, he probably should have changed his name."

I rolled my eyes. It was pronounced "wine-er" but . . . Gram will be Gram.

I stared at my best friend's earthy eyes while they filled with bullshit innocence. "You are a traitorous . . . snack smuggler," I said, unevenly.

It's early. I'm tired. The comebacks will improve as the day goes on.

Linc's lips pulled further as he held up his other hand, revealing an iced coffee, and extended it toward me. "For you, Lady Pip."

My mouth tilted. *Good move.* A peace treaty immediately following a breach of snackery.

Gram's cholesterol and blood pressure had been all over the place at her last check-up—the doctor was throwing out some scary words.

It was as surprising as it was terrifying. Because while Gram had a sweet tooth and a very deep love of California weed, she kept herself in good shape. Honestly, the woman barely ever sat still.

Sitting on my throne of hypocrisy, I was contemplating double-fisting my coffee. *Is this really a wise decision?*

Probably not. Linc's presence alone had already kickstarted my heart. My eyes were currently surfing the delicious waves of his mussed hair. The thick, dark strands were styled in an effortless way, but looked . . . freshly tugged.

The feeling swan dove into the deepest part of my stomach, and I shifted in my seat. *Fucking annoying.*

I rolled my eyes, willing myself to get a grip, and accepted his peace offering. I finally said, "Are you still going to call me *Pip* when we're Gram's age?"

Short for pipsqueak—which he'd started calling me after his first major growth spurt in sixth grade—the one that put—*and kept*—him in the lead by a landslide at just over six-feet-tall.

All that extra height went straight to his stupid head. Stupid hair.

"Till the end," he said, with a grin that made the gold flecks in his eyes flicker, just as I took a sip of the coffee he brought me.

I smiled through my pursed lips over the straw. He *must* have felt bad if he was quoting the forever forgotten but always remembered friendship oath. The one I wrote and notarized when we were ten. My notary seal was a *very official* lemon scratch-n-sniff sticker.

I didn't notice I was still staring at him until I felt Maisie tapping the tops of my thighs, her cheeks puffed.

I laughed. "I'm so sorry. Thank you for being so patient. What's up?"

"Ifinallywatched*Buffy!*" she yelled, all in one breath, and Gram laughed, popping one of her candies in her mouth.

I lifted my hand for a high five. "Oh, hell yeah! How many episodes did you watch?"

She tapped my hand, saying, "Just the first one," then finally made her way over to Gram, who pulled her up on her lap, and situated her braids behind her shoulders. "Brother's worried I'll get scared," Maisie mumbled pointedly at Linc.

I lifted my eyes to her brother, giving him a face. And he knew what it meant. We had watched *way* scarier shit than *Buffy* when we were her age. I gave him the silent message.

You disappoint me, Lincoln.

His eyes squinted back at me, and I swear to God, I think he subliminally told me, *"Don't call me Lincoln."*

We both laughed, whether it was from our silent conversation or not—sometimes it just happened. We'd known each other so long that sometimes it felt like our internal thoughts crossed paths.

"We should really get going. It's gonna get hot come noon, and we've gotta shoot tonight too," Linc said, then tilted his chin toward Maisie. "And I've gotta drop the bread loaf off."

"Liiinc! Stop calling me that!" Maisie whined, pouting, but Gram swayed her knees, tickling Maisie's sides, and it was quickly forgotten.

Poor Maisie. Also subjected to a Linc nickname, only hers was worse. But also sweet. He referred to her as bread loaf sometimes because when he found out he was getting a little sister, he practiced "holding a baby" with a bread loaf.

Yeah, damn. That was fucking cute.

The memory pushed me to stand quickly. Too quickly, and I stubbed my toe on the leg of the table. "Fuck!" I yelped, pulling my foot up instinctively before my eyes caught Maisie's. "Sorry, Mase."

She shrugged. "It's okay. Brother says it too."

My eyebrows scrunched before I swept an accusatory glance over to mister brother boy.

Is that so?

Linc looked genuinely confused. "I do not," he said—with only a fraction of the confidence of someone telling the truth—before he added, "When do you hear me say that?"

Maisie shrugged again. "That time you watched wrestling in your room."

My eyebrow cocked, and my eyes caught his, which were widening by the second as a quietly mortified glint appeared. I sucked my lips into my mouth to suffocate a laugh.

LINC

"Wrestling?!" Paige laughed. No, she *cackled* from the passenger's seat as soon as Maisie got out of the car.

"Hey," I chuckled, awkwardly, keeping my voice as even as possible. "It happened *one fucking time*, and now I use headphones."

Luckily, Darlene and Maisie were none the wiser, but of course, Paige caught what Maisie had accidentally heard from my room a few nights ago. And while I knew there was a possibility the bread loaf would bring it up at some point, I was just grateful I was able to hide any silent hints I may have given Paige that I "wrestled" myself to the thought of *her*.

I shifted my weight and pulled out my pack of cigarettes, grabbing one between my teeth as I opened the window.

My eyes floated over to my pretty best friend, watching her light, honey-colored hair blow in the wind as she begrudgingly rolled down her window. My eyes moved back to the road, but from the side of my eye, I could see delicate, sunkissed arms crossing over each other with an exaggerated huff.

I sighed, lighting the cigarette. "Wolverine smokes, ya know," I reminded her.

She glared at me with a side eye as the corner of her mouth

lifted. "Yeah, but *Hugh Jackman* doesn't. The image is hot, but the habit? Woof."

Goddammit, this girl was impossible. She was being extra bratty this morning, and *fuck me* if it didn't have something stirring deep in my stomach.

But of course, like a fucking pussy, I didn't say anything.

I didn't act on it.

I did nothing.

It wasn't the time anyway. We had a lot of shit to get done, and school was starting next week.

The sudden clearing of her throat commanded my attention, and my mouth pinched at the corner.

"What scenes are today?" she asked.

I flicked some ash out the window. "*Today* should be easy. It's just the swimming sequence. Tonight will be the challenge."

The sound of her laugh danced with the wind whipping from our open windows. "Worse than being dragged through the woods and covered in mud for four hours?"

My lips pulled back to the corner. She really was a trooper for that. And she'd never let me forget it either.

I shrugged. "Tonight's the hill scene."

I could see her nod in my peripherals. "What's so hard about that one?"

My mouth flattened, and I took a drag on my cigarette to stall. There wasn't a *non-weird* way to tell her that I wasn't exactly looking forward to watching her make out with Ellis for however long it took me to get the shot tonight.

Not that I was worried about something sparking between the

two of them or anything. This fun little garden of jealousy was unfortunately something I'd been dealing with since our freshman year, when Paige got her first part in a musical with a love interest.

Since then, I'd seen her in a handful of stage romances. And I'd wanted to kill every single one of her costars except Ellis. The two of them played lovers in last spring's black box show, and I think I was just so goddamn impressed that I couldn't focus on anything else.

Their friendship gave them this incredible, natural chemistry. And for as good as they were on stage, the camera ate them up.

Clearing my throat, I finally said, "Just really want to get the new moon in the shot naturally. Mr. Harris let me borrow a monitor so I can do some playbacks while we're there, but I won't know for sure if it worked until after I upload and mess with it a bit."

She nodded as I pulled into the small lot—a little patch of gravel. I saw Ellis's Jeep already parked, while the little hobbit-hole mouth to the trail to get to the cove was through a small clearing of trees just a couple feet off the lot.

It was kind of sad, actually. It was a cool little spot, but it was surprisingly dead during the day. There was usually a scattering of various trash around the area from some party the night before. Paige brought some bags just in case we had to clean up a bit.

Ellis got out of his car, his smile wide—looking every bit the part of Hollywood golden boy. Shirtless, tan, sandy blond hair. I huffed a chuckle. Asshole.

Paige whistled. "Damn, Batman. Someone's been hitting the gym."

So had I, but whatever.

He started toward my car, and my jaw tightened as I moved to my trunk, grabbing the camera bag and monitor.

"Me and this guy have been doing two-a-days for the last month," he said, and as I closed the trunk I saw the mischievous glint in his green eyes, sparkling in the damn sun as he looked at Paige. "Don't act like you haven't noticed Linc's man arms."

When my eyes fall to her, I'm prepared for one response, but I choke on my breath. Because . . .

I fucking saw that.

A beautiful rosy tint to Paige's cheeks. It was there, and then it was gone—the sight's only proof was the heatwave hitting my groin, and I almost coughed from the impact—like the wind had been knocked out of my lungs and into my dick.

It wasn't new for Ellis to make some sort of off-handed comment about me and Paige—it *was* however the first time I saw her do anything but roll her eyes or laugh it off.

So . . . what the fuck?

"Speaking of which," Ellis interrupted my spiral as he grabbed the monitor bag off the ground. "Let's get a move on with the shoot, otherwise we won't have time to get our second workout in before tonight's torture."

Paige scoffed. "Um, kissing me under the moon is torture? The *fuck?* Did *both* of you forget about dragging me through the woods for *hours?* I feel like no one cares enough about this."

"Okay. Now you're milking it," I told her. Then, unable to

help myself—I tapped her nose with my index finger before hiking the camera bag over my shoulder.

Her nose did a cute little twitch before her mouth gaped. "A *boop* on the nose is not hazard pay!" she cursed at me through a laugh while I passed by her, heading toward the tree clearing.

Over my shoulder, I reminded her, "I'm not paying you at all, Pip." Then glanced back, adding a smirk that would surely add fuel to the fire of this feisty, bashful, little-monster-mood she was in—a creature I was completely obsessed with.

My smile pulled further. It didn't matter that she was behind me, I could feel her eyes firing into my back like little ice blasters.

Freeze gun eyes.

It felt good on a hot day.

She growled, and I stifled the laugh. I wondered if she could hear me egging her on, even in my head. Sometimes I was certain we could read each other's minds.

Suddenly, 105 pounds of pouty Pip stomped past me and I chuckled.

Yeah. Our brains were just . . . synced. Entwined.

Her cute bubble butt tucked back and forth with each of her steps as she practically stomped ahead, and my own gait slowed.

"What's her problem?" Ellis muttered, catching up to me.

I watched her carry on through the hobbit-hole opening and shrugged, mumbling, "I don't know."

But I fucking loved it.

CHAPTER 5
LINC

My toes wiggle on the smooth wood below my bare feet, searching for some kind of roughness—*a bite.* But there's some kind of sealant on the wood. It's bumpy, but I can't feel any grooves or knots under my arches or toes.

The sliding glass door opens and closes as I hear Ellis say, "Hey," from behind me, and my body jerks—feeling like it quite literally lands back into place.

Through a series of blinks, I shake my head, glancing down at the penny I'm mindlessly flipping through my fingers. I blink a couple more times.

I'm at the house. On the porch.

Just as another moment passes, I snap the penny up, but quickly snatch it back, out of the air, then shove it into my pocket with the other few coins.

Ellis chuckles, and I breathe a laugh too, mostly to seem present—but I still feel *spacey as fuck.*

Peeking up into the early evening gray sky, I can't help but think it looks a bit darker than when I first came out here.

How long have *I been out here?*

My mind is always a bit of a flight risk, but add in the fact I didn't get back from Venice until almost three last night, tossed and turned till five, only to get a whopping *hour* of actual sleep.

My internal clock woke me back up at six, and it's made for a strange, delirious day—majority of which has been stuck in my fucking head.

Or floating in outer space.

Did I really lose the whole day to standing and staring?

Ellis clears his throat, then mutters, "Looks like rain," as he comes up beside me, leaning his forearms over the bannister.

Still feeling a bit . . . *far,* I clear my throat, mumbling. "P-People are gonna be pissed."

He snorts a laugh with a nod. "LA is the crankiest of bitches when it rains."

I huff with a nod. Digging my hand into my back pocket, I fish out my cigarettes, lighting one as I keep my gaze outward. Through the thick, foggy air, I'm only able to make out bits and pieces of the sprawling landscape.

The house Ellis bought is part of a private gated community, nestled deep in the Santa Monica mountains. On a clear day, it's 100 percent the *million-dollar view* he paid for. *Literally.*

Lush greenery surrounds a winding, paved road up the mountain. Past that, you can usually see a valley with some neighboring towns. And on really clear days, you can even see the faint skyline of the city.

The house itself isn't huge, but it's more than enough space with three bedrooms and four bathrooms. Ellis bought it as his first investment, and four years ago—after my year away at *the spa* as he refers to it—he offered up one of his spare rooms.

"The spa" is actually a place called Lending Lanterns. It's a mental health facility in Santa Barbara. And the only reason I can afford his spare room is because he gives me a *steep* friends-and-family discount.

Only two drags into my cigarette, he says, "Question," like it isn't a question at all. "Why are there like . . . six radio-actively-large lemons on the counter?"

Ah, fuck.

I never took them into my room last night like I meant to. You know, like a *normal* person does when they "visit" their ex-girlfriend's vacant house in the middle of the night to have panic attacks, throw mugs, and steal citrus fruits.

Totally fucking normal.

"I mean, they're massive," he says. "Kinda like the monster lemons from Darlene's tree . . ."

Motherfucker.

He knows. Of course he knows.

I avoided him yesterday—which makes me the shittiest friend ever, given everything he's done for me. But it would have pushed me over the edge. The risk of remembering was too high.

And he already knows I suck.

But I think he wanted some space too. He knew that backyard as well as I did. That house.

Them.

I feel his heavy sigh in my own chest. After a few seconds, he mumbles, "Is anyone living there?" It's a question, but there's this foreboding tone that makes it sound like he already knows the answer. My gaze finally pulls over to him and I see his green eyes, muted from the darkening sky. Another beat passes before he peeks over at me, waiting for an answer.

Or confirmation.

He's asking if *she's* living there.

My weight shifts, taking another drag as I shamefully dip my chin, giving my head a small shake.

Silence holds the moment, but in it, I can nearly *hear* the unspoken conversation between us. The one that happens nearly every time Paige even gets *indirectly* referenced . . .

He'd tell me to call her. I'd remind him of why I can't, *and his mouth would harden into a tight line, undoubtedly fighting back an obnoxious flood of frustration and exhaustion as the words would eventually just . . . evaporate.*

Cue my self-loathing, which would lead to more dumb decisions. So, we don't.

It used to be worse. I've *channeled* a lot of my bullshit—which is a lot like folding your clothes and organizing them into drawers, only to end up with a massive pile on the floor by the end of the day.

"And therapy is where you pick it all up and put it away again. Fun."

I groan at the thought of my *least* favorite therapist's words. The one who focused on my exposure therapy at the facility.

Truthfully, I can't be certain if he was my least favorite therapist or if it was because the therapy itself was a mild form of torture.

It was for a small group of us that had issues with . . . physical contact. And something about sucker-punching one of the guards—*upon arrival*—for tapping my shoulder, got me an immediate seat.

Or so I'm told. I don't know. That whole time is . . .

Fuzzy.

But therapists love to remind me that our mental well-being can't be *controlled*—just tamed. Managed.

And last night was the first time in . . .

Running my teeth along my bottom lip, I try to remember the last time I'd allowed myself to act out on a bad idea . . .

My chest lifts when I realize, *I can't.* And *fuck me* if that isn't a pathetic victory. That enough time has passed between my breakdowns, and I can't *easily* recall the last time it happened.

My free hand sinks into my pocket and fiddles with the change, as my toes wiggle again.

Ellis's audible yawn manages to fully bring me back—*Goddammit. I'm so fucking spacey.*

He crosses behind me to walk over to one of the four Adirondack chairs on the porch, plopping down in one, as another sigh pushes past his lips.

I see now that he's already in sweats and a T-shirt, beer in hand. In an attempt to side step any more talk about yesterday—*last night*—I ask him, "How'd it go today?"

His mouth tilts as he rustles a hand through his sandy blond hair. "Good. Should be all set. Becca says she'll make the deposits then bring the money during her monthly visits. But I might still do it when I can. Any excuse to go out there and see the family sometimes, ya know?"

My mouth ticks up, taking another drag as a warm hum spreads through my chest.

Ellis released his first documentary, *The 5,* a few months ago, and now he's getting ready to send it off for festival consideration.

A double entendre, *The 5* is about a family of five people who are *houseless*—a term they have asked to be used, not *homeless*—as their *home* is in a small covering under the 5 freeway. Their family's story is multigenerational and layered through some really compelling interviews—footage that addresses the shortage of affordable housing in LA.

He did a fucking great job. And given that the family he worked with has been living on the streets for decades, they don't feel comfortable managing money or dealing with banks. So Ellis entrusted the task to a social worker and their finance team to make sure it's taken care of.

But I know he'll miss working with them.

Ellis Casper may have been born to one of the wealthiest men in the country—maybe even the world—but he has a big fuckin' heart. *Even if it comes with a lot of* opinions.

A quality he's had since the day I met him.

Just a few days after I met her.

Ellis swipes the thought away when he says, "Oh, the lawyers sent me a bunch of shit for the copyright. You sure you don't want any sort of credit for the poster shot? I mean, it's a category at some festivals."

I shake my head immediately. It's *his* picture.

I mean, yes, it's a still shot that I fucked around with from one of my dailies. But I took the still with his narrative in mind.

It was my first attempt with mixed media photo editing, but luckily, I had three years to figure it out. And the transformation from the original to the finished movie poster is fucking cool.

It started out just as a shot of the family under the bridge. Then I was able to place photos I took of certain city landmarks—*some might argue excessive, unnecessary, and costly landmarks*—and I blended them into the family's skin. I was able to play with some transparency filters so you could still see their facial features, and I texturized the shit out of the photos of the landmarks so they were all gritty—which was the vibe Ellis wanted.

He smiles. "Well, thanks, man. It's fucking awesome."

A tightness bunches in my chest—a knot of warmth and itchiness. The gratitude, the praise.

I don't deserve it.

Not this *guy.*

I work to swallow, taking my last drag.

Ellis says, "Oh, Desmond called me earlier. Said he wants to come over and grill out tomorrow. You good with that?"

I nod, unevenly, as I smash my cigarette into the ashtray—a little harder than necessary.

I don't know why the mention of Ellis's dad stopping by always . . . I don't know—makes me stand up a little straighter.

It's an asinine response, seeing as Desmond's never been anything but kind to me. And like his son, he seems to have a soft spot for lost causes.

Ellis stands, looking down at his phone. He chews his bottom lip. "I've gotta take this. But do you wanna watch an episode of *Lost* after?"

My mouth twitches at the corner, stuttering, "S-Sounds good, man."

With a nod, he walks toward the sliding door, I hear him answer his call as he steps back inside the house, and my chin lifts back out to the mountain range.

In the time we've been out here, the cloudy day has become dusty twilight—the moon invisible through the fog.

A familiar ache buried inside me starts to stir in the deepest part of my chest—so much so that I clear my throat, and give my head a shake.

Don't.

Night has become something I crave and dread in equal measure. A nocturnal ache awakens as the things I *channel* and *put away* taunt the edges of my mind, skipping the perimeter of my awareness.

Like a monster under the bed, I think.

Waiting. Lurking. Hiding in the shadows.

I huff. *Sounds like me.*

CHAPTER 6
PAIGE

A groan pushes past my lips as I roll to my back. The soft mattress does nothing to soothe the immediate pain that shoots through—*everywhere*—as my eyes slowly blink, squinting to open. The vent in my ceiling comes into a blurry focus.

Ugh. Well, it's tomorrow.

And it's definitely worse than yesterday.

She's *still* gone—same as the last year—and *now* I feel like my body has been stretched by ancient torture devices.

Fucking hell.

Luckily, my apartment is closer to The Window than Venice, and traffic—*for fucking once*—was in my favor. I made it to my bed in about twenty minutes before immediately passing out.

But *fuck.* I can't go into the club today. *I don't think I can move.* I hear a small scuffle by the window, just beside the foot of my bed and decide to test the theory. Wincing and flinching, I take an eternity to sit up. "Oh, holy fuck—" I grit out, slowly dipping my chin and gently trying to rotate my neck.

Pain shoots through my arms, my back—but in trying to

move my neck, my eyes lock with the wide gray ones staring back at me from the *Fern Gully*-inspired terrarium.

Cheeto, my tiny house dragon—also known as my leopard gecko—is judging me. And I don't blame her.

Rookie mistake, we agree. I should know better from my experience with painful living. The day *after* the bad thing is always the worst—when you wake up and realize it wasn't a dream.

He left. He left you.

She's gone.

Still gone.

You're alone.

A whimper tightens in my throat as I twist my back, stopping quickly when the sharp pain at the base of my neck becomes too much, and I inhale deeply.

Ugh. Fuuuck.

Sitting still for a second, I breathe in through my nose, and out through my mouth—trying to let my body recover from the small bit of movement.

I think maybe there's some part of me that just *feels valid* wallowing on the day—*the anniversary of bad things*—and then the day after, when the world reminds you it's still turning, it feels even worse because you're *not done.*

I've been *"not done"* for seven years. And truthfully, I don't think I'll ever be done grieving my losses. They're *too big.* I'm just a piece of fucking Swiss cheese trying to not get blown away.

Cheeto is still watching me. Maybe she's worried. Being that we're both nocturnal creatures, I'll usually plop her on my shoulder while I stretch, and we'll watch a movie or listen to some music after I get home from the club.

"Sorry, girl," I say quietly. She takes my apology and climbs back under the cave of her rock.

I move, slowly. *So slowly*—my body flinches through every bit of it, as I push myself to stand, and swipe my phone from the nightstand.

It almost slips out of my hand, but I jerk to catch it, wincing and yelping at the abrupt movement. My muscles tense through the spasm between my shoulders. Once it finally subsides, I take another breath, and then hobble to the bathroom, catching an unfortunate glance of myself in the mirror.

Blue hair—*everywhere*. I didn't wash my face so my makeup is smeared over my cheeks, and my eyes are dark and heavy from sleep.

Adding insult to injury is the tiny nature of my bathroom, which allows me to see the top half of my head in the mirror as I sit on the can, wedged between the shower and the wall.

I sit, long after my business is done, mostly because it took me an hour to sit down, and text Rio.

Me: You were right.

I sigh, my body deflating at my *fucked*-meter—which is pretty much off the charts. I made a pitiful hundred bucks last night, and I truly think some of it only accidentally fell onto the bar counter.

Rio: I always am.
You know the drill—72 hours.

Fuck, fuck, fuck.

I knew it. But *goddammit.* She knew after her little evaluation last night that I had no shot of making it in today—giving me till the morning was a courtesy. But after a confirmed injury, I knew she'd dole out a mandatory seventy-two-hour leave. As a dancer herself, she takes injuries very seriously. Suddenly, another message comes through, and I look down again.

Rio: Take the break, Blue.
You need it.

My head leans into the wall, still sitting on the toilet, as a pathetic whine pushes past my lips. The plaster on the wall is cool to my clammy forehead, my body still tense, my muscles aching.

But something warm finds its way to my chest at the acknowledgment. *Rio knows about Gram.* She's the only person that knows *anything* real about me.

Last year, when I fled our house in Venice—it's all a bit of a blur. I know I ended up wandering into a coffee shop by the club, and she found me. Like a stray puppy. But she got me a job, helped me find this apartment.

Just like the wristbands she makes for me, it's a kindness, but even more so.

It's an *intuition* I've only noticed a few people possess. *Typically* people that are really paying attention. *Typically* other people who have been down on their luck.

They're a special breed of human that don't need words or

explanations for your brokenness. They just see it, acknowledge it, they recognize it's in the room.

Surprising myself, I feel my lips quirk at the corner.

I'm pretty sure Rio is that kind *of people.*

So was Gram.

My eyes squeeze shut again, and I try to shove the thought away. But no matter which way I turn, my mind is full.

I'm going to need to figure out how to make up for losing out on this much money. I'm still a good four hundred dollars away from making my rent for the month, and there's only a week left in September.

"You could always go home," I hear Gram's voice sneak through my mind and I tap my forehead into the wall.

I can't. Not yet, I tell her silently.

Even in the couple of weak moments where I've let myself run away back to Venice over the last year, I haven't been able to make it past the street before ours.

Everything is . . . *so fucked.*

But I can't do anything about it. Not right now, anyway. I wouldn't dare argue with Rio, but even if I did—there's no way I can dance tonight.

I finally push myself off the toilet. All I want to do is crawl back into bed, but that will just make it that much harder to move again later.

Just keep moving.

I did it again. I stared at the bad decision, I saw it cocking its eyebrow back at me—*daring* me to keep walking past the idea of spending money on things I don't need. Money I don't have. And then I did it anyway.

After falling back asleep then taking an hour to get out of bed, I limped down to the corner market and bought two bottles of champagne, a pack of Irish Silver cigarettes, and bath salts. Lemony ones.

And after soaking in them for about an hour, I've now shoved my pruny ass into some sweat pants and, currently, I have no regrets.

Though, that is probably in large part due to the fact that champagne bottle numero *one* is already down the hatch.

"*'Bout time you loosened up,*" Gram's snicker filters through my ears, and I huff a laugh.

My body wobbles a bit and there's a dull ache in my tailbone, just as I notice that I must have sat on the floor at some point.

My body still hurts, but my mind is too drunk to care. Which is *exactly* where I want it. A beat passes, and I sigh, suddenly, oddly, aware of my blinks. I can't tell if they're slow or fast.

Shaking my head, I lift my eyes, peeking around the perimeter of my dark, seven hundred-square-foot apartment, realizing *just now* that it's night time.

When did that happen?

I never turned the light on. Just the small lamp on my makeshift table by the door. A vintage, repurposed, moving box.

"*Look out, HGTV,*" Gram's voice sounds again and this time, I breathe a laugh. I can feel the film of moisture that's been over my eyes for the last hour—maybe longer—and I don't think it's the booze.

One of my many plights in life is my inability to not relive the most horrible days in blurry, fractured pieces. And fighting the memories from last year is as awful as . . .

My last day with him.

I groan, scrubbing my palms up and down my face. The alcohol feels like it's slowly sinking further into my bloodstream, and I gracelessly lie back, wincing through the dull ache my drunkenness has awarded my muscles for the moment. My eyes stare up at the ceiling.

The uneven planks of the wood floor poke at the back of my head, and my vision blurs and focuses, pointing at the light casting over the ceiling from the window just beside Cheeto's terrarium. Watching the light change ever so slightly is a little haunting.

The shadows flicker, pull . . .

Someone walking under a streetlight.

A car driving by.

Blink.

"Make sure her face catches the light."

My eyes slam shut.

What the fuck?

The sudden—*unexpected*—memory hits like a sandbag to my ribs and I gasp, curling my legs into my chest as I turn to my side.

Tightening to the fetal position does nothing to help even out my breathing, but I'm trying desperately to squeeze the thought away.

Why?

God, it would just be fucking polite if my bullshit could take turns.

Gram's voice finds me again, still too far as she says, *"This is why we ask Buffy for favors. God can be quite the fickle bitch."*

Just the thought of her response eases some of the tightening knots weaving and tugging through my body.

But still, I keep my eyes closed, focusing not on her words but her voice.

Swallowing the lump in my throat, I listen again.

I read somewhere once that the sound of a person's voice is the first thing you forget once they're gone.

And I can't let that happen.

My mind leans into my drunkenness and floats, it drifts to a softer surface. A better, bad day . . .

Warm arms held me as I woke up and suddenly registered I was screaming, crying—losing my fucking mind.

"Shh," a soft voice hushed, and my body loosened at the familiarity, but whimpers and cries still punched past my mouth as I grabbed onto soft, knit fabric. The big beige cardigan that was basically like a small throw blanket

Gram.

The smell of roses and black tea surrounded my terror. A terror I couldn't even let meet the air.

"Oh, my sweet girl," she said, her voice rich with tenderness.

But I was too consumed. I couldn't even remember what dream I'd been having—just that it was bad.

It was all so fucking bad.

Asleep. Awake. Alive.

Gram's cheek rested on the top of my head, she continued to run her fingers through my hair, and I did what I could to steady my breathing.

"Paigey May," she finally said through a sigh. "It's a hard lesson to learn, this one." She pressed a kiss to the top of my head and I winced. The tears continued to fall in thick drops, outlining my nose as I pressed myself harder into her side.

She thought this was from proverbial teenage heartbreak.

And holy fuck, did I wish that was true.

That's all she could think, though.

The truth was my own personal haunting that only I would know and I must keep.

Her soft sigh did something to at least ease some of the tension bunching between my brows as she said, "I know it sounds crazy right now, but . . . this experience. It's an important one."

I swallowed. Unable to say anything. My fingers curled into her, gripping her like a scared, helpless child.

"We rarely want life lessons, baby. And one of the hardest lessons to learn is that humans must separate."

My eyebrows pinched, holding her tighter.

"I mean, not from me. I'll haunt ya for eternity," she chuckled, and I tried to smile, but it didn't work. She took another deep breath, then said, "I just mean, in one way or another—through distance, time, death—humans separate. And learning that is far more difficult than enduring the separation. This will be the worst of it, my girl. Because after this—after you pick yourself up off the floor, you'll know you can survive. And that's worth the shitty lesson. I promise you."

I appreciated the comfort she was trying to give me. And God, had she been trying—coddling me for the last six months of my living nightmare.

One that seemed to have no sign of slowing down.
I couldn't respond. Just listen—but not even to the words. Just her voice.
Her voice.

My eyes open, blurry from tears, but I can see I'm in a kiss or kill moment with the dust along my floor.

Still on the floor.

My eyes shut again, willing the memory back, willing her voice back.

And I can still hear it, but it's further away, mixing with the other fallen voice I'd managed to somehow keep safe.

Deep breath.

In. Out.

Seven years ago, a deep well formed in my heart.

Some experiences force you to hide things even further inside yourself. With my heart as its safe, the well holds anything precious I've managed to keep.

But *this* pain . . .

I rub my palms up and down my face, fighting off another swelling ache tightening my throat.

God, I need her.

Through all of it. Everything. I've always *had her.* My eyes close again with a pained, long blink, sighing just as I hear her whisper through me, *"I'm here, baby."*

My eyes reopen, cheek to floor, devastation renewed as I stare across the empty space between me and the wall. I swallow back the new swell of tears before my voice croaks out, "But you're not."

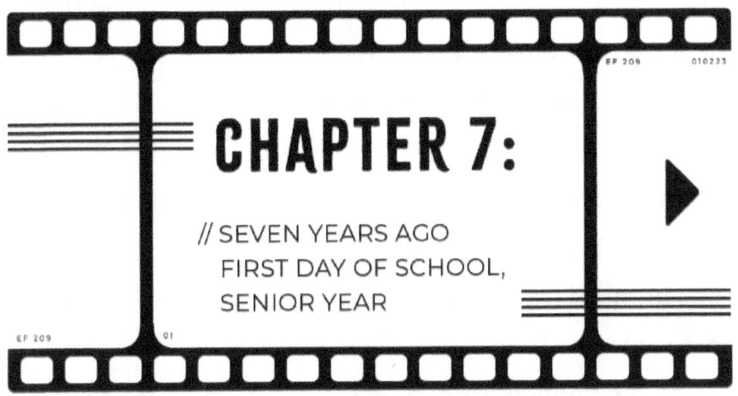

LINC

Ellis popped through the double doors to the cafeteria, carrying Paige bridal-style over to the table I had already snagged us outside. I liked being at a table that was close to the designated area for my *habit*, as Ellis affectionately called it.

I currently stood, hauling in a drag from my cigarette as Ellis plopped Paige's small body onto the bench, next to my backpack, and she giggled.

"Okay, that was fun," she laughed some more as she untied her flannel from her waist, shrugging it on over her shoulders and covering her plain white tank top.

"Audition went well?" I asked, knowing the answer already.

Her blue eyes were bright and shining and they met her smile in a way that made my heart race. Then her mouth ticked at the corner, more playfully, splaying her arms out in front of herself. "Hence the queen entrance."

"Don't get used to it," Ellis chuckled as he rounded the table to sit across from her. A laugh trickled through the exhale of my drag before I put out the cigarette, tossed it in the dispenser, and went over to the table.

I slid onto the bench, next to Paige, bumping her shoulder with mine. "What'd you sing?"

She bumped my shoulder back, and Ellis rolled his eyes while tapping away on his phone.

Paige dug through her backpack, pulling out a bag of dry cereal, muttering, "I went with 'You and I.' Lady Gaga felt like a good choice for a *Rent* audition." She added the last part as an afterthought before she finally found the other thing she'd been looking for.

A banana.

"Caroline would be crazy not to give you Maureen," Ellis said, putting his phone down.

While Ellis was a film student, he did some acting. Obviously, he had helped out on the moon movie, and he usually did the fall musicals with Paige, but he opted out this year because he was leaving in a couple weeks for a trip to Copenhagen with his dad.

Asshole got two weeks of virtual passes.

They're something Providence Academy gives out so that we can work professionally and not fall behind. But Desmond Casper also donated enough money to the school that Ellis could probably get credit for coming in and taking a shit everyday.

Not that he would. He worked as hard as anyone—*harder, I think, sometimes.* He didn't talk about it often but I'd known Ellis almost as long as I'd known Paige—and I knew he felt an extra sense of pressure to build a name for *himself.*

My eyes were still zoned out, my unfocused vision stared at Paige's measly little lunch. *Dry cereal and a banana.* She had a shift at Queenie's after school too.

Swear to God—this girl runs on iced coffee and Cheetos.

"I'll be right back," I told them, walking back toward the cafeteria door.

As I pushed through the doors, the loud clatter of sounds hit me like a wall. Twelve or so tables full of boisterous, dramatic conversation was . . . a lot.

At least it was the last *first week of school,* I reminded myself. That was, if I didn't do the college thing.

I started toward the cart with the premade peanut butter and jelly sandwiches, grabbing one, and then quickly got in line.

I could see Paige and Ellis through the windows on the far wall. Paige was laughing as she bent down to her backpack, beside the bench, grabbing something.

A sharp inhale pulled through my nose when I saw the top of her black lace thong peeking through the small gap between her shirt and her jeans.

A whistle sounded from behind me, landing in my head like a fucking arrow before a familiar voice said, "That flannel's not foolin' anyone, huh?"

I snorted, my teeth clenched. "Is flannel confusing for you, Kline?"

Martin Kline. Douchebag enemy number one—also an acting student. The asshole was already on my shit list for slipping his tongue into Paige's mouth last year when they had to kiss on stage.

Unprompted, unrehearsed, and un-fucking-acceptable.

Paige didn't want to make a big deal about it, but I was one rageful tick away from manually shoving the guy's lips down his throat and pulling them back through his asshole like a balloon animal.

Instead, I told Mr. Harris, and he helped me file a complaint. But Martin only got a slap on the wrist. Mommy and Daddy undoubtedly paid a bunch of money to make it go away.

And all it did was unleash another level of douchery.

I still hadn't turned around but the moron kept talking. "If you haven't hit that yet, I guess the rumors about you are true. Too busy blowin' Ellis to give hot little Paige what she needs."

My palm slammed into his chest before I twisted and pulled the material of his shirt.

Rose, the lunch lady, gasped, and I pulled Martin's stupid face closer. I was taller than him by an inch or two, so it took just a flick of my eyes to see him smirking.

My fist tightened, my anger intensifying, before I realized . . . he knew I couldn't *afford* to get in trouble.

I gave a small tug on his shirt before I shoved him—hard enough to knock him back a few steps, but not enough to be considered "violent behavior."

I couldn't decide if I wanted to call him out on the supposed *rumor* with strange, homophobic undertones but . . . *it wasn't worth it.*

He wasn't worth it. "Just keep that disease-ridden tongue to yourself, dickwipe."

I turned back around, apologized to Rose, and then paid for the sandwich. After pocketing the change, I gave it an extra jingle inside my pocket to try and release some of the adrenaline—*the urge* to turn around and beat that fucker into the floor.

But I forced my steps back toward the door. I tried to reroute my thoughts, calm myself down, and I absently wondered if that really was a rumor. If people really thought I was with Ellis.

It seemed impossible since everyone except for Paige seemed to know I was obsessed *with Paige.* Plus, as far as social statuses were concerned, mine was basically nonexistent at this school.

Paige and I were scholarship kids. It's the only reason we could afford to go to a place like Providence. Needless to say, I was sure there was far more scandalous gossip than an unknown film kid's sexuality.

I shook my head. It didn't matter—*what the fuck did I care.* In all likelihood, Martin was probably still pissed that someone held him accountable for being a fucking creep.

And yet, he was still a fucking creep.

"Hey, Pip," I said as I got back to the table. "Rose was giving away the last of the PB&Js. You want it?"

"*God,*" Ellis whined dramatically. "Are you *fucking* Rose or something? How do you always get the free shit?"

My eyes narrowed at him. "Drink your juice. You're getting grumpy."

His eyebrows furrowed over his green eyes, but he did in fact take a sip of apple juice, making me chuckle.

"You don't want it?" Paige asked, her eyes big and damn near twinkling at the sandwich.

I shook my head, my nose scrunching.

"Right," she sighed, taking it from me. "Sometimes I feel like your aversion to jelly should have an exception for PB&Js.

Peanut butter makes everything good," she said. "There's a rumor that it cures cancer."

My mouth pulled back as I sat down next to her. "Not *this* peanut butter, unfortunately," I chuckled.

She shrugged, unwrapping the sandwich. "Thank you." She smiled up at me. A smile that just made me fucking melt.

Food was her love language. She was a poor planner *and* she hated spending money. After her first bite, she leaned her head into my shoulder while I tipped my cheek on her head, her temple pulsing against the bottom of my jaw as she chewed.

My lips tilted at the corner, breathing in the slight spice to her smell, mixing with the peanut butter on her sandwich, and any remaining tension from inside the cafeteria fell to the ground.

Lifting my gaze, my eyebrows hitched when I saw that Ellis was sitting across from us, flicking curious glances our way as he tapped on his phone.

I knew we confused people. Ellis made his opinion very clear on my inability to make a move with Paige—and he was saying it silently now, witnessing our little *display.*

But *this* was also the very thing that made wanting her—*wanting her so fucking much*—all the more confusing. Complicated.

Because *this?* Sitting like this was just . . . how we'd always been.

Before we even knew what attraction was, this was a comfort thing. We'd been affectionate our whole lives and then hormones made it all fucking weird.

Deciding I needed to break the tension, I cleared my throat. "Hey, did you guys hear I'm gay?"

Paige sat up, chewing her bite slowly as her eyes scrunched.

Ellis choked on his apple juice and then chuckled. *"Buffy bless,* are gay rumors still a thing? *Here* of all places? The fuck?" He shook his head, and I shrugged.

"No one's ever said anything to me," Paige said.

Ellis smirked. "Of course not, babe. They think we're a freaky little threesome doing six-handed tricks."

Paige snorted a laugh. "Yeah, right."

Ellis tilted his chin.

Paige's eyes widened. "Wait, that's really something people are saying?"

Ellis shrugged again, taking another sip of his apple juice.

Paige stared at him, examining his features. Another second passed, and his smile crept up from the corner.

Paige balled up the cellophane from her sandwich and threw it at him—cracking me up.

"Asshole," she giggled, cradling her cheeks.

"Your face—" Ellis lost himself to more laughs, spurring me back on.

A quick glance at Paige had me catching the smallest hint of that blush again—the same fleeting one I'd noticed the other day when we were shooting at the cove.

I need to make a fucking move.

PAIGE

The sun was just setting as the citrus and lavender smells wafted through the small breeze as I walked through the backyard.

Our front door was kind of broken. Or . . . *nailed shut?* We couldn't figure it out, so we just used the back door.

As I walked up the steps to the small porch, a pretty melody softly played, pulling my lips up my cheeks—something deep and warm settling through me.

The piano.

I fucking loved listening to Gram play.

She didn't do *piano time* as much anymore—said it hurt her joints.

I opened the door slowly, and closed it behind me—*quuuiet*—listening, as I took off my beaten up, yellow Chucks.

When I started to make my way through the kitchen, the chorus to the song she was playing became clear.

"Vienna," by Billy Joel. A permanent member of Gram's "Lemon Lady Mix."

My smile lifted as I shrugged off my backpack, leaving it at the table before I walked the rest of the way to the living room. Her back was to me—sitting at the bench in front of the piano in the corner.

She was in her element in front of those keys—in a trance.

The lid of the piano had some of her house plants on it. Purple and blue smudges stained the walnut colored wood of the Spinet piano.

Luckily, we were able to clean most of the keys, but that one spot remained from the night Linc, Ellis, and I watched *Aristocats* for the first time.

My focus moved back to her. Her posture was poised, but you could see the flicks of excitement. The small jump of her shoulders, the languid sway of her chin in the transitions.

As I could hear the end of the song nearing, her movement slowed. Her light gray hair swayed down her back as she dipped her chin, plunking the last couple of notes. I stepped just behind the bench and hugged her over her shoulders.

Beautiful.

She clasped her hand over my arms that were crossed over her chest. "I still got it," she squeaked, with a small laugh.

I chuckled through my nose, straightening up. "Ah, Lemon Lady, you never lost *it.*"

It was just . . . harder for her to play.

She sighed, but a fondness lifted in her dark blue eyes. "A rap album. That's the dream," she said.

"It is," I agreed.

Lemon Lady was a self-appointed rap name. It was inspired by the *actual name* a few kids in the neighborhood had given Gram, on account of the fact that she handed out giant-ass lemons from her tree out back during trick-or-treat every year.

Truly witchy behavior.

"How was the first day as a big bad senior?" she asked.

My shoulders lifted with a sigh as I pushed back and leaned into the side of the piano. "It was like any other day," I shrugged. "It was fine."

"Just fiiine?" she whined. "Come on, no one's sleeping with a teacher or doing cocaine in the green room?" Her head shook. "Art school ain't what it used to be."

I giggled through a yawn. "My audition for *Rent* went well. I had a shift at Queenie's, but it was dead so she sent me home.

Oh, she wanted me to tell you that the library is looking for some extra mystery readers or something?"

"Oh, great. I'll call Leonard in the morning. Sweet man—but ya know, he and his husband had to move out to the deep valley. It's getting crazy, Paigey May."

I nodded. While I didn't know the librarian well, I was *very* aware of the ever-rising cost of living in the LA area. I mean, I went to school with some of the richest kids in the country.

We were lucky I had my scholarship and Gram owned our little shanty beach cottage—gifted to her from her grandmother. Her gift to me one day, as she always said.

And I loved our house—broken floorboards and all—but it was impossible to imagine living here without her.

God. I wouldn't *let* myself imagine that.

Either way, while the house might have been paid off, it was also in desperate need of some TLC.

I sighed. *A problem for another day.*

"Well, I've got some homework, so . . ."

"Ohh," Gram shooed, standing up. "I made some chili. Let's at least eat together." I could tell by her face that wasn't all she was asking, and I told her I knew that with my eyes, hitching my brows.

After another beat she said, "Can we watch *Practical Magic* while we eat?"

·◆ ·)· ·)· ·)· ·●· ·(· ·(· ·(· ◆·

Luckily, Gram had a couple of weed gummies after dinner and passed out pretty early on into *Practical Magic*.

Not that I didn't love a good kickoff into spooky season but . . . I had some shit to do.

Sitting at my desk, I fired up my laptop. My management class was requiring us to update our resumes and I had three roles to add since the last time I updated it.

Four if I included Linc's movie . . .

Which was good. It was a never ending critique on my re-sume.

Not enough film credits.

Ironic, given that Linc almost always had a camera in his hand. But those were different. They were just for us.

My laptop screen lit up with a picture of me and the other two-thirds of my *threesome* on Venice boardwalk—the night Ellis bought weed from a guy in a chalk circle that just said:

Stand here.

The picture cracked me the fuck up. We all looked really happy, but also wildly confused—*dumbwonderment* was what we titled the moment. And it was now a tradition on Linc's birthday.

We'd buy weed the old-fashioned way and get high at the cove.

Turning on some music, I lost myself to the bullshit for about an hour. I was in the middle of combing through some videos Linc had shot for me in a show I did at the beginning of the sum-mer, just as my phone rang.

My mouth pulled up at the name and I hit accept.

"What's up, punk? You called at the perfect time."

I could hear him taking a drag of his cigarette as he said, "This already sounds like a favor." I could hear his smile too.

My mouth twisted. "Well, it's all about perspective. Does splicing together and updating my reel sound like a favor or f-f-fuun?" I sang the last word half-heartedly.

I was met with the sound of light wind whipping in the background through the phone. He must have been driving, windows down. "That sounds *exactly* like a favor," he said. And I didn't quite care for his tone. It was . . . *dangly.*

Standing up, I walked toward my bed. "Fine, don't help me. When I'm shakin' my goods on Sunset because I couldn't get an agent, because my *best friend*—"

"Jesus," he said a little deeper than usual—rougher—and it sent a wave of something *un-fucking-expected* to my lady regions.

After what sounded like another drag, his voice lightened a bit. "The dramatics." He sighed through a light chuckle, "'Course I'll do it."

My mouth ticked up as I plopped down on the mattress and laid back. "Where are you going?"

"Home," he exhaled. "Just did our second workout over at Ellis's."

I nodded, but the mention of their little workout routine had my mind . . . *wandering.*

It immediately wandered down to the deep end of my thought pool, playing back his reaction—*to a joke.*

I'd never heard him sound so . . . possessive.

Ugh. My toes curl.

And then, it's like my little motherfucking, shithead of a brain, cannonballs into the pool—sending the water up and smacking the land hard with the splash of memories.

His cut biceps, smudged with dirt from the woods—the terrace of his abs glistening in the sun from the water in the cove. The downright-heartthrob smirk he flicked over his shoulder on the same day.

"What are you up to?"

"Nothing!" I yelped. A quick-reaction panic that definitely sounded like *something*.

I rubbed my forehead with the pads of my fingers. A poking feeling intensified in my brain, flinching my eyebrows. I could *just fucking feel it*, and I ground my teeth. "Stop smiling."

He laughed. "How the hell do you know? You're not even here!"

"Just stop. It's giving me a headache."

He laughed harder, but took a breath to say, "My smile makes your head hurt? But, like, not even my physical smile. *The thought of my smile?*"

I pinched between my brows. "I'm hanging up."

"No, wait!" he said, his laughter conceding.

I sat on the other end of the line but laid the phone next to me on speaker. We just . . . sat silently.

This was so weird.

This hormone hiccup wasn't fucking passing. It was *festering*.

It was just too hard to be . . . *sure*.

Sure that he was feeling this way too.

Sure that we weren't confusing the connection we'd always had with something fleeting—like *teenage goddamn hormones*.

And I couldn't really talk about it with anyone because everyone thought it was weird that we *weren't* together. No one understood. For all intents and purposes, we already acted like a couple. Just without the . . . physical stuff.

And it seemed as though *that* had been on the spotlight of my thoughts—just a full-moon fucking *light* around this intense attraction to the boy I'd known my whole life.

The sound of the light wind disappeared and made way for just his breathing. He must have rolled up the window.

His quiet sigh felt like it swept through the phone and blew over my eyelids, closing them, and I felt my limbs sink further into the mattress beneath me.

"Thanks for defending me today," I said, in a sedated adrenaline crash.

He huffed a small laugh. "What?"

"Jenna told me you almost lost your shit on Martin Kline for calling me a slut in the cafeteria."

"No, that's—" he stopped himself, and took a breath, but his tone was still tight when he added, "That's not exactly—" he stuttered again, then blew out a heavy exhale. "He made a comment about your—uh . . ."

Oh God, the places this could go . . .

"Your thong," he said, clearing his throat awkwardly.

My mouth gaped, but my nose scrunched. "Ew. What'd he say?"

He grunted. Another beat passed before he said, "It doesn't matter. Let's just steer clear of him." That deeper, grittier resonance in his voice was back, but the stir it caused earlier was either tired or he sounded too . . . angry.

My eyes fluttered back open, saying, "No arguments here." But I could feel him silently stewing through the phone like hot static in my temples. I sigh. "It's fine, Linc. We've always known he was a douche kabob."

He laughed humorlessly. Another beat passed before he muttered, "Yeah. It's just fucked. More should have been done. It's bullshit, and it all comes back to money."

I nodded through a yawn.

We shared this lament often—*some* variation about the injustices of being the poor kids. It was just a hard pill to swallow. And given where we lived and where we went to school—we had to take the pill fairly regularly over the years.

I yawned again. "Well, luckily, you and Ellis have been hitting the gym if we need to challenge him to a duel."

Linc snorted a laugh, followed by a sigh. Another few moments of silence lingered. After a deep breath pulled through my chest, I asked him, "Are you home?" My eyes closed again, practically falling asleep.

"Mhm," he said, his voice softer again. "You falling asleep?"

"Mhm," I said quietly.

I wasn't sure why we weren't hanging up. Hell, I wasn't even really sure why he called but there was just something keeping us on the line.

Waiting . . .

CHAPTER 8
LINC

Heavy. It's the only feeling that fully sinks in.

A fuzzy image plays in front of my eyes, slowly. Unfocused.

My lungs tighten while blurred figures spot my vision.

Heavy, heavy, heavy.

I think one of the figures is standing—no, kneeling—but sort of hunched over the other one.

For some reason, it feels like I'm one of them, but I can't tell which one, or what's happening.

"Easy," I hear someone say. "Nice and easy."

"Easy," Ellis's voice snaps through the fog.

Oh, fuck.

My untimely space out happens as I'm flat on my back, my inked arms starting to shake above me as I push the barbell back up and away from my chest.

The memory, in all of its blurriness, lingers as Ellis stands over me—*close*—which isn't helping, and then curls his fists around the bar, locking the weight back in place.

Okay, so I guess he was *helping.*

Blinking rapidly, a long hiss pushes through my clenched teeth and my muscles half-release.

"Is it as hard as you make it look?" he jabs with a chuckle.

A raspy laugh escapes, relieved he didn't seem to notice that I had zoned the fuck out. I cough to release the jolt of adrenaline. "Fuck y-you."

Another deep breath.

A residual laugh pushes past his lips, shrugging. "No, man. That was good. Benching two hundred ain't nothin'," then he mumbles, "Looked like you were about to kill someone."

The remnants of the disturbing coldness still feels like ice melting through my veins, and I shudder as I sit up and swipe the towel at the end of the bench.

"You doin' all right? You've seemed . . ." he trails off as his gaze flicks down to my bobbing knee.

I actively work to slow it down and nod.

Quickly. Too quickly. Fuck.

Exercise *usually* helps. *Lifting* in particular usually *demands* that I stay present—the physical weight, the rough almost-granular metal bar that bites into my palms, is usually enough to keep me *here.*

So, what the fuck was that?

I can sense Ellis's curious, possibly *concerned*, eyes on me, and a heavy sigh drops my shoulders—doing my best to appear indifferent.

Not too far, not too deep.

But Ellis has seen all the ugly parts of what I've become, *and* he's obnoxiously intuitive, so concealing *anything* is a bit of an art form.

I have to give him just enough honesty that he'll accept it and move on. But not enough that we'll accidentally stumble into "worried territory."

Luckily, I think my delayed response can be blamed on the fact that my body is still heaving from the exertion—*and* the realization that I was holding two hundred pounds while my mind was *who-the-fuck-knows* where.

I grab my water bottle off the floor, my voice hoarse as I mumble, "Just still a little m-messed up from going back to V-Venice."

He nods, keeping his chin dipped for a moment. I think he's satisfied with that answer. At least I'm actually *admitting* I went to Venice.

And to be fair, I do think it's at least partially true. I hadn't been back there in years, and I think it's fucking with me.

Mom and Maisie don't even live there anymore.

I've avoided going back for a reason, and now I know why. Revisiting a place where I wasn't *this version* of myself—*where my life was completely different*—it feels like it opened some kind of portal. One where the memories are teasing the edges of my mind—pulling my focus even more than usual.

And it's not that I can't handle the memories . . . they still hurt like a bitch, but I can handle them when they surface—it's more like what will happen if they *continue* to hit like this.

I cringe even thinking about it.

In the last five years—one of which being right before I went to Lending Lanterns—it's happened twice. Two times where the visions—*the memories*—have pooled, stormed, and then crashed like a tidal wave through my skull.

And then I float. For God knows how long. *And I can't let that happen.*

Popping up, I say, "W-Wanna hit the bag?" Flicking my eyes over to the boxing bag in the corner of the garage.

Ellis chuckles. "Ahh, man. Desmond's gonna be here in an hour . . ."

My fists clench. The reminder of Desmond's visit solidifies that I still need to work off some adrenaline, keep my mind busy.

The *idea* of the social aspect has already jacked up my heart rate, and I crack my neck. "It's c-cool," I stutter. *Fuck.*

That's been a little worse too. Not that I talk a whole lot as it is—but when it gets *hard* to talk . . .

It's cause for concern.

Taking a deep breath, I force a chuckle—*force* an easy tone. "It's cool if you can't hang," I jab, walking toward the bag.

Ellis groans, "Dick," but I hear his footsteps follow behind me.

"Linc. Good to see ya," Desmond says, standing from his seat at one of the bar stools at the counter, as I step out from my hallway.

He extends his hand and I accept it, swallowing hard and clenching my jaw.

No matter how many times I *visualize* this feeling—the tough, calloused feel of his hand brushes my skin and a rushing, itchiness crawls up my throat.

My bare feet press as hard as they can into the floor. I don't know what shit Ellis had them put in here—but it's fucking magical. The wood is imported from Madagascar or something, but it's always the perfect amount of coolness.

As soon as Desmond releases my hand, the tension pulling my body starts to loosen. "How's it goin'?" he asks, giving a clap to my shoulder that shoots down my spine like a whip.

My fists tighten at my sides, and I immediately feel the pressure from his hand on my shoulder release. "Oh, shit. Sorry, I wasn't thinking . . ."

Fuck, fuck, fuck.

Barely passed the handshake and I'm acting like a kicked puppy.

This is one of the many reasons I should just live in a fucking hole.

Ellis slides two beer bottles toward the edge of the counter, closer to Desmond and me, saying, "He's fine," casually to Desmond, but then looks at me. "*Cinderella Man* probably just tweaked something while he was wailing on the bag just before you got here."

Desmond's concern seems to fade away completely with one look at my cracked, raw knuckles.

Buffy bless Ellis.

Whoa.

Where the fuck did that come from?

The old phrase hits me with enough force to knock the wind out of me. I *do* need a fucking beer.

Giving Ellis an appreciative nod, I silently thank him for veering the attention away from me. I pick up the bottle, and he picks up his too. He gives a subtle, easy shrug just as Desmond says,

"Well, good for you, kid," with a smile, clinking his bottle with mine. "Cheers."

Ellis taps his bottle in too, and we all take a sip.

Well, I take a gulp.

I limit myself to one drink. Any more has the potential to get out of control—to send me *too far away.* But a single drink is usually enough to pull me out when I feel *too deep inside*—too lost in my own fucking head.

My toes push into the large grooves of the floorboard as the malty taste of the beer soothes down my throat.

Another perk to fancy flooring—*at least to weirdos like me*—is the unique grain pattern. A darker brown finish with *big* knots and grooves.

"I just saw this morning that *The 5* got selected for Outskirts Fest, that's pretty fuckin' big, son. Congrats." He tips his bottle toward Ellis before taking another sip.

My eyes widen, looking over at my friend, my mouth twitching at the corner. *Really?* I ask silently.

He gives a modest smile with a nod. "Yeah, it was definitely a *long-term* goal, so it's a little overwhelming, 'cause films that do the best have a *really* big following. So I'll have to step up the marketing, and it kinda delays the start of my next project."

Next project?

Damn. He doesn't waste any time. But it checks out. Sometimes it's like he can't turn his brain off. We have, like, the exact *opposite* problem.

My brain likely looks like an abandoned warehouse with an echoey voice asking, *"Is anyone home?"* While Ellis's brain probably looks like some sort of mod-podge gathering, with interesting stories, tinkering glassware, general amusement—all swirling around him while he picks up ideas and inspiration like party favors.

I envy it sometimes. I used to love creating shit like he does. But to let that part of myself fully back in feels risky. Like if I let *that* back in, I'd let *all* of it back in.

I take another sip of my beer just as Desmond says, "Actually, speaking of work—Linc, I wanted to talk to you about a potential opportunity."

Me?

My expression alone must show my confusion but Desmond says, "Let's fire up the grill and we can chat while we eat."

CHAPTER 9
LINC

I volunteer to take grill duty—figuring a quick breather will do me good, while my brain still fights to understand *what-in-the-fuck* kind of *opportunity* someone like Desmond Casper could have for *me.*

He owns . . . *well, everything.*

He has a foot in the film business with his production company, he owns *so many* restaurants and hotels, I can't even begin to list them all—tons of rental properties, his own private jets.

It's interesting how different he and Ellis are—but one similarity is this quality, I guess. While Ellis doesn't care much for excessive wealth like his dad, he is greedy for *more* in other ways—more justice, more discovery, more information.

Ambition, I think, just as I flip the patties.

I had that once too . . .

My mind threatens to slip off. The fuzzy memory starts to blur the corners of my vision, as a scratch of shame itches my throat.

My grip tightens around the rough wooden handle of the spatula I'm holding, and I focus down on the grill. The heat haze ripples the air—making the sight in front of me flicker with invisible waves.

The grill is hot, I think. Just a finger touch to that and I'm sure to singe the feeling away.

My hand lifts to do it, but at the last second I realize how epically *stupid* that idea is, and instead, I smack myself in the forehead.

Ow. Fuck.

Rubbing the skin, I groan. It's tender, but I'm certain it doesn't hurt as much as, oh . . . I don't know . . . *sticking my fucking finger on a blazing hot grill.*

I grunt and take another gulp of my beer, but I need to slow down—make sure I have enough to sip through whatever conversation I'm about to have with Desmond.

The smokey smell of the meat hits my nose, and I glance down to see they're ready. I slide the three patties onto the buns, then twist the knob to turn off the grill.

After a breath, I carry the plate back inside from the porch.

"Hey," Ellis says from the counter, his laptop open. I hear Desmond off in the background on the phone, but he's too far down the entryway hall for me to really hear anything.

"Burgers are d-done," I say, lifting the plate.

"Awesome, man, thanks," Ellis says, tapping the keys in front of him. My eyes scrunch curiously at the laptop and he says, "Got some info from the tech guy I contacted to help me with the new project—just wanted to respond quickly."

I nod. "D-Don't you have to delay the new one?"

Ellis blinks a couple of times down at his laptop screen, his green eyes studying something before he looks back up at me. "Yeah, I mean, I do. But if I can have him doing some research while I'm promoting *The 5,* then I won't lose traction."

My chin lifts with a half nod. Considering I didn't know he was actively working on anything new until about an hour ago, I obviously have no idea what this new project is. But I'm sure he'll tell me about it.

However blurry my memories may be, I know that he and I *used to* lose ourselves for hours, just "talking shop."

I'm not as good at it now. The ideas—or the talking for that matter. But he thanked me constantly for the little bit I helped with on *The 5*. He said I had been his *"brainstorming backboard"* and . . . it meant a lot to me.

I look forward to when he gets me on a good day, and tells me about the new one—maybe I can help him shoot some stuff again.

The sound of his laptop screen snapping closed pulls my attention back to him, and he says, "Let's eat."

After Desmond comes back from his phone call, the three of us fall into easy conversation, that is, until Desmond says, "Ya know, I'm actually heading up to San Francisco for a benefit at the end of the week. I should see if your mom and Bruce want to grab dinner."

I nod, awkwardly mumbling, "I-I'm sure they'd love to."

Ellis's eyes meet mine in the check-in way I'm used too, and I sigh my response.

I'm fine. As fine as *I'm* capable of, at least. Bruce is my mom's new husband. She'd started dating him my senior year of high school, and he proposed shortly after . . . I left. They moved up to the Bay area right before I came back.

I make a mental note to text Maisie later, just as Desmond angles himself more toward me. "Anyway," he says, clearing his throat, "that job I wanted to talk to you about . . ."

Swallowing my bite, I shift my eyes down to my beer, seeing I've got about a third of it left.

"S-Sure," I tell him, picking up the bottle and taking a sip, then ask, "What's up?"

Desmond leans forward. "Well, it's a bit unusual, and it'll be temporary. My buddy owns a club in the city and he called me a couple nights ago. I guess he's down a security guard."

"A bouncer?" Ellis says with a confused huff.

I'm not sure how to take his reaction, but it sits strangely in my head. *Does he think I* can't *do it or* shouldn't *do it? I can't tell.*

"Kind of," Desmond says, with a tilt to his head. "On the surface, you'd be a guard, but it's a little more involved than that. He suspects there may be something amiss at the club." He shifts his weight with a small sigh, then continues, "It's an exclusive place. Invite-only, and the guard they just terminated was let go because he was caught admitting uninvited guests. There's also been some second-hand chatter about multiple staff members being approached by people recruiting for some underground sex club. He's not totally sure on the details, but that's where you would come in."

"Underground sex club?" Ellis drawls.

Distantly, I see Desmond shrug as he says something else to

Ellis, but his words are taking an absurd amount of time to sink into my head.

"Wh-What would I have to do?" I ask. It's the only thing I *can* ask. This already sounds like something I'd be terrible at.

"Essentially, you'd work regular guard shifts. Discretion would be key," he says emphatically, then adds, "He's asked that you document anything that might allude to anything unsavory happening—any strange interactions you might notice among the staff. Any suspicious patrons . . ."

The fuck? How will I know what's not normal when I have no fucking clue what normal is? Not just in life but like, specifically, at this club.

My eyes squint, confused, and Desmond leans forward. "Look, I know this sounds kind of unusual. But if the club is being used to facilitate anything illegal, it's important that he gets out in front of it before it becomes a PR nightmare."

Ellis laughs humorlessly. "Why doesn't the guy just spend some time at his *beloved little joint*? Worried, but not worried enough to take the time and figure out what's going on for himself?"

My eyes widen a bit. Like me, Ellis has been a little on edge these last few days, but it's still a feistier response than I'm prepared for.

"Easy, kid," Desmond chuckles with a shake of his head. "It's true, he's a busy guy, but if shady shit *is* happening there, his presence will only throw a temporary blanket over it. People tend to be extra careful when the boss is around. And since his schedule won't allow him to be there all the time, he needs to get to the bottom of it as quickly as possible."

I don't even know . . . *what the fuck?*

Desmond sighs, adding, "He's an old friend, and he asked if I had anyone I trusted. Someone with good instincts. Strong. I thought of you immediately."

"Um . . . I am *right* here," Ellis says, and then laughs.

Desmond does too, and it eases some of the tension that came from this bizarre fucking offer.

Then Desmond says to Ellis, "I knew you'd be busy with *The 5.*"

Right. Ellis has *a job.*

I've mostly stuck to freelance editing jobs I can do from the house over the years. Picking up enough work to pay Ellis my measly excuse for rent.

Maybe that's what this is about. Ellis has stuck with me through all my bullshit for the last five years, but maybe he was getting sick of it, and didn't know how to tell me.

Or maybe after seeing the lemons yesterday, he's worried I'm slipping and talked to Desmond about it. He wouldn't be wrong, I've been worried about it myself. *The zone outs . . .*

Speaking of zone outs, Ellis clears his throat, bringing my attention back to the table

Desmond says, "Look, Linc, I've known you for a long time. You've been through a lot . . ." he trails off for a second before his spine stiffens. "I just think if there is anything going on there, you'll find out about it."

My unease swells with something else—something encouraging. I'm not sure if it's the result of a billionaire tycoon *working me,* or if it's sincere, but the way he said it made it really sound like he asked me because he believes the things he mentioned to be strengths I have, instead of just shit I've lived through.

The sound of Ellis picking up his bottle darts my eyes up, as he says. "Why don't you just think about it, Linc?"

Desmond nods. "Yes, of course."

I shake my head, quickly rasping, "I'll d-do it."

Truthfully, I went into the conversation preparing myself to accept whatever he threw on the table. It's the first thing Desmond is asking of me—something he's *entrusting* me with—and while I'm not sure of my ability to follow through, I owe it to him to at least try.

It's only temporary, and maybe something that gets me out of the house—a schedule—will help steer me back on track.

Maybe this will be good for me.

Desmond nods. "Really? That's great, Linc. I really appreciate it, man." Ellis gets up with his empty plate, and I follow, in need of a breather, when Desmond says, "Oh—uh—and just one more thing." I stop again, staring down at him as he says, "It's a burlesque club."

Fuck.

CHAPTER 10
PAIGE

Buzz. Buzz. Buzz.

Buffy, *fuck. What is that?*

I feel the vibration rattling in my head. My eyes peel open but immediately shut again when the heavy stream of light blinds me from the window.

Buzz. Buzz. Buzz.

Oh my God. I'm going to diiie.

Ugh. I could only be so lucky. My brain feels like it's bobbing in a pool of champagne and tears, and *holy fuck* I am not a fan.

It's then that I notice my temple is pressing against a hard surface, and I roll to my back.

Oh, holy shit.

A sharp twinge between my shoulder blades shoots a reminder of how monumentally stupid I am—up my spine and into my brain.

A whiney groan pushes past my lips. The aftereffects of getting shitfaced and sleeping on the floor.

And crying. Don't forget about the massive amounts of crying. Buffy fucking bless.

The buzzing finally stops. I now recognize it's my phone vibrating, but I think it's over on the counter and . . . I think I need to live on the floor.

I have the displeasure of not only feeling every tug and pinch in my back—but thanks to the full length mirror leaning on the wall across from me—I get to watch for a full minute while I flop and push my way to a standing position.

When I'm finally, kind of, upright, I stare at my bare legs, seeing a bruise on my calf from swinging it too hard around the pole. *Improper weight placement,* as Rio would say.

That catches my eye first, then my gaze drifts up to my black booty shorts and white tank top, covered by Gram's oversized cardigan from my dreams. Visions.

I'm going fucking mad.

My eyes are puffy and bloodshot, and the silverish-blue nest on my head falls a bit when I cradle my face in my palms, flinching when my neck spasms.

I tut through another whine at the pain—at the forty bucks I spent yesterday, *after* learning I'd be unexpectedly out of work for three days.

Stupid, stupid, stupid.

"Have to be young and stupid to become old and wise," I hear Gram's voice distantly, and it does the smallest bit to ease my aching body—my heart.

I moan and groan through my few steps to the small kitchenette, just beside my front door, deciding I need water and coffee immediately.

Between starting the coffee and grabbing the water pitcher out of my fridge, I pick up my phone from the counter and see that it's just after noon.

Yay for small victories, I guess. My little breakdown at least managed to get me a solid eight hours of sleep.

But then I see that the source of the buzzing was a missed call from Jackson.

He didn't leave a message but then texted—

Jackson: Call me.

Immediately, I want to ignore the message. Why he felt the need to text me something that's made pretty fucking clear by a missed call is beyond me—but this is Jackson Thorough Hardass III.

Maybe he's calling to see if I want to pick up a floor shift. The cocktail waitresses make next to nothing compared to the dancers—but I guess beggars can't be choosers.

I click on his name, calling him back as the coffee pot starts to bubble, the smell igniting a small excitement at the promise of its magical wakey-wakey powers.

On the third ring, he answers, "Jackson."

I snort. "God, you and the Hollywood sign."

"What?" he says back quickly.

I shake my head, wincing at the pinching pain between my shoulders. My teeth clench before I say, "Forget it. What's up?"

"Heard you were out the rest of the week."

I shake my head, wincing. "No, I'm okay," I lie. "I can come in."

I hear him blow a *"psh"* noise through the phone. He's probably having a cigarette, but says, "And risk the wrath of Rio? No thank you."

My mouth quirks at the corner. I don't know their history—just that they seem to have one. I don't think it's romantic, but there's a deep respect—*a fondness*—between them, that suggests they know each other outside The Window.

He clears his throat, ironing out his measured tone before he says, "Well, this might help. I just wanted to let you know that you have a Veranda gig on Saturday."

My eyes squint, studying the statement like I can see it in front of me—rearranging the letters and trying to make sense of it.

"Blue?" he says.

I nod, but then realize he can't see me and say, "Yeah. Um . . . who requested *me?*"

It wasn't a vanity question. I had only heard about Veranda gigs through *"someone, who knows someone, who knows someone."* But I knew enough to know that the "entertainment" was chosen by the patron booking the room.

"You know I can't tell you that. You'll get the information at the debriefing on Saturday, so be here by *six at the absolute latest.*"

He puts such a hard emphasis on the time that it quite literally shoves me into the decision to be purposefully late.

That, and the fact that he's telling me, not asking me, is twisting its way through my nerves, tightening my limbs and reawakening the soreness.

Veranda events aren't *"required."* They're more, *"You can say no, but you definitely shouldn't say no." Wink wink.*

I mean, there were rumors that the gig was a guaranteed five grand paycheck, plus tip—but no one can ever confirm anything because the engagements are tightly wound in nondisclosures.

That kind of money wouldn't cost nothing.

"Blue," Jackson barks through the phone.

"Huh?"

"I knew you weren't listening."

I was not.

I clear my throat, trying to shake the unease, muttering, "Got it. Be there by seven. Don't be late."

"If you're a minute after six—"

"Yeah, yeah. You'll huff and puff and blow my job away. Don't you think it'd be more fun to find something else to blow, Sergeant Hardass?"

I can practically feel the smoke coming out of his ears through the phone, and a blip of satisfaction finds its way to my chest, tilting the corner of my mouth up.

He's so fucking serious all the time that I can't help but push his buttons. It's my own measly form of entertainment—misery loves company and all that—but I'm nearly certain the enjoyment is one-sided.

"Get some rest," he says, tightly. "I'll see you Saturday."

"Wait—" I stop him and hear his impatient sigh through the phone.

I want to ask him for a bit more clarification. *The expectations of the Veranda,* but I can practically hear him tapping his metaphorical watch through the phone.

"Nevermind," I mutter. "Thanks."

His salutation is a grunt before he hangs up, and my mouth flattens.

Dick.

I lose the day, slipping in and out of painful consciousness. So by ten o'clock at night, I lay in bed, nowhere near sleep.

My mind is tossing when my body turns, then twisting and tumbling down my throat, rattling me like a raging river through a gorge.

"*Vibrating at a very high frequency,*" I hear Gram say.

I take a deep breath and twist toward my nightstand, grateful the movement is a little less painful—after my stretching session with Cheeto on my shoulder, between naps, my muscles still feel strained, but less actively *irritated.*

I pick up my phone and see that Rio texted me back. I had messaged her earlier, asking if she knew anything about the Veranda gigs.

Rio: They're just private shows.
Good $$. And since it's kink night,
the costume I'm making you
is basically leather dental floss lol.

I huff. *Great.* Still, my mouth ticks up, before I slide the phone back on the nightstand, staying curled on my side.

I guess if Rio isn't concerned, then it really isn't a big deal. And if Veranda events are as good of a payout as they're rumored to be, it'll help offset my little injury hiatus.

Gram's chuckle weaves its way through my chest. It feels as real as her cardigan I'm currently wrapped in. I hear her again, *"Such loud thoughts for a little thing."*

A heavy sigh pushes past my lips. "Just a bad feeling," I mumble out loud, responding to the voice in my head, but . . . I know I'm alone. Except for Cheeto, of course.

When I don't get a response, it's confirmed. This isn't a real conversation. *I know the difference.*

In the many times I've questioned my sanity in the last seven years—my imaginary conversations with *her* since her death have been the front-runner.

But every time I wonder if I've actually snapped, I'm faced with the unfortunate reality that I'm entirely aware these conversations with her are not real.

A heavy yawn stretches my mouth before I release it with an exhale. *And really, is that any better?*

God, I need to focus on something else.

My eyes drift just past my nightstand, just to the other side of it where the doorway to my small walk-in closet sits open.

Closing my eyes, I visualize my laptop, sitting on top of the small, three-drawer dresser, just inside the archway. *The top drawer that holds . . .*

I think about it. My eyes open, and I even sit up with the idea. I could open the drawer, take out the box—I could turn on the laptop.

But fear stops me. It keeps me in the bed.

It forces me to lie back down.

"Sleep now, my girl."

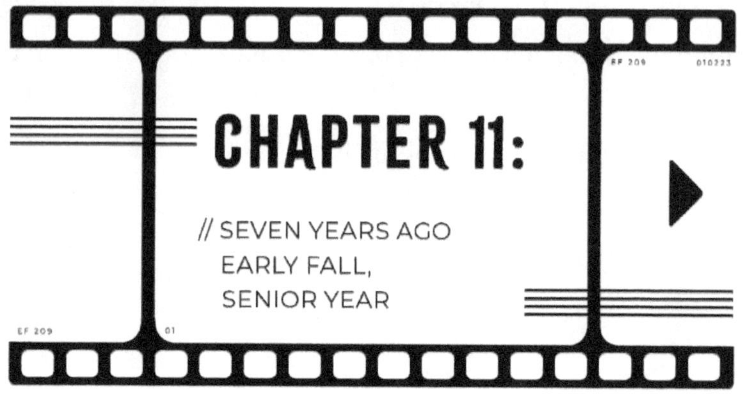

PAIGE

Boob to boob with Margaret Baylor first thing on a Saturday morning was a bit more than I was ready for.

Gram would probably be proud.

I shook my head, refocusing.

It would be a fun but exhausting day as we did a bunch of promotional shit for *Rent*, our musical theater ensemble class show, and the *fun* started with this photo shoot.

Margaret and I had just marked through our duet to get some still shots, and my character, Maureen, was currently pressed up against her girlfriend, Joanne—also known as, Margaret—my new boob buddy.

"Margaret, can you lift her up?" Mr. Harris asked.

Mr. Harris had recruited some film students—Linc included— to help run cameras while he directed the shoot.

A *"psh"* sound blew past Margaret's lips as she glanced down at me with a silent, *"Ready?"*

I smiled, placing my hands on her shoulders and then went as far to squeal *"Wee!"* before hopping into her arms, hugging my legs around her waist. She laughed, as did a few others around us, while she easily held me up with her arms hooked around my lower back.

"That's what I'm talking about," Martin said, loud enough that I could hear, and my eyes shot over to him.

"Fuck off, Kline," I heard Linc jab before Mr. Harris cleared his throat.

To which Martin obnoxiously blew out a drawn-out whistle like a Pepe LePew wannabe.

"Mr. Kline," Mr. Harris's voice raised, but only slightly, commanding attention. "Your lack of professionalism will undoubtedly be your downfall. These two young ladies are doing their job, so if you can't behave accordingly, you can do us all a favor and get the fuck off my set."

I snorted a laugh, appreciating the matter-of-fact delivery—and the curse. Linc told me Mr. Harris was relaxed with it, but dropping an *F* bomb right off the bat won him some points with me.

Margaret laughed too, hiking me farther up, holding me in place around her waist.

I actually thought she was a dance student during our freshman orientation. She was easily just under six feet tall and obnoxiously gorgeous.

Little did I know she was a badass singer. A video Linc had taken of our duet had gotten over ten thousand views online—which wasn't exactly viral, but still pretty cool.

Her character was a lawyer, so her costume was a dark gray

pantsuit. But she weaseled the wardrobe director into scrapping the coat for the shoot, and letting her wear suspenders. So she was dressed in the gray slacks, black suspender straps, and a black tank top.

My costume was easy—I wore a plain white tank top and some black leather pants that I could feel digging into the underside of my ass cheeks as she held me up.

"Paige, can you touch your forehead to hers?" Mr. Harris said. "And if you can, kind of hold her cheek? Margaret, move one of your hands just a little higher up her back. Imagine this is the moment their relationship becomes something real."

I took a deep breath, allowing myself a second to sink into the moment.

He added, "They've probably been feeling it for a while. But neither one was sure until this moment, when the veil drops."

I wasn't sure if I just related to that point-of-view, or if I really liked Mr. Harris's directing style. He was very specific with the blocking. And it didn't hurt that he seemed to have no tolerance for bullshit—even from smarmy rich kids.

But *intimate scenes* were the hardest for me. On top of trying to truly embody someone else, forcing affection had this way of bringing me back into myself. It was almost as if the intimacy *reminded* me that I was playing a part instead of letting myself fully emulate a human experience.

Focusing back, I gently tilted my forehead down against Margaret's, taking a breath. After another second, I pulled my gaze up to meet her pretty brown eyes, her flawless dark skin. I wondered if Maureen noticed Joanne's eyes first, or her beautiful complexion—maybe her voice—but then my mind started to wander . . .

I found my hands holding *her* nape, moving to cradle the side of *her* face, imagining . . . *what the light stubble of* his *jaw would feel like against the pad of my thumb*—his *arms wrapped around me like this.*

Wanting, yearning.

His *eyes. Swirls of green and brown with hints of gold when the light caught them just right. Like I was running through a field of pine trees, filled with fireflies.*

Running, running, running.

"Cut. Excellent," Mr. Harris's voice startled me, and my shoulders jumped as he muttered, "Great work, girls. We can move on." Then he walked over to some of the other cast members who were getting ready to shoot as Margaret put me down.

I was trying to recover from the whiplash of everything that just ran through my mind as I faintly registered Margaret giggling, "That was fun, lover," then gave me a playful swat on the bottom before flitting back toward the dressing rooms down the hall.

I released a breath with a small laugh. But as soon as my eyes pulled back from where she'd just left, I was met with the exact eyes I was just imagining.

Linc was standing on the other side of the room, watching me. My mouth felt dry as it nervously ticked up at the corner while something I couldn't place filled his expression.

In our first month back at school, we'd both been so busy that we weren't getting to see as much of each other, which seemed to be giving room for the ever-growing awkwardness to flourish.

Linc placed the camera he was holding on a tripod, locking it in place before he walked over to me with a casual but purposeful stride.

When he was right in front of me he looked kind of . . . *tense*—but not angry.

"Nice pants," he finally said with a smirk.

My legs crossed from the full-blown tingle that tightened in the deepest part of my stomach, and I coughed, mostly to release some tension but then tried to cover it up with nervous laughter.

Good fucking God. Paige Michaels, get your shit together!

I quickly said, "At least they didn't have to sew me into them."

What?!

My eyes widened as his eyebrows pinched, but a glint of amusement sparkled in the corner of his gaze.

"In *Grease*—" I quickly added. "They sewed Olivia Newton John into her leather pants."

The charge held his eyes for a moment more before he shrugged. "Sounds like a costly bathroom break."

It took me just a second to register what he meant, and then I barked a laugh, grateful that he broke the weird tension, and we both lost ourselves to the laughter.

Linc's gaze snagged on something behind me, and my eyes followed his line of sight, seeing Martin looking over in our direction—in a particularly southern region on my backside.

Fucking creep.

Linc's hazel eyes seethed back at him, silently daring him to say or do anything.

But Martin would be an even dumber asshole than I thought to say something after Mr. Harris already put him in his place. That, and if Linc's eyes could kill, Martin would already be six feet under.

"Hey," I piped up, and Linc's eyes came back to me. "With Daddy Ellis out of town we definitely don't have the financial backing for a brawl. Just ignore him."

Ellis had left us for a few weeks to go to Copenhagen with his dad, and his absence was already digging an unbearable void into both of us.

I moved out of the way as a couple other cast members passed behind me, putting me only an inch from Linc's chest, and I breathed in deep.

Silvers, sea salt. Woods.

He was the only person I'd ever met that somehow smelled like pine *and* ocean—just a hint of his Silver cigarettes.

I'd never admit it, but the smell ran like a tide through my limbs, crashing and curling my toes.

"You okay?" he said, and it was only then that I realized my eyes were closed.

They fluttered back open, and I saw my best friend's amused curiosity staring back at me in the way of playful eyes and an assuming grin.

Caught.

His smugness immediately lit my fuse, my lips pursing. With a lift of my eyebrows, I shrugged. "Thought I smelled something weird."

Pitiful. Not even a good response by sleepy standards.

Linc's eyebrow cocked as his teeth ran along his bottom lip. "Weird, huh?"

I swallowed, dipping my chin indignantly.

He stepped into me, eliminating the space between us as he dropped his lips just over my ear, "Does *weird* turn you on, Pip?" he said quietly, a gravelly whisper that was tickling that same deep place in my stomach.

Holy shit. Did he really just say that?

My eyes widened and pulled up to look at him, meeting his heated stare.

"Hey," Mr. Harris suddenly said from behind us and my shoulders jumped. "Can I get you on camera two, Linc?"

"Pine beaches," I said, abruptly. Awkwardly.

What the fucking fuck?!

Linc's eyes scrunched in my direction, as did Mr. Harris.

"A soap—a smell—that smells . . . good." *Oh my God, my brain is actually short-circuiting.*

I panicked. I was worried that Mr. Harris heard us talking, and I said the first thing that came to mind.

Linc laughed, rolling into a, "*What?*"

I growled, overwhelmed, and the confusion was fogging my brain. "Just get some soap!" I practically shrieked, storming off back toward the dressing rooms.

"I missed something . . ." I heard Mr. Harris say as I rounded the corner and then proceeded to smack my forehead for ten minutes straight.

LINC

My *still untitled* film project—the one my friends and I had spent nearly our whole summer shooting—was going to be the death of me.

I never thought my ending would come from trying to make a ten-minute short, based on a reimagining of *The Buried Moon*.

It's English folklore, but in our version it was a noir love story. Paige was playing the Moon, a beauty in the sky that the village worshiped, while Ellis played the lonely Fisherman, who is pulled to the same hill every night upon his arrival in the village by Moon's song.

Moon becomes curious about the handsome man on the hill—curious enough to make a journey down from the sky.

She covers her light with a cloak to blend in and falls in love with the Fisherman, and he loves her in return.

However, without the moon's light, the world becomes impossibly dark, unbalanced, and creatures that are otherwise kept away start to roam free.

They kidnap Moon, torture her, drag her through the woods, back to their dwelling.

The Fisherman saves her, but she must return to the sky to restore balance.

The Fisherman spends the rest of his days on the hill, visiting Moon at night until he's an old man.

When he dies, he becomes Sea, and he and Moon are reunited, forever bonded through nature.

But right now, the Moon looked like a high-voltage light

bulb. Heightening the exposure of Paige's dress wasn't having the desired effect. I groaned as I tapped the button to remove it.

"Shit," I muttered.

Leaning back in the chair, I whined again, rubbing my face at the computer screen in one of the smaller AV rooms.

After the *Rent* shoot wrapped, I asked Mr. Harris if I could try to get an hour of editing in, but this looked like *shit.*

Hunching my shoulders, I leaned in and clicked the next frame just as I heard, "Ah, mad scientist posture, I know it well," Mr. Harris's voice came from behind me.

I released a raspy chuckle. "It's the lighting. It was a new moon. And I wanted it that way—but it's all too dark. I never add enough—I just want it to look natural."

Mr. Harris's mouth ticked up at the corner as he walked over and peered down at the screen. After a moment, he made a *tick* sound, then said, "Damn, man. It's a really good shot, though, the angle, the breeze, the close up—what made you do a tight shot instead of the full landscape?"

I cleared my throat, nervously. The unofficial answer was, I was obsessed with the girl who was playing the Moon, and my camera lens couldn't help but try to capture every bit of her, but my less-weird answer was, "I prefer tight shots. And in this case, I like it because they're about to be separated forever—physically. It felt like that should be the audience's experience too," I said through an awkward shrug.

But his mouth pulled up. "Very cool, man. I love it."

The words lifted in my chest. Mr. Harris had been the one to help get me into this festival, and I really didn't want him to regret it. Not to mention, I loved the stuff I'd seen him shoot. His opinion meant a lot to me.

"There's gotta be a way to make it work. You already pulled up the exposure of the dress?" he asked.

I nodded. "It drowns out her face—and the glow isn't soft."

He makes another noise—a few clicks with his tongue on the roof of his mouth then sighs. "Can you play the scene?"

"I only just removed the external sounds, I haven't added any-thing—"

"That's okay. Raw footage is best, just play it."

I suddenly felt nervous. It wasn't anywhere near ready for some-one to see. But I took a deep breath and scrolled the footage back.

It was a quick scene, luckily. The Moon and the Fisherman's farewell before she returns back to the sky. But I scrolled back a little further than I meant to, landing at the end of the woods scene I'd edited last weekend.

"Just start there," Mr. Harris said, and I swallowed hard.

The woods scene looked the best so far, but I still hadn't added any sound. I take a breath and click play.

On the screen . . .

A close-up of a slim shoulder, beautifully flawless skin with gritty swipes of dirt as the camera slowly pulls up to her face. Her big blue eyes staring off just past the lens. Looking for him.

The beautiful Moon is covered in filth—creatures and other evil beings have covered her light with a heavy blanket of leaves and muck, dragging her away from the hill where she is to meet her beloved.

Her eyes fill slowly, and she blinks, releasing a single tear. It falls over the bridge of her nose, and she starts to sing softly, brokenly.

I'll be, I'll be
Waiting there for you
That's what you don't see
My love, I'm waiting for you
I'll be, I'll be

Darkness shadows the screen and then jaggedly cuts to the raw footage of Paige and Ellis on the hill.

The Moon stands, darkened, but safe in the arms of the man she's fallen in love with, the wind blows softly around them as the Fisherman holds her cheek.

Her big blue eyes are wide and full of longing as he leans down to brush his nose with hers. "Life without the Moon is too dark, my love."

Only a beat passes before the Fisherman kisses his beautiful Moon. The wind sails beneath their undying love.

"And that's where I'll fade her out. I've been messing with an effect, but it's . . . extreme. I'll have to play with it for a while to make it look like she's not being sucked away in a vacuum."

Mr. Harris snorted a laugh, with a shake of his head. "This is . . . this is some great stuff, Linc. The attention to detail in the shots alone are impressive."

My posture straightened at the praise. It was the boost I needed, honestly. Between trying to get this film edited, school starting back up—my growing attraction to my best friend, and my inability to make a move—I was feeling pretty overwhelmed at the moment.

"Tell ya what," he said. "Put it on a flash drive for me. I'll take a look at it this weekend and see if I can mess with it. If not, maybe a reshoot with some umbrella lights. But let me take a look first."

My eyes widened. Don't get me wrong, I'd be lucky to have his help but, it felt like a big favor. "Are you sure? I can just try to reshoot it when Ellis gets back."

He shakes his head. "Nah, let's at least see. I know you're busy—I'm happy to take a look."

My teeth tug my bottom lip. I'm not sure why I latch onto his acknowledgment of my busy schedule, but I do.

Most of the kids at Providence didn't have part-time jobs, or little sisters to watch at home, household responsibilities—they had *help* for those things.

My attention blinked back to the present as Mr. Harris handed me a flash drive.

Right.

I plugged it into the USB and synced it up to load as he leaned against the desk. "The camera loves them," he said, his eyes flicking to the screen, still locked on a dark image of Paige and Ellis, staring into each other's eyes.

"She mostly does theater, right?" he asked, looking toward Paige.

Any excuse I had to look at her, I did, then I nodded. "She's amazing on stage. But I wish she'd do more with film. She's so natural."

Her windswept blond hair, her parted, heart-shaped lips—the fucking gorgeous *yearn* to her big blue eyes. *I imagined her looking at me like that so many times.*

Mr. Harris gave a small tilt of his lips. "Some folks—older than me, of course—would say you've found your muse."

I snorted a laugh. Darlene had said it *only a thousand times,* and I would never argue it. It would be stupid when the evidence was literally caught on film—not just in the Moon movie but in everything I shot.

I suddenly found myself wondering, though, how old Mr. Harris was. His light brown hair was intact with no visible recession, a few fine lines around his brown eyes indicated some age, but not much. He looked younger than most of the faculty. And we liked a lot of the same movies, as I'd discovered through class—so maybe low-to-mid thirties?

It felt weird to ask, but the thought was interrupted when an alert noise from the screen pulled my attention to a prompt for the upload, and I clicked through it to safely eject the drive, then handed it back to Mr. Harris.

I stood, saying, "Thanks, again. I really appreciate it."

He pocketed the drive with an easy smile. "No problem."

"Liiinc," Maisie whined next to me. "One more! One more!" She tackled me to the side of the couch, and I tickled her off of me. She giggled and squealed, and when she was a tight ball of laughter, I swiped the remote.

Another whine. "It's Saturdaaay." She widened her big brown eyes—evil little thing that she was. She was cute, and she knew it.

But a schedule was important. I had to be responsible. "Sorry, Loafie. An hour later on weekends. Dems da rules."

She pouted more, crossing her arms. "You're just making me

go to bed 'cause Paigey is coming over and you guys wanna roll around and kiss."

Whoa. "What?!"

She shrugged. "That's what you do when you like someone, Brother. You roll around and kiss them."

I had no idea how to respond. Paige wasn't coming over, she had a shift at Queenie's, but my mind was caught with—*How does the little girl I rocked to sleep know what kissing is? Rolling around . . .*

My eyebrows flinched and the pads of my fingers rubbed against my forehead. This felt more like a parenting moment—something I'd unfortunately had to do a few times in the small loaf's life. But this one side-swiped me.

"Look, Mase. That's *part* of what happens when you like someone. But there's lots of other stuff before that. *Lots.* So no rushing into the kissing and . . . rolling *thing.* Got it? Not till you're eighteen."

She lifted her chin, squinting her eyes—*a little lawyer in the making we're pretty sure*—and said, "Ahh, so that's why you're waiting with Paigey? 'Cause you guys are *seven*teen?"

I was suddenly wondering if she was working an angle. It wouldn't surprise me if Darlene put her up to something.

But at this rate, she also wasn't wrong—though I certainly wasn't waiting for the golden age of eighteen to provide any sort of bravery in this area.

I was waiting on *me* to stop being such a pansy and just do it.

"Women like a man to take charge."

I shook my head, instantly annoyed. My dad's voice and the

shitty tidbits of *"advice"* he'd managed to toss out *before* I was Maisie's age didn't make it into my head often anymore, but it still pissed me off when it did. *What the fuck did he know?*

I truly didn't give a fuck that he was gone. He was a piece of shit, and we were better off without him. But every once in a while—with shit like this—I wish he didn't suck *so* much.

Maisie cleared her throat, reminding me that she'd asked me a question. And I told her the easiest thing I could—the thing that would reinforce the important part of this conversation. "Sure. We're waiting till we're eighteen."

Though, maybe the lie would help keep me accountable. With Paige's birthday only a month away, and mine the month after, we'd both be eighteen soon enough.

"I think you should kiss her sooner. Make it a surprise."

I smiled. "Ya think so?"

She nodded. After another few seconds passed, her smile stretched nervously, glancing back at the TV, then back to me.

I rolled my eyes. "Go brush your teeth, and you can lie out here and watch *half* of another episode."

She squealed, hugging me tightly, then ran off toward the bathroom, and I laughed.

CHAPTER 12
LINC

Walking down the sidewalk, I pass another parking lot. That makes *three* lots I could have parked in that were closer to this place.

The Window.

I grunt, flicking the last of my cigarette, then puff out an exhale, and pop my neck. It's been a *long minute* since I've made my way down to Hollywood, and the general *liveliness* is stacking on the anxiety already teetering in my spine.

My heart kicks up a notch as I reach the last building on the block—a big brick building.

I think this is it . . .

Glancing up, there's a wrought iron balcony on the corner of the building about two stories up, overlooking the cross-streets. When my eyes drift back down, I see a heavy metal door I assume is *not* the front entrance to a high-end burlesque club.

Continuing around the corner, my thoughts are confirmed when I see a massive set of double doors in the center of the dusty bricks.

Walking closer, I notice that the doors are a deep cabernet

color, with two rectangle cut outs on each, but they look too dark to be windows. They also have these intricate carvings on them—almost as if they're made to look like detailed shutters on an over-sized . . . window.

Hah. Nice touch.

But there's also no handle or door knob, and my eyebrows slope.

"Marble," a voice behind me says, and I twist. My fists tighten—one even rises on instinct—but I clench my forearm when I see a man standing on the other end of the sidewalk, closer to the street, smoking a cigarette.

My eyes squint, unsure if he's talking to me, but no one else on the block seems to be within ear shot.

Why do people talk to strangers?

It's like, the first rule you learn and then everyone fucking ignores it as an adult.

When I don't say anything, he lifts his silver eyes to the doors behind me, and I flick a glance back.

"Heavy as fuck," the man says.

Oh, he was saying the doors are marble. Heavy.

My throat works to swallow, my lungs searching for the air to get a few words out. Taking just a small step—*a lean toward him*—I blow out an exhale and ask, "D-Do you work here?"

Shaky on the lift off. Just keep breathing.

He nods, taking a drag of his cigarette, but it's not until he flicks the ash that I register he's built like a fucking wall.

I think he might be an inch or two shorter than me—and his graying buzz-cut suggests that he's older, but that's the only thing that gives away his age. His arms are massive, barely contained by his black T-shirt.

Tension bunches in my neck when I realize he's staring back at me.

Right. We were talking. Kind of.

I tilt my chin, trying to crack my neck, but it doesn't work and say, "I'm—I was hired for the security job."

The man nods, eyeing me curiously and it adds the slightest lift to his gaze. "You're Cook?"

I nod through the lie easily enough.

Norman Cook. My new alias—given to me by Ellis. When I asked why, he said that he liked that only the letter *R* separated it from, "No man cook," but he said it like a caveman.

I pull my lips into my mouth to suppress a chuckle from the memory as the man says, "I'm Jackson. I'll be training you." He then picks up his phone and starts tapping his thumb on the screen, still nursing the cigarette in his other hand.

A deep inhale pulls through my nose, trying to feed the tension still steadily building through my limbs.

The air seems thicker here, though I can't be sure if that's a *Hollywood* thing or a *me* thing. I haven't had to carry on any sort of prolonged conversation with someone I don't know in a long time.

Since the man—*Jackson*—seems preoccupied at the moment, I turn back toward the doors. Shoving one of my hands in my pocket, I jingle the change, then pull out a penny and run my thumb along the ridges of the perimeter.

Focusing on the door again, my eyes drift to the left, seeing a gold plaque next to the entrance.

THE WINDOW.

It's such a small sign. But then I guess a place that needs an invitation to be admitted doesn't need a big sign. Like swanky restaurants that don't put prices on the menu.

Twisting my chin, I lift my neck just the slightest bit to peer in through the small dark cutouts in the doors.

They're a rectangular shape, not much bigger than my face but they're so dark, they look—

My breath catches in my throat as my eyes are met with what looks like . . . a video of—a woman.

A video. In the door. That looks like a window.

Okay, so this place is fucking weird.

My eyes blink, squinting. The woman is sitting on a stool with her back turned, gently swaying her shoulders and slowly rolling her neck.

Her long red hair cascades down her back—with no sign of a bra beneath. She suddenly twists her chin over her shoulder, glancing back before she lifts a *"come hither"* finger in my direction.

I jerk my face away, and a low chuckle surprises me, suddenly a bit closer, and a sharp inhale pulls through my chest.

Right. Jackson. His steel-colored eyes meet mine and my jaw ticks. Another beat passes, and his stance loosens as he says, "Yeah, the monitors for the peep show aren't exactly light either. So, like I said, the doors are heavy as fuck. I'll show you where the back entrance is—that's where you'll come in for your shift."

With that, he turns, and I follow—relieved when he doesn't

reach out to shake my hand. That was another thing Ellis and I practiced over and fucking over again, just so I'd be ready for it.

Like Pinocchio learning to walk without his goddamn strings.

This place is fucking massive.

Not a hole-in-the-wall strip joint, I think. Though I guess the peekaboo doors at the front of the building should have told me that.

Jackson gave me a tour, and . . . this place should come with a map.

It's like the building was constructed for *The Borrowers.* Every room has hidden, back hallways for the staff in addition to the main halls that the guests use while moving between one of the four rooms.

Five rooms if you include the Veranda upstairs.

Currently, I'm in the Great Room, setting the extra tables and chairs we pulled from storage. A job Jackson entrusted me with while he ran to take care of something else.

I think he told me, but I can't remember. Most of my energy is going into just trying to act fucking normal and listen. I figure the more at ease I am doing whatever I'm expected to do, the more I can focus on what I'm actually here to do.

Which to be honest, I'm still a little unclear about. I know I'm supposed to document everything for right now, until I have a meeting with the owner, Desmond's friend Beck, I guess—but he's in New York till this weekend.

Desmond had said discretion is key, so maybe being clueless will help me appear to be inconspicuous.

I don't know. Either that, or I'll totally fuck it up and it'll be enough proof for both Casper men that I'm better off kept away from people—hidden away in the hills.

I place one of the small tables in a space just outside the performance area. This room reminds me of some kind of luxurious circus. Tall ceilings, red velvet booths, and matching curtains surrounding a large, open space in the middle of the room.

I guess they're anticipating the club to fill to capacity tonight—hence the extra seating.

As I pull two chairs over to the table I just set, I hear a heavy door open and close, seeing Jackson walk back through the room with a woman beside him.

She rivals Jackson in height, tall and statuesque, wearing a long, robe-looking thing, and her hair is tied up in an intricate bun on top of her head.

As they get a bit closer, I can see her eyes are brown—lighter than the rich, dark color of her skin.

Jackson gives a casual glance around, silently noting I've put out the remaining tables and then turns to the woman, saying, "Rio, this is Cook," but I notice that he signs it too.

Her warm brown eyes pull back over to me, and I clear my throat, then awkwardly sign, "Nice to meet you."

I'm by no means fluent in sign language, but I taught myself as much as I could when . . . when I could barely talk at all.

I sniff in an attempt to clear the thought away, especially while Rio's eyes are still studying me.

Not in a bad way, necessarily, but I'm paranoid—given that I have ulterior motives for being here.

You don't know what that is either. Just . . . be *a person.*

Also hard.

"Nice to meet you too, Cook," she signs. "You know sign language?"

Oh, wow. Watching her sign is . . . well, I don't know. It looks so natural, but there's a fluidity to it that's so captivating.

Suddenly, I'm aware I'm literally just standing and staring at her like a weirdo. With a shake of my head, I quickly sign, "Kind of—a little."

Her mouth tilts up, crinkling the corners of her eyes. She trails the ink down my arms, following it all the way to my knuckles, and then back up to my face. "Do you have a name sign?"

My eyebrows pinch, then I shake my head again. I read about them when I was teaching myself ASL. But name signs can only be given to you by a Deaf individual and they're usually some kind of physical feature or personality trait.

"I'll work on that," Rio signs. With a tilt to her head, in Jackson's direction, she adds, "I gave him G.I. J—insert whatever *J* word you deem appropriate. Mine is usually 'jackass.'"

I pull my lips into my mouth, fighting the chuckle stirring in my chest as Jackson shakes his head. "Nice," he mutters, but his gray eyes meet hers with the smallest flit of affection. It's so quick that it's gone between a blink. And I think it was only noticeable because even Jackson's *resting* face seems to be hard. Tense.

This time, Rio uses her voice to say, "He'll give you the rundown, but you'll stay on my good side as long as you keep your hands and eyes off my dancers." There's a fierce glint to her stare that makes her eyes almost bronze, glittering with caution.

I nod emphatically, my back stiffening—unsure if I did something in this small exchange that warranted such a warning.

The thought crawls from the depths of something rotten inside me, something that rolls my stomach and constricts my throat.

My face cools, telling me I've lost some color, just as Rio asks, "Are you okay, honey? I don't usually scare big burly men *so much* right away," she breathes a nervous laugh, but her eyes are still watching me, concern lifting her brows.

And I shake it off with a roll of my shoulders.

Operation *Don't-Look-Like-A-Fucking-Freak* is failing.

Finally I manage to shrug off the relentless pull of shit through my brain, and my hands move slowly, signing, "I'm fine. Sorry. Migraine." All lies, but I knew all the signs for them.

There's still unease holding her eyes, while Jackson's stern face looks more curious than anything—but I want to reassure them.

I'm not dangerous.

I won't touch or look at the dancers.

I clear my throat, preparing to sign to the best of my ability. "And no worries about that," I sign to Rio, awkwardly. Then I wiggle my jaw, loosening the clenched muscles so that she can read my lips. I don't know the sign, but I tell her, "I'm gay."

~~Peak: Slept mostly for three hours.~~
~~Peak: Thought about unpacking.~~

My mouth flattened, annoyed. The twenty minutes I'd grown to dread was just about up. A fucking therapy assignment where I had to write down the "peak" and the "pit" of my day.

And yes, it took twenty minutes. Usually more.

And my pit was always the same . . .

Pit. Missing her.

And eventually, after another long stretch of silent minutes and aimless staring up at the moon, I finally wrote.

Peak: The memory of her ~~smile laugh~~ voice.

My butt shifted on the seat, sitting out on the porch at Ellis's new house—where I'd been staying since I'd left Lending Lanterns a few days ago—meant to be some sort of emotional half-way house.

A year of the finest therapy money could buy and still, people were reluctant to let me live in a hole like I wanted to.

My mom and sister had moved up north, and . . . I didn't know her new husband. The idea of staying with them, trying to fit into a new family when there was barely anything left of the person I used to be, felt . . . *very* overwhelming. Unbearable. And while all I wanted was to be alone—no one in my life would allow it at this point.

My eyes flicked down to the paper again, and I sighed. The best and worst part of my barely-there existence was a ghost. One I was *terrified* would eventually stop haunting me . . .

The sound of the sliding door behind me jerked my shoulders, and I twisted just as I heard Ellis call out, "Hey!"

Breathe.

I didn't always need so many reminders to complete basic human functions, but the last three years of my life had turned me inside out. Despite the year away, everything still felt so raw. Exposed.

As Ellis started toward me, I scrambled for something to talk to him about. *Just act normal.*

I vaguely remembered him telling me he was starting to interview some unhoused families in different neighborhoods for his documentary.

I cleared my throat, and then opened my mouth, preparing

to ask him about it, only to shut it again when he extended a bottle toward me. A beer.

"I thought we could hang tonight," he said. "Sorry, I've been busy the last couple days—"

I cut him off by shaking my head. An instinctive grunt escaped, but I looked up at him from the chair I was sitting on.

Good fucking God, the last thing he should feel is guilty.

His green eyes looked darker with exhaustion, his sandy blond hair was a mop on his head. Subtly, I noticed he was wearing a shirt and sweats.

"Do you, like . . . turn into a sparkly vampire if you put on a shirt or something, or are you just morally opposed?" Paige asked him one day at the drive-in.

Ellis lay on the hood of his car, gazing down the landscape of his bare torso. "Don't be pissed just because, unlike you, it's socially acceptable for me to let my pecs peak out in the open and my belly button breathe."

Her face scrunched in the cute way it did when either one of us annoyed her. Like she was mentally throwing a sneeze at us—

Stop.

I had to cut off the memories—a tightrope of awareness.

But the sentiment lingered. Ellis had been that way since we were kids. He hated shirts and shoes. Which meant the only reason he was wearing his shirt *now* was because of me. Putting aside his own comfort just so *I* could be a little less twitchy. For reasons he had yet to ask me to explain.

God, I suck. I felt like I should tell him he could take it off, but . . . *that* would definitely be a fucking weird thing to say.

The cold condensation in my palm reminded me that I was holding a beer. Ellis sat in the chair beside me.

Right. He wanted to hang out.

Shifting my weight, I dug my hand into my back pocket and grabbed my lighter. Using the bottom part of the lighter, I placed it under the bottle cap, then pushed up and flicked my wrist. With my thumb as a makeshift fulcrum, I popped off the cap, and snatched it from the air before it fell.

Ellis chuckled, mumbling, "Nice."

Something passed through his expression but it was gone before I could even register what it was. "Cheers, man." He leaned toward me, extending his bottle and I clinked it with mine, then timidly took a sip.

Whoa. My mouth smacked at the heavy, malty taste.

Ellis chuckled again. "Not into IPAs?"

Shaking my head, I took another sip. I didn't want him to think I was ungrateful. Plus, I was hoping the liquid would help soothe the pathway of my throat so I could actually fucking contribute to this conversation.

My fingers fiddled with the bottle cap, pressing the wavy ridges into my thumb as he said, "I think there's some tequila in the freezer."

Clearing my throat, I felt the muscles in my neck pull and I shoved the bottle cap into my pocket. "Th-This is g-great. Thanks."

Fuck. Well. The talking thing only stands to get better. Hopefully.

I was already talking more than I did a year ago—so, that was something.

Ellis's mouth lifted at the corner, dropping his eyes down for a second. Just like before, a fleeting moment of *something* passed through the green color in his gaze, muting them, but it was like the emerald wave rushed back in just as quickly when he pulled them back up to me.

"Hey, I think I could use your help next week if you're up for it," he said, taking a sip. "I wanna shoot some exterior shots for the doc—mostly to get the vibes. I thought maybe I could get you to come with me? Could use some of your money-shots."

I huffed but nodded. Of course I'd help him in whatever way I could—*could* being the operative word.

But, me and a camera? It was different now than it once was. And I wasn't sure if I'd actually be any help to Ellis. I hadn't filmed anything in years . . .

Which sounded insane. It was the kind of thought that gave me the. . .*far-away* effect. Like the *me* from three years ago—*from before*—was staring back at the *me* now. *Confused.*

I'm confused.

That was the only constant in the last three years.

Ellis sat back, taking a sip of his beer as he shoved his hand up his shirt and scratched his chest.

I clenched my teeth, trying to stamp out all the voices in my head.

He's uncomfortable because of you.

You ruin everything.

Remember what you did to her?

I took another sip of my beer. The more I drank, the less I felt the bite on the back of my tongue. And hopefully the alcohol would quiet the intrusive thoughts.

Long seconds passed as we sat silently watching the sky.

The big moon. I couldn't help but wonder . . .

Even if she isn't in LA, she can still see it. Maybe she's looking at it right now too.

Just the *idea* that we were both looking at the same thing tugged at my heart, just as Ellis said, "Do you remember that one Halloween? I think we were thirteen . . . it was Paige's year to pick the costumes—"

My sharp inhale cut him off. Tension bunched at the base of my neck, and I felt my heart's mighty thump pounding in the walls of my chest.

The silence thickened. Another beat passed before Ellis quietly said, "Everything I've read says it's good to talk about your memories."

Fucking hell. I clamped my eyes shut, shaking my head quickly. The idea that he'd researched *anything* made my stomach turn.

And *thinking* about her was one thing—but *talking* about her? Talking about *before*? It was a sure-fire way to fling myself into the ravine just below the house.

"Maybe it'll help," Ellis whispered.

I had to remind myself that he was encouraging me to *talk*. Reminisce. *Not* throw myself over the side of the porch and plunge to my death.

Is there a difference?

"Linc," he said again, his voice edging with caution, but the sound of my own name clicked something inside me, jumpstarting my heart and accelerating my pulse as I pushed to stand.

Tick. Tick. Tick.

"Shh." A different voice slithered through my head—not *one of the therapists. Not Paige. Not Ellis . . .*

"I can help you. You don't want to hurt anyone, right?"

"No," I croaked out, screwing my eyes shut. The voice was close—*too close*—mixing with the voice next to me.

"I'm here, Linc. I've got you."

"Let me help you."

I couldn't tell who was talking . . .

What the fuck is real?

My eyes bulged open as I felt a grip on my forearm. Lunging my hands at the chest in front of me, I kept my gaze on the white-cotton fabric, twisting it in my fists, instinctively pulling the body in front of me closer. The fabric, *closer.*

Wringing, twisting, grabbing.

I know this.

Distantly, I was aware that the person wearing the shirt—*the shirt I was wrestling*—didn't *want* to be wearing it.

My brain felt like an exposed film reel, blotchy and unfocused, with bursts of light—*awareness.*

I was too scared to look up. Too scared to see . . . *someone else in a white T-shirt.*

"What are you doing?" the familiar voice in front of me rasped.

Ellis. It's Ellis.

Right?

A stuttered inhale pulled through my chest, still too scared to look up as my knuckles turned white. The shirt I was still holding stretched between my shaky fists.

"You have to try, Linc."

"T-Take this off." My voice sounded different.

Is that me?

"My shirt?" His response was tunneled, but I recognized the voice. Confirming that the deep, monotone voice before it *was* me.

My eyes were still down at his chest, but we were essentially the same height, so I could still see him trying to meet my eyes.

"*Why* exactly do you want me to take off my shirt?" he asked, his voice low. If he was alarmed, he didn't sound like it. Just curious.

Because you don't like it, I thought.

But the words got trapped in my throat, and I pulled the hem of the shirt up, awkwardly lifting it over his head.

He said something, but he helped me by shrugging out of it. I balled the fabric in my hands, pulling the soft material through my fingers and bunching it between my clenched fists.

My gaze shifted up just the slightest bit to his mouth, but it was as if my eyes hit a ceiling before they could make it to his eyes.

Just focus.

His lips moved like he was saying something, but I couldn't hear it over the whooshing in my head, my thunderous heart. The intrusive thoughts now had a haunting melody—*a taunting song*—wailing at an ear-shattering volume through my head.

Maybe . . .

I took a deep breath in and out, cracked my neck to the side, and then grabbed the hips in front of me. Every part of me was shaking through the robotic, jagged movement. He grunted, roughly, "What—"

But his words got cut off by me—leaning in, grabbing his

face, and slamming my mouth against his. His surprised whimper, his lips, his taste, sent a freezing cold blast through my limbs immediately.

Wrong.

So, so, wrong.

But everything feels wrong. The things that felt right were wrong.

On autopilot, I prepared to add my tongue into the mix just as the lips against mine gently pulled away, stepping back.

The second my eyes opened, my breath caught in my throat.

Green eyes and spearmint smacked my senses, and I suddenly felt like I was crashing through every layer of the Earth—plummeting toward the heated core.

Burning, burning, burning.

That—that isn't . . . What . . .

"Linc, look at me," Ellis's voice snapped my attention back to him, and everything sharpened. Focused.

Oh my god. Oh my god, oh my god.

It *was* me. *That* was *me.* I just fucking kissed Ellis.

The adrenaline pumped through me, still reeling, but the look on his face was a blow I wasn't expecting.

He looked so . . . *so fucking sad.* So confused.

His seaglass eyes had a shattered glaze over them as he stared back at me like I was a million miles away. It looked like he was fighting back tears. After another second, he slowly reached out to me, but I flinched, tripping over myself as I cowered away like a wounded animal.

He yanked his hand back, his face breaking further. "Shit. I'm sor—" he lost his breath, but then said, "I won't touch you." A quiet, croaked sob broke through his voice at the end, and he shook his head, but he said it again, almost to himself, "I won't touch you."

Dread prickled like tiny pieces of glass just beneath my skin.

Why—why is he acting like this?

He should have been outraged—*pissed*—but not . . .

My breath stuttered. "W-Why are you looking at me like that?"

He shook his head, swiping his palm down his face, seemingly trying to rid himself of the emotion. He took a breath, then took a step back. "Why did you kiss me, Linc?"

My mouth sloped down and my throat tightened. I worked to swallow.

I don't know how to answer his question. He won't understand. That it's just . . . easier—better—if people think—if I try—

God, even my thoughts are a fucking trainwreck. But I took a breath just as another beat passed, and I cleared my throat. "'Cause—I'm . . ." but the sound fell off. I suddenly felt my awareness splintering again. Like Ellis could see side-by-side versions of me—*then and now*—and he was studying them like a venn diagram.

The crease between his brows deepened before he said, "'Cause you're what? You're gay now?"

He didn't say it in any sort of way—but for some reason I winced. Probably because it felt ridiculous—giving air to something like that with *him* of all people. Someone who had a front row seat to my obsession with Paige Michaels.

My breath shook. A beat passed before one of my shoulders lifted with a shrug, but I didn't say anything.

What can I say?

Ellis's chin dropped with a curse, shuffling his feet. It was probably only seconds, but it felt like hours stretched on with thick, suffocating quietness. Not even the typically steady breeze dared to whirl around the tension stacking in the weighted silence of this moment, but it slowly started to fill as Ellis's eyes darkened.

Tick. Tick. Tick.

My heart dropped, as the sound stabbed its way through my head again. It always found me when I was teetering . . .

No. No, no, no.

Ellis's gaze suddenly locked back with mine, holding my eyes hostage. "Did Jeremy tell you that?"

The name hit like a cannon blowing through my skull. The *ticking* intensified, but I could barely hear it through the roaring whoosh in my ears. I charged toward the body that let the name escape—*the voice that gave it life.* Then, a black hole of time took hold, and everything went dark.

CHAPTER 14
PAIGE

My path to self-destruction is paved and apparently, bound-less. That much is clear as I pull off my old freeway exit.

Back to Venice.

After spending *more money* I don't have to gas-up the Cabrio and make the drive out here again, I sigh as I pull off to the exit ramp.

Hopefully my Veranda gig tomorrow is as good of a payout as I've been led to believe, otherwise these shitty decisions are going to be a real bitch for future Paige.

I had to get out, I remind myself. Another day holed up in my apartment would have sent me sufficiently into madness. *Deeper* madness.

"Welcome, the water's fine!" I hear Gram's snicker, and I turn up the music in an attempt to drown it out. *I can't. Not right now.*

She's undoubtedly going to invade every part of my brain if I somehow manage to make it to our street this time, and I can't be on the verge of a breakdown *before* I get there.

Because then I definitely won't go.

A swell of irritation weighs heavily in my chest as I think about the three other times I've come out here this year. *Driven past the canal, past Main Street.*

Only to get to the unpaved road that would lead me to our house, only to then bang a U-turn right the hell out of there.

The music is just noise between my ears, so I turn it down. *I can't get fucking comfortable.* Everything just feels . . . *awake.*

Everything. And not in a good way.

My hair feels itchy on my neck, but it felt like it was adding to my headache when it was pulled up. My wrists are sufficiently covered in case I get out of the car, but the lace fabric and brace-lets feel more suffocating than usual.

I groan as I come to a red light. My palms cradle my face and my bracelets bump together, jingling, and I wince. I usually like the sound. It's grounding. But right now it feels like it's clashing my head between two orchestra cymbals.

Grabbing the steering wheel again, I hold my arms out straight and roll the tension stacking in my neck. Thankfully, the soreness from the club has pretty much passed because my anxi-ety is winding me up *something fierce.*

It's pathetic, really. I always thought I'd be stronger. Braver.

More like her.

Darlene Hansen was a woman who lived. She survived the loss of her husband and her daughter. She was never rich, her life was never easy—but she still managed to be the most alive person I've ever met.

The stoplight turns green, and I press on the gas, driving past the intersection. *Passing Main Street . . .*

Keep going, I tell myself, but my pulse picks up.

I ease the pressure on the gas, going slower, but still moving.

Another moment passes, and I suddenly hear, *"Keep going, Pip,"* and my spine straightens. That voice sounded more like . . . *him.*

But I listen to it. I keep going, despite the sweat breaking at my hairline. My breath quickens as I reach the road, and I slam on the break.

Luckily, I wasn't going very fast, and I quickly flick on my hazards before my shaking hands grip the steering wheel harder. My chin stays down.

Breathe.

After another moment passes, I peer up, looking at the opening to the road that used to take me to our house, and my vision blurs as my eyes fill.

I can't. I can't. I fucking can't.

But just when I think the panic is about to take hold, something strange happens. Something stupid.

Maybe she's actually back there . . .

Maybe he is too. Linc. Ellis. Everyone.

Maybe my old life still exists back there and I just don't know it. Maybe this is life's greatest trial.

It stripped me of everything, but maybe these past seven years without Linc—this last year without her—was just a test. One I failed, and if I can just make it back to the house, the universe will give them all back to me.

My hopeful bubble blows away as a car speeds past me. A small pathetic sound aches in my throat as my forehead falls to the back of my hands on the steering wheel. Waves of frosty blue strands curtain my face, and my eyes slam shut, my tears falling immediately.

Goddammit.

The delusion sounds *so fucking good.* And I want it. I want it so badly that my mind can't help but keep playing it out.

I imagine driving down the road, to our cul-de-sac. Just a short drive. The sight of our pale yellow beach cottage would come into view. It would look the way it used to.

Homey, well-lived in. Warm. There'd be music filtering in as I walked up the stairs to the back porch. The smells from Gram's garden would meet my nose and hurry my steps.

As I'd push through the door, Gram would be at the piano playing something familiar. A song from her Lemon Lady Mix, while Ellis sang and Linc stood by, capturing it all on film.

I could watch it later—see everything I missed.

Everyone would be laughing. They'd be waiting for me.

Linc would find me first—the way he always did. Like there was a radar in his mind that was fully synced to me. His hazel eyes would light and he'd look at me . . .

Like before. *How he looked at me* before *what happened to us.*

There wouldn't be any disgust or revulsion—no shame to his handsome face.

The experience would be forgotten, and he'd sweep me up in his arms and hold me tight. So tight, that nothing could ever take us away from each other again.

We'd turn to stone in that house, locked together in the kitchen as the sound of Gram's piano solidified our embrace.

An eternity in his arms.

I blink rapidly, gasping when I see . . .

The pale yellow beach cottage.

I . . .

My chin twists from the left to the right, seeing I'm parked in the driveway, and my heart rate blasts off.

What the fuck?! I fucking drove here?

My breathing becomes rapid, my lungs feel like they're the size of fucking golf balls. *I can't breathe.* But I can't drive. I shouldn't have driven *here.*

I pop the door open, letting the air from outside fill the car. I take a deep breath, and my chest heaves against the seatbelt. My hand fumbles to hit the release button, but I get it off, and immediately push myself from the car.

Fuck me, I can't believe I drove here. I don't even remember . . .

I take another breath. *I can't think about that right now.* The time lapse is only going to spiral my panic. I close the car door quickly and stumble my way toward the fence.

The tiny pebbles of asphalt shift under my worn yellow Chucks just as I reach the fence. A stuttered inhale tuts through my nose as I fumble the latch to open the door, then close it and screw my eyes shut, falling to the ground just inside the fence. My body shakes, still struggling to breathe.

The wetness on my cheeks registers, and I realize I'm also crying. My fingers sink into the dirt at my sides, like maybe I'll find the air buried down there.

I struggle through multiple failed attempts, but after several painful seconds, my lungs finally find a small bit of air, and I get a hint of citrus.

I take another breath, my lips shaking, but the smell becomes a little bit stronger, and my lungs start to expand.

Keeping my body still, I stay seated on the ground with my back against the fence. Eyes closed.

I'm in our backyard.

Not in my dreams or thoughts. I'm sitting on the ground. And the realization . . . *doesn't* make me flee immediately.

The only thought that finds me is . . . *I wish I'd brought Gram's cardigan.* It's a temperate September day, and I don't need it. But suddenly the smell is making me wish I'd shared it with her sweater. Like maybe it would have helped keep the smell longer . . .

"A lemon tree can live to be a hundred years old with proper care. I always thought that was kinda neat," Gram had said to me, admiring her garden while I sat on her lap in the yard on a blanket. "This one could maybe make it to see your granddaughter."

We were having a picnic in the backyard. It was our thing.

I giggled to myself, then asked, "Can we make lemonade?"

"That's why I planted a lemon tree, silly. So we could always make lemonade." She snuggled into my cheek, tickling my sides while I sat on her lap.

She stopped the tickling quickly, then pushed one of my honey-colored braids behind my back and said, "Why the sudden interest in lemonade?"

My cheeks felt warm, but I didn't know why. "My new friend likes it."

"Oh, you made a new friend? Well, that's nice, Paigey. What's your new friend's name?"

My mouth tilted. "Linc-on, except when he's sleeping," I giggled.

My eyes snap open, with the breeze that sweeps through, carrying the laughter—*the memory*—and I look out at the dry, overgrown yard.

A yard I've done nothing to take care of.

Though, to be fair, I had let the gardening slip far before Gram was gone. My priority was taking care of her, and keeping my own small will to live, everything else just . . . had to wait.

Wait for what? I wonder silently, as my eyes drag along the yard. The lemon tree stands tall and somehow fruitful in the back corner, and a small smile pulls up my cheek. It matured years ago, and didn't need much upkeep. And it was still in good shape when I left a year ago, but . . . you never know.

My shaky legs push to stand, and I step slowly, cautiously, toward it, following the sight like a lighthouse. As I get closer, though, my heart stops.

Stuck in a web of weeds and vines in the tattered old hammock—the one that looks haunted—was a forest green mug with a simple mountain peak design.

Linc's mug.

What the fuck?

My body twists, looking for . . . *What? I don't know.* But . . . how did this get out here?

I literally abandoned ship when I left a year ago—only taking the bare essentials and leaving the rest behind.

There's no way . . .

Linc left. He's gone. Chicago, last I heard. Though, that was second-hand information from Maisie Morrow six years ago—before Bruce swept them away too.

I stupidly followed the tip, though. I spent a shit ton of money to spend two weeks shelter-hopping around the Windy City only to come back feeling even more hopeless than when I left.

But it wasn't until I came home, no closer to finding him that it really sank in . . .

Linc doesn't want me to find him.

You disgust him.

I swat the intrusive thought away by swiping the mug out of the garden of weeds, looking down at it like it can somehow tell me how it got here.

How did *you get here?*

It tells me nothing, obviously, and I don't know if it's just because it's Linc's mug, or that I know for a fact I didn't randomly leave it out here, but I suddenly feel like I'm being watched.

My eyes peek around again, looking for anyone—*anything*—but there's not even random critter noises.

My grip tightens around the mug I'm still holding, and I look back down at it. *I remember now, I left it on the table.*

I thought about bringing it with me, but then didn't. My eyes float up to the back door, remembering . . .

I never locked it.

An unease suddenly tightens through my limbs, and my heart begins to pick up momentum again. In an instant, I race back toward the fence. To the driveway, toward my car.

Coward, a voice I can't decipher mutters through my mind. It sounds like me. *Kind of.* But I try to shake it off as I tear open the car door and toss the mug onto the passenger seat.

Starting the car, I pull out of the driveway.

Drive away, I command inwardly.

I try to calm myself down from the stampede of adrenaline that just found me, taking breaths in through my nose and out through my mouth.

In all likelihood, I just freaked myself out. It happens all the time. My imagination can be a bit . . . much.

"Never too much," I hear Linc say, his voice lingering in my mind, and I look down at the mug.

I have a split second where I genuinely wonder if Linc *is* the mug, before I remind myself—*I think I'm having some sort of breakdown.*

I groan, smacking my forehead and then yelping. "Damn," I mutter, rubbing the skin, trying to refocus.

Watch the road. Think about something else.

I made it to the street this time, I praise myself. The yard. The tree. That's progress.

For today, it's enough.

I stir, barely awake, but I feel an arm slide under the small of my back, wedging between me and the mattress, just as a rough, familiar palm anchors my hips, and I gasp.

With my lower half encased by strong arms, the smell of ocean and pine invades the sheets beneath me, hitting my nose like a wave, and my heavy limbs sink further into the mattress.

There's no question who it is.

I sigh, but sleepy excitement wades low in my belly as soft lips trail the skin of my inner thigh, followed by his nose dragging, breathing with a deep rumble. My core tightens and I inhale sharply.

But I keep my eyes closed—something tells me he wants me to.

His low, muffled groan makes me squirm, and his grip around me tightens just as I feel a small bite at the crest of my inner thigh and pelvis—waking me up—or maybe he's making sure I'm awake—and I whimper my awareness.

Christ, keep going.

When he finally reaches my apex, my hot beating core is already begging for his mouth. The urge to dig my hands through the thick terrain of his hair is strong, but my arms feel too heavy.

He kisses me there, sweetly, then adds his tongue, kissing my pussy like he kisses my mouth. He flicks my clit and my moan mixes with his hungry groan. My eyes finally open as the sound vibrates into me.

I make a noise—a breathless needy thing—as my gaze travels down between my legs, and my heart erupts at the sight of his wicked hazel eyes, gleaming. "Oh good," he rasps, pressing another kiss to my pulsing center, followed by a gentle lick. "You're awake."

My mind can't conjure a response, and he doesn't wait for one. His nose toys with my slit, his hooded eyes stay locked with mine. I whimper again, a desperate, "Please . . ." wheezing past my lips.

He groans, licking, nibbling—fuck, he sniffs me, but he's just teasing my entrance. Teasing me.

"God, Pip. You're so wet. Were you dreaming about me?"

Always, I think in my head, but the word doesn't surface. Something about this doesn't feel real, but I don't care.

Any rational thought falls away. The only thing that registers is his smug smirk nearly twinkling up at me. But in an instant, he fully buries his face into my damp heat, his hot tongue plunging into me as he uses his shoulders to spread me farther.

His untamed hunger as he devours me sends a buzz through my body, despite my heavy limbs. I can't seem to move at all, but my hips grind into him. His tongue fucks me slowly, meticulously, reverently, and I can't move. Can't do anything but surrender to the pleasure.

"You feel like heaven, Pip," he says, his voice wrecked as he barely comes up for air.

I whimper, but my eyebrows flinch.

Feel?

The thought dislodges from my mind in an instant, though, as he flips me onto my stomach. My arms cross at my wrists as he shoves my ass into the air, but he relentlessly continues to eat me from behind. "Fuck," I gasp. "Wh—"

My words cut off as the sensation builds, tickling and knotting in the deepest part of my stomach with each delicious noise he's making from behind me. My cheeks heat, knowing my asshole is also on display.

But fuck it feels good. Carnal. So . . . dirty.

The word tumbles through my mind, quite literally shifting the air in the room.

Cold, damp, musky.

The warmth to my lower half shifts like a drift in the wind pattern—a sailboat off course—and the sound of chains clanking against steel blows through my mind like the fucking Kraken.

The pillows I was shoving my face into, the soft sheets below me become rougher.

Stale. Couch cushions.

Hard, unforgiving, heavy metal weighs down my wrists. Blood trickles down my forearm like an icy path, and my blood runs cold.

The sight, the feeling, the smell. It all hits with a stark, terrifying awareness.

No. Please, no.

A large hand bites into the back of my scalp, pushing my face into the cushion, and I fight against it, but it's half hearted.

"Stay down," the deep, rough voice behind me grunts.

It sounds like him, but different. Like if a sound you loved was put through a wood chipper.

Uneven, sharp, broken.

"That's it," a different voice—not his—slithers its way through, slinking like a toxic fog through an already horrific scene. The same voice says something else, but I can't hear it. And I can feel now that the intrusion behind me is no longer soft, warm, worshiping lips, but slow, deep thrusts.

I whimper, shoving my face into the cushions—he told me to stay down. The chains around my wrists make it difficult to move, and one of the hands holding me down closes over my own hand.

The gentleness of his thumb's movements along the soft skin between my thumb and my forefinger are crescent moon strokes of comfort—a contrast to everything else happening.

Muffled sounds of the other voice—somewhere next to us—distract me, saying something else, but I tune it out—living in the fluid strokes of the thumb tracing hope into my hand.

His body tenses for a moment behind me, just before the broken sound of his voice pulls through. "Take it, you filthy fucking tease." My eyebrows flinch as a strong hand connects with the bare skin of my ass, a resounding smack forces my mouth open on a silent gasp into the cushion.

"Lift her up," the voice off to the side says, and I cringe. It's a deep voice—masculine—and my eyes screw tighter shut when he adds. "Make sure her face catches the light."

I wake up with a gasp, my body clammy *and* cold.

Only a second passes before I'm stumbling out of the bed. I bump into the nightstand, nearly knocking over my haunted mug. I barely make it to the toilet before I immediately puke.

I haven't eaten much today, so it's a lot of retching, my body violently contracting as the memory, the smell, the pain spews out of me.

Get it out, I think.

And still, the desire the dream began with still sits heavily in my gut, adding to the sickness. A whine breaks free as I continue to heave, but I've got *less* than nothing left. My body slumps to the linoleum floor. It isn't as cold as tile, but I can't get up yet.

I'm so drained that blinking feels like an effort, but another jagged whine pushes past my lips as I realize . . . I really can't seem to get off the fucking floor.

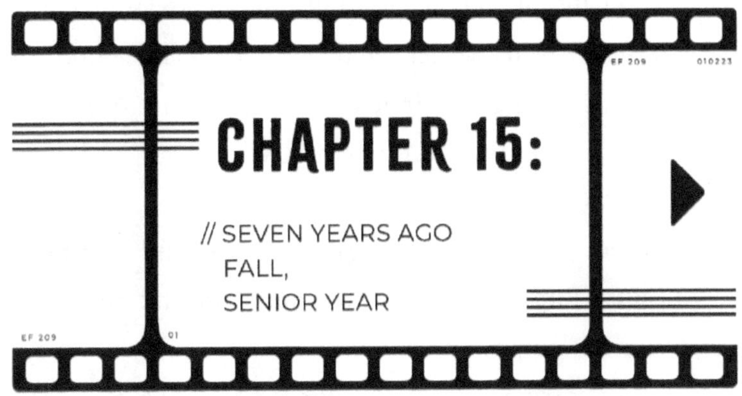

PAIGE

God, there was nothing like it.

Curtain call after a *kick-ass* opening night.

As soon as we all spilled out from the stage door, the cast was a pile of embraces, I was falling from one set of arms into another—not caring who it was.

That was one of the most visceral experiences I had ever had performing. We were all so in tune with our characters and each other. It really felt like we became that group of people in New York City for a few hours.

It sounded cliché as fuck, but it was true.

It was perfect.

"Girl!" Margaret squealed, pulling me in for a tight hug and I returned it. "An encore on opening night!"

I squealed too. *That* was fucking amazing. There was a small section of the crowd that erupted after our duet, "Take Me or

Leave Me," chanting "encore!" And like the well-seasoned, badass little actresses we were, we delivered. It was a high like none other.

Suddenly, strong arms circled me from behind, pulling me from Margaret and I twisted immediately.

Ellis.

I screamed, jumping into his arms as a forceful huff pushed past his lips. But he wrapped his arms around me. "Jesus, woman! I'm jet-lagged."

"Sorry not sorry, you prick!" I hugged him but it was also a punishment squeeze. "I'm chaining you to my porch."

"Sounds fun. And kinky," he growled, and I laughed.

Ellis traveled a lot—for as long as I'd known him—so I'd gotten used to missing him. But it felt harder this time for some reason. Probably because he always did the musicals with me. And while opening night fucking rocked, I wish we'd gotten to be on stage together.

"You were amazing, Paige. Just like always," he said quietly.

"Missed you," I whispered back, squeezing him tighter.

He put me down, giving a playful swat to my thigh, "Those pants do wonders for your pancake ass."

I snorted. Despite years of regular dance lessons and my many private mirror-twerks, my butt refused to plump and lift.

"Paige," I suddenly heard, at the same time Louis pretty much tackled Ellis and I turned to find who was calling me, seeing Mr. Harris.

I smiled, taking a few steps toward him and he said, "That was some good shit."

Laughing awkwardly, I stuttered, "Th-Thanks."

"I did a regional production of *Rent* about five years ago," he said. "And the girl who played Maureen never did *that.*" His eyes moved to the stage door, and I smiled.

I hadn't had Mr. Harris as a teacher yet. I was excited to take his film acting class in the spring. But I knew Linc really liked him so it felt good to know I impressed him.

My eyes scanned around the crowd, looking for the tall kid with a mop of messy dark hair just as I heard, "He's wrapping up the equipment from the mezzanine."

I focus back on Mr. Harris in front of me. *Did I ask him where Linc was?*

The knowing grin on his face told me *No, but you're obviously looking for him,* and I felt my cheeks heat.

Jesus Christ.

Mr. Harris chuckled, stepping off as he said, "Great opening, Paige. Enjoy your night."

I gave him a weird nod, thanking him, before I peeked around again for Linc when I heard another familiar voice, chant-singing, "Over the moon, over the moon . . ."

Gram. Singing part of one of my songs—the one I knew she'd love because in the scene, my character Maureen, was basically holding a protest. There was a cowbell—it was a whole thing.

Gram held out her arms before she actually reached me and basically hugged me the rest of the way to her. "Did you hear me mooin'?!"

I snort. *I really did.*

As part of Maureen's protest, I invited the crowd to moo with me—like I said, it was a whole thing.

Ellis rejoined me, and Gram hugged on him too, throwing out similar threats so that he wouldn't leave us again, then she asked, "You kids partyin' tonight?"

Ellis shook his head, yawning. "I just wanted to see Paige kill it. I'm still on Denmark time."

Gram started humming something . . . something I'd heard before but couldn't place. Ellis smiled and started singing the words.

"*Wonderful Copenhagen.*" I couldn't help but laugh. I didn't know the song. It was probably from some obscure old musical. Ellis would tell you himself that his love of musicals was the first clue he had to his homosexuality. Though, it happened when we were ten and saw the recording of Hugh Jackman playing Curly in *Oklahoma!*, so I can't be sure if it was the musical or the beautiful man that caused his awakening. And I can't prove it, but I'm pretty sure Hugh Jackman's attraction is appealing to nearly every orientation.

"Where's Lincleton?" Gram asked, scooping the long gray waves of her hair, twisting it and tying it up.

I sighed, looking around again. When I still didn't see him, I shrugged. "Not sure. He was in the mezzanine filming the show for the archives tonight. Mr. Harris said he was cleaning up."

She nodded. "Well, I'm gonna head home. It's Friday night and I've got a spicy new romance book and a gummy with my name on it."

Jesus. Note to stay out of the house.

I wasn't sure if I wanted to go to the party. Ellis was the only reason I ever went to parties and he was too tired—maybe Linc and I could just go hang at the creek. *A night hike.*

If I can find him.

Back in the dressing room, I wiped the stage makeup off my face. I was so bad at wearing makeup. It was like the second I had it on—a fixation with rubbing my eyes immediately ignited.

The room was empty. Clean. I was pretty sure everyone had already cleared out to go to Louis's for the party.

But I still hadn't seen Linc.

Maybe he had to get home for Maisie.

I checked my phone again to see if I had a message from him, but there was nothing. Wet naps coated in makeup rivaled the sight of a small crime scene as they sat in a pile on the counter beside me, and I sighed, which trickled into a small laugh.

My gaze lifted to the mirror. I wasn't able to get all of the eyeliner off so my blue eyes looked a little darker than usual, sharper. I had curled the blond strands of my hair so it was wild and bouncy.

I looked like me, but not.

Pulling out another wipe, I was just about to scrub at the dark maroon color on my lips, when I suddenly saw familiar, earthy-colored eyes staring back at me in the mirror.

Gasping, our gazes collided and then locked through the reflection.

I was too breathless to even say "hey," or some sort of quip about how creepy it was that he appeared out of fucking no-where.

Because that would be a lie.

I'd been looking for him since the show ended, but something felt . . . different right now, as he stared back at me.

"I saw that," he finally said.

My captured eyes stayed with his, but my eyebrows pinched. I still hadn't turned around, just watched him through the reflective glass as he leaned against the archway.

He smirked, and the tick of his lips felt like a zap to something deep in my stomach. My legs crossed under the small vanity counter, as I finally said, "Saw what?"

"At the end of Act One," he said. "When you looked right at me."

I sure did. But for some reason his shadowy-self was edging something . . . *devious* in me.

"I have no idea what you're talking about." I shrugged, allowing my lips to tilt ever so slightly.

Linc stared for a moment longer before he slowly fished through the back pocket of his jeans, pulling out his phone, keeping his eyes on me. He flicked them down to the phone for only half a second before he was holding it up, just in front of him.

"Keep going, Pip," he said quietly as I heard the light beep of the camera starting to record.

Eyeing the wipe I was still holding in my hand, I stared back at him through the mirror.

What. Is. Happening?

LINC

I wasn't sure what led me down *this* path on the road to confronting my feelings for Paige, but here we were.

The steady pounding in my chest shook my limbs, but I worked to steady my hand. All I could do was follow my instincts, and every single one of them was telling me she wanted me watching her.

I liked to watch her. And she let me.

It was the way we'd always been. *She showed off, and let me watch.*

But this was different. And we both knew it.

I knew I was going to talk to her tonight—about where my head was—or where I thought it was. But when I saw her looking for me in the abyss of the crowd—her blue eyes landing on me like a target while I watched her—I was done for. I knew I would kiss her tonight.

Her face had this soft curiosity. It was similar to the *flip* I'd see in her expression when she was listening to a new song—a glow-up. Her eyes would light, her plump rosy lips would part, ever-so-slightly, before her best smile emerged.

Only this time, there was no smile.

Surprise still lit the corners of her gaze, but there was also . . . *heat.* This fiery force that blazed back at me.

And just like that—the beautiful face staring back at me—the yearning *want* in her eyes became its own expression.

Her lips tilted slightly, and I zoomed in with the camera so that I was only getting her face as she wiped the color away from her mouth. Her movement was careful, measured, trying to avoid smudging the dark color onto her skin.

It was so quiet, and the tension crackled as I stepped farther into the dressing room, closer to her. Her eyes flicked up to me, and I saw her shoulders tighten from behind, tugging at my smirk as I peeked down at the screen.

She sucked her lips into her mouth for just a second before her teeth pinned her bottom lip, and I found myself eagerly awaiting the release.

I zoomed in to just her mouth, as the rosy flesh was finally free, and I felt my own teeth scraping across my lip.

Damn.

As I zoomed back out, the same, charged expression held her features and I propped the phone up on the small counter, flipping the view so that the camera lens was recording toward us.

Paige's eyes floated down to it for just a second, before they drifted back up—*back at me, behind her in the mirror.*

I looked for any sign that she was uncomfortable, but all I saw was this gorgeous curiosity. And yet there was a shadow of something darker—something that had my fingers moving lightly, trailing along her shoulder.

A sharp inhale dropped my eyes to her chest, as my own lips pulled up. I basked in the silky feeling of her skin beneath my fingers.

I almost felt like I was in a dream, moments away from waking up.

Fuck, I don't want to wake up.

Her blue eyes sparkled up at me in the reflection, and I felt her jaw tense as I ran the back of my knuckle over it.

My eyes traced the full outline of her lips, her small delicate nose, landing back on her ocean blue gaze. Leaning down, I pressed my cheek to her temple, keeping my eyes on her in the mirror. "You're so beautiful, Pip."

My voice was hoarse—wrecked. I was so fucking nervous, but the adrenaline felt like kerosene on the open flame of my soul.

The smallest noise escaped her, something between a whimper and a sigh and *oh my fucking God, her smell.* The soft hints of cinnamon were mixing with sweat in the most intoxicating way, and I felt my weight wobble.

I glanced up at her again, checking in, when an idea suddenly came to me. Collecting her curls, I moved the soft blond strands off of her shoulder, before my hand slid to the row of freckles. Swallowing hard, I started to trace letters on the thin skin—still keeping my eyes on her.

T-I-L-L

The blue in her eyes softened, and her mouth pulled into the sweetest smile—nearly bringing me to my knees. But I carried on, fueled by the beautiful girl watching me—barely blinking, barely breathing.

T-H-E, I continued to spell, but I upped the challenge by boldly running my other hand down her shoulder as I spelled out the last word.

E-N-D

Without even a thought, I found myself dropping my lips to the freckles as she inhaled sharply.

"Linc," she breathlessly whispered on her exhale. The sound

twitched my dick against my jeans, as a low, involuntary groan rumbled on my lips against her neck.

Never had I ever heard my name from her lips like fucking *that*. In an instant, I hauled her off the seat and pulled her up so she was pressed right up against me.

My hand moved to her chin, pinching it between my thumb and my finger, while my other arm hooked around her lower back.

She stared up at me, and her eyes widened when she felt my hardness pressing into her. Our noses were brushing, our breaths mixing. After another couple seconds, I finally told her, "I've wanted to kiss you for so long."

Paige moved her hand to mine on her chin and slid it to her cheek. Leaning her face into my palm, she finally asked, "Why didn't you?"

I brushed my thumb over her cheek. It felt surreal—like a literal dream coming true.

"I wasn't sure you . . ." I trailed off, drowning in the depths of her eyes, deep shades of blue surrounded me, just as a small pinch on my thumb snapped me back.

My mouth fucking *dropped* when I saw Paige's teeth clamped lightly down, nibbling, on my thumb as her hands held my wrist.

The corners of her lips pulled up, her expression turning mischievous as she released my thumb. "Are you sure now?"

I twisted her so that her back was flush with the wall and leaned into her. She gasped as her hips instinctively swiveled against mine.

Jesus, fuck.

This wasn't at all how I expected this to go. But to fight it felt as useless as trying to stop lit dynamite. It felt explosive. *It felt fucking right.*

My grip on her jaw tightened.

One, two, three blinks. One breath.

And my lips crashed against hers. A deep, inhuman noise scraped through my throat but she swallowed the sound before plunging her tongue into my mouth. I stroked it with mine, pulling another moan from deep in my chest as she whimpered around our tangled tongues.

It was ravenous, untamed. *So fucking hot*—and she was fighting me for dominance—which was . . . *unexpected* and driving me fucking mad in the best possible way.

Truthfully, I didn't know *what* to expect when I finally kissed Paige—but she was matching me, pushing back instead of melting, and I was already addicted to her lips.

"So fucking sweet," I whispered against her mouth.

She combated that too, by nibbling gently on my bottom lip, but then she did this thing with her tongue—where she'd lightly run it along my lip, over the bite.

I'm a goddamn dead man.

"Fuck," I grit out and then pressed my lips against hers again.

We kissed.

And kissed.

And *fucking kissed.*

Our mouths moved until they were numb. I wasn't sure how long we had been at it, but finally we slowed, pulled apart, both of us panting and clutching each other.

My neck bent down, continuing to press my forehead to hers.

"Wow," she whispered breathlessly, still close enough that I could taste the words. Taste *her*.

As much as I wanted to keep kissing her, I had to cool down. This had already gone way further than I was expecting.

I just meant to come down here and see if she wanted to go for a drive so I could finally tell her where my head was—talk some shit out. If it went well—kiss her.

I wasn't expecting . . . *this*.

Not that I was complaining—not at all—but . . .

Oh shit.

I twisted back to my phone on the vanity and saw it was still recording us. We were still in shot, just farther away, and I reluctantly let go of her to go stop it, picking it up.

I turned back to Paige, my lips pulling back as I quickly said, "I'll delete it."

She still had this dazed look in her eyes, almost like she was settling back—coming down. And I felt it too. It was like the feeling you had after you'd just jumped on a trampoline.

The ground felt different.

I slid my phone in my pocket and took unsteady steps back toward her.

"Hey, was . . ." I trailed off awkwardly. The muscles in my neck bunched and my hand moved to rub it as I said, "Uh—was that . . . okay?"

I knew she kissed me back. It *felt* okay. It felt fucking incredible, but I was having a hard time getting a read on her.

When she still hadn't said anything, I said, "Pip?" and she blinked over at me.

Finally, a playful light found her eyes, and she smiled. She closed the distance between us in a few small steps. My chin dropped to meet her eyes just before her mouth ticked up. "How the hell did you learn to kiss like that?"

CHAPTER 16
LINC

You're kidding me! *No* nudity?!" Ellis balks.

I snort, shrugging as I sag into the couch, and Ellis sits on the other side. He's been busy pounding the pavement for *The 5* since I started at The Window a couple of days ago, and our schedules finally allowed us to hang for a bit before my shift tonight.

Ellis flicks his lighter and holds it over the weed in his pipe, *Blackfish*. He'll claim he named it that because it's black and white, and he has a genuine love of orcas. And that's all true but . . . he *cried hard* watching that documentary—didn't get the pipe till after, so jury's still out on that one.

Just as he exhales, he says, "You're telling me these people— some that probably partied at Studio 54—are dropping *thousands* at an invite-only burlesque club with no *tits?*"

My body shifts. *Fidgets.* I keep my hand out of my pocket, but I push the change around over the material of my black jeans. Clearing my throat, I tell him, "Well, I—uh—I think there's topless acts. I-I just haven't seen them. Plus, th-there's a policy against looking."

Ellis's eyes widen, but his brows furrow. "Looking? Isn't it like . . . your job? What if there's a threat to one of the performers—"

"Watching—" I grit out. "I guess it's a policy against w-watching the dancers. Jackson said that—uh . . ." I shake my head and take a second to gather my thoughts.

One thing I've noticed in my small time of interacting with actual people—*aside from Ellis, of course*—is that I'm *capable* of talking more.

My two nights at The Window are the only prolonged time I've spent with people I don't know since I was at Lending Lanterns, and that was . . . different.

There have been a few times I've been signing something to Rio where it comes out no problem, or I just take a second and visualize the words before I say them out loud. *Take my time.*

If I speak slower, it helps get the words out.

In the past, I usually got too frustrated or impatient—or I've been with Ellis, who knows me well enough to understand what I mean most of the time anyway. I think somewhere along the way, I just stopped trying to work on it.

But last night, when Jackson asked me to explain the procedure of removing a potentially dangerous guest—*something he'd explained to me the night before*—at first, I got overwhelmed. But then I thought about how I'd sign it to Rio, and it helped me come up with keywords. And slowly—I mean, at a snail's pace—I realized I *could* do it.

And now that I know I can, I find myself wanting to . . . try.

Ellis sits patiently, tending to *Blackfish*, as I clear my throat and organize my thoughts. I think about it with the preparation I give myself to sign something to Rio.

After another exhale, I slowly say, "Jackson takes the safety stuff seriously. And he says keeping our eyes on the floor is the best use of our reflexes. Plus, he said it's the most respectful thing we can do for our coworkers. Th-They're not dancing for us." I take a deep breath, it almost feels like the words deplete my air supply. But . . . I got them out.

Ellis's eyes widen, but crease at the corners with a smile and I try to capture the image in my brain. A *"mind glint,"* as I've taken to calling them.

It's my own version of a "brief shining moment." Like the wind blows a curtain and a little ray of light sneaks through.

Light. Easy. Like before.

Ellis says, "Are the people cool?"

I nod, telling him about how I'm getting to make good use of sign language with Rio, then add, "And the building is huge. A little confusing. Th-There are staff hallways and stairwells so it's a little bit like a maze. I haven't even been upstairs yet, but there's a private party up there tonight."

Ellis's eyebrows lift. "Sounds cool, though."

I nod. It *is* cool. If nothing else, there's an other-worldly feel to the building. Like how I imagine it would feel stepping into the elephant at the Moulin Rouge.

Something does feel kind of *off*, but I still can't tell if that's just because I'm not used to being around people. Maybe *I'm* what's off.

"I-I've been writing stuff down," I tell him. "Documenting what I can, but, I'm still not really sure what I'm looking . . ."

He sucks his lips into his mouth, and turns toward me. His emerald eyes peer up, a little glassy, and I can tell the weed has hit. But if there's anyone that can handle their pot intake, it's Ellis Casper.

After another second, he sighs. "I wouldn't overthink it. If something devious really is happening there, it'll make itself known, and you'll be paying attention."

I nod, absently. The words reverberate through my brain. He's said something . . . Or *someone* has said something similar to me before, but I can't place the memory.

My head shakes, and I blink, shoving my hand into my pocket and jingling the change to rattle the feeling away.

It was better before.

"Hey," Ellis's voice brings me back to now, and my eyes dart up. I take a breath as our stares hold, and he adds, "You know you don't *have* to do this, right? I mean, if you're enjoying it, then I think you should, but I just want to make sure you know you don't *have to.*"

My eyebrows pinch. The way he's saying it feels heavier than what we're actually talking about, but it's like the meaning— *whatever* he means *behind* what he's saying—is hidden. Like it's behind a wall I can't edge my vision far enough around to see.

I blink and shake my head again, then nod, jaggedly.

Jesus. "N-No, I know I don't have t-to." *Slow down.*

I take another breath, I think about the words, the signs. I see them. "It will make me feel good to h-help." *Almost.*

Still, Ellis smiles. It's a stoned goofy thing, but it makes me laugh. And I tuck the victory in my back pocket for my next low day.

"I'll be, I'll be
Waiting there for you
That's what you don't see
My love, I'm waiting for you
I'll be, I'll be"

"Cook!" someone barks, and I blink rapidly.
That's me.
I'm at The Window.
On door duty.
Fuck.
My mind returns with the urgency of a fucking feather—loftily swaying, swaying, swaying, before pile-driving into my head.

My heart races as the broken melody still plays through my mind, but I give my head a quick shake. When my feet feel sturdy, it finally registers that two guys on the other door are working to close it, so I brace myself before lifting up, and then pulling, while another guard pushes from the front of the door.

Holy shit, Jackson wasn't kidding.
The doors are fucking heavy.
My eyes peer up from the floor to see the other guy who's working the door tonight . . . *Collins, I think his name is.*

"You wanna stay here while I do the sweep?" he asks, clearly doing his best to pretend closing that door didn't just feel like moving a fucking school bus.

I nod, doing my best to pretend the same. I'm also certain that staying here is less fuck-up-able than doing a *sweep,* and he leaves with a simple nod.

With another heavy breath, my feet rock slightly, my toes wiggling in my boots. As I glance around, I notice a few people lingering in the lobby, taking pictures by the giant photowall of a mural painted in the foyer.

An LA landscape under a night sky, Capitol Records kissing the corner of the moon while stars dot distant mountain ranges.

The artist did a beautiful job. The colors are dark purples, blues, and blacks, highlighted with moonlit grays and stormy white swirls of clouds. All peering through big, cabernet-colored shutters. Like the behemoth door I just closed.

"Cook." I hear a clipped voice that I recognize as Jackson's, and my chin twists to see him walking back with Collins—*I think.* "Did you see this man come in?" He holds up his phone, and I see a guy with reddish hair—shorter, but muscular.

Fuck. I don't know, *maybe.*

Don't panic, take your time.

I look down at Jackson's phone again, back at the man's face, studying it a bit more. It's kink night, so everyone's dressed in an assortment of leather and mesh—but the man in this picture looks like he's wearing a security uniform.

He does look kind of familiar, though—*the hooked nose*—I re-member wondering if he broke it or if it was naturally like that.

"Y-Yeah," I say, my throat tightening. "He had an invitation. Came in with the first wave."

"Shit," Jackson mutters.

My eyebrows scrunch. "Why? What's going on?"

I'm getting the idea that I fucked up by letting this guy in, but I scan my memory of the wall Jackson showed me a couple of days ago.

In the back room of the Saloon, there's a picture wall of people banned from the club for various violations.

Jackson shakes his head. "His name is Seth. He was recently terminated and was asked not to return."

Well, fuck me.

Jackson's mouth flattens into a tight line. "There's a private party in the Veranda tonight. We need to find him but not cause alarm. I'm gonna go to Beck's office and take a look at the cameras."

My weight shifts, and I shove my hand into my pocket, grabbing the first coin I can and letting it fall between my fingers, but I keep my hand in my pocket. I feel like I should apologize, but I can already feel my throat closing up.

Jackson looks at me. "I need you to check the staff hallways, and the stage stairwell up to the Veranda. Collins, you take the front building guest rooms. Dev can take the others. If anyone sees Rio, let her know."

My chest stutters through an inhale, wiggling my jaw. I wish I had some water so I could *fucking say something*, but Jackson is in go-mode, only adding to my anxiety before he adds, "He was never violent. I don't expect it will come to that for any reason, so if you find him, just bring him to Beck's office and tell him I'd like to speak with him. Walkie me immediately."

Day three on the job and I've already caused a fucking security breach. And just because this Seth guy wasn't violent while he was *at work* doesn't mean he isn't.

I mean, he was asked not to return, so he must have done something shitty.

"The complexity of people is life's meanest joke."

The thought makes me cringe, but I finally say, "I-If he doesn't come willingly?"

Jackson hands me a nightstick and some handcuffs. "Fists first, though."

CHAPTER 17
PAIGE

I stare back in the mirror, trying to follow the winding paths of leather twined around my body.

Leather dental floss, indeed. I huff a laugh at Rio's text.

She did warn me. *And Buffy bless her*—she basically crafted a leather chastity belt around my crotch, while the rest of the rough material is crossed tightly over my body.

X formations hold over my nipples, tying around my neck, while an open diamond shape displays over my belly button— my thighs bare.

As always, she made me wrist cuffs—*leather ones this time*— and she'd made them loose enough that I was able to sneak a band with my mace inside.

It's not easily accessible by any means, but I figure in a dire situation . . .

Something the owner, Beck Davis, doesn't seem to have a lick of worry about—at least, that's what I gathered during our *debriefing* when I showed up here at six o'clock *sharp*.

Give or take a few minutes—in my mind, I was mostly on time.

I learned that I'll be working the Veranda for Beck's *associates*—no more explanation required, I guess—and that he'll be joining the other three gentlemen for the first hour.

I'm not sure what to make of it.

I hadn't met Beck Davis before tonight. He only made appearances at the club during big industry nights—more during award season, since there was usually a production company or two that held their party here.

But I'd only ever seen him from afar before tonight. His thick head of blond hair, shorter on the sides, longer on top, and styled to sit perfectly between his ears. A smile with straight white teeth that suggest he's never missed a cleaning, and his tall, commanding stature now have a voice in my head.

And it's *meh*.

I see a few dancers passing behind me, wearing similar bondage-inspired get-ups—the whole place smells like leather—kind of smokey.

I take a steadying breath, fluffing up my hair, which is rocking its usual mussed up waves, then I outline my lips with a dark purple lipstick.

"Oh my God, Blue, you look so hot." I hear a familiar voice—*Selene*—somewhere off behind me and my eyes pull up, meeting her piercing blue eyes through the mirror.

It's Selene! is how her name is saved in my phone, and I'm pretty sure it's the *only* reason I can actually remember her name. *Her club name, anyway.*

After a few text exchanges where she had asked me to cover her shift—only to have me text back *every time*—*WHO ARE YOU?*—she took my phone and saved the contact information herself.

"Heard you were out on leave," she says—not in any sort of way, but it just *reminds* me of how broke I am.

How much I need this stupid night to go well.

Picking up a brush, I open the lid to the glitter, seeing her still lingering by the doorway that leads to the Great Room. "What room are you in tonight?" I ask her. Mostly just to kill the silence.

Music has been amping up my anxiety. Every song has felt like it's feeding the nerves—but the quietness is filling in the blank spaces with thoughts of what awaits me upstairs.

"I'm doing an hour in the Saloon and then the after-hour in the Drawing Room."

I nod my response, then flex and lift the brush to my bicep, tracing the curves of the muscles with the soft end of the brush. Selene smiles behind me.

I'm not sure how old she is. Somewhere in the twenty to thirty range, but it's hard to tell with her blond bombshell hair and show makeup.

After a second, her eyes light up with a gasp. "You haven't been here! You haven't seen the new security guard!"

My eyebrows pinch. I barely know the *current* security guards. Just Jackson and his trusty stick.

"So hot," she gushes, nearly bending at the knee. "Tattoos, scowls—*oof.*"

Yippy. God, I don't care and I think it shows.

Another moment passes, and I *will* this conversation to die—cursing myself for starting it in the first place as she asks, "You're working the Veranda tonight, right?"

My eyebrow lifts. For a place that boasts about discretion, it appears Selene happens to know a whole fucking lot. I was under the impression that Veranda events were pretty hush-hush—you know, for morale sake.

Avoiding a sequel to Showgirls, I imagine.

I continue with my ritual, trying to politely end the conversation with my slight scowl.

But she smiles, saying, "Well, that's awesome. I heard a girl got such a good payout from a Veranda gig that she quit the next day. She's like . . . a pop singer in Canada or something now."

My eyebrows scrunch. It's so specific that I *have* to believe it's true, but I ask, "Where did you hear that?"

She shrugs, nervously. "I don't know. Around."

Someone who knows someone.

Seems she knows *a few* "someones."

Inhaling deep, she must take my silence as a cue to move along, and I absently wonder what kind of payout it would take for me to leave.

Leave The Window? That wouldn't be hard. I'm not particularly attached to this place—just the paycheck. I'd miss Rio. Jackson . . . sometimes.

But leave California? That's harder. Leaving here means leaving Gram's house.

And if I leave, how will he *find me?*

Such a stupid, hopeless thought that I *can't seem to drown the fuck out.* Not in the deep, cavernous bottom of my most sacred space—not ever, it seems—and it's *fucking pathetic.*

My head shakes. I can't stumble down that hole.

Not tonight.

I have to keep my wits about me.

If tonight goes well, I'll have some money in the bank. Maybe I can start to make a plan. And I already have a celebratory bottle of champagne chilling in the fridge.

·•·)·)·)·•·(·(·(·•·

The Veranda is . . . stunning.

But also kind of creepy. There's floor to ceiling-length openings with sheer white curtains.

Through them, I can see it leads to a spacious balcony with the wrought-iron railings I've seen a hundred times from the street below.

My steps are slow on the floor. It looks almost like cobblestone, but it's white and not as jagged. They vary in color a bit too. Some more ivory, others with a yellow tinge to them—kind of reminds me of big, flattened teeth.

Ugh. The thought sends a shiver through me, and my throat works to swallow as my eyes sweep to the oversized fireplace, then to the various lounge furniture surrounding it.

No poles . . .

Convenient way to get a lap dance—*just take away the poles.*

As my eyes take in the perimeter of the room, I see two doors. The one I came in, that leads down to the stairwell that takes you back toward the dressing rooms. The other one leads to the stairwell the guests are led in by and that's when I see the bar cart.

But no bartender. There's no way these assholes are going to pour their own drinks.

That will likely be your job, jigsaw.

I huff a small laugh with the soft click of my black pumps against the floor, walking toward the bar as suddenly music starts to play.

But . . .

What the fuck is this?

It's not dance music. It's . . . it's instrumental. Some kind of light jazz. A crooning saxophone softly wafts through the speakers, sending an ominous chill up my spine.

There's a certain melancholy to the notes that heightens my nerves, and I instantly pull the mace down a bit, so it's just a bit looser.

I need to calm down.

It's just a private show. I let Rio's words resound through my racing heart—feed the reassurance to my tightened limbs.

Theatrics aside, there's a cold, almost dead feeling to this room and the sensation prickles down my spine.

The moment happens quickly, but slow enough to pull my attention completely. The doors push open, and my eyes snap up to see four men walking in. Once they make it past the first two windows, shadows no longer cover their faces and I scan their features.

My heart pounds with possibility as the adrenaline tries to

shake its way down to my knees, but I lock them and hold all the tension in my core, my jaw.

My eyes find Beck first—every bit the put-together man I saw earlier, with his hair combed back and his three-piece charcoal suit.

He pretends to be a gentleman and lifts his dark blue eyes to my hair, smirking before lowering his gaze back to mine as he says, "Blue. So lovely to see you again."

He says it like it's a regular occurrence. Like he didn't learn my name—*my club name*—an hour or so ago.

But . . . he literally owns the place.

I swallow my pride. I tuck it in, promising to make up with it later. *Just make the money.*

It's as if I can feel the muscles in my face creak and turn like gears on an old clock, but I manage to pull my lips, extend my hand. "Pleasure's all mine, Mr. Davis."

·•·))·)·)•●·((·((·•

The first half hour or so passes by uneventfully—if you don't count the massive amounts of cocaine Beck's *associate,* Tariel, has been bumping away on over there.

I've already renamed him Sharktooth in my mind, seeing as you can see *every single one* of his big fucking teeth.

It's unnerving.

The jazz music still plays, but it's light.

And as it turns out, I *am* the bartender.

Luckily, the group settled on the furniture in front of the fireplace, only requesting expensive bourbon while carrying on some kind of circle jerk. Truthfully, it doesn't even sound like a conversation.

They've been talking about some art collection—how much money they've spent, made—*who the hell knows.*

Ugh. Why the fuck am I here?

I've tried to tune them out, and instead started singing some made-up lyrics to the music playing over the speakers.

Humming, I turn my attention back to the group. One thing I've noticed from my spot behind the bar cart is the other two guys that came with Sharktooth look young—really young.

Not underage—but just by a chin stubble. And they don't seem to be adding too much to the conversation.

"Blue," Beck's voice carries over, and I shift my eyes to him. "You sing?" he asks, pleasantly.

My eyes squint. It's a strange thing to ask, seeing as the only way he knows that is because he *heard me* just now.

"You tell me," I say, attempting playfulness, but I think it mostly just comes off as bratty and confused. Which I am.

Beck's shoulders lift the slightest bit, his vest creasing in the same way sketch artists draw the lines with the pencil, and for some reason, it annoys me as he chuckles. "I'd say your reputation precedes you."

Reputation? As what? As The Window Witch?

Actually, that sounds kind of accurate. And he's probably getting his information from Jackson—who, let's face it, *would* say that.

Sharktooth sits on the green-velvet settee, closest to the fire-place, while the boys sit in arm chairs—their backs on an angle away from me, while Beck stands casually by the fireplace.

"Pour yourself a drink and come on over," he says, gesturing to the seat across from the two boys whose names I've already forgotten.

CHAPTER 18
PAIGE

It's a palpable feeling.

Men with power. *Powering.*

A *buzz* some are immune to from naivete, or worse, experience.

Aware of the current, I skip the drink, but accept the man's invitation—*just get this fucking over with.*

As I wander toward them, I try to dip my hips in a way that hopefully makes it look more like a strut than trepidation.

Strupidation.

The old *ism—for once—*doesn't make me wince, but twitches the corner of my mouth and sparks my step. Discreetly, my eyes peer back toward the guest entrance door—just keeping tabs on how far away it is.

Probably no more than the intro to "Sunday Morning."

The No Doubt song plays in my head, my stilettos clicking to the internal drum taps, as I reach the center of the room, mostly naked and on display for four strangers—one of which is technically my boss.

No more naked than you are downstairs. In front of hundreds of people.

I mean, typically I was a *little* more than a steady breeze away from a nip-slip—but whatever. Haven't cared about nudity since . . . *ever*, basically.

But this is strange . . .

"Take a seat," Sharktooth finally says, and now that I'm close enough, I can confirm, I hate his voice. It just . . . *sounds like* it talks too much.

Just make the money.

I move to sit, and the leather stretches in crazy, fairly invasive ways, least of all the straps that are protecting my crotch.

A discomfort I am grateful for, I remind myself.

Beck's eyes meet mine with another smile and I absently wonder if it's real. You can't tell with some people. *Jaws* over there *looks* creepy, but maybe he's just the only one not pretending. Maybe he's not creepy at all . . .

"So, Blue, do you have a singing background?" Beck asks.

Aaand why do I suddenly feel like I'm at a job interview?

Crossing my ankles like the lady I am *not,* I lean my elbow on the arm of the chair in an attempt to appear at ease—while also trying to find a position that doesn't feel uncomfortable.

But this is fucking uncomfortable.

When he continues to look at me, expectantly, I breathe and then easily say, "Church choir."

Beck chuckles again. "And I'd bet everyone showed up to hear you."

Seriously, what the fuck is this?

The movement to my right catches my attention, seeing the two boys get up and head over toward the bar. As my eyes scoot back, Sharktooth seems only half-invested just as Beck clears his throat. "Well, anyway, I've got to get going—I'm meeting some colleagues at the Chateau."

Sharktooth stands, with a cackle, saying, "Oh, last time I went there, I pissed next to Harrison Ford," all but stumbling off to the other two by the bar.

Beck smiles, glancing over at me, "It was probably the bathroom attendant, who . . . *does* surprisingly look a good bit like Indiana Jones."

My eyebrows pinch. *Does he think we're having a moment right now or something?* He's about to leave me up here with his coked-out friend and two barely-men!

It's a battle of blues between our eyes but my face must look some sort of way because he says, "Look, I know these guys. Tariel is a little wild, but those two are his nephews, he's just trying to show off for them. I assure you, this will be the easiest money you've ever made."

I think my brain might explode from the amount of words I'm holding back, so I can't help it when it just slips out. "And what's the easiest money you've ever made?"

He huffs, amused, then simply says, "That's easy. You."

Again, the control over my face is wearing thin, but he quickly clarifies, "All of you. You're all employees of The Window, and therefore, I pay you. And I think money is best spent on people. Invest in good people, less turnover, you work less—easy money."

Simple and idealistic as it might be, I don't like that I don't *hate* his answer. It has a veil of humility I wasn't expecting.

"How about this," he says. "I'll grab Jackson and tell him to come do a check-in in about a half hour? He can pass it off as a bar cart check."

Pass it off?

Why should it matter if a security guard is checking on a room in a building under his watch?

"Anyway, I really have to go. But I do hope to see you again soon."

My mouth doesn't work, and in just a few steps, he's over by the bar cart, shaking the *gentlemen's* hands before striding back toward the guest entrance door and pushing through it and I just can't shake the feeling that . . .

The babysitter left.

As my eyes pull over to the bar cart, Sharktooth's dark eyes sink into me, emphasized by the heavy door shutting behind Beck.

I'm just on edge. *It's fine.*

I can handle it. Jackson will be coming by.

You're trusting the million-dollar man that goes to places like the Chateau, *getting mints and condoms from Captain Dynamite. Smart.*

Straightening my spine, I dig my feet into the ground as the men come back over to where I'm sitting. Sharktooth is carrying a decanter of bourbon and an extra glass.

He's lost what's left of his blitzed-out mind if he thinks I'm going to drink anything he offers.

So he doesn't. He just pours. A subtle power move as he slides it to my end of the table.

I ignore it, and instead, stand up, mostly just to release some nervous energy, but then I say, "Why don't we switch up the music? I can give you a little taste of the fun we have downstairs."

God, even saying it out loud sounds like a deal I'm striking with a toddler.

"Why would we want the downstairs experience *upstairs?*" Sharktooth asks, displaying his long rows of straight white teeth. A haunted, maddening xylophone trill plays through my mind at the sight. I can't tell if it's my anxiety mixing with the adrenaline, but he seems more . . . menacing.

My eyes narrow. "Well, I think they have a deck of cards in the bar cart. Go fish?"

He chuckles, flicking a glance to the boys, who are settling back into their seats. It's out of my mouth before I even realize it—"How old are you?"

"They're twenty-three today," Sharktooth says cheerfully. The boys share a smirk, then continue to mostly have a staring contest with their glasses as he continues, "I have a feeling you can dance to this, Bluebird. Why don't you give it a shot? I love this song."

The nickname *Bluebird* makes me wish I could peck his eyes out, but I side-step it, and turn back into the music. It's still jazz, but more upbeat—I recognize this song, actually. *Whiplash*—the Don Ellis version.

Fuck it, let's see how this goes.

Remembering an idea from earlier when I was becoming BFFs with the bar cart, I start to walk toward the floor-to-ceiling windows, planning to use the curtains somehow, but I'm stopped by Sharktooth's voice, "Uhh—"

My chin twists to him. He looks but says nothing else.

My eyebrows lift, expectantly, and he grins—*Jesus, I wish he wouldn't do that*—then pats his lap.

Of course.

Something I've already thought about, and I take a breath, trying to shake away the unease as I shrug. "There's a strict no touching policy here. I'd hate for you and the birthday boys to get banned from the club."

He laughs like it's the funniest thing he's fucking heard, while the boys look over, watching me, but in more of a studying way.

This whole thing is just fucking bizarre.

My eyes pull over to the door—just a little bit farther than I was last time I checked.

If I kick off my heels, it's still a quick run.

I stay where I am, and my eyes lock with his for the first time tonight. Dark—his pupils are massive. No doubt from the blow, but I can barely tell *what* color they are.

It doesn't matter. I straighten my spine, narrow my eyes. "You're . . . some sort of businessman, yes?"

His smile stretches, sending another chill down my spine when he says, "I'd like to think I'm more of an artist."

Great. A Renaissance creep.

My jaw tightens. "And how do you fund your art? With all

due respect"—*which is none*—"I don't think I've had the pleasure of seeing your . . ." I trail off because *fuck* if I know what he does.

You're here to make money, dipshit.

A flutter of irritation passes through his eyes, but he just as quickly sniffs his nose, his smile returning. "It's not likely you've seen my work, Bluebird." He takes a sip from his glass before he leans back. "But going back to your initial inquiry," he pauses, while reaching into the inside pocket of his jacket, and pulls a stack of cash. "We were talking business."

A deep inhale loosens my shoulders. For some reason, the presence of the money brings me some ease. This has been a strange-as-fuck exchange and dancing for money sounds like the most normal thing I've heard all night.

I take one step, one click of my heel, before Sharktooth says, "Full transparency," he smiles. "I was prepared to give you a thousand just for getting on my lap—your hesitation cost ya five hundred." My eyes widen as he quickly adds, "But don't worry. You'll have a chance to earn it back."

The idea of *earning back* something that I didn't actually ask for shifts strangely in my stomach as he continues, "Actually, ya know what?" He claps, and the unexpected noise pulses in my chest as he says, "It's kink night. I'll bump it right back up if you crawl to me in that little number." His blackened eyes drag along the lines of leather.

I don't know why, but my eyes flick over to the boys—who are now wholly focused on me.

This is . . . weird. I mean, it isn't *normal* to watch your uncle get a lap dance, right?

Watch me crawl to him.

But this is the first time they've even looked remotely interested in being here. Maybe what Beck said was right—Sharktooth is just a bougie guy giving his nephews an exclusive night.

Showing off.

And I only stand to make more money. I have to make up for missing work . . . the impulse purchases.

If I make enough, I can make a plan.

Swallowing hard, I see that all eyes are on me, and a cringe drags slowly through my shoulders, up my neck, and spreads through my skull as I slowly sink down to the floor.

It's hard on my knees, my palms, but the most painful part of it is my vantage point, as I slowly crawl toward the green velvet settee—on my hands and knees—toward the pinstripe dress slacks to earn my one thousand dollars.

Luckily, the floor seems clean.

As I reach him and begin to stand, he says, "Ahh, right there is good."

On my knees . . .

I blink as everything slows down, waves swell between my ears, disorienting me as Sharktooth smiles.

Ice becomes my spine. In an instant, I know I've made a mistake.

I just do.

The music blasts just as everything speeds back up and two sets of hands are grabbing each of my arms.

The urge to kick and scream—flail and spit—it all bubbles up, but I don't panic.

Jerking my arms just once, the boys' grips tighten, and I wait for the slight release that comes with the offensive move.

It's not enough to break free, but it's just enough to lean forward and shoot my leg out behind me, angling my toes outward so the sharp pick of the stiletto hits him.

"Agh," he growls, but unfortunately for me, only lets go with one of his hands. My shoes are ripped from my feet before I hear, "Bitch!"

Smack.

My face whips in the opposite direction as pain radiates across my cheek, taking a second to realize the guy fucking slapped me.

What the fuck?

I fight against their holds as fury pummels through me just as Sharktooth coos, "Easy." He leans back like he hasn't a care in the world before his eyes pull up to the boys holding my arms. "Remember. We're looking for *nonviolent* restraint. They'll almost always fight back. You're disturbing comfort—*expectancy*—which is usually met with resistance."

What in the ever-loving-fuck is this?

Am I seriously part of some *demonstration* of how to *peacefully* assault someone?

"*Forcing* is different than *taking*," he adds, then drops his eyes to me. "Isn't that right?" His stubby finger brushes over the still-heated skin on my cheek and I snap my teeth, missing. "Ooo," he says, practically giddy. "Not the Bluebird on your shoulder."

"Fuck you!" I spit back, blood boiling, blackness curling the edges of my vision.

How the fuck did I let this happen?

After everything I know about this shithole of a world, how *is this happening?*

Intrusive thoughts find me in every form as Sharktooth tosses the remote to the side, raising the cash he's still holding, just slightly, before placing it in a neat stack on his knee.

"Is ten grand enough for us to see what that pretty voice sounds like when your mouth is stuffed with my cock?"

The blunt vulgarity of the question immediately burns my throat. A pressure builds behind my eyes . . .

"Filthy fucking tease."

Fuck you, fuck you, fuck you.

The sight of the money bounces around my vision like a screen saver.

Ten thousand dollars.

Just as a light breeze blows the sheer white curtains in the room, I gasp when I see Sharktooth has taken his dick out—unimpressive *and* offensive—just as the movement in the room slows again. Like it's pliable, stretchable, rubber.

The man in front of me smiles with a slight nod to the boys still holding me.

"We got her."

Rage relights just as they release my arms, and a resounding *boom* echoes like a gunshot through the room.

In an instant, my arms are free, and I don't hesitate. My hand snatches the money off the knee in front of me, and without my heels on, I bolt toward the door.

My eyes flinch as the leather lodges farther up my ass crack, but I don't care. I can't help but look at the scene that just broke up my assault from the other side of the room. I see a guy. The security guard that just got fired . . . *Seth.*

What the fuck?

Jackson has him pinned down, chest to floor, cuffing him—but I'm still running toward the other door—the one closest to the stairwell that will lead me down to the dressing room.

"Blue!" I hear Jackson yell, twisting my neck. Still, I keep running.

I have ten grand. I'll just fucking leave. Become a popstar in Canada.

The stupid thought quite literally gets knocked out of my head when I run face first into a plank of rock solid chest.

A yelp breaks free as the hard, toothy-looking floor connects with my bare ass. The ache in my tailbone throbs, but I try to shake it off, clenching my fist around the money in my hand. Keeping my head down for a second, I catch my breath.

A hand extends in front of me, the back of which is covered in ink—but I don't accept the help.

I hate everyone right now, including you, new hot security guard. Pushing to my feet, I'm just about to take off again, but my eyes flick up on instinct and . . . my breath leaves me completely.

No. It's *stolen.*

Everything stops.

Memories cast through my veins and then hook into my heart, sinking me to the spot.

I can't breathe, I can't blink, I can't fucking move.

Dark hazel eyes trap mine, blazing down at me. A perfect wave of almost-black hair falls to his forehead, and it flicks my gaze downward, taking in the tapestry of ink sprawling down his cut arms—all the way to his knuckles.

Chaos erupts around us, but my eyes are voyagers on new land. *Old* land.

It can't be.

And at the same time, there's no mistaking it. The devastatingly handsome *man* stares at me in awe as his deep, hoarse voice rasps out, "P-Pip?"

CHAPTER 19
LINC

I thought I'd checked-out again—that I'd somehow conjured up an even more breathtaking girl than the one who had spent the last seven years inhabiting my brain.

Drawing on the walls of my skull, singing between my ears.

She has . . . she has blue hair.

I love it. *It's so beautiful—like she'd dipped the strands in moonlight.*

And she's here. Actually *here.*

How the fuck is she here?!

It suddenly registers how much darker her eyes look right now. An icy glint. One of her cheeks is red . . .

My eyes finally drop to her barely covered body. The straps of leather wrap around her delicate curves like a smooth road between sun-kissed terrain.

Holy fuck.

An ancient, brain-tilting rush, immediately hits my groin and I nearly grunt from the impact, blinking rapidly.

Tick, tick, tick.

No. No, fucking no.

I blink hard again, and suddenly, the room snaps back into focus. My eyes lock with hers and my breath catches—finally putting together that the girl I walked in on—the one who was being held down by two guys and then running away at full speed was *her.*

A snarl pulls at my lips, reverberating through my chest as my eyes cut to the men in the middle of the room—specifically, the one buttoning his pants and staring in our direction.

Dead. His creepy Joker-ass is fucking dead.

I can feel a pull inside, grasping for something tranquil, but it's too late. I'm taking heavy steps before I even realize I'm moving. I can barely hear anything over the heavy metronome of my heart, but distantly, I'm aware of a door opening and closing somewhere behind me.

As I reach the man, his mouth opens, showcasing a straight line of horse teeth. With zero hesitation, my fist winds back, and the resounding *crack* of his cheek echoes through the room.

I hear commotion behind me, but my vision is tunneled with one target. Visions of stepping on the guy's neck, pulling back his arms, and ripping him in fucking half, thunder through my mind.

Suddenly, his two pups come tearing after me. I easily shove the one away with one arm and the other guy lands a sloppy punch to the back corner of my jaw.

I'm just about to flatten him out when a strong grip pulls on my shoulder.

I can barely see anything right now. Everything is splotchy, blurry—a maddening abyss of fury. My fist plows into the body holding my shoulder, but I'm stopped by an iron grip around my wrist, bending my arm so that if I move it at all, *something* will snap.

"Everyone. Calm the fuck down," Jackson growls, still restraining me, and I hiss through my teeth.

"Th-They w-were—"

"Shut up," he says, clenching his teeth. "You three. I imagine Beck will like to see you. I'll give him a call, and we can discuss what happened here tonight."

The big-tooth man laughs incredulously. "One of your employees just assaulted me. The slut took ten grand off my lap. You bet your ass I'll be talking to him."

My body jerks with a need to beat the fucker's face in, but Jackson's hold on me tightens, only jacking up my adrenaline more.

"I'll follow you out," he says tensely, twisting his chin, silently directing them toward the door. The one he'd sent Collins through with Seth. It took us for-fucking-ever to find him. Didn't help that the asshole *knows* the building, and I definitely do not.

As the men push through the door, Jackson finally releases me, pushing me forward a bit, and I whip around.

His tense silver eyes meet mine, and I swallow hard, the severity of what I've just done settling around me. *I hit him.*

"Go check out for the night," he says. "You're done."

Done? Done as in fired or done for the night?

My immediate thought is to call Desmond. But it's late. And I should wait till I'm not here. I don't know if Jackson's privy to this little covert operation that Desmond assigned me. Something I'm royally fucking up.

But . . . this was something I never could have seen coming.

How had I not seen her before now?

I clear my throat. "The girl—the girl that was in here . . ."

Jackson's jaw ticks. "Blue."

My mind works to accept that. Paige is Blue. "I should go see if she's . . . o-okay."

Jackson's eyes shut for a second. He runs his hand over his buzzed hair, while also shaking his head. "Check on her. Tell her to call me ASAP. And then check out for the night. I'll touch base with you once I speak with Beck."

I run my teeth over my bottom lip. I was ready to throw those assholes off the balcony before I even knew it was Paige. But . . .

My mouth flattens, and I work my jaw for a second before I dare to ask, "W-Why was there no security in here?"

Jackson's steel eyes look not so much angry as . . . *distressed.* But he doesn't answer me. His eyes flick to the door that the men just left through before he says, "I'll call you after I review the footage with Beck."

My molars grind, but I nod tightly. I guess I should be grateful I'm not in any immediate trouble. Though, after they *review the footage* I'm sure that will change.

I can't even find it in me to care at the moment.

Jackson heads toward the guest doors, and I take that as my cue to start toward the one that leads down to the dressing room.

But my steps falter as I get closer to the door. The wave of everything that lies below floats to the surface of my mind, and I bend at the waist, holding my weight on my thighs.

With my hands braced just above my knees, I stare at the tattoos—the Celtic knots—searching for the hidden lens peeking between them.

I blink a couple of times, trying to get my heart to calm the fuck down. Taking a breath, I still focus on my hand, but this time, it's on the knuckle tattoo with the mountain . . . the *M* from my mug.

"Mmmorrow."

Pip . . . she's downstairs. She's *right downstairs*. I can't ignore that.

I should. But I can't. My fingers flatten, rubbing into the rough denim of my pants, as I take another deep breath.

A moment later, I straighten back up and push through the door into the bright fluorescent lights of the stairwell, but the cavernous echo of the space immediately sways my body.

The unease from *just a fucking* second ago resurges, and my flat palm meets the cold concrete of the wall, instantly magnifying the clammy sweat breaking at my hairline.

My eyes clamp shut but an image slowly focuses behind my eyelids.

Her crystal blue eyes peeking up at me from windblown strands of light blond hair as we drive. Her hand on my knee, my hand on hers.

A hiccup in my chest forces me to grip the railing for balance, but it's not the thought of her that's jacking up my heart rate. It's . . .

I shake my head. Usually even the *idea* of physical contact is enough to turn my anxiety up—but the thought of her hand in mine, driving, it's actually . . . calming me down right now.

She's downstairs . . .

Maybe. Or maybe she left . . .

My eyes snap back open when I think about the terror that lit her gaze, a charged electric blue just now . . .

The vision tumbles immediately into what was happening before I came in, and my anger taps back into the ring. With a grunt, *I fucking move.*

My pace picks up momentum down the steps, nearly stumbling down the last couple. The ones just outside the dressing room.

Another breath. Paige could be in there but . . . other scantily-dressed dancers could be too.

Deep breath. Keep your eyes angled down.

The words roll through my head with a sickening familiarity, but I swallow it.

After a few more stuttered inhales and exhales, I release one just as I open the door and walk into the room.

It's quiet, which I guess is to be expected now that the club's open. It seems impossible that there's an entire nightlife experience happening on the other side of these walls.

My eyes timidly pull up to see the line of vanity mirrors with various articles of clothing dripping from chairs. Only one of the two overhead lights is on, and I walk slowly through the space. "Pa—" I stop myself, shaking my head. "B-Blue?"

Seems stupid, but if there is someone else around, I don't want to be caught breaking another rule—since I'm still not sure where my last violation landed me.

Crossing through the room, I push open the bathroom door, listening for the showers, but I hear nothing. Still, I say, "Blue?" again.

When there's still no answer, I turn out of the room and immediately run into Rio.

"Oh, sorry," she says, stepping aside in an attempt to not collide with me.

I've never felt more like a wall.

A frown pulls at my lips, and I sign with my free hand, "Have you seen Blue?"

Rio's eyes drop. "I didn't even see her. Selene said she ran out of here with her costume still on."

The surge that hits me at the idea of her, running down the sidewalk in *that,* is immediate. I have no fucking clue what the protocol is here, but I don't really give a shit. My mind works to string together a sentence, and I jaggedly sign, "I need to know where she lives. Do you have her address?"

The crease between Rio's eyebrows deepens, and she shakes her head. "I can't give you that information. What happened upstairs?" She uses her voice and her tone is sharp, serious.

I swallow hard, then make sure I'm facing her head on, enunciating, "I-I don't know. When I got in there it looked like things could have been . . . inappropriate. And I just want to make sure she's okay." My speech is slow, mostly because it takes me an eternity to talk, but hopefully it's helpful for her too.

Rio's mouth flattens to a tight line, crossing her arms over her chest as she shakes her head again, signing, "I'll text her."

I release a heavy exhale, then sign, "Rio, please. I just . . ." but I trail off.

How the hell do I ask for this?

I've spent years keeping myself away from her, and I know I have my reasons but, *fuck.* She was here. *I saw her.* And now . . .

I don't know. She's existed only in my mind for so many years at this point, it's almost hard to believe it was real.

I *need* to find her.

Rio slips her phone back in her pocket, but her caramel eyes study me, clearly trying to connect some dots.

A heavy, stuttered sigh pushes past my lips, and I shake my head again, as I do my best to sign, "I just need to see her, Rio. She could be hurt. She's my . . ." My hands drop. I have no idea how to simply *finish* that sentence, and my fists tighten at my sides, overwhelmed.

Rio releases a long sigh, her hug around herself tightening, before she signs, "I can't. I'm sorry."

I lift my chin, wondering if I should call Desmond tonight. Tell him about what happened and then see if one of *his* people can find Paige's address for me.

"But you know, there's this great little bar over at the corner of Las Palmas and Fountain," she signs. "Maybe you should go blow off some steam."

My eyes squint, trying to follow her signs, but she fingerspells the street names, so it helps. I'm confused for only a second before what she's telling me sinks in.

Las Palmas and Fountain.

I don't have an apartment number, but I'll knock on every door on the block if I have to.

Because she's here. She literally ran directly back into my life tonight, and . . . I *can't* ignore it.

I toss my third cigarette in the twenty-minute drive over here—it should have probably only been ten, but I had to pull over twice to puke. My jaw ticks as I pull onto Las Palmas, inching my way down the road.

As if I needed more deterrents, now I'm going to show up smelling like . . .

Ugh.

Luckily, I keep some mints handy and I pop the container open before pouring half of it in my mouth.

Crunchy mouthwash, I think, and my shoulders loosen.

The *"Pip-ism"* doesn't send the lung-gripping despair it usually does, and some stupid, off-the-fucking-charts *dilluted* part of myself wonders—*hopes*—that maybe it's because she's not far. Some stupid internal pull, like waves shifting with the moon. *We're closer.*

Now I just have to find her.

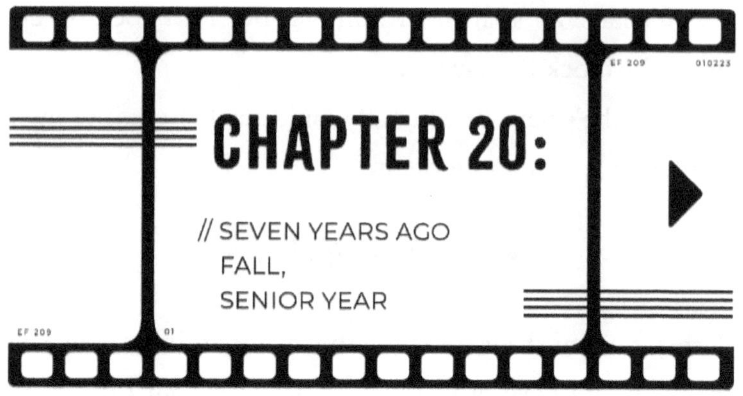

PAIGE

We'd done this trail probably a hundred times, but I think it was technically trespassing if they caught us here after dark.

When I had mentioned the night hike idea to Linc, there was no changing his mind, and I was too giddy to care at the moment. Still reeling from an *epic* first kiss.

My smile stretched as I followed behind him through the rocky climb to the creek. Soft cuts of moonlight snagged on tufts of his dark, wavy hair—just as grabbable as I'd imagined.

Buffy bless. He laughed it off earlier, but I really did want to know *how the hell* he learned to kiss. He was really fucking good at it.

His lips were so soft, but commanding. It felt like he wove an entire new thread to our existence between our mouths by the time we had pulled apart.

We kissed like we laughed—with everything we had.

I failed to recognize—or maybe with all of the uncertainty, I just wouldn't *let* myself think about it—but kissing someone who knew you inside and out was a far more visceral experience than I could have expected.

For some reason, I wasn't sure if our telekinesis would transfer in that way.

But *holy fucking hell*—did it ever. He seemed to know *exactly* what he was doing, and filming it was . . . well, it was pretty fucking hot.

He lifted himself up onto the boulder—just at the mouth of the creek—and then extended his hand out to me. I took it, my breath hitching at the contact but I swallowed it down as he lifted me, while I used my feet to scurry my bottom half up, and Linc chuckled.

"Maybe I need to start doing at least *one-a-days* with you and Batman," I laughed.

Linc laughed too but wasted no time pulling me into his arms, twisting me so that I was sitting in the *V* of his legs. My back pressed to his chest as he held me from behind.

Truth be told, it wasn't the first time we'd sat like this, but it *was* different somehow. His hold always felt protective, but there was this small bit of distance we'd always kept between us—just a paper-thin breezeway that was no longer there.

His arms tightened, as if hearing my thoughts—*though he probably was*—and my head naturally leaned into his shoulder.

"To think, we could have been doing that for years," he whispered to the shell of my ear, and I felt his lips pull up.

I smiled too, shoving my nose into his shoulder with a small laugh. We'd stayed silent on our way over here. Just listened to some music and held hands in the car. But it was good to know the mind-reading waves were open and clear.

"When did it change?" I asked, absently.

Without any clarification, Linc cleared his throat. "Four years ago for me."

My eyes bulged, twisting to look at him like the deranged human he was. He'd been wanting to do *that* with me since we were thirteen?! That was *before* my boobs came in.

Which made me curious. "When?"

He snorted a laugh, *"God,* I hate that I have to tell you this but . . . it was Halloween that year."

My smile pulled hard before I clutched his arms to me, laughing and squirming as he chuckled through a sigh behind me. "Yeah, yeah, laugh it up. You're the one that stuffed your bra—it's really your fault."

I snorted another laugh, tilting my head with a half-agreeance. I *did* stuff my bra that night. It was *my* year to pick the Halloween costumes, and I picked Buffy, of course. Linc went as Angel, and Ellis went as Spike.

"How about you?" he asked.

My lips pulled in, suddenly a bit nervous. I hadn't really been thinking about any of this until more recently—not really—*not for four years.*

I shifted my weight a bit in his arms, and he turned me so that I was looking back at him.

My eyes had adjusted to the dark, plus he was right in front of me, his nose practically grazing mine. "Pip, you can tell me no. You know that, right?"

I shook my head quickly to that, and he added, testingly, "Or . . . that you're not ready? I mean, just because—" he fumbled over his words, shook his head and then said, "I know four years seems like a long time, but . . ." he trailed off, moving one of his arms only to brush a rogue curl out of my eyes, then released a nervous-sounding breath. "It's not. Not with things like the *almighty forever* out there."

Till the end.

Even through the shadows of nightfall, I could see the sincerity gleaming back at me in his eyes—he meant what he was saying and it settled my moment of anxiety.

But . . . it sounded like he'd waited long enough. *I* didn't want to wait. I was ready. Just nervous.

I cleared my throat. "My voice recital. Last spring."

The corner of his mouth ticked up. A small sigh mixed with something throatier, rumbled against my forehead before he tilted his chin back down to look at me. "You looked so pretty that day—that dress." His face dropped to my neck, breathing deep.

A shiver ran down my spine, trying to think about how I could secretly wear that dress under every outfit.

I was more of a T-shirt and jeans kind of girl, but if it got *that* response? I'd order that dress in every fucking color.

Wishful thinking, of course. It was Gram's.

Luckily, we were able to sew up the hole. While I was petite, Gram was a *bean pole* when she was my age. My tits weren't big by any means, but they were big enough to rip the back of the dress a few days before the recital.

It definitely wasn't anything sexy—just a pretty, vintage, A-line powder blue dress that flared out a bit when I twirled.

Linc chuckled, his lips pressing to my temple, pulling both of our gazes back to the distanced water running through rocks along the creek, the sound of nocturnal critters singing and dancing.

Now that we weren't talking, only listening, the surrounding noise was *so loud,* and we both burst out laughing.

"This would be so much more romantic without the symphony of frogs and bugs," he laughed and then buried his nose in my hair, fueling the fire in my chest.

I laughed too, but it hiccupped with some of that earlier anxiety resurfacing. How did this feel so normal? *So good.*

The steady beat of his heart echoed the rhythm of our woodsy song and it slowly helped to steady my nerves.

Sighing, I finally said, "I don't know, I kind of like it. It can be our song."

His arms held me tighter, his voice a bit raspy as he said, "We already have a song."

My smile widened, still staring off, with him behind me. Maybe that's why this seemed so easy. Maybe this wasn't us *changing* so much as settling into where we always belonged. Maybe just the *idea* of it was big.

We had already sat like this. Now we'd kissed.

We'd already had a song.

"Fast Car."

Another calming wave washed through me as I took a deep breath. Quietly, I started to hum the intro chords, lazily matching it as best I could to the *symphony,* as Linc called it, surrounding us.

I couldn't be too scared. Nervous, yes. But scared?

How could I be?

Not in his arms . . .

LINC

Listening to her sing, like this. In my arms, *like this,* was fucking nirvana.

She had started to sing the lyrics quietly, playing with my fingers in hers, staring off in the same direction I was looking—the black abyss of a deeper trail, farther upstream.

Endless.

But I still felt like she wasn't quite where I was. Maybe I was just nervous because it all happened so fast. Or maybe it freaked her out to know *how long* I'd felt like this.

But it's not like I was miserable through those four years. I just loved her the way I always had, but with new, bonus affection.

"Pip," I said, hating that I had to cut off her singing, but I had to make sure, "You don't regret it, right?"

Her chin lifted, twisting before she pushed back a bit, but only so she could turn to fully face me. "Of course not," she said, her voice cracking a bit, and she shook her head. "Sorry. My voice is just tired. From the show."

My heart settled a bit, knowing for a fact that happened sometimes, and it wasn't just a coverup of her unease. She'd had to nurse a tired voice with honey and lemon juice before—vocal rest. It was usually pretty brutal because she talked *a lot* for being such a pipsqueak.

I was about to encourage her to not talk, that this could wait, but she said, "What we have is special."

My chin dipped, agreeing. "This doesn't change that."

Her teeth pinned her bottom lip, and I darted my eyes away for a second. I felt like I'd been staring at her mouth a lot, and I didn't want her to feel like I was expecting anything. But I also couldn't stop thinking about how fucking *good* they felt against my own lips. How they fit perfectly together with mine.

"Doesn't it?" she finally asked. "We won't be friends with a special connection anymore. Our hugs—*this*—it won't be rooted to *that* connection. It'll be led by . . . other stuff."

Pulling in a deep inhale, I let her words settle into my mind.

Honestly, it made me feel good. Even if I wanted *so badly* to be together the way we were earlier in the dressing room, it felt so fucking good to know, *to confirm*, that what we already had was so precious to her, she felt the need to protect it.

But . . .

"I don't think that's how it works. I think—" I said, but then stopped—my throat suddenly feeling dry. I swallowed, flicking my eyes to her. She was still sitting between my legs, but facing me with her legs crisscrossed, her yellow Chucks peeking out in the darkness.

After another second passed, she gave me a little nod, encouraging me to keep going. After another breath, I said, "I just think attraction, desire, they only intensify with time. Fighting it or holding it off doesn't stop it, it just . . . gives it time to burn." Then I shrugged and finished with, "And what we have? You're damn right it's special, but being together like this doesn't make it less special. I mean, if we were special friends, don't you think we might be special this way too?"

Her lips had stretched and pulled up her cheeks through my little speech. She'd moved closer to me—close enough that I could feel her breath hit my lips. She nodded, but moved her chin in that extra inch so that her nose ran lightly up and down mine.

God, her beauty was undeniable. She was a fucking knock-out—but nothing prepared me for how effortlessly sexy she'd be. It was like our kiss had shifted her light in my mind, bringing forth this whole other part of her that was hidden in the shadows. But I somehow knew it was there. It was a part of her that I desperately wanted to belong to me.

But only if she wanted that too.

Surprising me, she leaned in and pressed her lips against mine. She deepened it by shifting her legs, and sitting in a high kneel, angling my head. My fingers grabbed onto her waist without a second thought as my tongue parted her lips.

She sighed into me and my hips instinctively rocked. I groaned as she did the thing again—biting my bottom lip and then licking over the bite. I kissed her again, an *"mmm"* sound rumbling my chest before I rasped, "I fucking love that."

I felt her smile against my lips. "I—" she started to say, but then looked down. It was too dark to see, but I was pretty sure I felt her cheeks heating as my hands cradled her face.

"What?" I asked her quietly, kissing the corner of her mouth.

She shook her head, "No, forget it—it's—" she huffed, and I chuckled.

Okay, now I need to know. I pulled her into me. "Tell me."

Her eyes traced mine through the darkness, her lips pulling into her mouth, and she shrugged. "I sort of . . . had a dream where I did it to you, and you liked it."

I'm gone. Orbiting the earth with no fucking signal.

I worked to temper the sheer fucking giddiness that shot through my veins, and I cleared my throat. "What else happened in this dream?"

"Oh, God, I can't—" she shook her head through a nervous laugh before covering her face.

I easily pulled them away and dipped my chin, forcing her to meet my eyes. "How about I tell you a dream I had about you, and then you can tell me the rest of yours?"

Her lips pursed, twisting adorably, and I fought the urge to lean in and kiss her again. Only because I really wanted to know the rest of her dream.

Finally, she nodded, and I searched for a . . . *tame* dream I'd had of her. She was pretty much the star of my subconscious— and, I guess, my conscious world.

I sniffed my nose, just as I found one. "Okay. Well, one of them was here, actually. There was a party at the cove and you and I snuck off to the waterfall." My eyes shifted farther down the trail to where the waterfall actually was.

"We could barely hear the party once we were behind it, but they still weren't far. We could still hear the music, but you . . ." I stopped, suddenly feeling what I guess she'd been feeling.

When I looked up at her, her eyes sparkled back at me, despite the darkness surrounding us, unhelped by the small, crescent moon in the sky.

She silently told me to keep going, seemingly hanging on my words, and I swallowed hard, then continued. "You shoved me up against the rock and kissed me.

"When I reminded you that someone could find us—hear us—I got . . . excited and you knew it. You kissed me again, while you unbuttoned my pants and then . . ."

She gasped. "I blew you behind a waterfall with a cove full of drunk teenagers nearby?" she asked, gaping, but amused, and I suddenly felt my own neck heat. She quickly moved into me, whispering, "*Dream me* sounds like a lot of fun."

I shook my head. Nothing compared to this.

The real her.

A few seconds passed before I said, "Your turn."

She sighed, pressing her forehead to mine. "You're gonna think it's weird."

I had crazier dreams I could have shared with her too. I got that this was a little uncomfortable, but maybe it would help with the transition. Knowing things like this was a privilege that came with adding *this* to our relationship. And I, for one, wanted to know everything.

I cleared my throat. "I bet I'll love it."

She released a shaky exhale, then slowly started to say, "I was in my bed. I was uh—sleeping—and I . . ." she stuttered, then blew out a breath, and I picked up her hand, giving a small peck to the back of her knuckle and her shoulders dropped.

"I was sleeping, and I woke up to you—um—your face . . ." Her eyes drifted down between us, and my eyes widened, but when she clarified, "between my legs," it sent an immediate rush to my dick.

And if it weren't so dark, it would be pretty fucking obvious—given that I was sitting with my legs spread. I bent my knees, but since I couldn't exactly *readjust* right now without being glaringly obvious—all the movement did was strain my cock harder, and a grunt pushed past my lips.

"See! I told you!" She lowered her chin, and I swallowed the discomfort, immediately pulling her into me.

"Hey," I said, my voice rough from the unexpected surge of arousal, my jaw tightened. "Nothing you could ever imagine me doing to you is weird. Got it?"

She nodded, and I took another breath.

I pulled her closer, so that she was on my lap. "And I would *love* to do that," I told her, kissing her temple, but I pulled my face away in an attempt to not make the boner I was poking into her any worse.

Silence followed—save for the echoing "woods song"—*our song*—the soundtrack to our thoughts.

After what felt like minutes of no more words, just wandering fingers, a random press of each other's lips to an area of skin before she finally said, "Hey, Linc?" I squeezed my response, hugging her a bit tighter and she said, "Don't delete the video."

My lips turned up, as my nose ran along her hairline, confessing, "I can't wait to watch it."

She shifts a bit. "Will you—uh . . . will you send it to me?"

Running my hand through her hair, I told her, "Why don't I upload it on a drive for you?"

She snorted. "Are you reinventing the mixed tape?"

I shook my head. "Just to be safe. You never know—shit sent like that ends up in the wrong hands all the time. Better to be safe, right?"

She nodded. Melting into me as she sighed. Another beat passed before she said, "I'm tired."

It had been a long night, and she had shows the next three weekends. We still had to walk back to the car.

Again, like she was in my mind, she asked, "Does girlfriend status get me carried back to the car?"

I snorted. I could probably carry her if it was just the beach, or a field, but the rocky, steep descent back down . . .

"I *will* carry you, but you should probably know, we *will* probably plummet to our death."

She giggled and the sound danced between my ears before she said, "Sounds like you're coming down with me."

CHAPTER 21
PAIGE

Well, it finally happened.

I've snapped.

Something I wish *the leather still twisted around me would fucking do.*

I can nearly hear Gram cheering and wooing through the air whipping around me in the driver's seat while my brain backfires through the last . . . *hour? Who the fuck knows!*

I grabbed my shit and quite literally tore ass out of The Window, only able to slip on my zip-up and shrug on some leggings a block before I got to my car.

A heavy sickness is still sitting in my gut, but at least the old lady that lives in my head is having fucking fun.

"*Keep going.*" I keep hearing *that* in my head too. Just like yesterday when I went home. But I'm not sure if the voice is Gram. Me. *Him.* Maybe a weird, dissonant harmony of all three.

It's driving me fucking crazy, that's for sure.

It's *literally* driving me somewhere else too. Somewhere even more insane—surely only meant to send me over the edge completely.

Maybe that's what *"keep going"* means. The reckoning of my soul is about to send me fully into madness, and honestly, I find myself welcoming it.

Which is why when I left The Window, I texted the only person I could think of that might know Linc's address.

I found the contact and texted—

> **Me:** Any chance you can find the new security guard's address?

It's Selene!: Gimme 10 minutes.

And the bitch got it to me with two minutes to spare.

I mean, *we'll see.* When she texted me the address—when I saw it was to a house *way the fuck* out here—well, I thought if nothing else, the drive might help me calm down.

But I suddenly come to where I need to turn and see a small security booth. *A gate.*

Pulling off to the curb, putting on my hazards, I blink.

Fuck.

How the hell does he live in a gated community? In Hidden Hills?!

I'm sure Oprah and her dogs live somewhere nearby, a Kardashian or two . . . *How?*

The sick feeling in my gut from earlier twists at the sudden thought. *What if he's married?*

I scan my memory of him. I was in too much shock to really

pay attention to anything other than the rugged, man-version of the boy I once knew, but . . . I don't think I saw a ring.

Just tattoos.

Lots of them.

After a small shudder from the memory, a buzz hums below my skin. I use the current to force the idea that Linc is married—*or attached in any way*—out of my head.

It's not true. It can't be true because it threatens to reason with my bizarre *need* to drive out here and maybe take an illegal peek around.

Just to see . . .

But *fuck. This* is not a complication I saw coming, and my chest deflates.

I can't go back to the apartment yet, either. Even through the whirlwind of seeing my *runaway* soulmate, there's been a very real fear that the men I just stole ten grand from—*without providing the . . . service*—will be looking for me.

Beck knows them, and he has access to my address.

Fuck.

But the infuriating reality is, it's probably not even the *money* that will send one of them after me. The massive amount I've tucked in my backpack, in my trunk, is chump change to someone like Sharktooth. But it's the fact that I *took* it. Swiped it right off his lap and bolted away before he could force me to suck his dick.

I'm sorry—*take,* not *force.*

What the fuck was that?

Cringing, my mind works to shove the memory away and I

refocus, eyeing the security booth again. My weight shifts, and the leather rubber band wound around me digs into every nook and cranny, sparking an idea. A shitty one, but it's the only one I've got.

If Linc does have a wife, this is definitely going to fuck shit up.

Unzipping my hoodie, I keep it on my shoulders, but reveal the front of my leather get-up, then finally pull back onto the street and turn onto the small road leading up to the mountain, rolling my window down as I reach the booth.

Taking a deep breath, I tick my lips up in a practiced way.

"Good evenin'," the man says.

"Hi, there," I say quietly. I'm trying to temper any shake out of my voice as I say, "Someone ordered my services for Lincoln Morrow, 22 Hilltop."

The man looks older. White hair, brown eyes. Looks to be about retirement age, and harmless, but gives a small chuckle. "'S that so?" he muses, then shrugs. "Well, I'll just give him a quick call—"

"—Wait!" I say, too quickly.

Shit . . .

"Uh—they said they'd like to keep it a surprise. Uhh—" I fumble, gracelessly opening my glove compartment, as *every* fast-food napkin imaginable falls out of it.

But so does my emergency twenty dollar bill. I don't want to break into the trunk stash, but I'll do it if I have to. My curiosity is on another plane of sanity. *Clearly,* as I try to bribe my way into an exclusive community with twenty fucking dollars.

And still, I timidly hold it out asking, "Will this keep it

between us?" My speck of dirt on the mountain of millions in front of me.

Keep going, keep going.

Keep going, Pip.

The words thrum through me, allowing my sheer *will* to let this happen. *Please, let this happen. I just . . . I need to see . . .*

I don't know who I'm begging to—like any other silent plea to Buffy and the universe, I expect this to go the same, but then the man smiles again and says, "Sounds good, darlin'."

Wait—really?

That worked?

He walks back to his little booth, tucking the twenty into his pocket as he hits the button to open the gate.

"You have yourself a good night. Give my best to Mr. Morrow."

Un. Fucking. Believable.

After parking at a vista point about a half a mile from the address Selene gave me, I walk the rest of the way.

Now, I can see the house that belongs to my destination—about three hundred feet away. And it looks . . . intense.

A dark charcoal gray cube, nearly wedged into the cliff with a giant balcony overlooking the mountain range.

Must be fucking nice.

How does he live here?

The Lincoln Morrow I knew could *never* afford this . . .

I reject the idea, again, that he married some rich bitch with

Daddy's money. The idea stops me right outside the fence—which seems more like a wall surrounding the property line.

Maybe I can slink onto the balcony. Worst thing that happens is I plummet—something I can't be certain I'm *not* already doing just by being here.

I start to move toward the balcony, slowly, pulling my hood over my head. I take a tiny step, then another, and in an instant, a bright light turns on in the corner where the wall meets the house.

Motion sensors—*fuck!*

At the grip of my panic, I remind myself, *no one's home.*

No one *can be* home, because if they are, then I really will just take the next couple steps.

"*Not funny,*" I distantly hear—I think it's Gram's voice, but I can't be sure with the blood whooshing through my head as I curl into the shadowy corner.

But it's too late. The door to the massive wall starts to slide over, creating an opening like a new-age castle, and I swallow hard.

Oh my God, oh my God, oh my God.

I prepare to see some big-titted, silk-wearing bitch that I'm about to throw down on—*for no other reason than I've lost my mind*—but for the *third fucking time tonight,* I'm struck speechless.

Paralyzed, when I see who walks through the opening.

No tits. No silk. No woman.

Familiar, sandy blond hair finally meets the light shining above me, but the shadows of night mute the green eyes I remember so well.

"E-Ellis?" I croak out.

Like Linc, he's filled out even more, but I'm too . . . *fucking rocked* to fully take in all of his differences as he casually crosses his arms over his chest.

His expression is studying, also confused, and while there's a tiny glint to something resembling warmth, he mostly looks irritated. "When Ted called ten minutes ago and told me there was a hooker on her way up, I got worried the poor girl had driven straight off the mountain or something. Got lost."

My irritation with *Ted* deflates completely at the weighted feeling of his last two words. They almost come out as accusatory, and I swallow hard.

"I—" I start, but then shake my head.

Goddammit. I wasn't prepared for this.

Which is crazy because a reunion with these two assholes has been at the forefront of my mind for years.

Since it all fell apart.

"Well, you're here," he finally says, a cold and matter-of-fact tone.

And I deserve it. I deserve all of his anger.

I nod. "I—" I'm cut off, as suddenly he's right in front of me, grabbing my chin, looking at my cheek.

Fuck me. I barely felt the pain from the slap anymore, but the growing rage in his eyes is enough to send cold, hard dread through me.

"What happened?" Ellis says quietly, still holding my chin.

My breath leaves me at the contact, swallowing hard at his question. And so does any semblance of control as my limbs start to shake.

He looks at it a second longer, his jaw ticking, and his eyes flick down to meet mine.

"I work at . . . The Window," I tell him, absently, like that somehow explains it, and his eyebrows pinch.

"And hitting women is normal practice there? Linc left that part out," he mutters, and a zap of *something* happens in my chest at the mention of Linc.

But his statement reminds me. "You guys—you live together?" Dumb question, but it's the only one that surfaces through the shock.

He nods, and I feel my weight wobbling again, but Ellis's hold on me tightens as he feels my body sway.

I feel like I went to work and left the building into a new fucking reality.

Two ghosts have reemerged tonight.

Ellis. My oldest friend. A friend I was no longer able to *be a friend to,* as of seven years ago.

He sighs. "Come inside. Let's put some ice on this."

Surprise lifts my eyebrows. *He's inviting me in?*

The bad-idea alarm in my head starts up, but something bigger and warmer knocks it away like a bumper car.

He finally steps back and tilts his chin toward the opening. I walk behind him. A few silent steps force the leather somehow even farther up my ass, the Xs crossed over my nipples burn again and I grunt, "Uh—do you have scissors?"

CHAPTER 22
LINC

The four-corner intersection of the cross-streets Rio told me did in fact have a bar on the corner of one, a small red market on another, and the other one had tall, trimmed hedges with no structure.

By process of elimination, I think *this* is Paige's building.

Though, it's all up in the air seeing as I still haven't found the balls to get out of the car and take a look.

It's a small building—almost looks like a motel. There's an open breezeway I can see from the street and there's two levels of four, maybe five doors on each level.

Being that it's just about midnight, there's been virtually no foot traffic. But sitting out here and lurking for the last hour, I've managed to rule out the corner unit on the bottom right given the very . . . handsy couple that just pummeled their way through the door.

Why is she living here?

I knew she'd stayed with Darlene until she passed, but when I saw Darlene's empty house last weekend, I thought maybe she'd left California . . .

I suddenly wondered if that was the reason for the onslaught of the spaciness that's been giving me whiplash.

I wonder if my brain was trying to make peace with the fact that Paige had actually left. If it was my mind's way of coping with *more* distance. It was probably the same dumb part of me that believed we still somehow felt that internal, gravitational pull, after all these years.

The thought alone swells an ache through my chest.

She's still here, I remind myself.

She was right downstairs tonight.

Now, she's right across the street. *Somewhere.* And I just need to get out of the car and find her apartment.

My reasons for keeping myself away are complicated—in an agonizing sort of way—something I can't even acknowledge if I have any hope of getting out of the car.

But I think at the beating center of it, past details aside, I know it's *fear* that's kept me from seeking her out *this* long.

The steep, mountainous *fear* of seeing her again—a fear that's been given endless time to grow and become more daunting and treacherous.

What I did to her.

What happened . . .

Where I went.

I'm not prepared to meet a single one of those truths tonight. And as it stands now—*not ever.*

But she could be hurt, a voice reminds me again.

A heavy breath pushes past my lips, looking again at the

apartments, noticing an iron gate with a detail at the tip of the spears that would hurt if you lost your footing while hopping it.

Which is exactly what I'll have to do if I want to find her.

Fuck me.

I'm not worried about falling, just the whole trespassing thing . . . seems like something I shouldn't be doing *twice* in the span of a week.

Stop making excuses. You've trespassed before, and you will likely do it again.

I clench my teeth as a frustrated growl rumbles through my chest. I'm just about to stall for a few more seconds, when I suddenly see a guy walking up to the entrance gate.

I'm too far away to jump out and have him hold it open for me without being suspicious, but I can watch what apartment he goes into, eliminating another.

Or not . . .

The lighting on the breezeway is dim, but I can now see the guy looks to be about my age—*her age, too*—give or take a couple years, with shaggy brown hair shadowing his eyes.

He's wearing a brown leather jacket, and walking purposefully up the stairs, onto the second level breezeway, then casually strides to the end unit, farthest from the street.

But he doesn't go in.

That same pull that's reawakened *deep, deep* inside of me tingles with awareness. My eyes squint, watching as he knocks on the door.

A few seconds pass, and nothing happens, but I'm ready to explode. For some reason, I'm certain that's her apartment.

A vision of her opening the door and pulling the guy inside flashes through my mind and I grunt, blinking.

My chest settles when I see, still, no one answers the door, and he tries the doorknob.

My eyebrows pinch. *If he's allowed in without a knock, why didn't he do that first?*

When the door appears to be locked, he moves over to the window to the right of the door. He stretches onto his toes, straining his neck a bit to look inside the window, and a prickling sensation rolls through me.

I have no confirmation if that's Paige's apartment, but my body is buzzing. The window he's looking through is dark and the small light by the door is also off.

Though, if the girl I saw tonight is anything like the girl I knew before, she'd keep that light off even if she was home.

After another few seconds, I see the guy take out his phone, holding it up in front of him.

Is he taking pictures?

My body jerks. I'm not ready to see her, but if that's her apartment, I need to beat that asshole's face in. My hand moves to the door, I'm just about to push it open, as my phone buzzes from my pocket.

Fuck.

It could be Jackson . . . maybe he's heard from her.

Keeping my eyes on the guy, now walking down toward the gate, I quickly pull my phone out to check the text. But my heart thuds when I see it's a message from Ellis.

Ellis: We have company.

PAIGE

A light knock at the door woke me up, and I whined, but then I heard, *"Happy birthday to you, happy birthday to you . . ."*

Gram was wiggling into my room, coffee in hand, finishing her song, and a sleepy chuckle pushed past my lips.

This woman. The energy. Is the sun even out yet?

I sat up, accepting her caffeinated gift, murmuring, "So early. Why?"

"Gotta enjoy the whole day, my girl. It's the best day of the whole year." My chest warmed as I took a sip of my coffee. Early or not, that was sweet. "Plus your *boyfriend* asked that I make sure you're up and ready to go by six."

My heavy eyes blinked up at her. She was wrapped in her signature cardigan, her hair was up in a wild sea of gray curls. "You look like Ursula the sea witch right now," I mumbled.

She clapped triumphantly, twisting toward my mirror above my dresser. "I love it!"

Ugh. The energy.

She sat down on the bed next to me, while I took another sip from my mug, willing myself to be awake, as her words finally sunk in. Her little teasing tone with the word *boyfriend.*

To say no one was surprised by me and Linc getting together was the understatement of the century. Reactions ranged from, *"'Bout fucking time,"* to *"Weren't you already dating?"*

The latter came mostly from classmates, the former from Ellis and Gram. I hadn't seen Christine since Linc told her, but he'd said she was happy about it.

We were still insanely busy. *Rent* had closed last weekend, so that freed up *some* of my time, but Linc had been working any spare moment he had to finish editing his film for the festival— *Without the Moon* was the decided title.

Gram's palm extending toward me brought my attention back to now, and I glanced down, seeing a bracelet . . . it looked like black pearls, but a little more jagged—rough. My eyes pulled up to Gram.

"I know the rule is no birthday gifts, but . . . I got these lava stones when your Grandpa and I went to Iceland. I'd always wanted to do something special with them, and, well, nothing is more special than my girl stepping into womanhood."

Oh wow. My smile pulled as she held it open. I lifted my hand and she slid it on my wrist.

"Lava rock is a stone of protection and strength," she explained. "But I just think it looks cool. And I added a little charm to the middle."

"A penny," I said.

"For luck," she said with a wink.

I loved it. It really did look cool. The black stones were a little grittier than the average beads, heavier, and the black and copper was a color combination I loved.

I placed my coffee on the nightstand and quickly scurried to hug her. "Thank you," I said.

"You're welcome, Paigey May. Happy birthday."

I smiled into our hug, before she gave me a quick double pat. "Okay, chop chop! I had strict orders, and I will not let my Lincleton down."

I breathed a laugh, immediately reaching back for my coffee as she started toward my closet. "Now, what does an eighteen-year-old with a hot new stud on her arm wear?" she mused.

I took Gram's advice and didn't wear my jeans and T-shirt combo. I opted for a short, dark purple skirt with some black tights—ripped, but not intentionally—and I finished the look off with my black combat boots and a tight, light gray Runaways T-shirt tied at the side of my waist.

I was just slipping on my jean jacket as Linc walked in through the mudroom.

It was still dark outside, and the only light was the small one over the sink, but his eyes locked on me immediately, suddenly making my knees shake a bit.

I tried to release some of the tension by pulling my hair out from under the denim collar of my jacket, saying, "Morning," with a small smile.

But damn, he's so hot. How I hadn't been all over him for years was beyond me, but it was like the moment we kissed, it became a pulsing fact any time he entered a room.

As Gram put it, Lincoln Morrow, my best friend, now boyfriend—was a complete stud.

And the extra layer of appreciation for his brown flannel jacket—the one he always wore around this time of year—was on another level.

His hazel eyes twinkled in the soft light as he smirked and finally walked over, reaching out to me and pulling me into him, but he stopped before hugging me.

Instead, he leaned down and pressed a sweet kiss to the corner of my lips. "You look hot, birthday girl."

I giggled, awkwardly. It was the damndest thing. I never thought of myself as *hot*. My big blue eyes and blond hair often landed me parts in shows where I was playing some version of the "hot girl," but me—Paige Michaels—I always thought I was more of a tomboy.

But the way *he* looked at me—*the way he kissed me*—had me thinking . . . maybe I was hot to him.

I cut off my own wandering thoughts and finally asked, "So, where are you taking me at this ungodly hour?"

He chuckled. "I thought we'd go on a drive before school."

My eyes lifted with the corners of my lips. *A drive.*

It'd been a while since we did one.

A proper *drive* in our universe involved an unknown destination, an unknown playlist, but it had to end with a piece of treasure and discovering a new song.

"Perfect," I said, and he smiled.

We found our destination at sunrise on the PCH. California was so beautiful, and views like this almost made it seem worth the exorbitant amount of money it cost to live here.

Ocean and mountains. Purples and yellows.

I peeked to my side. *Linc and Paige.*

He had thought of everything. We were sitting in the bed of his pickup on a blanket, facing out toward the beach. And he'd even stopped for breakfast sandwiches and coffee before he picked me up.

His sandwich was long gone, but he waited until I was chewing my final bite to say, "Do you want your present now or later?"

My lips stretched. I had tried to make the no-presents rule with him a few years ago, but he never listened. And I secretly loved that he didn't.

Still, I pretended. "It's a rebellion this year. First Gram, now you."

"What'd she give you?"

Wiggling my jacket sleeve up, I showed him the bracelet and he held my wrist, looking at it, but his thumb rubbed softly along the thin skin on my hand. "Gram said she found them on a hike to some volcano in Iceland."

"So pretty. I'd love to go to Iceland."

"Me too. Gram says it's the most magical place in the world. Apparently they're really into fairy and troll folklore too."

"Let's go one day," he said, looking up at me.

It felt like a big promise—or it felt like it *should be* a big promise—but only because he was my boyfriend now.

Still, I couldn't deny that I wanted to do that someday. *With him.* So I nodded with a smile, leaning in to kiss him on the cheek. "Deal. Plus, I think you could totally rock the viking look."

I smirked, and he pulled me into him, onto his lap. "Oh yeah?" he mused, playfully.

My mouth ticked up teasingly, and I lifted my hand to his hair. "Oh yeah, these locks have serious potential," I said, then ran my fingers over the light sprinkling of facial hair. "This too."

He smiled up at me. "You didn't answer me. Present now or later?"

I twisted my mouth, pretending to contemplate, but then my lips tilted up at the corner.

"Now it is," he said. I started to move, but he held my thighs tightly. "Don't you dare move," he said with a hint of challenge, that same dark glint hit his eyes with the sun slowly rising over the ocean beside us.

I stayed put, because *holy fuck* was I into his bossy-man routine.

I had never let my mind wander too far with how he'd be if we were ever together like this, but I guess it wasn't exactly surprising that he was possessive. Dominant.

We've both always been fiercely protective of one another. Ellis too. But this was different.

After rustling through his bag, he finally pulled out a square package wrapped in black wrapping paper with glittery stars on it and an electric blue bow.

"Maisie picked the wrapping paper," he said as he handed it to me.

I smiled. "It's badass. She's turning out all right, huh?"

He nodded, smiling too, then said, "Open it."

I tugged my lip between my teeth but then unwrapped the package. Opening it, I gasped as I saw what looked like some sort of old-world antique box.

It had this gold crescent moon with stars dangling on the lid. I pulled it out of the box he wrapped it in to get a closer look.

It was a hexagon shape and around the perimeter there were carvings of the moon phases.

I was speechless. It was . . . so pretty. So unique.

His hand lifted, opening the lid, and as he did I gasped again. The inside of the lid was black with stars dotted along it, and an iron-looking ballerina figurine rose up. Linc twisted what sounded like a spring being wound, and a song started to plunk through the box.

I listened for a few seconds, realizing . . .

"'The Killing Moon,'" I said quietly.

Echo & the Bunnymen. It was on a few of our playlists.

This was . . . *so cool.* So *creepy and cool* and . . . I loved it so much, but it looked . . . expensive.

"Do you like it?" he asked.

I blinked, trying not to cry. "I love it, Linc. I wish you wouldn't have spent the money—"

He cut me off with a kiss, then whispered, "You're worth every penny, Pip," then flicked the penny on my new bracelet.

I smiled and put the box back down safely so I could properly thank him.

The second I put it down, I grabbed each side of his face and pressed my lips to his. With my hands cradling his jaw, I positioned his face so I could fully taste every bit of him.

Coffee and Silvers.

He gripped my waist with one hand while the other one moved to my nape, fighting me for dominance.

I did the thing he liked. Nibbling along his bottom lip and licking behind the bites as he groaned, his fist gripping my hair.

I pulled my lips away from his, and a small whine escaped him.

I smirked as I slid my hand to the back of his hair and tugged—*God, it really was so grabbable it should come with a warning or something*—but he looked up at me with curious, lustful eyes, and I put on an admonishing face. "I'm trying to thank you, so stop fighting me."

His eyes darkened, but he just gave a small, devious pinch to his cheek. "You wanna be in charge?" he asked.

I pulled my lips into my mouth. Other than our little dirty dreams exchange a few weeks ago, we'd never talked about what we liked—what we were into—I wasn't sure I knew, honestly.

I knew I was into *him.* The way he looked at me. And I liked when he took charge, but I shrugged. "Maybe sometimes?"

He smirked, pulling my face closer to his. "Baby, you can order me around any day." And then he kissed me again.

He took the control back, but my grip on it might as well have been a dolphin trying to hold onto a ketchup bottle.

Impossible.

Baby? God, do I love that. And he was kissing me like the *hot girl* he claimed I was earlier.

Eighteen was looking pretty fucking great.

LINC

"Reese Witherspoon driving off in the Jaguar at the end of *Cruel Intentions,*" Jenna said.

A few people clapped, and Mr. Harris chuckled at the front of the room. It was last period, and film class had run a little off course. We'd somehow managed to veer off to iconic film shots.

"Oh, no way," Ellis said. "From *that* movie, it's definitely Sarah Michelle Gellar's close-up tears—*Bittersweet Symphony. God.* The nineties were a revolution."

I snorted a laugh, as Mr. Harris said, "Well, I guess that's an interesting question. What makes the shot iconic? Like, how can we all be sure—if we step on a boat, that someone is going to stand at the front of the ship and yell, 'I'm the king of the world!' What do we think that is?"

The class chattered a bit, then Ellis spoke up. "It's a vibe."

"Simple as that?" Mr. Harris asked with an amused huff.

I cleared my throat, but I didn't say anything. Honestly, I was just counting down the minutes until I got to see Paige again.

This morning was amazing. I was so fucking happy she liked the music box—and *God,* did she thank me. She kissed me for so long and so hard that my lips buzzed the whole way back to school. I could still feel her through first period.

The bell rang and, like I'd summoned her, Paige suddenly walked to the doorway just as Mr. Harris said, "We'll start tomorrow with your establishing shots. Don't think I forgot—but well played, Ellis." He gave a tilt of his chin toward Ellis, chuckling.

I guess he *was* the one who mentioned the "king of the world" shot that started the whole thing.

But I was more curious as to why Paige was here.

I watched as she walked over to Mr. Harris with a slip of paper, my eyes squinting. "Ah, Paige. Perfect," I heard him say.

Her eyes flicked over to me, giving a small smile, but then directed her attention back to Mr. Harris. Shoving the rest of my shit in my bag, I started in her direction, but waited off to the side.

Mr. Harris noticed and said, "You can come on over, Linc," and I awkwardly shuffled over.

To be fair, I was driving her home after we stopped by Queenie's for a piece of pumpkin pie. Her favorite—and with a November birthday, it was always available.

As I came up beside her, I shoved my hands in my pockets to keep myself from pulling her into me.

I was certifiably *obsessed* with her little punk-rock princess look.

So. Fucking. Cute.

"I was just telling Paige that an old colleague of mine is doing *American Idiot* at the Wilturn in the city, and he needs someone to step into the *Whatshername* role pretty quickly. The show opens in three weeks," he said to Paige.

Her eyes widened. "I mean, I know most of the music, I think," she said. "Does he want me to send him a few bars of something?"

Mr. Harris smiled. "I think that would be great. Send it to me, and I'll send it to him. I've already told him about you, but this way my recommendation doesn't get lost in the shuffle."

"I can shoot it after Queenie's," I told her.

She tossed me a small closed-mouth smile before she looked back at Mr. Harris. "Thank you so much, Mr. Harris. This is awesome. I appreciate it so much."

"Of course, Paige. I think you'd be perfect for the part. In fact, you should probably wear exactly what you're wearing now when you film the audition."

She pulled her eyes down, examining her outfit, "Yeah, you're right. Though, I do have a 'Jesus of Suburbia' shirt I could put on."

Mr. Harris chuckled. "Sounds great. It's a paid gig too. A stipend, but it's something. And it'll be a regional theater credit on your resume."

There were a thousand reasons I liked Mr. Harris, but *this* was a great opportunity. I didn't know much about the show other than it was the Green Day musical, but shows that came through the Wiltern had a great reputation.

"Linc, do you need the AV room today?" Mr. Harris asked, just as Ellis joined the little gathering at the front of the room.

I shook my head. "No, it's Pip's birthday, so color correction will have to wait till tomorrow. I've just got the last scene—which should be pretty easy since you fixed it."

He shook his head. "You shot it, man. I just had some software that I've . . . *permanently borrowed* from an old colleague," he chuckled.

Ellis laughed. "Careful wording. I like it."

Mr. Harris waved us off, "Well, happy birthday, Paige. You guys have fun."

•• ·)··)·)· ·● · (· ·((·(· ••

We took her pumpkin pie to go, and brought it back to Darlene's. I brought my camera in and had been filming Darlene playing the piano while Paige ran through her thirty-two bars of music.

I loved watching them do this. Darlene didn't play as much as she used to, but it was an artistry of its own just to watch them. They were in their element when they were in front of that piano.

They flowed better and better with each pass at the song, and after three tries, I stopped filming.

"Okay, stand in front of the bay windows—face out toward the street," I told her.

"Such a bossy director," she teased, a twinkle in her eye as she passed me. I gave her a look, my eyebrow lifting.

With Darlene distracted by the sheet music, I leaned down over Paige's ear, "You only get to be in charge *sometimes,* remember?"

I fucking loved that she wanted to take the lead that way—or at least seemed open to it—but it shouldn't have surprised me.

She was the one who climbed the tree without peeking back

and jumped off the small cliffs at the watering hole by the creek without a second thought.

Got on stage in front of thousands of people.

She smiled again and moved in front of the window like I told her and the light was perfect.

The sun was just setting so it lit her face naturally from behind me. She ran her fingers through her hair and readjusted her clothes. "You look perfect, Pip," I told her.

"Aww," Darlene said from the piano, and I snorted.

Paige rolled her eyes but laughed. She turned back to me, and the sun caught her eyes like a wave, and I stopped and stared.

"All right, Linc-on. Let's do this. I need to get a slice of pie in before Ellis gets here and eats half of it."

And just like that, she was back in charge.

I had pretty much made a habit of following her lead in most other things. But the urges I had with her had four years to dance around as *just ideas* in my head.

I wanted to do anything and everything with her.

But there was no need to rush. We had time.

CHAPTER 24
PAIGE

"You good?" Ellis's voice sounds from the other side of the door, and my body jerks upright.

I've been in the bathroom for at least fifteen minutes while I literally cut the leather off of my body. As I toss the scraps in the trash can, I huff a small laugh as I think—just like *Olivia Newton John in Grease.*

My mouth quirks at the corner. I'll have to make sure to pay Rio for the material.

Not that she pays for costume supplies with her own money, but I don't want them to do something shitty like take it out of her paycheck.

Ellis clears his throat, reminding me that he asked a question.

"Yeah, sorry," I finally rasp, then grunt. "I'll be right out."

The relief I feel at not being twisted up is short-lived when I catch sight of myself in the mirror.

Buffy bless, I can't believe he let me in the house.

The wild blue strands of my hair are unruly and knotted—*bed head to the extreme from driving full speed down the freeway*—I see now that there's one part of my cheek, right near my lip that's still red, a little swollen, and there's a cut there, but I think that's because I bit it.

My eyes are also glassy, picking up on the gray from my zip-up, but it's also evident that I've been crying, which doesn't surprise me but . . . I don't remember it happening, or for how long, or when it stopped.

Feeling my eyes well again, I shake my head and then run my fingers through my hair. After I've pulled through most of the knots, I shove it up in a bun, allowing some of the shorter pieces to fall around my face.

After wiping under my eyes and cleaning up my lip, I take another breath. I'm certain this is the most *okay* I'm capable of looking right now. And I just . . . don't think it's enough. Not for *who* is waiting on the other side of this door.

Linc and Ellis are living together.

In a house in the mountains. Just under an hour drive from the city—from Venice.

My eyes peer around the swanky bathroom with modern finishes, then back at myself in the mirror.

That same inward chant keeps finding me, *"Keep going,"* but it's more of a feeling than the words themselves now, a wound-up feeling, like the crank on a music box.

With that, I take an inhale, swipe the scissors off the counter and open the door.

The bathroom is conveniently located right in the entry hall. I head in the opposite direction of the door we came in, and walk toward the slate gray cabinetry I see just past the hallway. When

I reach the kitchen, I'm unprepared for the fucking beauty that is *this view.*

The dark tunnel you enter through is like a portal. The house has a fully-open concept and the entire wall opposite the kitchen, next to the living room, is floor-to-ceiling windows overlooking . . . well, it's night right now—so all I can see is a dark, forestry landscape down the mountain, dotted with lights like fireflies from other homes, I assume. But the vast depth of the dark mountain range is still breathtaking.

I see Ellis out there in a pool of light, standing with his back to me, and my shoulders hunch.

This is going to suck.

"There's good and bad suck, this we know," Gram reminds me somewhere inside, and my lungs expand. I hold her words, I feel that inward pull, and timidly cross through the living room, toward the sliding door.

Opening it, Ellis's chin jerks in my direction, but my breath gets caught in my throat once I step on the balcony, looking up.

"The stars . . ." I gasp.

And oh my God, the moon. It feels so close, I feel like I could just lift my hand and run my thumb along the smooth, inner curve of its crescent shape.

Wow . . .

Suddenly, Ellis is in front of me, handing me a small ice pack. With the natural nocturnal glow and the small corner light from the balcony, I can see him a little better now. His gorgeous boy face, but with some lines of manhood that weren't there before. Still clean-shaven. And while he's barefoot, I'm surprised to see him in a tank top. The Ellis I knew is the reason businesses put *"Must wear shoes and shirt"* on their doors.

I don't say anything though. That would be weird.

I take the pack from him, but mumble, "Thanks, but I don't really need it."

He shrugs. "It'll help with any swelling."

Shuffling my feet, I nod, holding the pack up to the corner of my lip. He sits in one chair, so I sit in another. The silence is a living, breathing part of this moment.

It's so quiet up here . . .

It seems like an eternity passes before I finally work up the courage to ask, "How long?"

Ellis sighs, leaning back. His green eyes catch the light from behind me with a glint, eyebrow lifting. "Me and Linc?"

My jaw tightens. *Why did he say it like that?*

He holds the challenge in his eyes for a moment more before his mouth quirks at the corner, and he shrugs. "He's been living here for four years, but we reconnected five years ago."

Five years ago?

"If you'd have answered one of my seven-hundred calls or texts, I would have told you."

My eyes clamp shut with a small shake of my head. It's terrible. *The fucking worst.* And even worse than that? I don't even have a good explanation for why I stopped talking to him.

I didn't mean to.

But I did.

He was away when Linc left and I didn't want to talk about it. Then it quickly became about taking care of Gram, and then one day it felt too overwhelming to even pick up the phone and try to call him, so I just . . . didn't.

Another casualty of the life pause.

The one I always knew would restart with a vengeance if it restarted at all.

But I miss it—him, us—so fucking much.

"I'm sorry," I whisper, barely audible, but he hears it. I can tell in the way his shoulders sink. His chin drops, and he breathes deep.

"What are you doing here, Paige?" he asks, quietly.

The tone isn't harsh but tight. And of all the things he can ask me right now, I guess that's the least spiral-bound.

I clear my throat. "Something . . . happened at The Window. I saw Linc, but only for a second, then I—uh . . ." I trail off, jaggedly explaining myself. "I ran away. Got his address from a coworker."

He studies me a second, he looks like he wants to ask me something else, but then thinks better of it. After another sigh, he says, "Full disclosure, Linc will probably be here soon. I texted him while you were in the bathroom."

Jesus. How is this happening?

How is this all *happening?*

Pushing my heels into the floor of the porch, I resist the urge to jump up and book it back down the mountain, back to my car, and instead take a breath. "H-How did you guys end up living together?" I ask timidly.

Fuck. I feel like I'm stepping on a frozen lake—just the right amount of pressure will break the ice and send me sailing down.

He clears his throat, then shrugs. "The usual way. I bought a house, he needed a room to rent."

Glib asshole. He's being vague on purpose.

Standing up, I drop the ice pack on the chair and step in front of him. "Look. I know you're mad at me. And you have every right to be, I . . ." I shake my head, realizing at this very minute. I did to him what Linc did to me.

I just . . . disappeared.

He stands too, his scowl deepening, but I continue, the words barely scraping past my lips, "Something happened . . . after graduation."

His chest inflates with a deep breath. "A lot of *somethings* seem to happen to you," he mutters, and I wince. He takes a deep breath, then says, "Sorry. That wasn't cool." He shakes his head. He again, looks like he wants to say something else, but doesn't. Instead, he pulls me into him, surprising me with . . . *a hug.*

It finds *that* part of me instantly—the deep, deep part I keep hidden. Like it *knew* the way. *And holy fuck*—it's like the embrace taps the outer barrier of my well with a pick, piercing it, and a small sputtering of sadness trickles out. A stream of pain I've been feeling *by myself* for the last year.

Since Gram . . .

My eyes fill and tears race from the corners and down my cheeks as I bury myself in his shoulder. *I'm sorry, I'm sorry, I'm sorry.*

"I know," he sighs.

I didn't realize I had been saying it out loud, but I shove myself into him harder and he holds me back, rubbing his hand up and down my back.

Oh my God, I can feel my body crumbling.

Breathe.

Ellis hugs me tighter as another moment passes, and he leans his cheek on the top of my head. "I'm sorry about Darlene."

A gasp stutters through my tearful breaths, realizing now *that's* why I'm quaking and crumbling to the ground.

A hug. A real one. From someone who used to care about me. I haven't felt this comfort since she died last year.

My hands twist and pull at the soft material of his tank top. "Me too," I croak, feeling even worse. I didn't plan a funeral, but people all over Venice did stuff in Gram's memory. I didn't go to any of it because I suck.

"I went to the celebration of life at Queenie's. Thought maybe I'd see you there," he says. With my cheek still pressed against his chest, a shaky, shameful inhale is my only response, then he whispers, "We still talked sometimes, ya know."

My wet eyes pull up, looking at him, my brow furrowing. "You did?"

He nods. "Not a lot. Less after her stroke. I know whatever happened after graduation fucked you up, Paige. Him too," he mutters, then shakes his head. "I'm still so fucking mad at you for shutting me out. But . . . I still thought about you. I've *missed* you. We were . . ."

"Family," I say brokenly.

I feel his nod. We *were* a family. *All of us.* And it twists the knife in my gut, amplifying my stupidity. I could have had *years* of Ellis hugs.

I would have known *five years ago* that Linc was back. Not that

I was sure what any of that meant since he still left in the first place.

Left me.

"How is this happening?" I wonder absently, feeling close enough to the sky up here, yet safe, protected in Ellis's arms, that my voice comes out a bit dreamy.

Ellis takes a steadying breath, looking off the porch as a car whips in through the opening.

I feel a twitch in his hand just before he drops them from me. "Fuck, this is—I really don't know how this is gonna go, Paige."

My eyebrows pinch. "What do you mean?"

He releases a long, drawn out exhale with another shake of his head. "I wanna give you guys some time to talk and whatnot, but . . ." he trails off, looking unbearably conflicted about something as he rubs the back of his neck. "Just . . . if you notice him start to space out, or blink a lot—don't . . ." he groans. "Just don't touch him, okay?"

What?! Don't touch him?

The confusion on my face must be apparent because Ellis shakes his head. "This isn't my business to tell. And the only reason I'm telling you this right now is for your safety. Just . . . be cautious with physical contact. Feel it out."

So many things shoot forward like a firework, and it's hard for me to grasp onto one thing. So I don't. I watch all the thoughts crackle and fizzle in the air in front of me.

Can't touch him?

How the hell will I kick his ass if I can't touch him?

I hate that Ellis knows something about him that I don't know. So many things, probably.

Does Ellis know what happened after graduation?

I hate that they've been living this close—for four years—becoming closer while I've been disappearing deeper and deeper into the abyss of loneliness.

And it's all my fault.

But wait . . .

We graduated seven years ago, they've been living here for four years, but reconnected five years ago . . .

My awareness returns and the question that surfaces is, "Where was he for the other two years?"

Ellis shakes his head immediately. "Nope. Not touchin' that."

He gives no further explanation and his tone is definitive, pulling at my nerve endings like loose rope, but the thought falls when I hear the faint beep from inside the house.

The security system. It did the same thing when Ellis brought me inside.

My pulse skyrockets as my head suddenly feels like it's in a fucking blender—whirling and slicing through any bit of strength I've managed to build through these years.

Ellis was a casualty of my inability to cope—and I always knew if I saw him again, I'd have to face that shitty part of myself that allowed it to happen. That *made* it happen.

The sound of the sliding door, opening and then closing knocks me back to now, but I can't look over.

"He's here," I faintly hear Gram and clench my teeth.

Yeah, no shit, I think, and I swear to God, I hear her joyful humming to "Daydream Believer," but the sound quickly distances in my head, and I finally turn my chin and look up.

CHAPTER 25
LINC

It didn't matter that her face had basically formed a permanent film over my vision.

It didn't matter that I'd thought about her every day for the last seven years. Just like earlier in the Veranda, my brain processes the sight before me through some kind of filter, one that captures the past in the shadows of the present.

Blinking rapidly, my mind flicks between seeing the two of them, standing not even a foot apart, backdropped with the starry night sky. When I blink again, they're seventeen. The memory of them on the hill, playing the Moon and the Fisherman takes its place.

Back and forth, back and forth.

"Linc," Ellis says, and I breathe deep, pulling my awareness to the voice. "Did you come from the club?"

He's a step closer to me now, I can feel myself settling back into the moment—*into reality*—but unlike usual times, *she's* still here. Ellis stares at me, expectantly, and my eyebrows pinch, just as his eyes widen a bit.

Right. This isn't actual curiosity about where I've been.

He can tell I'm zoning out, and he's trying to get me to stay alert. *Aware.* Which I know I need to do if I have any hope of making it through whatever is about to happen.

It seems impossible that she's here. *Why did she come here?* She should have called the cops. Gone back to her place. Maybe that . . . *guy* I saw was looking for her.

But she came here . . .

Swallowing hard, I shake my head. "I-I was at your apartment," I croak, speaking directly to her for the first time and her eyes shoot up.

I can't even begin to dissect the dark indigo swirls of anger, the icy glint of hurt that matches her hair. Her nose scrunches in the exact way I remember. "How do you know where I live?"

I shake my head. "I d-don't. N-Not really," I stutter. *Shit.* It's impossible to breathe right now, let alone make a sentence.

And her voice—oh my God. In all my imaginings—*rememberings*—nothing's prepared me for the warmth that shoots through my veins at the sound of her voice. It has an angry edge I remember well, a bit deeper, but the sound is fucking music to my soul. A full breath to my lungs. After another deep inhale, I add, "Rio gave me the cross streets."

She huffs, crossing her arms over her petite body, thankfully now covered with a slouchy gray zip-up and leggings. A flash of her outfit from earlier blinks past my vision but I clear my throat in an attempt to force it away.

If I get a boner right now, I'll throw myself off the balcony.

But God, in all the times I imagined seeing her again, I never thought my physical reaction would be so . . . *fucking insistent.*

Yes, you did. That's why you had to stay away.

The voice finds me, the words choking me like there's a hand gripping my neck.

It's true. Any thought I've had of her for the last seven years has always elicited *some kind* of reaction, but I . . .

Ellis clears his throat louder than necessary, and I'm aware enough to know it's *again* for my benefit.

Fucking stay here.

I swallow again, working my jaw to loosen the tension gathering at the base of my neck and crawling up to my clenched teeth. "I th-think I saw someone there."

Her brows drop, the angry dark swirls of her eyes cloud just a bit with confusion before she says, "At my apartment? Someone from the club?"

I shake my head. The relief that she doesn't immediately assume it's someone—*like a boyfriend*—gives me an irrational wave of calm.

Paige's eyes widen, flicking to Ellis, then to me before they settle on the wood planks of the floor. *God, she's so close.* I think my knuckles are about to split from the restraint it's taking to not pull her into me and crash my lips into hers. Sink my tongue into her mouth.

Fucking no.

"You should stay here tonight," Ellis says quickly. "Until you talk to people at The Window and find out what's been done about the . . . situation."

My heart drops. *Stay here?*

It's like my greatest, deepest wish is dangling in front of me but it's wrapped in the electrical barbed-wire of my bullshit.

"I—I can't," she says, quietly. "I have . . . Cheeto."

"I've got Cheetos," Ellis says, easily. And he does. Of every variety.

"No, she's my gecko . . ."

Well goddammit, if that's not the cutest thing.

I take a steadying inhale. Even though it will be a mild form of torture to know she's sleeping walls away, I know Ellis is right. She can't go back there.

He says, "Well, let's all pile in the batmobile and go get your lizard."

"Gecko," she corrects him. "But I shouldn't—I can't—"

"Paige," Ellis cuts her off. "We're sidestepping our bullshit for a minute. We're gonna forget that I'm mad at you, and you're mad at him, and he's mad at . . . well, he's just mad," he says, and I huff. *Asshole.* "There may have been a guy lurking around your place after an . . . *incident* at the club. Better to be safe for right now. Okay?"

The reminder of how I'd first seen her in the Veranda ticks a knot in my already tense body, but I'm still somehow able to appreciate Ellis's "take charge" attitude. I need him to take the reins right now because I'm floating between my realms—her eyes my only anchor.

An unsteady one at that. She's been looking at me on and off since I came out here—never too long, but also frequent. She sighs slowly, looking at Ellis, then again to me before she says, "This is really happening?" as she walks toward the sliding door.

And all I can think is the *same fucking thing.*

I think I'm about to defy the laws of science and start a fire with the way I am rubbing the small bumpy surface along the penny in my hand. I swear I can *feel* her eyes on me from the backseat. Ellis is driving, his jaw tight as his eyes flick between the rearview mirror and the road. Like he can't believe she's really here either.

This whole night feels surreal and now, with her in the backseat, and Ellis and I up front, it feels like we're *sitting* in the Bermuda Triangle of our past, colliding with our present— rattling awkwardly in our seats as we drive to Hollywood.

"So this *incident* tonight," Ellis says, cautiously, then angles his chin just slightly toward me. "Was there security there?"

I swallow hard. My own eyes flick up to the rearview and see hers meeting mine. An itchiness crawls up my throat and I dig my thumb into the ridges of the penny. "No," I finally say, then take a breath. "Th-There was a breach with an old security guard that I guess has been banned."

"Banned? I thought he was just fired?" Paige pipes up from the backseat.

My eyes meet hers through the mirror again, and I shrug. "Jackson said they asked him not to come back."

Paige mumbles something and I pull my gaze over to Ellis to give myself a breather.

But, like a magnet, my eyes pull back to the mirror, unable to ignore her reflection. I take another breath, then say, "Either way, it ended up being a shitshow. A-And we only ended up at the Veranda because we were chasing him a-around the building.

When I talked to Jackson after, he made it sound like there's n-never security in there."

"What?!" Ellis barks.

I shrug, just as Paige says, "It's the VIP room. The guy who rented it knows the owner."

Ellis shakes his head, muttering, "What the fuck?" then wipes a palm down his face as we come to a red light.

"What was the guy's name?" he asks.

Paige's eyes squint, she seems to be dazed too—I can't blame her. This is the night that will never end. But at the same time, I'm not sure I want it to. It's like in between all of this speculating and silence, little pockets of light find me, reminding me that she's *really* here.

"Tariel," she finally says.

"Could he have been the guy that came to her building?" Ellis asks me.

I shake my head. "He looked y-younger than the guy in the Veranda. Shaggy brown hair, t-taller—I think he was wearing a leather jacket."

Ellis's eyes peek into the rearview mirror. "Sound familiar?"

My eyes also move to the mirror again, seeing her shake her head.

Another few seconds pass as Ellis mutters a curse. Peering around the cross-streets, I can see now that we're only a few blocks away from where I had staked out a couple hours earlier.

The silence through the car thickens again. It starts to feel suffocating, and my steady rotation of the penny between my fingers is barely enough.

The cool air hits my face, and I breathe deep and close my eyes for a second.

As the car slows to a stop, Ellis puts on his hazard lights, then says, "I'll wait here. You guys go grab her Cheeto."

CHAPTER 26
PAIGE

The long walk of the breezeway to the far end of the building is a charged stride. My back is straightened, my muscles feel like a fucking zipline—*knowing* he's right behind me.

In a pathetic attempt to replace him in my mind for years, there were so many times when I just imagined him watching me.

Him, watching me make this very walk. Drinking coffee in my bed. Stretching with Cheeto. Dancing at the club.

All the time.

My body is having a strange reaction to the utter madness of this night though. A dog whistle moment—so high it's silent.

Like right now. I should be shitting my pants because Linc and I are about to be alone for the first time in seven years. *The first time since . . .*

"Th-This one's yours," he says, cutting off my thought. It's not a question, but a statement and I stop, turning toward him.

The stutter is new. It's not super noticeable because he kind of mumbles anyway, which is also different. My mind aches to know when that started. But I don't ask. I don't say *anything*.

"This is where he was," Linc says, his teeth clenching, and I get lost in the cut lines of his chiseled jaw, the speckled coarse scruff leading to his full angular lips.

Buffy bless, he's gorgeous. And if that doesn't just piss me the fuck off.

I shake my head, reminding myself that he's confirming there was some creep poking around my apartment. With new urgency, I unlock the door, and immediately look across the way to the wall opposite me—at the terrarium.

The small scuffle of Cheeto's feet immediately settles my nerves, and I release a breath before moving toward her. "Hi," I whisper. "I'm sorry if you were scared."

Linc clears his throat from behind me and my chin twists back to see him still standing in the doorway.

My eyes squint. "Are you a vampire? Do I need to invite you in?"

Actually, it would explain a lot.

The dark eyebrows. The constant tension in his face. He looks so . . . serious. His hazel eyes are a hypnotic combination of green and brown—like earth's venom paralyzing me.

I blink a couple times, unsure if I'm seeing things, but it suddenly looks like he's smirking. My eyes squint in his direction, a few seconds passing, before I realize . . .

Right. I called him a vampire.

And he thought I *was a vampire the day we met.*

I fight my mouth's instinct to pull up as well, and instead take a breath and look around. My chest quivers, but at a glance, everything looks normal. One of the perks to owning next-to-nothing is it's easy to see if there's anything out of place. And it helps that the studio is just a single room except for the closet and bathroom.

Still, it's unsettling that someone was here.

After an initial sweep, I see Linc still hasn't moved, and I roll my eyes, grumbling, "You can come in," then head toward my closet.

My laptop sits on the dresser with its power cord and I move to the top drawer of the chest, opening it.

The tension in my shoulders loosens when I see my music box sitting inside with the gold crescent moon and stars dangling on it. I'm not sure what compels me to open it, but I do, easing a bit more when I see the stacks of pictures, sentimental shit, hauntings.

I close it up and pull it out, packing it along with my laptop. I don't have a plan, but I can go anywhere if I have my box and Cheeto.

I grab my bigger duffle bag, and pack my meager collection of clothes, Gram's cardigan, and after tossing literally everything in the bag aside from Cheeto herself, I wonder . . .

Is this really a good idea?

I mean, I can't stay here, obviously. And aside from driving out to Venice once we get back to the mountain—the only other option would be to sleep in my car.

I take a breath, then peek back out of the closet, seeing Linc now inside, staring down at Cheeto's terrarium. "D-Does it bite?" he asks.

I blink a few times, and my mind feels like it skips . . .

"Does it bite?" he asked, his floppy dark hair falling over his furrowed brow.

My new friend had never been down to the pond at the end of our road, and I was so excited to show him the ducks. Well, the ducklings!

"Probably," I laughed. "Just don't go near her babies. She's protective."

He smiled, his eyes glistening in the late afternoon sun. "Pro-tective," he said slowly.

"It means she'll always take care of them. No matter what," I told him, and he gave me a funny smile.

I blink again, realizing he's still looking at me. Nineteen years later, still asking the same questions. Walking a few steps toward him, I correct him with, "*She* is usually pretty chill."

His eyes snap over at the sound of my voice, like somewhere between asking the question and my zone out, he forgot I was even here.

Though the *way* he's looking at me makes me feel like he hasn't taken his eyes off me. Or like he's memorizing me. His eyes keep floating up to my hair and it loosens the tension in his eyebrows every time he does it.

There is so much we should talk about—so much that *needs* to be talked about—and despite all the time I've spent imagining this moment, I can't help but feel like I'm drowning in the heavy current of the reality.

He's here. But he left. He left me, and found Ellis. Or maybe Ellis found him.

Either way, it all fucking hurts.

I blow out a heavy breath. "It looks like everything is undisturbed," I say awkwardly, glancing around the apartment. "Maybe I don't need to—"

"No," he clips.

My eyebrows pinch. "You don't know what I was gonna say."

"You're not staying here, P-Paige." The small hiccup in his voice hitches in my chest, but the deep rasp is a command. And God, *fuck me,* if it doesn't curl my toes.

But it also licks fire down my spine, charging forth an anger I can't even grasp before it's out of my mouth, "Your concern for my safety after a near-decade of abandonment is touching," I snap, my tone seeped in disdain.

Linc's jaw ticks, his mouth flattening. In just a few steps, he's right in front of me. I gasp but surprisingly, I don't flinch. I'm not sure I blink. *Breathe.*

A stuttered inhale pulls through my chest.

God. Sea salt and forest. I breathe deeper. *He still hasn't kicked the smoking habit. I can smell the Silver cigarettes too.*

A noise—*only partially human*—pushes past my lips and it's followed by a rumble from him too—a noise so quiet and low that I have to wonder if I imagined it.

"Don't touch him."

I see Ellis's warning, but my mind lifts it to a dare. In direct violation, I raise a shaky hand and press it to Linc's chest, unsure if I'm pushing him away or pulling him closer.

His hands immediately dig into my sides, his fingertips bruising as one of his hands drags along my lower back. His breathing increases and I can feel it wheeze against my temple.

"Don't—" he croaks through a whisper, but his arms tighten, shaking around me like there's an actual earthquake erupting through his body.

He's panicking. I recognize it instantly.

But I can barely fight off my own panic, let alone someone else's.

He's not just someone else.

Instincts, divine intervention—call it whatever—*something* snaps into focus. I move my hand to the back of his neck, feeling a film of sweat gathering just below the thick, dark strands, and I give them the smallest tug.

Our eyes lock. The green and brown swirls in his eyes meet my blue, like rainfall hitting the earth.

I'm here. You're here.

He chokes on a breath, but doesn't pull away. In fact, his grip only becomes more punishing, pulling me closer. The hand that was holding my back has now slipped under my zip-up, just barely, but it's skin-to-skin, and I feel his breath even out just a bit.

His fingertips are hot to the touch and so is the curve in my lower back. The sensation nearly sizzles in my stomach and I gasp.

We stand there for long seconds, holding each other like we're falling.

Or maybe we're about to land.

I hope for it. For the years I've spent lost in space, the release of touching down sounds damn near euphoric.

His grip around me becomes suffocating, but I don't want the air. I want *this*. This feeling—*this person*—taking my breath.

The one who's holding me like he used to. *Harder*, even. *Like we were before.*

I know that's impossible now. Not with all the time. Not with all that's happened . . .

I shove the thought away—denying it with a low hum. A hum that turns into lightly singing an unknown melody. His hold loosens just a bit, and his nose buries into my hair. "P-Please, keep going," Linc pleads in a hoarse, nearly-desperate whisper, his face shoved into my hair.

And me . . . well, I'm caught in the current of his forest and ocean smell, riding my de-lu-lu tidal wave as high as she will take me.

Without a single thought, I hum an acoustic intro that feeds through my veins. To the song I never listen to—the one that surprises my vocal cords with a breathy air behind my voice.

It lasts for a few seconds. My cheek is now pressed roughly against his chest, and I can feel his heart still racing. Fingers still run and fidget along my lower back. If this were any other situation, with any other person, the touch would probably be weird.

But it's not. With him, it's never *weird* . . .

"God, Pip," he croaks. "Y-You're—" he stutters, and his grip re-tightens. "*How* are you not scared of me?"

Scared of him?

What?

A dread similar to the one that found me earlier—the one when Ellis told me not to touch him—finds me again. Except this time, I can feel the shadow of what's to come.

Like an overhead bombing.

Even so, it doesn't make sense. My eyes narrow and my chin lifts to look up at him as my eyebrows pinch. "Why would I be *scared* of you?"

His eyes flicker and then mute with a murky haunting. He swallows hard as a look of complete confusion passes through his gaze. A deep, wounded, utterly devastated expression that aches in my own chest stares back at me.

"You don't remember?" he asks, his eyes moving from one of my eyes to the other, and it feels like it's only rattling my confusion.

What the fuck is he talking about?

I *remember* what happened . . . there hasn't been a day we've been apart that I haven't thought about what happened.

But I still don't understand what he's saying.

His throat bobs through a swallow and suddenly I feel the shortness of breath, my pulse exploding as his face only becomes more broken, still holding me tight.

His forehead falls to mine and my hands grip his shirt between our chests, feeling like my knees are moments away from giving out.

"Please, don't be afraid of me," he pleads, holding me tighter.

God, the roughness in his voice, the desperation is so fucking sad that I just . . . I can't take it. *I don't understand.*

Yes, I'm mad at him—but . . .

"Linc—" I croak, then take a breath, steadying my voice. "*Why* would I be afraid of you?"

I feel his head shake slightly with his forehead still pressed to mine.

And just when I think I can't break anymore, just when I think my heart is already a pile of dust—he blows it into the wind when he chokes on a guttural whisper, and says, "Because I raped you."

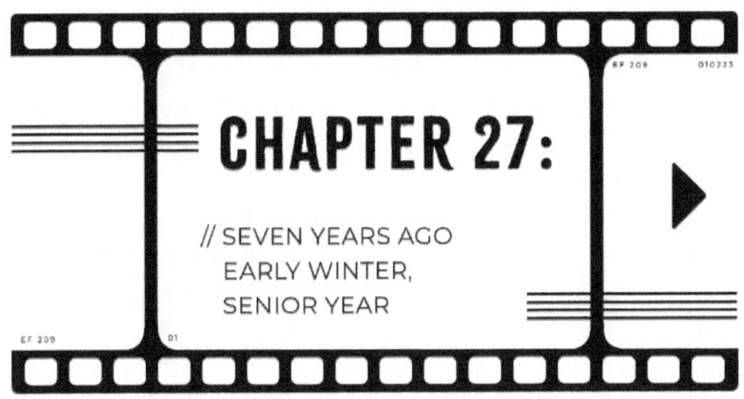

PAIGE

"What's up, punk?" Climbing into Ellis's car, I shoved my bag into the backseat as Flyleaf blasted through his speakers. My eyebrows lifted. "Ooo. Are we having some feelings tonight?" I said loudly over the music and he turned it down.

"Sorry," he mumbled with a half-hearted chuckle.

As I clipped in my seatbelt, I asked, "Everything okay?" My words dragged with caution.

He didn't respond as he peeked behind us, backing the car out of the driveway and then slowly driving down my small road.

By the time we got to the stop sign, I could *hear* him thinking. *Chomping on his gum.*

"Dude, you sound like a yeti chewing tinfoil. What's up?"

"Nice," he snorted, then sighed. "It's nothing. Just got into it with Desmond."

My mouth sloped at the corner, but I stayed quiet. Waiting.

Ellis was picking me up for what had become my regular gig at Queenie's. I didn't end up getting the part in *American Idiot*. But two weeks ago, Queenie's off-season band went on a permanent hiatus—*our suspicions are of the Fleetwood Mac variety*—but she let me step in, and her husband, Jack, played guitar for me.

Performing there was different from what I was used to. The setting was smaller, I could see everyone, and I wasn't playing a part. It was just . . . me and Jack.

My nerves started to find my limbs again, my knee bouncing, but Ellis's sigh brought me back to now before he said, "I guess one of my dad's old business partners is suing him. A company he's not even a part of anymore."

Shit. That sucks.

My throat worked to swallow. I didn't really know what to say, but something told me he just needed to vent. So, I stayed quiet.

He shrugged. "They settled it out of court this afternoon."

Oh. My eyebrows hitched, but then furrowed when I saw his jaw tick, his grip on the steering wheel tighten. "That's good, right?" I asked.

It sounded like the problem was solved, but I knew that couldn't be the case because only a second later, Ellis scoffed. "Every fucking time," he muttered quietly, then spoke up a bit. "He told me he was gonna fight this one. *Actually* take this asshole to court. But he didn't. He spent an asinine amount of money to keep it *private* and it just . . ."

My eyes squinted. I didn't understand. For lack of anything better to say, I asked, "Why are they suing him?"

Ellis chuckled, but there wasn't any humor to it. "Great

question. And since he didn't actually go through the system there's no record—" He stopped himself shaking his head. "Sorry."

I put my hand on his knee. "Hey, don't be sorry. We can pull over at a vista point and beat our chests—yell into a canyon. *Tony Robbins* this shit out."

He snorted. "No, definitely not." The small hint of a smile he had, dropped. After a second, he ran his teeth over his bottom lip, then said, "It's not like I think he's guilty of anything. It just makes him *look* guilty when he handles shit this way. I get that he doesn't want the publicity but . . ." he trailed off.

I squeezed his knee. "I get it. That makes sense."

And it really did. I'm sure he did believe in Desmond's innocence. But they were all each other had. Like me and Gram. And Gram and I made most of our big decisions together. They usually involved what home appliance we could live without.

Ellis shook his head. "He just . . . he'll *always* be a target. And I feel like it would at least scare *some* people off if he publicly— *just once*—tore an accusation to shreds."

"Aw, buddy, I'm sorry." I rested my head on his shoulder, and he leaned his temple against mine, still driving us leisurely.

He blew out a breath. "Ugh. No, *I'm* sorry. Let's change the subject." He cleared his throat, his eyes flicking to me before going back to the road. "I, for one, *cannot fucking wait* to watch Linc go all alpha male when he sees that little get-up."

My eyes drifted down to my outfit. I had taken some old fishnets and cut the crotch, wearing it over my head so the net material stretched down my arms under a metallic purple tank top

I was wearing. I rounded out the outfit with some ripped, black skinny jeans and my combat boots.

Gram also glitter-bombed my hair. A fact I think Ellis was too preoccupied to notice, or he may have not let me get in the car.

I breathed a laugh, rolling my eyes. Before I had time to really think about it too much, Ellis asked, "What's on the set list tonight? If there isn't any Avril Lavigne, can there be some Avril Lavigne?"

I snorted a laugh. "I'll have to see if Jack knows any. But 'You Oughta Know' is on my list."

"Oh, fuck yeah. Alanis Morissette. A *whole mood*," he said, as we pulled into the parking lot. After he grabbed a spot near the back, I unbuckled my seatbelt, then saw him reaching into his pocket, "I'm gonna burn one real quick," he said, pulling a joint out, and I smirked.

"Hot boxing? How millennial of you," I teased. But I grabbed my bag from the back and flicked my eyes back over at him. His stare looked distracted, staring off for a second and I finally said, "Sure you're okay, Batman?"

He chuckled, but nodded and then looked over at me. "Totally. This'll just give me the final shove into rock-out mode. I plan on moshing."

I rolled my eyes. *Jesus.* "Queenie's gonna kick your ass out," I muttered, finally pushing the door open.

"You underestimate my charm," he called out as I closed the door and laughed again.

I was in the back room, warming up—I think Queenie was trying to make this a green room, but real estate was expensive here, so it was about the size of a walk-in closet, with a single arm chair and a mini-fridge.

I took a sip of water just as I heard the door open and Linc slipped in.

My smile pulled. I knew he was working tonight—he'd made it a point to work Tuesdays after I got the singing gig.

"Goddamn, Pip, you look . . ."

My heart stuttered and a timid smile shook my lips.

Ellis's claim earlier sounded through my mind as Linc's hazel eyes seared into me. *Alpha male, indeed.*

". . . Like you've got stars in your hair." His lips tilted as his eyes lingered on my wild curls, tracing them like constellations before his gaze fell back to my face. The deep desire in his eyes lifted my chest. My confidence.

I grinned. "Fitting for the moon, huh?"

The *way* his eyes drifted from my hair to lips nearly knocked the wind out of me.

I had only recently started dressing up a little. Well, *my* version of dressing up, anyway, and it still felt a little awkward.

But the response I got from him was *so damn good,* I think I was unofficially trying to up my game each time—see if I could get his jaw to actually drop—*cartoon style.*

In general, nothing quite curled my toes like the way he watched me. *Knowing* his eyes were on me. The fact that he had such a natural artistic eye, and *I* seemed to be one of his favorite subjects, was a kick to the clit I didn't quite expect.

"There's a lot of guys out there tonight, ya know," he said, inching closer to me, in the already small room.

But I welcomed his closeness. It'd been a week since we'd been alone—*and he was just about to go up my shirt when Maisie knocked on the door.*

He hooked his arm around my back, pulling me into him, reminding me that he'd made . . . *an observation.*

I cleared my throat. "Guys, huh? Interesting, seeing as I sing a lot of moody girl bangers."

His nose brushed against mine, and I shivered at the contact as he chuckled softly. "Something tells me you could sing a full set of Wiggles music and they still wouldn't blink through the whole thing." He kissed me lightly, teasingly, but pulled away, and I whined.

He chuckled, brushing some hair off my face. "Queenie asked me to give you your half-hour warning," he said, still holding me to him.

"Did Ellis come in?" I asked.

Linc nodded. "Yeah—fucking *blazed,*" he chuckled. "And he ordered like, the rest of the pastry case—so we have that to look forward to when the high rolls off."

I breathed a small laugh, but my mouth tilted downward. "I feel bad. He seemed upset on the way here. I guess him and Desmond had some sort of fight."

He pushed some of my hair over my shoulder and sighed. "I thought I heard some *tense talk* when I was leaving after our workout earlier. But I wouldn't worry about it. Happens all the time."

My eyebrows pinched. I didn't know that. In fact, Ellis rarely talked to me about Desmond. Maybe Linc just *saw more* since he made his way over to the estate more often than I did. Ellis preferred to come to my house. See Gram.

A soft brush of Linc's thumb over my lips hitched my breath, and I blinked up at him. His eyes scanned me again, and a playful glint turned his eyes slightly more green.

Another silent beat passed as a reminding tilt to his brows angled down at me. Confusion filled my eyes for just a second before I finally caught on, and smirked.

When Queenie offered me the opportunity to sing on Tuesdays, I immediately said yes. But in the week that followed, I had almost talked myself out of it multiple times.

"The bar setting—live band thing. I'm not used to just standing up there—not unless it's a recital or something. And that's different."

We had been lying on my bed, "doing homework." But homework had come in the way of roaming fingers, stolen kisses—confessions.

His fingers had been making steady little designs on the small of my back—on the sliver of skin between the waistline of my jeans and my tank top—but he stopped and pulled me into him.

"What's to say you can't pretend you're just playing a part at Queenie's," he smirked. "The hot local singer—catching the eye of the bus boy."

I giggled, pressing my forehead to his. "Ooo. I like it. She has a troubled past—sees the bus boy on his smoke break by the dumpster as she leaves."

"He'd been watching her all night," he said against my mouth as I giggled more.

Linc's lips zapped me back to the present when he suddenly pressed them to the soft spot just below my ear and I gasped. Then he kissed again, just a little lower, and my mouth ticked up. He was kissing down my freckles. A part of my body I'd only ever seen through his camera lens.

An aroused chuckle tickled the bottom of my earlobe and a shiver ran through me. "I'd better go," he said quietly, gravelly—like he definitely didn't *want* to go.

I didn't want him to either. But it was probably for the best. We didn't need to get caught making out in the make-shift green room.

Still, another thrill ran through me—remembering our game, remembering he'd be watching me, and I smiled. "Gotta give my bus boy a show, right?"

"*Mmf,*" he grunted, taking my lips. His tongue just barely breached the seam of my mouth and I whimpered.

God, I was a needy mess for him. It was kind of crazy, especially because we hadn't even made it to a proper second base yet. He had me hot and fucking bothered with just his mouth.

I felt him smile against my lips before he reluctantly pulled away, taking a single step back to the door—physically putting distance between us before he said, "I'll see ya out there," and left.

LINC

After beelining to the bathroom to tuck my boner away as best I could, I walked out to see Ellis cutting the muffin tops off a carrot muffin and a lemon poppyseed, coating the undersides in jelly, slapping them together, and eating them.

My eyes flinched as I got closer. It was all pretty gross. I grabbed a water from the cooler and put it on the table. "Hey, man. Why don't I make you an americano?"

"The Oscar statue—*the Academy Award*—is naked," he said, looking at something on his phone, then up at me.

My eyes squinted. *Ugh.* I was not prepared to deal with a blitzed-out-of-his-skull Ellis. Not while I was at work. Not when Paige was performing.

With nothing else to say, I shrugged. "Yeah, man. They are. Americano?"

"So maybe, it's not Oscar *buzz,* but Oscar *butts!*" He barked out a laugh, cracking himself up.

I laughed too. *Okaaay.* "I'm gonna go make you an americano," I made the decision for him.

"Cool," he said with another bite of his . . . muffin-top sandwich? *Ugh.* With jelly.

Gross.

I started back toward the entrance and hopped behind the coffee bar. I wasn't a barista—that was usually Paige's job, but I could make drinks if I needed to.

Luckily, majority of the customers were visiting the bar that served alcohol over by the stage.

I poured some hot water in a mug, and then started to dial in the shots. Once they were pulling the way Paige had shown me— *blonding,* as she said—I stopped the shots and poured them in the mug over the water.

As I tapped out the espresso in the filter, I heard the front door open, and looked over, surprised, when I saw Mr. Harris walking in with a younger brunette woman.

His brown eyes found me behind the bar, giving me a small wave, and my mouth tilted as he walked up to the counter.

"Hey, Linc." He extended his hand out for a handshake and I reciprocated.

The exchange straightened my spine. Since our interactions were always at school, it wasn't common practice for teachers to shake our hands—so I was a bit surprised at the grip of his handshake—firm, commanding. I made a note to work on mine.

Just as he released my hand, I asked, "Are you guys here for the show? Or are you grabbing drinks?"

Mr. Harris smiled. "Our rehearsal finished up early, so I thought we'd catch Paige's set. But I was hoping you'd be here. San Diego invitations went out today and *Without the Moon* got a screening."

My eyes widened. "No fucking way! Seriously?!"

He nodded and everything in me clenched. I fought the urge to haul ass back over to the room Paige was hanging out in—I wanted to tell her immediately.

But I must have been staring off because I suddenly noticed Mr. Harris tilting his chin down, trying to meet my eyes, and I blinked back up at him. I could feel the pull of my muscles in my mouth, still smiling as he said, "Congratulations, Linc. You deserve it."

A warmth spread through me, pride lifting my chest. I'd second-guessed going to Providence pretty much on a daily basis.

Given the fact that Paige and I were both scholarship kids, the school knew we weren't good for any other sponsorship or donations—and that meant the faculty overlooked us for shit like this.

But *he* didn't, and the gratitude that filled with that thought was enough to cause a stutter through my chest. "Thanks, Mr. Harris. I wouldn't have even gotten a shot if it weren't for you. I really appreciate it." I extended my hand again, ready this time.

When he took my hand again, I shook first, tightening my grip and he smiled wider. "It was all you, man. You can lead a horse to water, or some shit."

We both chuckled, and after we released the handshake, a small silence passed and my eyes awkwardly flicked to the woman who was with him again.

She was pretty. She looked older than me, but younger than him, dressed casually in a tight black T-shirt and jeans.

He clicked his tongue. "I'm sorry. I'm running on fumes, I swear. Josie, this is Linc." He leaned into her, quietly saying, "My best film student by a landslide."

My face worked to control its shock. Not just at the claim, but . . . *should he say stuff like that?*

Not that it didn't make me feel fucking great. If there was any faculty at Providence I cared about impressing, it was him. *And it sounded like I had.*

I felt my mouth tilt. I guess it was okay. It's not like he said it at school, in front of everyone.

"Nice to meet you, Linc," the woman said with a timid smile.

Mr. Harris looked over at her. "Josie's in that new immersive project I was telling you guys about."

My chin lifted with recognition. He'd mentioned something about doing a show—some kind of experimental piece, where performances were happening all through an apartment building.

I told him, "Oh, we're pumped to see it. Paige, Ellis, and I are all gonna go."

Josie smiled, but Mr. Harris nodded. "Oh, excellent. You'll have to tell me what night, maybe we can all come here and chat after. I'd love to know what all of you think."

Nodding, I said, "Sounds great," then heard some whoops and miscellaneous noise from the seating area.

"Anyway," Mr. Harris said, glancing toward the commotion. "Just sit anywhere?"

"Yeah, anywhere is fine," I said with a shrug, picking up Ellis's mug and rounding the espresso bar.

As we got back to the seating area, I placed the mug on Ellis's table, but saw a high-top table in the corner of the room, and pointed it out to Mr. Harris and Josie.

He gave me a wave and they walked over, just as everyone started clapping.

I turned to see Paige was on the platform, under the lights.

God, she really did look cute. The glitter in her hair. Those tight black jeans hugging her waist.

She smiled. "Jack brought the Fender tonight *and* a drummer," she said, leaning toward a younger guy behind the drum set. "What's your name, dude? I need to know the name of the guy keeping time."

The crowd chuckled, and before the drummer could answer her, some asshole yelled, "I'll keep time for you, baby!"

My chin snapped in the direction of the voice, but I couldn't see. Paige's eyes squinted out among the crowd, finding me immediately, but only for a second before she narrowed her gaze toward where the voice came from, cocking her eyebrow "Something tells me you can't keep up."

A group of bro-like *"Ooos"* came from the huddle of guys up near the front of the stage. Jack gave a dramatic strum to his electric guitar, and the drummer gave a small rolling tap as the crowd got even louder.

My mouth inched up, watching Paige as she whispered something to Jack. She was fucking amazing. *I* knew she was nervous, but to the average eye, you'd never know it when she was in front of an audience—only made more convincing by her clap back at that dipshit.

Just as another moment passed, she gave a, "3-2-1," and the drummer took off as Jack immediately joined in on guitar. After a small intro, Paige started to sing, "That's What You Get" by Paramore, and the crowd erupted—myself included.

Pulling out my phone, I turned on the camera, zooming in on her hand holding the microphone—like it was an extension of her own arm, holding it to her mouth, and amping magic through the speakers as I started to record.

I stayed on her, then moved the phone slowly, sweeping over the crowd—a sea of shadowed bodies jumping and singing along—fully loving the pretty girl rocking the fuck out on stage right now.

My girl.

My eyes made their way over to the area in front of the

performance space—the mass that belonged to that group of guys. I didn't condone assholes who openly hit on girls like that guy had just done to Paige—*not ever*—but something about my reaction to it had . . . *shifted* since we got together.

I used to have silent, rageful fits when I noticed guys checking her out—*a Linc-down,* as Ellis affectionately coined the term. But now that I knew Paige wanted me like I wanted her . . . well, some devious, barbaric part of me kind of loved watching other guys drool over her. Knowing they could look at her, but it was *me* she let touch her. Kiss her.

Goddamn. I had just gotten rid of my *last* erection and I already felt my dick twitching below my jeans.

My eyes dragged along the crowd again, but I kept the camera steady on her. *What else is a bus boy who's obsessed with the hot local singer to do?*

Ellis ended up crashing pretty hard by the end of Paige's set list, so he'd left. I just came back in from the final trash run and turned off the espresso machine as I saw Mr. Harris and Josie walking toward the café area.

"Hey," he said, with an easy smile. "Your girl's a bit of a rockstar, huh?"

I nodded, peeking back over toward the seating area. "Is she still stuck schmoozing?"

It was her least favorite part of "the biz" but I had promised to rescue her by the time I finished cleaning up.

Mr. Harris nodded. "It seems so, unfortunately, and we've gotta run. But she really was great. Pass along the message for me, okay?"

"Sure," I said, then looked over to Josie saying, "It was nice to meet you," before I shifted my eyes back to him. "And thanks again for everything, Mr. Harris—just send me anything I need to do before the screening and I'll get it done."

He smiled, nodding. "Will do, Linc. Congrats again."

It was the first time I noticed I was actually a little taller than him. I wasn't sure if it was something I had just never noticed before or if we were standing closer than we typically were at school.

He was still standing about a foot away, but then he leaned in just a little closer and said, "And you can call me Jeremy when we're not at school, okay?"

I nodded with a smile. *Cool.*

CHAPTER 28
LINC

Sitting on the floor, I watch through the small TV screen. My best friend . . . my girlfriend. Naked. Her big blue eyes are full of tears, her arms chained to a pole, wrists bleeding.

"Please, no. No, no, no," she cries.

The fucker on top of her pushes her face into the cushions, leaning down so his mouth hovers over her ear.

Did he say something to her?

The angle makes it to where I can't see his face. Just dark hair. Grabbing. Driving into her from behind.

The camera angle shifts closer. A moment later, the guy grabs her hair and twists her face away from the back of the couch, toward the camera.

The crystal pools in her eyes are haunting—even more blue when they're heavy and red from tears.

He's fucking raping her. Filming it.

The sight is decimating me with every thrust, and I slam my eyes shut.

I can't help her. I can't fucking help her.

Why? Why is this happening?

Why am I watching this?

The constant chill to the room I'm in somehow gets colder, but the sudden sound of a smack pulls my attention back up to the screen, and Paige jerks, her bare ass clenching as it quickly turns a little pink.

"That's it. Take it, you filthy fucking tease."

The sound of the voice drops my heart. My eyes freeze, blur, then focus.

The guy. The guy holding Paige down. That piece of shit, scum of the earth on the screen is . . . me.

It's fucking me.

My chest shakes, and a roar erupts from my throat as I wobble to stand, hooking my hands behind the TV. I shove it over, watching it crash to the ground and shatter.

He was right.

My eyes shoot open and I gasp for air. The smallest movement tells me I'm lying in a pool of sweat and I roll over, cringing at the damp feeling surrounding me as I check the time . . . 7:08 a.m.

I finally catch my breath, then groan. *Goddammit. An hour of sleep.*

Just enough time for my subconscious to torture me with another memory I wish I could forget.

Adding to the collection would be last night—*what I said . . .*

My palm smacks my face, dragging it down and wiping away the sweat before I pull my tank top up and over my head. Yanking it off, I ball it up and toss it to the floor, releasing a heavy exhale.

Truth or not, there's a little thing called tact—something that was completely absent when I reminded her of what happened.

She looked horrified—*retchedly* shocked. And it's so fucking confusing that all I can do is chalk it up to a trauma response. I know the mind is capable of blocking out all sorts of things.

My heart quickens, and I blink up at the ceiling, taking another deep inhale.

I'm kind of surprised she came back with us. *With me.*

She also didn't say another word.

Ellis tried with a couple of small-talk questions when we got back in the car, but gave up and just put on some music when he realized she wasn't going to say anything.

Her gaze caught mine a few times through the mirror, but she looked so painfully stuck in her mind that all I could do was mentally beat the shit out of my own brain.

When we got home, she immediately locked herself in the extra room, and I spent two hours bare-knuckling the boxing bag in the garage before taking a cold shower and memorizing the exact layout of my bedroom ceiling.

Shoving myself out of bed, I shuffle to the bathroom, take a piss then open my bedroom door. I cleaned up my hands last night, but I should go make sure there's no blood on the bag.

As my hallway opens up to the living room and I start toward the garage, the extra bedroom door down the hallway—the one that's usually open—is closed.

She's right behind that door.

My bare feet take timid steps toward the bedroom, letting my toes drag through the pathways of the grooves in the floor.

Part of me wonders if I'm secretly hoping the floor stops me from continuing. *Maybe I'll hit a knot in the wood and stub my toe.*

Turn around.

But I don't, *of course.*

Bad ideas.

The door is suddenly right in front of me, and I stare down at the knob. A worn brass device that will open with a simple twist, unveiling my singular paradise.

If I could just watch her sleep . . .

The wavy mess of silvery blue hair sprawled over the pillows, her face peaceful with softly parted lips as she breathes.

In my mind, my eyes travel, curious . . .

Her beautiful body tucked and nestled.

A sharp inhale comes with a thought that plows through my imaginings. *"I sleep naked most of the time."*

She'd said that once. I remember . . .

Holy fuck.

I turn away from the door, preparing to run from the memory like the coward I am, but suddenly every bit of *anything* I'm feeling pools and circulates to my groin, and I grab the wall, grunting.

Jesus, fuck. I'm sick.

After what I did—*what I said to her last night*—and now I'm getting a raging hard-on outside her door.

Suddenly, I hear a throat clear, and my eyes shoot up, seeing Ellis standing there, yawning through my painfully fast and aggressive erection. I work to straighten myself up.

Try not to bring attention to it.

A small bit of relief finds me when I see his eyes drift just behind me, but it disappears when I realize his gaze is lingering on the door.

There's a longing there too, but it's stifled by something I can't quite place. Another beat passes before he says, "So, what are you gonna do about that?" his eyes pointing toward the door.

There's a challenge lit in his gaze, but it's not exactly playful. Just like with most things, Ellis is steady until he's not. And right now, I'm gathering from his expression that there's an answer that will keep him steady, and an answer that will tip the scale. And right now, that realization is only jacking up my discomfort.

My eyes squint and my weight shifts, studying him. But really—how can he be so . . . *calm* about this?

Given the fact that Paige was typically a *"no fly zone"* as far as conversation was concerned, and the fact that I was gone for the couple of years they seemed to lose touch means I'm not exactly sure how he feels about seeing her again.

But . . . *he's* the one that offered to let her stay here.

And he knows what I did to her.

I don't even remember telling him. It was the night I . . . kissed him. He said . . . something, and I blacked out.

But he told me the next morning. And I'll never forget the haunted look in his eyes . . .

I cringe at just the thought of the fuzzy memory as Ellis crosses his arms over his chest, awaiting my response.

I take a deep breath and my hand digs through the pocket of my sweatpants, searching, but I don't have any change. "I—" I start but then stop.

Slow.

I take another breath, but my jaw tightens, my throat narrows.

Ellis knows what I did to her, but he doesn't believe it. Just like her. *That much* is clear from her reaction last night.

They just don't want *to believe it.*

And I don't either—but you can't deny what you've seen in plain sight.

I wonder if she's seen it . . .

The thought strangles the air in my throat, and Ellis dips his chin, reminding me that he's standing right in front of me—that he asked me a question.

"Sh-She doesn't remember," I say quietly, jaggedly. I feel lightheaded, but my hand is still on the wall, helping me stay upright.

"Linc," Ellis says through a sigh. It has the tone of . . . *disappointment? Frustration?* I can't be sure. He rustles his hair on the back of his head, looking like he wants to say something, but then releases a heavy exhale. "Just promise me you'll actually talk to her. Take a few days, get your thoughts together, let the initial shock settle, and then talk to her."

I gnaw on my lip. Ellis has been dealing with my shit for years, and I know he's delicately side-stepping what I told him in that blackout. Not ignoring it exactly, but he doesn't acknowledge it.

And I can tell he's being . . . *cautious* with his wording. He doesn't coddle me in any areas of my slow, painful attempt at recovery, and I genuinely appreciate it. But this is the only thing I've noticed he *will* tiptoe around.

Probably because you blacked out and scared the shit out of him last time he brought it up.

And I imagine it's because he tries to avoid the reminder that his best friend is a monster. When he doesn't think about it—without her around—it's probably easy enough to just hold onto the person I used to be—deny the truth of what happened.

His mind probably won't *let him* accept it, and he's looking at Paige's return like some beacon—something to shed light on an event I wish I could physically capture and bury at the bottom of the fucking ocean.

But unfortunately, no matter how lightly you tread around the truth, no matter how much you try to keep your eyes off the reality, there's no denying it.

It will surface and then they'll see.

I *am* a monster.

CHAPTER 29
PAIGE

Fucking hell.

I think I'll die in this room. Death from hiding. A cowardly stripper and her gecko on the luxury thread-count sheets. But I can't leave this room until I'm sure Linc's left for work.

The art of avoidance is a discomfort I know well.

My back sinks into the mattress and I stare up at the ceiling, trying to trick my body into calming down as the fucked carousel playing through my brain starts back up. The whiplash as the words hit me again.

"Because I raped you."

Nothing—not even the event itself—was as devastating as the deep agony on his face as he said that. The haunted—absolutely wrecked— glaze in his hazel eyes. His unshakeable belief intensified the devastation.

It rocked me to my core, and the certainty of his expression only lit one thing inside of me.

Rage.

I don't know why, but it was the only emotion that registered, and the anger still finds me now, tightening my fists at my sides.

He seemed . . . so sure.

A shiver runs down my spine as a lump settles in my throat.

After years of speculation, I had my own thoughts and theories as to why Linc left—why he left *me.*

But I could have never imagined this might be it.

If *that's* what he believes—if that's what he truly thinks happened . . .

I feel a trickle of moisture drip down my cheek and I sniff, realizing I'm crying. *Again.*

I wipe my eyes, groaning. My own inability to cope always makes things worse. I'm not going to get anywhere by *wondering to the fucking walls* about it.

As I've learned from my brief but oh-so-needed hug from Ellis last night, there's a *chance* I'm terribly lonely. There's a *chance* I'm completely fucking lost.

But . . . the other thing I felt in our embrace was—*maybe* there's a *chance* Ellis might forgive me. Maybe not right away. But . . . maybe.

And in Linc's arms last night, before he dropped the bomb on me, I felt it too.

Like, maybe we can all get back on track.

Gram always believed we would—even at the end, she'd always tell me, *"It's just because so much time has passed. Sometimes our minds confuse bravery and fear, Paigey May. And it's easy to do because the things that require bravery often terrify us."*

The thought of her voice soothes me and I sigh, my shoulders loosening with some relief. I haven't heard her as much. Though, my head barely feels attached to my body at this point.

My phone buzzes, bringing me back to the room, but I ignore the call. I'm certain it's Jackson. He's been calling *all fucking day.*

I know I need to talk to them. Honestly, I should talk to them *soon.* Ellis knocked on the door earlier to tell me he moved my car up to the driveway and even from here, I swear I can hear the money banging around in the trunk like the drums from fucking *Jumanji.*

But I've decided to give myself the day. *Just a day.*

A moment passes and I stare at the ceiling, wondering if they're the same in every room. The ceiling gets the aerial view. The haunted thoughts on each side of the pillow. It probably even sees the shit you stash under the bed with the monsters.

Is this what he's looked at the last four years while he's fallen asleep?

And the years before that . . .

"Where did he go?"

My mind floats to Ellis's response, *"Nope. Not touchin' that,"* and a sharp inhale pulls through my chest.

Where Linc went after our shared horror was a hard limit for Ellis. Why?

If Linc had moved to Australia to live among the koalas or decided to film ant hills deep in the valley for a couple of years—*what's with the secrecy?*

Unless he was *with someone?*

No. My mind rejects it right along with his hypothetical, big-titted, Malibu bitch.

But then *why?*

Ugh. I swear I'm burning calories with the hole my mind is running through the floors of my skull. Groaning, I sit up. After a breath, I break my rule and look at my phone, seeing ten missed calls. No voicemails. Seven texts.

All of them say "call me" except for the last ones.

Jackson: I'm sorry, Blue.

Rio: Any tattooed visitors last night?
I knew that boy wasn't gay!

What?

It takes my mind a few seconds to figure out what the hell she's talking about, then it dawns on me—*Linc?*

Right. Linc works at The Window.

But why would she think he's gay?

God, my head is pounding with all the *new* boiling over.

In need of a distraction, I ignore Rio's message for the moment and instead focus on Jackson's uncharacteristically apologetic message. It surprises me at first, but then I realize . . .

He knows they fucked up.

That's got to be it. After reviewing the footage, they must have seen the crystal clear evidence of an attempted sexual assault—*not a security guard in sight*—and now they're trying to "make nice" before I "make noise." Something I have no intention of doing, regardless.

But if they watched the footage, that also means they saw me take the money. *Right?*

Maybe not . . .

Either way, the creeps were friends of Beck's, so there's no doubt he at least knows about it.

I pin my lip between my teeth, my eyes flicking to the time on my phone, seeing that it's six. That's usually call-time for the guards and out here, we're an hour away when the traffic is perfect—*which happens right along with unicorn sightings.*

I take a breath and stand up. I should run to the store, grab some food. I think I've earned some carbs. Maybe a box of wine. I can drink on the fancy sheets.

Tomorrow, I'll call Jackson back, resume reality.

I text Rio back three question marks, mostly as a proof of life, but also kind of hoping she'll enlighten me a bit.

My socks press against the floor gingerly. I'm not sure if Ellis is home, but I just want to go to the market and come back.

I also have a bone to pick with Teddy boy at the bottom of the mountain.

I make it to the kitchen, turning toward the entry hall when I hear, "Your sneaky walk is reminiscent of a noodle starting to boil."

I yelp but stop midstep, unable to *not* snort a laugh and turn around, seeing Ellis sitting in one of the bar chairs at the counter.

"That is—" I rasp with a shake of my head. But then take what feels like the first deep breath all day, before I say, "So fucking specific."

The emerald glow to his eyes is closer to what I remember—less muted than last night—as he smirks. "Evidence that I've consistently reached a point of hunger where I *watch* my food cook."

I breathe another laugh through a nod. "I was—uh . . . I was gonna go get some food, actually. From the—store. Do you . . . do you want anything from . . . the store?" His chin dips further, the longer it takes me to sputter through the sentence.

"Wow." He closes his laptop. "That was painful."

I cringe. *Yes. Yes it was.* But I can't help it.

This is so fucking crazy.

Ellis and Linc were the only two people aside from Gram that required zero social battery, and now it feels like a second with either one of them drains me instantly.

Tomorrow. I need to call Jackson. And I need to figure out a game plan for where I'm going to go.

"I've got shit for grilled cheese," he offers with a lift of his shoulder.

My mouth twitches, wanting to smile but still fighting it for some reason. I squint my eyes in his direction. "You don't know how to make grilled cheese."

He volleys a glare back at me. "That was *one* time. And you know as well as I do that Crisco was a great fucking idea. It was just . . . poorly executed."

I break, barking out a laugh. *The cheesy fail of 2007.*

A movie marathon night back in middle school where Ellis got a strong desire to prove to us he wasn't a spoiled little rich boy by making us grilled cheese. And then burnt the ever-loving shit out of them.

After losing myself to the laughter, I shrug, telling him, "People don't forget."

He laughs this time. It's a quote from *Superbad.* A stupid one, mostly made funny by our irrelevant and frequent use of the line.

"Pop a squat, Michaels. I'll make you earn your keep. I have some questions . . ." he says, standing and rounding the counter, rummaging through the cabinets. But the tension that fell away with our easy conversation suddenly returns, and my spine straightens.

Ellis must notice because he stops before he opens the fridge. "Purely present questions," he clarifies, and my breath still sticks in my throat before I swallow.

I'm not sure that's much better.

Still, I walk back toward the kitchen. I don't deserve the olive branch he's extending, but I take it as I slide onto one of the other bar stools, sitting across from him while he opens the bread. "How long have you been working at The Window?"

My eyebrows pinch. I used to be a pro at spotting when Ellis was working an angle. But I have no earthly idea what that could possibly be—why *that* matters at all.

I clear my throat. "A year. I started right after Gram . . ."

He's quiet for a second, buttering the bread, then his eyes flick up to me. "And the *incident* that happened last night . . . that's the first time anything like that has ever happened there?"

I nod, swallowing again. "In *my* experience. Why?"

Ellis shakes his head with a long pause before he sighs and shrugs, laying the cheese on the bread. He seems to be lost in thought for the moment. My eyes drift absently, but they catch on the pile of yellow fruit tucked into a corner of the counter space next to the fridge.

He notices my sight line and twists around to see, but a strange combination—equal parts shock *and* solace— warms my chest.

It *was* him. He left the mug out in the ratty old hammock back at the house.

I have no idea why he left the mug outside, but those are lemons from Gram's tree. I fucking *know it.* I just do. Ellis twists his chin back toward me, his eyes shining brilliantly from the wall-length windows behind me. He doesn't say anything. He doesn't have to. His face confirms my suspicions and the feeling tightens in my chest.

I'm so . . . *fucking* confused. I feel like all the blanks I've worked to fill in through all these years were all wrong.

I didn't think Linc was even in California—*at The Window.*

Which reminds me . . .

"Can I ask *you* something?"

Ellis bends down and grabs a pan, his eyes halting with caution, and I quickly say, "Purely present," parroting his earlier words.

He huffs a small laugh, then nods.

I take a breath. "Any thoughts on why my coworker thought Linc was gay?"

Ellis stops moving completely. Any nervous energy he was putting into redeeming his grilled cheese rankings just stops.

I see his Adam's apple bob as the silence holds for a few more seconds. I'm suddenly terrified. I expected him to laugh or at least display some of the wild confusion I had when I read Rio's text, but his palpable . . . *something* is making me regret asking.

Quickly he says, "Uhh—" then shakes his head. Rubbing the back of his neck, he adds, "He—uh . . . he does that sometimes."

What?!

Linc's played *gay before? And Ellis knows about it?!*

My estranged friend is still looking at me, but his even expression is only confusing me more. My eyes and nose scrunch—*completely fucking lost*—just before I exclaim, "Why?!"

Ellis shoves a hand through his hair, then leans one palm against the counter. His eyes study mine a moment more and I see caution take to his gaze before he shrugs. "He thinks it makes people feel . . . safer," he says quietly, jaggedly, as his eyes drift down to the plates with the sandwiches.

Now the caution in his eyes makes sense. He knew his explanation was only going to give me more questions.

"This isn't my business to tell," he had told me last night. Right before he warned me not to touch Linc . . . which I did.

And Linc touched me too.

Goddammit. My brain feels like a swirled soft-serve, and I press my thumbs to my temples as the sizzle from the grilled cheese makes me flinch in my seat. My empty stomach and my hunger are twisting and shifting into nausea.

The sound of the freezer door closing pulls my eyes back up to Ellis as he then opens the cabinet just to the side, putting two shot glasses on the counter. "You know what goes great with grilled cheese?"

My eyes move to see . . .

Tequila.

CHAPTER 30
LINC

I take a heavy drag of my cigarette, coughing a bit on my exhale before it tapers into a groan.

Ugh. Walking to The Window is the last fucking thing I want to be doing.

After hanging up from an hour-long talk with Desmond to catch him up on the shitshow that was last night, I'm running a little late. But I told him every detail I could think of. I *did* omit the fact that Paige is currently our third roommate for . . . well, I don't know how long she's planning on staying at the house.

She stayed in her room all *day.*

Hiding, probably.

I shake my head at the voice and try to focus back on my conversation with Desmond. He seemed surprised to hear she's working there, but given the fact that he knows little to nothing of what happened between us, he seemed to only consider it an interesting coincidence rather than an earth-shattering event like I did.

Or Ellis for that matter. After our exchange this morning, I noticed that he seemed quiet before I left. Like he was memorizing every pixel in his laptop screen. If I know him like I think I do, he's probably pooling some resources to see if he can get more information on the guys from the Veranda.

Something I'm hoping to get a little clarity on today. That is, if I'm not knee-deep in shit for hitting my boss.

Desmond seemed unfazed when I told him that, but who knows. This whole thing is fucking bizarre.

Just as I toss my cigarette out, I get to the back corner of the building and see Jackson out on the sidewalk. He's pulling his cigarettes out of his pocket and my eyebrows pinch.

I've only been here for a few days, but I've never seen the guy out here for a smoke break this close to opening the house.

He lifts his chin, pulling out a cigarette as he gives me a nod, which I think is meant to be a greeting, but then he leans his head to the side—a subtle movement requesting I join him . . . *I think?*

Going with it, I walk in his direction, shoving my hand in my pocket and jingling the loose change between my fingers.

The light clash of the sound helps. I focus on trying to catch all the coins as I pick them up and drop them inside my pocket, and the distraction is enough to steady my heart rate.

Even if I hadn't hit him last night—Jackson's pretty fucking intimidating. Dude looks like he could wrestle an anaconda. But from the small action I've seen him take, I think it's his ability to stay level-headed that probably gives him the upper hand in fights.

He looked like he *wanted* to tear someone's head off last

night—whether or not that was *me* is still to be determined—but he didn't. He simply *diffused* the situation.

But something tells me his anger doesn't evaporate.

As I reach him on the far end of the sidewalk, I find myself absently glancing down at his knuckles, checking for evidence to see if maybe he spent two hours punching shit last night.

But of course, his knuckles are knobs of clean, unbroken skin—a visual aid of someone with *actual* control. I pull my own cigarettes out and light one up.

Why the fuck not?

"Cook," Jackson says, a bit clipped but no more than usual.

I inhale, dipping my chin in a return greeting. Luckily, I don't see any marks on his face. His eyes flit up to mine and I dart my gaze out toward the street. Not at anything in particular, but the eye-contact, the proximity, it's making my skin crawl.

But I take a breath, then start to tell him, "I—uh . . . I'm s-sorry, about—"

"You know her," he says decisively, letting smoke blow through his nose.

I can only assume Jackson doesn't know about my *hidden agenda* for working here, so I'm unsure of how much I should divulge. But if he's seen the tapes there's a good chance he saw me mentally shoot off to the moon when Paige stood right in front of me—wrapped in leather.

The thought stirs, but halts as he clears his throat and finally, I nod, shuffling my feet.

"Is she okay? I've called her twelve times today. I swear to God, that girl—" He clenches his teeth with a shake of his head, blowing out a heavy breath, taking another drag of his cigarette.

Worried. He's worried. It's just being rerouted to frustration. I recognize it since I'm basically made of fucking detours.

"S-She's okay. She's with a friend," I tell him. Only another beat passes before I finish what I was about to say, "I'm s-sorry I hit you."

He stays quiet for a second, then clears his throat. "That happen a lot?"

My eyes squint, confused. I look over at him and his expression remains steady, his silver eyes sharp in the hazy sunset blanketing the street.

When I still look lost, he says, "I was—" he stops, then continues, "Ex-marine. I—uh . . . I recognize a blackout when I see one."

My throat works to swallow. My free hand moves back to my pocket, fiddling with the change, while simultaneously taking a drag off my cigarette.

"Look, we don't have to talk about it. In fact, I'm totally fucking good *not* talking about it. But, remove yourself from now on if you feel that slip. You have anything that helps it?"

My weight shifts uncomfortably, but I don't think it's because of him. It's actually a really kind thing to do—to ask. I haven't been around people enough that a need to address my . . . *issues* has ever come up.

I release the puff on my cigarette and then swallow hard. "Coins," I tell him, jingling my pocket.

I keep the fact that sometimes nothing helps to myself. It's nice that he's asking at all—I don't need him to know I'm a *constant* flight risk.

I can handle this.

Jackson's hardened features stay firm as he nods. "Okay. Well, use your judgment." He takes another drag himself, then says, "And if you see Blue, can you please tell her to call me?"

I nod again, taking a breath, grateful for the subject change. I flick some ash to the street and take a second to visualize my words, then ask, "What happened with the guys last night?"

Jackson's jaw tightens. "We reviewed the footage and filed a police report. Beck is insistent that we get Blue back here before proceeding with anything else. He'd also like to speak with you."

My eyebrows lift. It doesn't shock me that Beck wants to meet with me. I assumed we would at some point, but I *am* surprised they've already filed a police report.

My knowledge about the world of powerful men like Beck is limited, but I do know one thing—they're *careful.*

Desmond always says wealthy people need to exercise more caution than the average person—that success on certain scales is a balancing act—a vital one if you want to keep the upper hand.

But I wonder if that's what's happening here. Maybe they've filed a police report as a ruse to get Paige to come in so they could settle it all *quietly.*

I toss my cigarette out. *Well,* I guess that's *another* reason it's good that Beck wants to meet with me—because if Paige *does* decide to take the meeting, they've lost their goddamn minds if they think I'll leave her alone with them.

Jackson tosses his cigarette too and a pinch of remorse

squeezes in my chest. I shouldn't be lumping Jackson in with Beck. Granted, I don't know Beck either, but he *did* leave the most precious human in the world, alone and defenseless in a room with three men.

But from what I've seen of Jackson—he seems okay. Works hard, takes his job seriously—*he's called Paige twelve times today.* He's worried about her.

Something about *that* settles me, despite the fact that there's something about this place I don't trust.

Jackson turns back toward the building and murmurs, "Be alert tonight, okay?" The order is basically under his breath, and I have to remind myself that he's talking to me.

Me. Alert. The guy who got an hour of sleep and what's left of him is still standing outside Paige's door. *Imagining.*

I am fucking wiped.

And I'm not done yet.

I push open the door to the storage closet and release a heavy exhale.

Luckily, it seems like a far less *eventful* night.

And I have tomorrow off, I remind myself.

One of the many reasons I was probably a shitty choice for this job is the whole consistent schedule thing. It conflicts with the very *inconsistent* way my brain shuts on and off.

And while the club itself seems to be less chaotic tonight, the whispers and following stares from other staff members has been a bit rough, mostly because the voices in my head are having a fucking rave.

I take a breath. There's a chance I'm on edge. And truly, I don't give a fuck what any of them are saying about me.

They can say whatever they want about *Cook,* but I almost lost my shit an hour ago when some twat was running her mouth about how Blue—*Paige*—probably scowled at the VIP until he lost his hard-on or something. I don't know, it was some bitchy comment at Paige's expense, and I . . . *removed* myself, as Jackson had suggested I do when I felt myself *slipping.*

I just want to be back at the house. Back with her. Even if she stays in her room.

And I know Ellis is right. I *know* I need to talk to her. But it feels like it will take me fucking years to visualize those words. *Like last night. I tried to find more delicate words, but I . . .*

My pulse ticks and my eyebrows flinch.

Fuck, I can't believe I said it—*like that*—on a night where she was already in shock, recently traumatized. *Goddammit.* I just . . . I hope she's okay.

She's with Ellis, I remind myself.

Another sigh pushes past my lips and I shake my head, then grab one of the chairs to stack it into the storage closet.

I've spent four fucking years *dwelling* as a hermit and she comes crashing back into my life when I actually have to leave the house for something!

I grunt as I put the last of the extra seating into the closet, turning off the light before I step back out and lock it.

Walking back through the staff hallway, I head toward the

dressing rooms to return the keys to the hub when I see Rio walking toward me, her light green robe billowing at her sides.

Her mouth pulls back and her caramel brown eyes are wide, but also like she might be about to laugh. "Hi," she says, but also signs.

My eyebrows pinch, confused as to why she might look guilty. Her posture is still impeccable, but her chin is just slightly tilted down, and I wonder if she's talked to Paige.

My nerves tick up, but then she smiles, signing, "How's it going?"

Rubbing the back of my neck, I sigh through a small, nervous chuckle, then shrug.

A moment passes between us, I'm not sure what. Her presence just carries this . . . warmth. Not cozy, but it's like a glow of knowingness. And strangely enough, my delirium finds it oddly comforting.

I think I find *Rio* comforting. Which is crazy because I don't even know her.

She surprises me when she doesn't ask me about Paige, but instead signs, "I thought of your name sign."

It takes me a second to remember what she's talking about.

Then I remember a few days ago when we met. She had asked me if I had a name sign.

It seems like a hundred years ago at this point.

The tired, heavy feeling of my eyelids lifts, eyebrows too.

Rio raises her right hand, just in front of her face, with her palm facing toward her. Curling her index finger and thumb into a loose *C* handshape, she swoops her hand farther away from her face. It's the sign for *"watch."*

Using the same hand, she lightly taps her thumb to her forehead, then her chest, ending the name with the sign I recognize for "*man.*"

Watch. Man.

My mouth stretches. A smile. I like it.

But my eyebrows pinch. I'm not sure if it's rude to ask why she chose that name, but luckily, she doesn't make me when she signs, "I've seen enough to recognize a man who's paying attention."

She signs it slow, pointedly. Her eyes meet mine in a way that seems like they're alluding more to now in this moment, but there's also a chance I'm sleeping with my eyes open.

Still, I give her a tired smile, and she pats my shoulder as she passes by. I flinch, but I think I'm too tired to fully react. Plus, her calming witchcraft seems to be keeping the unease from making it past a blip in my chest.

Checking my phone, I don't know what I'm expecting, but I'm disappointed when I don't see it, which makes no fucking sense.

My eyes instead find the time, seeing it's almost midnight. Just a half hour left before I can head home.

And it can't come soon enough.

Apparently the recipe for a temporary friendship bandage is a grilled cheese, two and a half margaritas, and a musical theater playlist.

We drowned out the uncomfortable moment from before by singing and dancing—*not unlike when we were kids*—and now we're just tapering off with, "Happy Days are Here Again," while I cradle Cheeto in my palm.

A serenade.

Just as the song ends, Ellis plops on the couch and I sit next to him. "Agh!" he scoffs. "Can you put that thing back in its little box now?" He eyes Cheeto with a glare.

She's curled up in my hand, being perfect, and with the pad of my finger, I give her a gentle rub. "I don't want her to feel left out."

"Oh, God," he groans. "Fiiine. But just sit over in the chair. If it moves too quickly I'll spill my drink and this sugar-crack-mix will be a bitch to get out of the couch."

I snort, picking up my drink and walking over to the chair across from the couch, which faces out toward the big windows, while the chair I plop into faces inward, on an angle facing the TV on the wall.

"Don't you get a glare?" I ask, my eyes flicking to the TV.

I mean, who needs a TV when you've got this view? I think if I could, I'd just listen to music all day and watch the mountain.

"There's a remote for the shades, but we almost never use them."

Reality settles among the showtunes dust, and I take a big gulp of my drink.

We. Them.

And then there's me.

Goddammit. More tequila.

Although, *that* could be a recipe for disaster.

Linc will be home at *some* point, and it's probably wise if I'm not sloshed.

Plus, I have to hold Cheeto.

Still, I take another sip of my existing drink, then try to cozy back into the chair. After a few seconds pass, I chew my lip, then ask, "So how'd you and Linc meet back up?" I try to sound as casual as possible.

"Smooth," he jabs, and my eyes narrow.

He chuckles and I watch him. The two-year gap between when everything fell apart and they found their way back to each other is itching at the underside of my brain, but I already know he won't tell me about that.

I shrug, giving him an expectant look and he pulls in a long inhale, rubbing the back of his neck. "Desmond and I were up at his property in Maine and we—uh—ran into Linc."

"Maine?" It escapes before I even have time to process.

Why was he in Maine?!

He'd literally never mentioned *anything* about Maine to me.

The word Maine is starting to sound weird in my head.

But not in our entire lives had I ever heard him mention anything about it. Though, he'd never mentioned Chicago either and he was at least there for a little bit.

Chicago, then Maine.

It's slightly more information than I had before, so I poke a little more. "What was he doing in Maine?" I ask, my voice is tighter this time.

Ellis takes a sip, and his eyes float down to his glass before he lifts them back up, the emerald color only sinks into my gaze for a second before he shrugs. "Filming something."

Lying.

Why is he lying?

New plan. Stop drinking and offer to play bartender. Get Ellis smashed and collect intel.

In an attempt to not appear too eager with my new plan, my eyes drift for a second, absently wondering whether or not Linc still films anything. He was just . . . so fucking good. *Money-Shot Morrow,* as Ellis always called him.

I suddenly take note of some small . . . *posters* on the coffee table. A photograph of five different people, but it's been edited so that their skin has some landmarks imposed through a grainy filter. My eyes float to the text that reads *The 5,* then see the name attached to it, and my eyes shoot up.

Ellis is already looking at me, but then his eyes flick down to the posters. "Linc did the cover shot," he says, pulling his gaze back up. "Shot a bunch of exterior stuff too."

The pang of jealousy doesn't even compare to the warmth that immediately floods through me.

The idea that they're still shooting stuff together speaks to the *us* before and I just . . . I can't be anything but *over-fucking-joyed* about that. That some part of us is still trying to float to the surface.

I smile. A real one. "You really did it. You really made a documentary." *With Linc's help.*

My chest tightens again and he sighs with a nod. "I mean, it really is the product of a ton of fucking people, but yeah." He smiles and *God*, it hits.

A flash of the boy who organized "Pennies for Primates" in second grade flutters past my vision. Outraged that monkeys had been moved to the local zoo without proper space, Ellis took action.

It was just the start, I think. But that deep part of me fills a bit, knowing he's still at it—feeding his hard opinions and anti-establishment ways. And I'm so goddamn proud of him.

"That's amazing, Ba—" I stop myself. *Holy shit.* I almost called him Batman. I shake my head and quickly say, "I—uh—I can't wait to watch it."

And I mean it. Another margarita or two, and I'll watch it and cry later. But I already feel my eyes misting and my head shakes.

God, do not become the weepy, tipsy girl.

Ellis is kind enough to not insult me by asking if I'm still acting or singing. Clearly, my performances are of a different variety these days.

After a few more seconds, I fill the slightly awkward pause with, "Are you working on anything new?"

He takes a long pull on his drink, nodding. After he clears his throat, he says, "Yeah, but I'm still researching shit at the moment. I keep hitting walls, so I hired a tech guy to help."

"Like a hacker?"

Ellis nods, a smirk pulling up. "Yes, but that makes it sound more nefarious."

A laugh pushes past my nose. "Nefarious, huh? You been watching *Dawson's Creek*?"

"*Fucking no*," he groans. "I only ever watched that shit because you and Darlene *made* me, and 'cause Linc couldn't take it." I laugh again just as his watch beeps and he looks at the screen, eyes squinting, then stands up and walks over to the counter to check his phone.

I take the moment to appreciate—*no, fucking relish*—that the thought of Gram isn't filling me with despair—*for once*. And the warmth isn't from some pathetic, fake voice filling my head either. Don't get me wrong, thinking about her—imagining her voice—it makes me feel good too, but . . . Buffy bless, *this* feels great—that she just gets to *exist* amongst the conversation.

This exchange—hanging out with Ellis—is *interesting*. Our past, our familiarity, our connection—it's almost like it keeps coming up for air in between awkward waves in the room. The current wading around everything we're not talking about.

Just as Ellis comes back to the couch, I put my drink on the small table next to me and try to keep the conversation going— keep it easy. "What are you researching? Must be kind of crazy if you're enlisting a hacker."

His mouth slopes as he runs his fingers over the edge of his glass. "That's the thing, I'm not really sure. It sort of happened by accident. I was looking into—something else," he says, a bit jaggedly and then stands back up, wobbling a bit this time as he tilts his glass toward me. A silent offer for another.

I shake my head, standing too. I should probably sit this round out seeing as that grilled cheese is the most I've eaten in two days.

I leave Ellis to make his next drink, and return Cheeto to her terrarium. Placing the sweet little nugget just beside her rock, I close it up and leave her to her nap.

She's probably tired from running back and forth for *three hours* early this morning. I felt so bad. She was probably freaked out. But now she's more than happy in her corner just beside the bed.

We can't get used to it, I think to myself and telepathically tell her on my way out of the room.

"*Why not? It could be like a '90s sitcom? But dark and twisted,*" Gram's voice slurs through my head and I chuckle, wondering if that's the booze or if she's *somehow* a little drunk too. The thought makes me giggle.

I wish I had taken part in more wine nights with her.

"*It made the few times we did special,*" I think—or maybe she says . . . I don't know. Standing up seemed to shoot all the alcohol straight to my head.

I stagger back toward the kitchen, seeing Ellis back in front of his laptop as he waves me over, sipping on a fresh drink. But I suddenly feel like I'm trying really hard *not* to look fucked up and it's *making me* look fucked up.

You were fine literally *a minute ago.* Still, I grab my water bottle from earlier off the counter and walk over to him, taking a sip as I look at the screen.

It's a nondescript website—just a red symbol in the center. There's a small diamond sitting in a half-circle, floating just above something that looks like the letter *M*.

And the website doesn't have any links or tabs; it looks like it's just a single page with no other content. My eyebrows pinch as Ellis clicks on the symbol, and a prompt comes up for a password.

Hm. "Weird. What do you think it is?"

Ellis shrugs. "I can't find the symbol circulating anywhere and I've sent the image off to a few semiotic specialists. I'm collecting it all to go through together. But it's fucking weird that you can't see anything on their website without a password and there's seemingly nowhere of regular consumption where you can *find* the password. So, that's where Wade comes in."

"The hacker," I confirm.

He nods, taking another sip, then says, "Even *he's* having some trouble—I don't know, we're meeting tomorrow to talk about it. Who the fuck knows. It may all be for nothing."

It does look weird—maybe cult-ish? But I'm barely an expert on this shit. For lack of anything better to say, I ask, "What led you to it?"

His thumb taps a couple times on the counter. "Just a hunch."

My chin dips with a lazy nod as his eyes stay on the screen, but his focus drifts in a way that tells me he's not really looking at it anymore.

Another silence passes—but I swear, I can feel it shifting—to what, I'm not sure, and it dims the energy around us. Something only made more clear when Ellis sucks on his lower lip, turning the skin red, before he finally releases it and sighs. "Paige. At The Window last night. Did . . . did they—"

"No," I answer quickly, then say it again, "No."

Shit. I feel terrible. I can only imagine the assumptions he made when he saw me outside last night.

Your estranged friend—now a stripper—shows up at midnight with a busted lip and twirled up in leather.

It'd be fair to make some assumptions.

And still, even after ghosting him for seven years, he welcomed me into his house and didn't make me explain myself.

"Like family," I hear Gram say distantly.

Sighing, I continue telling him, "They—well, it was mostly just Tariel—"

Ellis stands on the base of his chair and leans over the counter, swiping another glass and pouring some tequila in it for me. Straight. And I take it.

Whoops.

My mouth clenches back and I go on to explain the insanity of what happened in the Veranda, but I conveniently leave out the money I stole.

Ellis's face fills with disgust and I suddenly feel itchy, but then he says, "Ew, it was like . . . a demonstration?"

Cringing through my shrug, I blow out a heavy exhale. "I honestly have no idea."

Ellis's eyes squint. "And he—Tariel—he knows the owner? Beck?" I nod, timidly, and he clicks his tongue. After another second passes, he says, "Linc is only working at The Window to help Desmond. I guess my dad knows one of the owners, who suspects there might be people doing some kind of shady dealings. I guess the guy asked my dad for help."

"Owners? Plural?" I ask.

Not that I know anything about anything, but I thought Beck Davis was the only owner of The Window.

Ellis shrugs. "I don't know. Either way, it sounds like there could be *something* going on. I mean, last night sounds pretty fucked."

I want to ask him what he meant by shady dealings, but I also don't really want to talk about The Window anymore. If difficult conversations were to be had, they didn't need to be about a burlesque club that meant nothing to me.

Another silence stretches. This one is less comfortable as what Linc said to me last night scoots to the edge of my brain, the words flicking their curious toes in the pool of tequila sloshing through my head.

"He—Linc," I stutter. And like the *fucking champion* that he is, Ellis pours another shot into my glass.

I knock it back. My mouth stretches, hissing until the shot drops to my stomach—coating the words. I take a breath, then look up at Ellis. "Linc thinks he raped me."

A sharp inhale is his only immediate reaction. But slowly, his eyes darken to a deep hunter green, his stare hollowing as he finally says, "I know," his voice gravelly.

My stomach rolls as a burn ignites in my chest. It's a full ten seconds before my mouth even moves to say something. "You know about what happened?"

"No," he says quickly, then tilts his chin. "I mean, I don't *know*. But I know enough."

I stare at my empty glass, wishing I could just *see* what he knows—summon it to appear like a crystal ball so I don't have to ask him.

It doesn't work, so I have to ask, "What did he tell you?"

Ellis takes a shot himself, shaking his head a bit and then swiping a palm down his face. He fidgets a second more by ruffling his hair, before he says, "Look, Paige. I told you—I don't feel right talking about this. If *you* want to ask him about it, you can, but . . . you—need to be careful. Take it slow."

My heart deflates at his resolve, but my face scrunches when the last part of his sentence registers. "Careful?"

Another warning. Though, he'd warned me about touching Linc, and I did it anyway.

Ellis's weight shifts on the chair, taking another breath. "He was in really rough shape when he moved in here," he says.

"Four years ago?" I confirm, mostly for my drunk mind.

He nods. "A few nights after he moved in, we were hanging out on the porch, and he—" He tugs on his lip with his teeth, then gives a quick shake of his head. "I was just trying to—jog his memory a bit. But . . . something happened, and I—*pushed* too far."

My eyes blink rapidly. There's a lot of vagueness in what he's saying, but I guess that's to be expected seeing as he's already told me he won't talk about this.

And I just can't understand *why*. I understand wanting to protect Linc's privacy but . . . *I'm* the other party involved here.

Which makes me feel like I'm missing something . . .

And I also know there's absolutely *no* breaking Ellis's moral code. It'd be admirable if it wasn't information I was absolutely starved for.

Deciding to see how far I can push it, I ask, "Wh-What happened?"

Ellis's face winces and I swear I even see a chill sweep through his shoulders. He sits silently for a few seconds before he quietly says, "Blackout rage. Literally . . . like a light blew out. I've—I've never seen anything like it."

The cold look in his eyes feels like ice in my own chest, and I silently wonder if Ellis has ever talked about this with anyone. It has the raw emotion of secrecy—a haunting I know well.

But the other part of me just can't believe this is *Lincoln Morrow* we're talking about.

I'm almost afraid to ask, given the disturbed look still on his face. "Did he hurt you?"

"No," he says immediately, then adds, "I mean, not really. He did swing a couple of times but he was too disoriented to really do any damage."

I gasp and my eyebrows scrunch. There's . . . there's *no way* Linc would hit Ellis. Not intentionally.

He stares off for a moment, just out in front of him on the counter, and his eyes grow darker—almost like he's *watching* the memory replay in front of him.

Have a few memories like that myself.

A heaviness rolls through me, and my voice shakes a bit as I ask, "S-So what did he say?"

Whatever images Ellis is watching still hold his focus for a few seconds, before he blinks, then clears his throat. "I think he thought I was . . . someone else."

His speculative eyes weave something silently, and I can't be sure, but I don't think he's being *intentionally* vague.

I swallow hard and dread prickles under my skin in the same way it has for the last twenty-four hours. There's something in Ellis's eyes that tells me he knows *exactly* who Linc mistook him for during his episode—but he says nothing.

And honestly, I'm grateful. I wasn't there, so I don't know, but I have thoughts on who Linc thought Ellis was too, and I can feel my body temperature rise as my throat works to swallow the idea.

Another beat passes and Ellis sighs. "Look, nothing like that has happened in a long time," he says, carefully. "But the reason I'm telling you is—his memory recall can be . . . temperamental. He really has been doing okay—*good*—and I think reconnecting with you will help. All of us. We just have to be—"

"Careful," I say, but I'm already standing, wrapping my arms around him.

How can I not?

I'm not used to seeing him stumble over his words. Ellis has always been the very definition of someone who never let you see them sweat.

But my hold around him tightens, hoping—*nearly believing*—that he's letting his guard down only because he's talking to *me.*

The familiarity of his arms, his smell. Mint. *And tequila, but I think that's both of us.*

God, I missed him.

I know we're not fixed, but it *feels* like we are in this moment. The hugs feel the same. *Stronger, even.*

"You've been working out," I tell him. If it hadn't been evident in the big muscles that rival his roommate's, it'd be apparent in his embrace.

He's always given the best hugs.

His slightly sad chuckle tickles my ear. "I love the blue," he murmurs, sifting some of my hair between his fingers, and I hug him tighter.

We stand, silently holding each other for long seconds—maybe a minute, but I'm in no hurry.

My mind tries to work through everything he's said, exploring between the words when I realize, "You don't believe he raped me either."

He sighs, holding me tighter. "I knew whatever happened must have been . . . fucking awful."

I can feel the regret in his limbs. Ellis is a do-er. He takes action. And his two shattered best friends might be one of the few things he *can't* fix.

It'd be poetic if it wasn't so fucking tragic.

My body tenses at the thought, but I hum to clear it from creeping too far in, and Ellis lets me. My mouth ticks up at the corner, but he can't see me since I'm pretty much buried in his chest.

Right now, I'm safe. Batman's got me.

I'm happy Linc had him.

The gratitude surprises me, but it's there. Despite all my hurt—the jealousy, the anger—in *this* moment, I find myself grateful. I had Gram and Linc had Ellis. And now, maybe . . .

We can rebuild. Carefully.

My eyes mist again and I groan. "Goddammit. I'm the drunk weepy girl."

He gives me a small squeeze. "All right. Then, enough of this." He just as quickly unlocks from me, swipes the bottle of tequila, and starts toward the living room.

He grabs a blanket off the couch, and then opens the sliding door. "Let's get wasted-er and sing on the porch."

Just today, I remind myself again. *Just take today.*

The stubborn tears stay in my eyes, but my mouth lifts.

I don't know what I did to deserve Ellis Casper . . . but I'll keep him.

PAIGE

Using my key, I twisted the lock to the front door of the Morrow house, then quietly closed it behind me. As I tiptoed through the living room, I held my hands out with the grocery bags—trying to keep them from rustling.

Quiiiet.

I knew Christine was working, but the house was silent aside from the small creaks the floor was making under my feet. And there was only a small bit of gray overcast light trickling in from the window beside the big comfy chair I loved.

My mouth pulled up at the sight of the Christmas tree. Their house may have been small, but it had the perfect spot, just beside the blanket chest for their little tree. My eyes peered down the hallway toward the bedrooms.

There was no question in my mind that Linc would still be sleeping if he could—but if Maisie was up, there was *no way* he *would* still be sleeping.

All of my excitement rushed straight to my abs and tightened, shaking my hands a bit—fighting a happy dance—and the bags rattled.

I made it to the kitchen and put down my supplies, smiling. I still had a shot at the birthday breakfast invasion. Underneath all of my shit on the kitchen table, I saw a piece of paper peeking out under one of the bags.

I pulled it out, noticing it was a card . . . with a Polaroid taped to it. My smile stretched.

A picture of Linc from when he was . . . *nine,* I think.

I could tell because he was sporting the scar under his chin he got from his *skateboarding phase.*

I snort a small laugh at the memory. Ellis tried too.

Kerplunk one, kerplunk two.

In the picture, Linc's sitting in front of the Christmas tree, road-burned chin lifted high. His hazel eyes peek out under shaggy dark hair, while a one-year-old Maisie stares adoringly at her older brother.

My eyes traveled to the note written in black marker on the white strip below the image.

> Her hero and mine.
> Love you always, Little Man.
> Love, Momma

My eyes immediately misted. *Jesus.*

I knew Christine was proud of Linc—*how could she not be?*—

but I loved seeing this. I knew it would mean so much to him, and I just . . .

Ugh. I grunted, giving a quick shake of my head, before I put the card back down on the table, suddenly realizing . . .

Nine years old, which would make this picture from the last Christmas with their dad . . .

Fucking loser.

I start to unpack the bags, letting the small bit of movement try to cycle through my jolt of anger.

"If nothing else, we kept his treasure," Gram had snickered to me once when I was on a tangent about Mr. Morrow. *His treasure* being Linc and Maisie.

My mouth twisted with an idea. It would take more energy from me, but I couldn't fight the urge once I had it.

I slowly walked out of the kitchen, passing quickly through the living room to the hallway with the bedrooms.

It took some serious restraint not to slip into Linc's room and wake him up the way I wanted to—but Maisie was home. Which is why I kept walking to her room.

I opened the door slowly. Her walls were decked out in purple—*everything.* My mouth ticked up as I saw the paper mache panda bear. A project I'm pretty sure earned me and Linc a Brownie badge.

It was for her class's China chapter at school. Maisie offered to make the classroom panda and Linc and I got . . . fucking creative. *Cutting up a wire hanger for the nails was a nice touch, though, if I do say so myself.*

How she slept with it in here was beyond me, though. The googly eyes were the shit of horror movies.

But she was Linc's sister after all.

I walked up to her bed. Her brown hair was . . . everywhere, and her little body was fully starfished on the bed. I leaned down, gently patting her back.

She jerked up quickly with a gasp, brushing her hair out of her blinking, sleepy brown eyes. After her face was clear she said, "Paigey?"

I smiled. "Hey, babe. Wanna make a surprise breakfast for Brother?"

Ellis's eyebrow lifted. "Breakfast in bed?" he mused, not so-subtly. "I see you, Michaels. Wasting no time."

I snorted as Linc worked to hold the inhale he'd just taken off the joint we were passing around. "Dude," he scoffed, still holding his breath, then released. "My sister was there too."

Ellis made an *ooo* noise, and I laughed as we all sat bundled in a little huddle at the cove.

After Maisie and I surprised Linc with french toast and bacon, the three of us went to the old movie theater. Since it was Christmas Eve, they always played a few holiday classics—*for only three bucks a person*—you just had to dodge any ceiling tiles that may fall on you.

Like a game.

Then we met up with Ellis back at my house, so Gram could watch Maisie while we went and took part in our *other* birthday tradition.

Smoking weed we found the old-fashioned sketchy way—on a side street near the boardwalk.

Linc handed me the joint next and I took my little baby puff, coughing through both the inhale and the exhale, passing it to Ellis, while simultaneously trying to breathe.

"Your perfect lungs always reject the fun, Pip," Linc chuckled, pulling me into him as he used one of the big rocks as a backrest.

His hands around my waist relaxed me a bit, and my lungs slowly expanded. It reminded me of the night we came here after we kissed for the first time a couple of months ago, and a warmth settled in my chest

He was right, though. I pretty much only smoked on his birthday, and it showed.

Ellis took his puff, then another, then handed the joint back to Linc. "Did you get him a creepy little moon box too?"

"Hey," I said as Linc chuckled. "I love my music box."

The truth was, I hadn't given Linc his present yet. I'd spent an obscene amount of time on it, and up until today, I was sure he'd love it. But I was hoping the weed would relax me enough to actually give it to him when we went back to my house.

Linc took a drag off the joint, I could see the tip illuminating in my peripherals. A moment later, his hand lifted to my cheek, pulling me toward his mouth.

I thought he just wanted a kiss, which I was always down to give him, but then a trickle of smoke caught in my throat. His hand was still hooked around my waist, and his fingers were dancing just below my three layers—jean jacket, flannel, tank top.

I breathed in, the smoke burned a bit, but I held it in my chest as he gave me a small peck, then pulled his face away, and I coughed through the heavy exhale but no smoke came out.

"Damn," I muttered, and the boys chuckled.

Linc handed the joint over to Ellis and I sat up, suddenly.

I felt bad . . . for a second, I kind of forgot he was here.

Still, sitting up, something about the quick movement made me feel even higher, and I giggled at the floaty feeling in my head.

"Uh oh," Ellis chuckled.

"We lost her," Linc laughed, still holding my waist.

I huffed another laugh, glancing back and forth between them, then at the joint. "Think we can pass it between all three of us?" my floaty brain wondered out loud.

Ellis let out a sound—*of praise or surprise, I couldn't be sure*— then he said, "Paige Michaels wants to try a three-way shotgun? You turn eighteen, get a boyfriend, and think you're a little badass or something?"

My eyes narrowed. "Always been a badass, Batman."

Ellis chuckled. "You're damn right." Then he sat up. "All right. What's the order? My vote is Paige goes last." He looked at me. "No offense—just from a lung capacity standpoint."

"How is that not offensive?" I interjected, but it was ignored when Ellis simply looked at Linc.

Linc's chin tilted toward me, studying me for a second, a silent question of consent—*"You want to do this?"*

I guess I hadn't really thought about it. It was just a silly little path my brain decided to take in an attempt to make sure Ellis wasn't feeling left out—which I wasn't even sure if he was or if I was just . . . high.

I was probably just high.

But I gave a small shrug, suddenly curious. *"Why not?"* I silently told him back with a small tilt of my chin.

After another second, Linc said, "Ellis, me, Pip. That's the order."

I nodded and a sudden rush of excitement took me by surprise. It was the same feeling I got when Linc was watching me or when we were telling each other about our dirty dreams—it was lit with that same deep dark desire I had kept all to myself until recently when Linc wanted to know any and everything I've ever fantasized about. It was sweet—how much he wanted to turn me on.

And I was suddenly *very* curious to see my two favorite guys in a near-kiss.

LINC

Ellis's eyes lifted back at me with challenge and I chuckled, taking one more peek down at my pretty girlfriend, high as a fucking kite.

Her big blue eyes were curiously glancing between Ellis and me, and Ellis said, "We can use our hands."

Paige inhaled sharply. It wasn't audible, but I could feel it because my arm was still around her waist.

She didn't want us to use our hands.

My eyebrows lifted and so did my lips.

She liked watching two guys?

I fucking loved learning something new about her. It happened less and less the longer we knew each other, but since we'd started officially dating, there'd been a few surprises.

I wasn't sure I could really deliver on this one since I had zero interest in kissing anyone but her, but . . . I could shotgun with Ellis.

My fingers snuck back under Paige's jean jacket, and then under her other layers, just enough to lightly rub the soft skin above her hip, letting the warmth of our bodies fuel my objective.

Give my girl what she wants.

She let me watch her all the time. It was the least I could do.

When I turned to Ellis and didn't lift my hand, he understood and scooted a little closer.

Paige sat forward a bit, still in the *V* of my legs, as Ellis leaned into me. His mouth ticked up in the corner, and after a second, so did mine. I understood silently that *he knew* this was working Paige up too.

I mean, he was her other best friend. Maybe she'd talked to him about this stuff before.

Either way, it felt like some early-2000s movie where two hot girls were about to make out on a dare or something.

But it didn't matter—turning Paige on in *any* capacity turned me on. My obsession with her was endless.

Ellis took the drag, inhaled deep, and then closed the last bit of distance between us.

With my arm still around Paige, my fingers lightly brushed along her hip as I opened my mouth, not even an inch from my friend's lips, and I accepted the smoke.

Our lips brushed, his breath was hot and foreign on my tongue, tasting like the skunky weed we were passing around.

But I inhaled deep and kept my face close to his. Paige's fingers gripped my thigh a little tighter, and the corners of my mouth ticked up, stirring the erection that was pretty much ready to tag in any time she was around.

I could *feel* more than *see* her mystified gaze as Ellis released the rest of his exhale, and I closed my mouth. He smiled, just as the smallest noise from Paige turned both of our faces toward her, our noses bumping slightly in the process.

Ellis chuckled softly, but I was still holding the smoke. He clapped my shoulder and gave me the smallest nudge toward her, but said, "I see adventure in your future, bud."

My smile grew as I inched my face toward Paige. She did too, though there was a blazing heat in her eyes that made me crash my lips against hers.

I still released the smoke slowly, in waves, so she could breathe it in between my kisses. I licked my tongue inside her mouth—*I couldn't help it*—before I pulled my lips from hers.

She released one small cough, and a puff of smoke came with it before we cheered, falling into a pile on the rocks, laughing.

Laughing, laughing, laughing.

After a few long seconds with Paige on my lap, Ellis on hers and my torso draped over Ellis's legs, Paige said, "Oh man, guys. The threesome rumors . . ."

Only a beat passed before we all burst into laughter again.

Hours later, I laid in Paige's bed, her cheek on my chest, while I ran my fingers through her messy blond waves.

Ellis came back for the holiday fun until his dad called and asked him to come home. Darlene and Maisie had passed out about halfway through *The Muppets' Christmas Carol* and that's when Paige and I snuck away for a bit.

It had been a great fucking day. It always was—*she* always made it special—but we hadn't had a second alone. I nestled my nose into her hair and took a deep breath.

"You liked watching me and Ellis earlier," I said, in a half-dazed state.

Her hold around my torso tightened as she shoved her nose into my chest with a small whine, "Why are you always paying attention?"

I chuckled. "It was hard to miss," I murmured against her hair, then pressed my lips to kiss her head.

She cleared her throat and sat up a bit. "I—uh . . ." she trailed off, then gave a quick shake of her head. "I hope you don't think it's weird. I just . . ." She seemed to lose her words again.

Nervous.

I sat up too and pulled her into me, quickly saying, "No." I hugged her closer. "Never weird."

God, I was a fucking simp for her—*and I didn't care.* I literally couldn't help but touch her now that I was allowed to. I just had to trust her that she'd tell me if I was being too much.

She hadn't yet. She met my touch with one of her own, running her fingers through my hair. "It's not like I want you running around making out with dudes," she said quietly.

I chuckled, pressing my lips to hers. "It's fine, Pip. I knew you were into it."

She sighed. "You're both just so . . . *obnoxiously* hot. And I just—" she stopped herself, but then released her breath.

I smiled. "You think I'm hot?"

Her palms dragged down her face but her eyes glared. Another second passed, and I decided to take pity on her. "No explanation necessary, Pip. I just wanted to make sure I wasn't reading it wrong."

Her blue eyes became a bit lighter in the soft glow of her bedroom, and her mouth ticked up at the corner. Her eyes flicked down, then back up, and she shrugged. "I don't know. I definitely wouldn't like seeing you kiss some girl—or *some guy*, for that matter," she said, quietly. "But I was just . . . *curious* and we trust Ellis. I knew he wouldn't take it too far."

My mouth pinched at the corner, and I pressed my lips to her hairline, then leaned back against the headboard and brought her with me, breathing deep.

I huffed a small laugh at a sudden thought, and she said, "What?"

I sighed, threading our fingers together. "It's just . . . interesting. You've been in a bunch of plays where you had to kiss guys and it only ever made me crazy jealous. Though, I guess I see what you mean. I definitely paused the *Rent* stills on your kiss with Margaret."

Shamefully, I'd "wrestled" to that image too.

She gave me a playful elbow nudge and sat up quickly, turning toward me. Her eyes looked the tiniest bit heavier—tired, but intrigued. "You were jealous?" A smirk tilted her mouth, and my eyes followed the curve of her pillowy bottom lip, but I laughed.

"Uh-yeah, Pip. Where do you think two-a-days came from?" I chuckled again.

Her mouth sloped with a small shake of her head. "Aw, I'm sorry . . ."

I leaned in, kissing her lips—trying to catch the apology and eat it—but then I pulled back a bit, keeping my forehead pressed against hers. "Don't feel bad. You're amazing on stage. All I've ever wanted is for you to look at me the way you looked at them."

Her eyes pinched. "At them?"

I shrugged. "Yeah, like in the moon movie with Ellis, when you're staring up at him on the hill."

I kept the fact that I'd paused on that frame so many times I felt like the computer itself was judging me—for more *wholesome* reasons than the still of her and Margaret.

The expression she gave at the end of the movie was devastating. The big blue eyes staring up at the Fisherman like he was her whole world.

She lifted her chin, a small smile pulling. "But that's fake."

I shrugged, awkwardly. "You make it look real."

In an instant, she straddled my lap and held my jaw with each of her hands. My fingers gripped her waist immediately.

I grazed the soft sweatpants she'd changed into before the earlier game of charades, and my hands traveled up to her bare skin on her lower belly, peeking out below her *Nightmare Before Christmas* crop top.

So. Fucking. Cute.

And I was hers.

She leaned down, taking my lips, and her tongue slid to mine, caressing and tangling. A low hum buzzed through my chest as she raked her fingers through my hair—*tugging*—something I'd gathered she loved, *and fuck, so did I.*

There was possession in her touch as she held me in place, exploring my mouth with licks and nibbles—we could lose ourselves to it for hours.

But she gave a small bite to my bottom lip, then kissed me again before she pulled back. "I love you, Linc. I've been feeling weird about saying it . . ."

I pulled her into me, hugging her this time. She was basically in a sloth formation around my torso while I held her, sitting on the bed, and I shoved my face into her neck. "I love you too, Paige. You know that. I was nervous to say it too."

She tightened her hold around me, and we stayed there for long seconds, wrapped in each other, wrapped in love.

After another moment passed, she exhaled hard. "Do you want your birthday present?"

My fingers trailed along her lower back. *I already have everything I need,* I thought.

She laughed. "*I* am not your present, you goob."

I chuckled too. "Okay, but do you have to get off my lap to give it to me?"

A soft laugh pulled her away. She gave me a kiss and stood up. "Stay there," she said.

I sat up, adjusting my boner. I was getting pretty good at it—like a card trick.

Paige shuffled over to her closet and pulled out a guitar, turning around. "The guitar isn't the present. It's—it's Jack's—he let me borrow it."

My eyes widened. "You're learning guitar?"

She shook her head. "No, not really. I mean, maybe—but . . ." she trailed off, and I smiled. She took another breath and sat down at the foot of the bed. "I just learned one song."

I fought the urge to take out my camera. She seemed nervous, so I sat back, already filled with wonderment as she took a deep breath, then started to strum.

My smile stretched at the intro chords—*her face*—as she watched her fingers. The moonlight from the window caught her profile and outlined her lips as she started to sing.

And *good fucking God,* it was *beautiful.*

Everything about it.

She sang about *being someone,* belonging—finding hope through the tragedy of circumstance.

As I watched her, my beautiful girl singing *our* song, I couldn't help but remember the first time we heard it, right after my dad left.

Paige suggested a drive, but we were ten . . .

We were sitting in Darlene's parked station wagon in their driveway, pretending we were on a road trip.

"Guess it's not just the musical Oklahoma! *that sucks. So does the weather," Paige mumbled from the passenger's seat just as a series of acoustic chords repeated through the speakers a few times, and a raspy voice started to sing.*

We stopped talking or looking out the windows. We just listened.

The words found their way to my chest, swelling and mixing all of the nervous and unknown feelings while the hand holding mine—her hand—ironed the anger, the fear, into something softer. Warmer.

I looked down at the music player, seeing "Fast Car" by Tracy Chapman running across the screen.

It felt like the kind of song that existed just so people could play it loudly, windows down, cruising down the freeway—and like the imaginary wind from our trip, the chords blew a refreshing breeze through me.

I wasn't sure if it was just what I needed to hear or if there was magic in the music.

Darlene had said that once. She said, "Songs were songs, but moments made the music," and I think it stuck with us.

The feeling of the song had the essence of escape while carrying the weight of something real. Steadfast.

Hopeful.

My mom was going to need me. My sister needed me.

But my breaths filled with a different air as I looked at Paige, as I listened to the song. I realized that it wasn't the fact that we were pretending to be on a road trip—pretending to escape—that was making me feel better.

I realized I was in the presence of someone I didn't have to pretend with. That this moment steadily and surely sucked, and I didn't have to pretend it didn't.

Not with her.

Even though she was really good at make-believe, I thought, just as her song ended. Emotion clogged my throat as I stared back at her. She learned the song that was ours, but the song itself was just so special.

That day, when he left, it felt like any room I'd made for him in my heart freed up and she slid in seamlessly. Like it was her place all along.

I leaned into her, kissing her again, telling her I loved her.

And I did. I loved her so fucking much.

"Happy birthday, baby," she said, and I melted.

CHAPTER 33
LINC

I have no words.

Fuck, I thought they were dead. Thankfully, they're just sleeping. A deep sleep, it would seem. I came in and saw them through the windows, lying in a pile on the porch.

In front of them now, I see the bottle of tequila with a healthy dent missing. Empty glasses sit on either side of their heads, as they lie—*limbs akimbo*—on a blanket below me.

Paige's arm is over Ellis's face, and one of his legs is crossed over both of hers, while their other hands are loosely holding each other's between them. They look like they're fighting *and* snuggling.

If I play with the light, fill in some shadows on their faces . . .

I pull out my phone and take a couple of shots. After I take a few, I scroll through them, zooming in on her in the last picture.

Her cropped black tank top is showing off her toned stomach—but her arms are covered by a copper-colored flannel. It looks so pretty against her blue hair.

I zoom in on her face, peaceful with sleep, then I blink—remembering the sight is right in front of me.

She's right in front of me.

Slowly, I move to the side of the blanket that she's lying on and crouch down just a little bit.

God, she's so pretty. The thoughts I've carried of her for years just don't do her justice. My memories *miss* things—like the small part in her lips, the deeper breaths she takes when a small breeze swirls around us. Her smell.

My Pip.

Not yours anymore.

My fingers twitch with need. An urge so insistent, I stand up quickly, shoving my hands in my pockets.

God, I want to touch her—even more than that, I want her to touch me. *Her hands, her touch, her fingers.*

The feeling is still heightened, but unlike other people who have unfortunately made the mistake of touching me in the last few years, it's not an . . . *unhinged,* explosive feeling.

Last night, when she let me hold her. When she held me back . . .

Her touch is a landing—a small pocket of gravity where none existed. *Her* fingers threaten to pull everything that's only lived in the clouds of my brain for years down to the ground.

And don't even get me started on what it feels like to touch *her.*

It's fucking everything.

And *that's* the kind of obsessive-thinking that I can't trust.

I can't risk it. Just because our embrace last night didn't turn into that explosive, trapped panic doesn't mean it won't—and it's even riskier with her.

I've hurt her before. I hurt her, and I loved her more than anything or anyone. So, if I'm capable of that, then there's just no fucking way I can be trusted.

But I can't just leave them out here.

I walk over to Ellis and nudge his foot with mine. It only gets me a grunt from him before I do it again, a little harder, and he snorts. "No, why," he groans.

Paige curls into him, taking away the *fight* part of their position and only leaving the snuggle. But he blinks slowly with another stuttered groan, "You are not a Hemsworth," but still, he pulls her into him for a second with a hug, and she returns it.

Her eyes flutter but they still barely open when she whispers, "Ellis," through a sleepy smile.

Do they even know I'm here yet?

It feels like I'm watching a private moment and a dark whirl of jealousy spins through my stomach—a punch to the gut. It's the first time I've been *envious* of close proximity. But it . . . it looks nice with them. *Comfortable.*

I clear my throat, awkwardly, to make my presence known.

Ellis is the only one that reacts. Paige looks like she fell back asleep, but her body is so curled into his, I can't quite tell.

He stays lying down for another second, then wobbles to sit up. Using the heel of his palm, he rubs one of his eyes and shakes his head. The only light is at the corner of the door, but even now I can see his eyes are bloodshot, glassy. *Still drunk.*

It takes about ten minutes to put the drunk giraffe—*Ellis*—to bed before I'm standing outside again.

Part of me wonders if I should just let her sleep out here. I can sit in the chair, make sure she's okay . . .

But the ground can't be comfortable.

I crouch down in front of her. She's curled up on her side, but her face is mostly covered by a wild drape of silvery-blue mayhem. My fingers twitch again, and this time, I allow my shaky hand to reach out.

My fingers inch toward her face—but a flashing fear that I'll find bloodshot, watery eyes, breaking and crumbling, makes me pause. I take a breath, remembering the picture I just took. Her soft lips, her peaceful face.

After another breath, I continue my way to her face and push back her hair, seeing that her eyes are closed, and my shoulders relax a bit.

"P-Pip?" I rasp.

Her eyes stay closed, but they flinch and her eyebrows scrunch. After a second, she sighs heavily and mumbles, "Still on the floor."

Fuck. I don't know what that means, but I think it means the only way she's getting up is with help . . .

My help.

I swallow hard, looking at the sliding door, then back through the windows, past the kitchen, down the hall that leads to her room. That's my route.

My next plan is to figure out how I'll pick her up. I'm not worried about lifting her, but I'm plotting where I'll put my hands.

One arm under the knees, the other behind her back, both hands will touch her too.

And God, do I want it. *Too much.*

I take another breath and stand again, walking behind her, I release an exhale and bend, inhaling sharply when I cradle her small weight in my arms and easily lift her.

She clutches onto me, her fingers charging my skin, rippling goosebumps down my arms and fire through my veins. A grunt pushes past my lips just as her head settles in the crook of my neck.

Holy fuck.

I didn't anticipate that. I hold her tighter, squeezing her so hard—*fuck, I might be hurting her*—the thought loosens my grip, but I lock my knees.

Jesus. Her smell. Not even the heavy dose of tequila takes away from the spice and citrus. It's just . . . *fucking ethereal.*

I want to live in a cloud of it. Encased in the sky, in a space where *this* is my only air.

Her featherlight fingers wiggle a bit on the fabric of my T-shirt over my chest, and then loosen, bringing me back to now— to *her in my arms.*

I look back up at my route.

After I put her to bed, I won't get to hold her anymore.

You shouldn't be holding her now.

With a heavy exhale, I walk us through the living room. Slowly. *Dying* to keep *this. This* exact weight in my arms, *this* smell, *this* person. *My person.*

Not yours anymore, my asshole brain reminds me *again.*

But why does she still feel like mine?

My mouth flattens as I slow my steps even more once we reach her hallway.

"You have to let go, Linc."

I cringe, stopping in my tracks and slamming my eyes shut. *Fuck. I can't—that voice—*

I hear a small inhale below me and my eyes shoot open, peering down, my chest jumping when I find Paige's tired, hooded eyes staring up at me.

Two sapphires shining from their sleepy cave.

I just want to keep holding her. Breathing her in. Maybe hear her sing again.

My room . . . I could take her to my room.

The thought whips past my brain too fast to do anything but tighten my jaw. My hand below her ass grips her tighter, same with the one hooked around her back, as she lifts her hand. My fingers dig into her skin harder but she's undeterred, as she softly cups my cheek with her hand.

My teeth clench to keep what I can only assume would have been a humiliating moan from pushing past my lips. But an inhale pulls through my nose, and just before the adrenaline has a chance to take a turn, her thumb . . . *rubs.* It's a soft touch, using just the pad to lightly massage the tension at the back of my jaw.

She doesn't say anything, and I don't either. But . . . it's helping—what she's doing. She's helping.

I wiggle my jaw a bit as the tightness soothes all the way down through my neck and shoulders.

The corners of her perfect rosy lips lift as her eyes remain barely open. She whispers, *"I can touch you,"* in a daze, and I wish I could keep the small sparkle in her eyes—keep it with the change in my pocket to hold when everything's becoming too much. And something about the realization really sinks its teeth into me.

She's right.

She can touch me.

I'm certain of it now more than ever that *her* hands aren't the same as others, and I lean my face into her palm. I also realize that if she's saying *that,* she recognizes me as *this* person. The one who hurt her.

And somehow, sleepy or not, she's still looking at me like I'm not a monster.

Jesus, I can't believe I'm still standing.

Put her to bed.

Begrudgingly, I listen to myself, and I find it in me to move again just as Paige's hand drops. I want it back, but I *have* to move or the last of my self-control will snap.

And that's when it will *definitely* get bad.

I push through her door, carrying her over to the bed. I pause another second, looking down at her and see she's fallen back asleep, her mouth open wider now.

I sigh, finally placing her down on the mattress, daring again to push some hair off her face before I pull the blanket at the foot of the bed over her.

A small pitter-patter sound slopes my eyebrows down, but then I quickly remember—*Cheeto.* Peeking around to the other side of the bed, I see the whimsical little terrarium, and two big gray eyes meet mine through the glass.

It's a strange eye-contact, but I find myself dipping my chin in a quick greeting, finding a pile of Paige's clothes at my feet.

I guess she emptied out her bag. *Maybe that means she's planning to stay?*

Before I have time to decide whether or not that's a good thing, my eyes catch on a specific article of clothing.

A pair of underwear I recognize . . .

My heart free falls, spiraling endlessly as my unblinking eyes widen down at them. They're simple and white, with honey bees and little dotted lines along the waistline, marking their flight patterns.

My eyes jerk along the dotted line.

Tick. Tick. Tick.

A myriad of images shutter through my brain, each one flashing into the next and I slam my eyes shut.

Yanking the panties off. Throwing them to the floor. Her.

I cringe, but my dick also hardens, and a shaky inhale tuts through my nose.

Sick, sick, sick.

A coldness sweeps my limbs and something darker takes hold. The sensation almost feels like it's taking the images I'm fighting off and baring its teeth at the memories like a feral animal, and my eyes snap back open, wide and unblinking at the small piece of cotton.

Bad ideas . . .

Don't do it.

Don't do it, don't do it.

But I do.

In one fluid movement—like I'm dancing *Swan fucking Lake*—I swipe the panties off the floor. Just the *feel* of the fabric sends a chill down my spine, and I quickly walk out of the room, shoving them in my pocket as I keep my chin down.

Ugh. It feels like the walls are staring at me and I don't blame them.

I'm sick. Disgusting.

I squeeze the fabric tighter in my hand, in my pocket, my steps becoming quicker toward my room.

I make it—pushing through the door and inhaling deep as I press my back to close it behind me. My eyes blink past the spots in my vision. My hips swiveling, seeking friction against my painfully hard dick.

I groan, tightening my hold on the panties in my pocket, rubbing the material between my fingers.

"Fuck *me,*" I grit out. Holding onto the underwear, I drop my bottoms.

Shirt.

I follow the silent, inner command without question, my breathing picking up. I glance around my dark bedroom for a minute, reminding myself of where I am.

Alone. Alone in my room.

I groan as my arousal swells, but with it also comes . . . disturbance.

Paige. Chained. Writhing on a couch beneath me. On her stomach.

But I gasp, when I see . . . *the vision is . . . different.*

Her blond hair is . . . blue. She twists so that she's on her back, crossing her wrists above her head and stretching her gorgeous body out below me. Her face isn't devastated, her eyes aren't filled with tears.

They're a glittering sea of fucking want.

She moans this breathy noise and arches her tits up to me in offering.

I cover the calluses on my hand the best I can with the help of the soft material clutched in my palm, shielding the roughness, stroking myself slowly up and down.

A sharp inhale pulls through my nose.

Fucking Christ.

My eyes squeeze tighter shut. Grasping at the thought of her . . . *her blue eyes begging.*

I suck one of her nipples into my mouth, teasing it with my tongue.

Her arms are chained but there's no blood or cuts. She's just fucking gorgeous and squirming and warm and . . . willing.

We're alone. We're alone in my room.

My hand moves faster at the thought of her below me, her warmth, her wet, her *fucking smell.*

My hand pumps faster.

Hot, tight.

Her. Paige. Pip . . .

And I feel it. My breathing picks up. It starts low and rises furiously as I fucking *erupt*—coming so hard I swear to God, I'm floating the Milky Way—unable to touch back down.

Falling into the wall, the rough surface scratches against my bare ass and knocks me back to Earth.

Back to my room.

"Fuuuck," I hiss.

I came *immediately*. And so fucking hard. Even now I'm see-ing stars. Guess it's been longer than I thought.

But I blink suddenly and my eyes pull down, scrunching at the sight.

Paige's underwear are a sticky mess in my hand, wrapped around my dick.

I am so fucked.

CHAPTER 34
PAIGE

Stumbling out of my room, my feet drag toward the kitchen—*definitely* still drunk.

I need water.

Ugh. I'm supposed to make a plan today. *Past* Paige really is a bitch. But the first of my plans should be a detox.

My head tilts with heaviness, my eyes blinking, following the early-morning twilight spilling through the massive windows. As I reach the kitchen, I grab a water bottle from the fridge and drink the whole thing, then grab another one.

Just as I start to take a few sips, the sound of a door opening startles me. My body twists toward the noise and I see Linc walking in from what I *think* is the garage.

Buffy fucking bless . . .

My eyes bulge at the rugged sweaty man closing the door, his hazel gaze immediately finding me, penetrating through the fog of my drunkenness, and I'm stuck to the spot. Keeping his eyes on me, he pulls out his ear buds and says, "H-Hey," through a heavy breath, but my eyes are trapped.

He's fucking *ripped.* In my mind, I've already run my fingers along the divots and ridges. *And the tattoos . . .*

Obviously, I've seen them already, but I haven't really *looked* at them.

That's the thing with avoidance . . . you don't get to explore if you're hiding. I'm still too far to really make out any details, but I want to study them like hieroglyphics.

He'd always wanted tattoos, but said he thought they should come with stories.

Maybe *they'd* tell me what the hell is going on.

"Was just getting some water," I slur through a mumble.

Well, if there was any question—I am *definitely* still hammered. Looking at the clock on the stove, I see it's just after six, and I yawn at the sight.

"Y-You feeling okay?" Linc takes a couple steps closer to me, and my chest jumps again. He steps into the light of the kitchen, and I take another breath, trying to get my shit together.

Luckily, he still keeps some distance—I don't trust my leftover drunkenness not to lean over and lick him or something.

When my eyes float up from his sweaty rippled torso, I meet his stare, tilting my head when I see him looking at me, expectantly. *Right. He asked me if I was feeling okay.*

I nod, jaggedly. It's the only response I seem to be able to give, but as a greenish glint in his eyes catches the morning light from the windows, an image of his face flashes through my mind.

This version of him. His piercing, haunted eyes, his inked fingers holding me in the dark, carrying me.

"You carried me to bed," I say quietly, through my haze.

Linc's jaw tightens, and I vaguely remember the feeling of his stubble beneath my fingertips. *I touched him.*

"You guys fell asleep on the porch," he says slowly.

That checks out. The tequila took a turn and it ended up being a "Gram's Best Hits" night—tumbling through our favorite memories, songs. I cried, of course, but it felt good. And I wasn't alone.

Which was . . . nice.

And infuriating. It happened so many times last night—I was struck over and over again with how it could have been this way all along. And all it does is remind me.

Of *why* Linc's kept me away.

The thought turns my stomach, as it has *every time* since I've thought about it since he spewed the vile combination of words to me a couple nights ago.

But even through the tequila haze, I'm able to recall what Ellis said last night.

Careful. Take it slow.

As Linc's eyes watch me cautiously, I feel mine sharpen the longer I study his features. It feels like I'm watching different versions of him flickering through slides before me.

Six, in his Batman shirt.

Nine, with his skateboard scar.

Thirteen, dressed as Angel from Buffy *on Halloween.*

Sixteen, in the driver's seat. Our first real *drive.*

And eighteen, where he looked at me like I was everything. And then it disappeared.

It was stolen, some deep part of myself reminds me, and I feel the anger push past my buzz. A sobering rock in my chest.

And now there's just this. Just him, just me. *These* versions of us. Another beat passes, but our eyes hold each other's, it's just long enough for my hurt to deepen a bit more before I whisper, "I'm so mad at you."

His eyes drop with a frown as he releases a pained sigh. It's only a second before his eyes pull back up, murmuring, "I-I deserve your anger." He shoves his hands into his pockets and *God. I just want to shake him.*

I physically move to do so, but stop myself as he tenses. My feet halt a few inches away—not touching him—and his eyes are only able to keep mine for a few seconds at a time

"I'm not mad at you for *that*," I tell him, honestly.

Heeding Ellis's warning, I can't breach *that* subject right now and honestly, it's *not* why I'm mad at him. But the pause is just enough that I lose some of my nerve. My body suddenly wobbles a bit, and I grab onto the counter to steady myself.

"A-Are you okay? Do y-you need to sit?"

A low noise rumbles in my throat. *God,* he's always been *so fucking sweet* to me, and it's squeezing my tequila-soaked brain at the moment.

My deep breath only makes things worse, sending a delirious wave through my head. I swear, I actually get high from the addition of sweat to his oceany-forest smell. My fingers grip the counter harder, and I finally force my eyes up to his.

I take another deep breath, then use the remaining booze and my *sheer will* to make this happen.

To confront this.

"*Fear and bravery—tomato, tomato,*" I hear Gram say in my mind, and it straightens my posture.

My knees shake, but I lock them and stand my ground as I finally say, "I'm mad at you for leaving me, Linc." My voice is hoarse and ready to break.

Just looking at him *while* I'm telling him this is breaking my heart. I've imagined this moment so many times, but *never* did it feel like this.

Like I can feel all my pain from the past seven years staring right back at me. In the form of a face I've longed to see since he left.

His eyes are glassy, distraught, and It looks like every muscle in his body is being tightened. His jaw ticks, and he grits out, "I-I'm sorry, P-Pip. I-I h-had to go."

Because of "what he did."

My eyes fill at the impossibility of this task. *How* do I convince him he's wrong when I can't talk to him about the memory we're disputing? Not without the risk of a traumatic blackout, anyway, according to Ellis.

And the only argument I have is my word against his.

But I *know* I'm right.

Suddenly, an idea comes to mind. A new tactic, but it will require more fear-bravery.

I take a sip of water as he still stares down at me, unmoving, and then I breathe deeply.

Keep going. Till the end.

Two affirmations find and fuel my cause, straighten my spine. I clear my throat, and then my voice rasps, "I—I thought," I choke on air, terrified to give voice to the thing I've *thought* kept him away.

Like our dirty dream confessions when we first started dating. *If I share mine, maybe he'll share his.*

But the shame feels as real as the morning I woke up and found his note. The day I locked all of my hauntings in the music box he gave me and hid anything I could keep deep inside myself.

"Rage. Rage, against the dying of the light."

Linc steps just a bit closer, and I take another breath. "I thought, after what happened, after I . . ." I trail off, but somehow manage to push the rest of the words through. "I thought you were disgusted by me. And I thought . . . leaving was easier than telling me." The words barely make it past my lips.

There's a wounded, childish tone to my voice, but I can't help it. It hurts *so fucking much.*

"God, no, Pip." In an instant, Linc is scooping me up. The heat from his biceps shoots a spark somewhere deep just as he places me on the counter.

The browns and greens in his eyes lock with mine, directly in front of me as our noses graze, and I gasp. "Fuck," he grits between clenched teeth, as his hands release my hips.

But they only move to grip the edge of the counter on either side of me. Our panting breath tangles between us, and I suddenly feel even more drunk.

Holy shit.

The charge between our eyes holds like bottled lightning. He blinks, only once, before his deep, hoarse voice takes my breath. "Never. I could *never* think that about you."

I don't have time to respond because his mouth collides with mine. In an earth-shattering, soaring, sky-rocketing moment—I feel locked and loaded.

Fucking blast off.

My anger evaporates and the shame curling my limbs releases. A noise aches in my throat as my mouth moves against his, sipping his lips like they're the fountain to my soul—drinking him in and swallowing his hungry groans as he pushes his tongue past my lips.

Knocking my head against the cabinet behind me, I latch onto his jaw, fingernails burrowing and scraping across his coarse stubble.

"Perfect," he growls under his breath while he's devouring my mouth, positioning my neck in a way where he can reach every inch, murmuring, "My perfect, *beautiful*, fucking girl."

God, his praise—the rough reverence in his voice makes me want to get down on my goddamn knees. To hear him call me *his.* A hand moves to my throat, and I whimper around his tongue—*his fucking words*—as he licks into my mouth again.

Good fucking God, I forgot how good he was at this. *Even better than he used to be,* I think.

Maybe he's had practice . . .

I flinch, and the thought pulls my mouth from his, but we're both panting heavily, gasping.

"I'm sorry—" he says, backing away.

I hop down from the counter, "No, it's not—"

"No, I shouldn't—I'm sorry," he says again, and before I can even fucking exhale, he's rushing down the hallway toward his room.

Shit.

After tossing and turning on the bed and getting exactly *zero* more hours of sleep, I've finally showered and I think *mostly* sobered up.

Standing in front of the mirror of the en suite bathroom, I take in my cleaner appearance. My eyes look a little closer to a Robin's egg blue—*brighter*—than they have in my last couple of reflections. And the damp, frosty-colored waves spilling over my bare shoulders look at least moderately tame. My eyes stare back at myself, following the neckline of my tank top.

I can nearly feel *his breath on my collar bone—*hear *the echo of his deep voice pulling through me.*

"My perfect, beautiful, fucking girl."

A shiver runs down my spine and I give my head a quick shake. Sliding a hair tie on my wrist, I snap it once—mostly as an attempt to *snap me* out of *Morrowland*—but the *snap* jingles the rest of the bracelets.

My eyes flick down to the purple lace wrapped around my wrists, counting the assortment of bracelets stacked together on top of them.

I step back into the bedroom, shuffling over toward my clothing pile.

Bending down, I grab the first flannel I see from the heap, a soft, dark blue, and I shrug it over my shoulders then take a breath.

"Dark Blue" by Jack's Mannequin starts to play in my head because it's just one of those things that you can't help but hear anytime the combination of words make themselves known. Plus, what a great fucking song.

After fidgeting and lingering in front of the door for a few more seconds, I finally push through it, and my feet carry me slowly down the hall, toward the kitchen. As I get closer, the images from mine and Linc's kiss start to come roaring back, and my steps wobble.

It fucking rocked me, and I still don't feel great, but I think that's at least partially from the anticipation of what awaits me at The Window.

When sleep seemed to be out of the question, I finally texted Jackson back.

Today, I'm supposed to make a plan.

I still don't have any plans for this plan—but dealing with the shit at The Window is a start.

In perfect Jackson fashion, he responded to my text with a phone call about an hour ago, telling me that Beck wants to speak with me before he leaves for India later this afternoon—which instantly made me want to tell him I was busy until midnight, but then Jackson threw me a curveball.

"I'm sorry, Blue. It's my responsibility to make sure you're safe when you're here. And I didn't do that. I'm truly sorry."

And it seemed . . . genuine. Sincere.

I immediately don't trust it. Though, I'm not sure it's Jackson I don't trust in this scenario. But I have to deal with it at some point.

I clear my throat—pushing the nagging feeling away as I reach the kitchen. I can see Ellis sprawled out on the couch in the living room, a small towel over his forehead. "How are you vertical?" he groans, his eyes seemingly hidden under the washcloth.

I breathe a laugh. "I'm diagonal," I mutter, slightly hunched. Walking over to the fridge, I grab a water bottle for the road just as footsteps sound from Linc's hallway to the right of the kitchen.

"*Ugh.* Duuude you sound like the fucking Megazord stomping around," Ellis groans.

I think it's a *Power Rangers* reference, but I can't be sure. I dipped out on most of the superhero stuff when Linc came into the picture, but my breath catches in my throat as soon as I see him come into view.

At first, Linc's eyes are on Ellis, a smirk as he takes in his very hungover friend, before he sees me standing off to the side.

I suddenly want to see him smile more than anything. *He almost did it just now.* He looks at the keys in my hand, then asks, "Are y-you going to The Window?"

My brain is mush.

He's so goddamn gorgeous. And right now, his dark, thick hair looks damp, giving a shine to his earthy eyes. The chiseled corners of his jaw have the most delicious sprinkling of scruff.

My mind tumbles to the feeling of the coarse hair biting my cheeks—his mouth, his tongue.

"Earth to Paige," Ellis whines from the couch, and I swallow hard, blinking rapidly.

My eyes flick between Ellis still lying on the couch and Linc standing at the mouth of his hallway.

Finally, I nod like a dipshit, and I don't miss a groggy snicker from the *general couch direction.*

But my eyes anchor to Linc, the balance of colors in his eyes is heavy on the brown against his dark gray T-shirt, and he says, "They wanna see me too."

A sharp inhale pulls through my nose, my heart fluttering. I mean, I guess it makes sense, seeing as he was there. But I wonder why they didn't talk to him last night while he was at the club. "They want to meet with us together?"

Ellis's groan interrupts us as he sits up, rubbing his eyes with a pinching motion of his fingers. Despite rubbing them a few times, they're still glassy and red as he squints down to the floor. "Do they know you two know each other?"

I'm about to tell him I have no idea when Linc speaks up, "Jackson does."

"Does Jackson know about your arrangement with Desmond?" I ask.

"How do *y-you know* about my arrangement with Desmond?"

My eyes flick to Ellis, and he sighs. Linc's eyes follow the noise and his mouth slopes down before his throat bobs. "A-Anything else you guys talked about that I should know before we go into this thing?"

It's Ellis's turn to look at me, and like the weird little wave of dominos this conversation has become, I look back over at Linc.

My mind works to sift through everything Ellis and I talked about last night. The only thing that seems relevant is the Veranda. So, I timidly explain what happened in the room— which at this point feels like ancient history.

When I get to the part where the boys were forcing me down on my knees, Linc barks out a cough. Or maybe a hybrid between a grunt and a gag, I'm not sure. Whatever the sound is, it's *unpleasant.*

"And that's when we came in?" he asks raggedly.

I nod quickly, and he exhales hard, almost like listening to my recount was as strenuous of a workout as he'd had this morning.

Before he kissed me.

The thought gets taken when Ellis says, "Try to see if either of you can get any more information on that Tariel guy. Even just a last name. I'm meeting with Wade this afternoon, maybe he can do a little digging."

"Wade?" Linc asks.

"His hacker," I clarify at the same time Ellis says, "Tech guy," while narrowing his eyes at me.

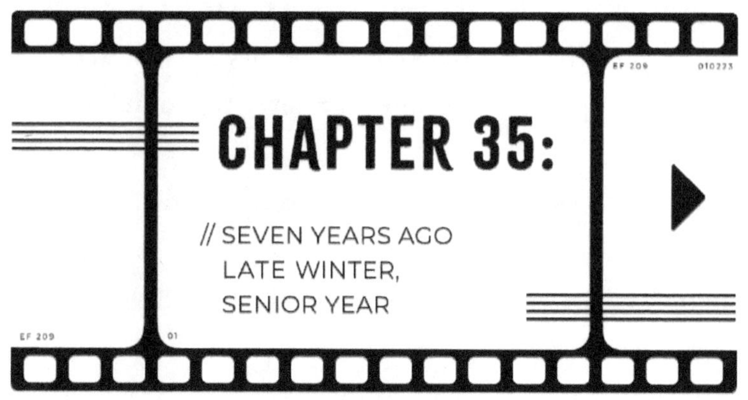

PAIGE

I walked between Ellis and Linc, holding Linc's hand down at my side, as we took hurried steps toward the building—*the venue*—for the play Mr. Harris was directing.

"So is it the whole apartment building?" I asked.

Ellis shook his head, peeking across me, toward Linc. "I don't think so," he said with a shrug. "I don't know. The only thing Mr. Harris said was that it's experimental, but the performances are only in certain units, and the doors will be physically open. I guess you're supposed to visit them in order."

Ugh. "This sounds weird for weird's sake," I whined.

Ellis groaned too. "Agreed."

"Hey, some of the best shit comes from weird ideas," Linc said through a chuckle.

I smirked, then scrunched my nose at him. "Did your pal *Jeremy* tell you that?"

His chest rumbled as he hugged me into him, whispering, "Such a brat," over my ear, and I giggled.

We'd recently learned that Linc and Mr. Harris were on a *first name basis,* and I couldn't help but give him shit.

I mean, we were all *pretty sure* Linc was Mr. Harris's star pupil, *but . . .*

I don't know. It *did* seem a little weird. But there were also plenty of faculty members at Providence that *I* called by their first name. *Caroline, the music director. Tam, the prop queen.*

I probably only thought it was strange because I didn't know Mr. Harris very well.

Being February, we were only about a month and a half into spring semester, so I had just started taking his film acting class a few weeks ago. And my only other interactions were the brief ones we'd had about *Without the Moon.*

A topic we were currently avoiding since all Linc could do was wait until the screening next month.

As we reached the building to the address, the three of us stood at the bottom of the stoop, our chins tilting up toward the three-story building like a haunted house.

I wasn't exactly looking forward to this, but I saw the value in supporting Mr. Harris. I mean, he'd already tried to get me a professional job with the *American Idiot* audition, and he hadn't even worked with me in any sort of official capacity.

But honestly, I was so fucking grateful for him just for having a vested interest in Linc—that *someone* at Providence looked past his empty pockets and saw his incredible talent.

Ellis walked up the few steps first, and Linc and I followed before Ellis looked at the security pad. My eyes squinted over him.

STORIES

A QR code.

Ellis pulled out his phone, and scanned it, then looked down at the screen, reading, "Welcome to a night of immersive raw performance. You, the audience, will simply be a fly on the wall as you visit the homes of the characters. Please visit the rooms in order, and do not interact with the talent. Your code to enter the building is below. We hope you enjoy our *Stories.*" He rolls his eyes. "I am not high enough for this."

"Yep, definitely gonna be weird," I said.

Linc sighed through a small laugh, "Maybe it'll be cool! You came around on *Donnie Darko.*"

"I came around on Jake Gyllenhaal," I muttered as Ellis put in the code to the door, then opened it.

He walked through and I followed. But just as we got inside, Linc pulled me into him, putting my back to his front, as he leaned down, his lips hovering over my ear. "Jake Gyllenhaal, huh?"

I pulled my lips into my mouth and twisted my chin toward him, shrugging playfully. "I'd watch you shotgun him."

Linc chuckled, then kissed the corner of my mouth, but our eyes simultaneously drifted up, realizing we were in the building, and we finally took in the space.

It wasn't very big. There was a staircase right by the entrance with three rows of mailboxes—about ten in each row. *Buffy bless, I can only hope the performances are in less than half of the units in the building.*

We started on the first floor, per the instructions, basically moving as one through the first four apartments, the last of which was empty.

Linc and I stood in the living room as Ellis walked through the archway into the kitchen, then started opening the cabinets.

"Hey!" I whisper-yelled, then wondered why. We were the only ones in here.

Ellis's eyes met mine, the green color lifting mischievously, then shrugged. "He said it was immersive."

I started toward the kitchen to pull Ellis out—*move this along.* I was promised a grilled cheese at Queenie's if I cooperated, but I gasped as I reached the kitchen. Through the window, I could see across the street, in another building, there was a guy staring into this apartment.

What the fuck?

"Linc," I said, but he was already right behind me.

"Whoa," Ellis said as he turned around, and I gathered that he saw the man too.

The guy was sitting at a table, well lit. He looked to be about thirty or so, and he was smoking a cigarette by his open window, just staring.

"Fucking creepy," Linc muttered, and we suddenly heard the door open, followed by violent arguing between a man and a woman.

Linc grabbed my waist and pulled me into him, as we heard what I *assumed* were the actors, playing out the scene in the living room.

Is it the actors?

The door was definitely open, and that meant this apartment is part of the show, right?

They came into view from the doorway in the kitchen, and I saw a younger woman with brown hair, she looked like she was crying, and a tall guy, built and bearded.

They were an attractive couple. A bit younger than the creepy guy staring into their apartment.

The man in the living room stormed past us, toward the fridge, and grabbed a beer. I looked back through the window, but saw the guy was gone.

I grabbed Linc's hand and started to inch our steps toward the door. Since the actors weren't acknowledging us—*thank God*—I felt fairly confident we could move.

When I heard some small chatter from what I could only assume was a few more audience members, I kept moving, pulling Linc with me, knowing he'd grab Ellis.

I kept my chin down, feeling awkward as fuck as we passed the girl crying in the living room, then a few more people walked in and started to watch.

As soon as we were in the hall, I took a deep breath.

"Jeez," Ellis said, and I nodded.

Linc's eyes squinted, still looking in the room.

"What?" I asked, fidgeting, still feeling . . . I don't know, *itchy.*

Linc's eyes peered down to me, with a small shake of his head. "I met that girl. The night Mr. Harris came to your show at Queenie's, she was with him."

My eyes scrunched, glancing back through the doorway, but I couldn't see the girl anymore. She was blocked by audience members.

"Huh," I said. "Is she his girlfriend, 'cause she might have a stalker."

Linc shrugged. "Not sure."

Ellis sighed. "All right, we've got four more rooms, you guys ready for floor two?"

Ugh. I just want grilled cheese.

By the final room, I was about ready to jump out of the window. We'd seen a young man living with his alcoholic and abusive mother, a woman ordering a male prostitute—it was just . . . uncomfortable.

"Last one," Linc said over my ear, and I whined into his neck.

This room looked crowded, at least—something I never thought I'd be grateful for.

This kind of shit went over my head. It wasn't entertaining to me. There was something just . . . *unsettling* about watching a "performance" in a nontheatrical space.

It was similar to a feeling I'd had watching a kid in our stage combat class turn reckless with the choreography—where we, the audience, were no longer engaged in the scene, but worried for his scene partner's safety. *This* had felt like an hour of *that* discomfort.

A crowd at least helped it feel more like a show.

We walked in, and the audience members seemed to be crowded to the far corner of the room. I was too short to see over people's heads, but I was able to see the arms of a couch.

There were whispers, I could hear a squeak—*maybe from the*

springs from the couch? But a sharp inhale pulled through my chest as I heard the unmistakable sound of a moan.

The heavy breathing filtered through my ears, and I grabbed onto Linc's hand and pulled myself into him. Tilting his chin down, he whispered, "Are you okay?"

I cleared my throat as quietly as I could, nodding. *Jesus,* I hadn't even seen anything, but I could feel a blush spreading up my neck and to my cheeks.

It's a scene, I reminded myself. They weren't actually having sex. *Right?*

I'd read about that once. Some A-list actor was talking about sex scenes in some magazine, and she just casually threw out there, that some scene partners agreed to actually have sex when they were filming a movie—which I found to be insane.

I mean, to each their own—but no thank you.

A few people toward the front of the audience moved away, and I finally saw the scene. My eyes widened, unable to look away.

The guy we had seen earlier—through the window and across the street—was on top of the girl who stormed in with that other guy downstairs. *Her name is Josie,* Linc had said.

She was below the creepy guy, their waists were covered by a blanket, but their hips were moving. You could see her tits any time he lifted himself up, before thrusting back down.

"Should we invite your husband up here so he can see how good you take a real dick?" the guy growled.

I looked over at Ellis, who stared with flinching eyebrows at the scene. I couldn't see Linc, since I was using him as a partial shield.

After another second, I felt him slide his hand down to mine and pull. He must have signaled something to Ellis because he followed just behind us, and we walked back out of the apartment, silently.

No one said anything as we walked down the three flights of stairs and then back outside.

Just as we walked down the steps, I peered back at the apartment building and then stopped for a second. "That was . . ." I shook my head. I had no words.

"Intense," Linc said.

"That's one word for it," I said with a breathy, awkward laugh.

Ellis shook his head, but I could see the tick of his jaw just before he barked out, "How is there no warning *anywhere* about an explicit sex scene at the end of that shit? Fucking *anyone* can walk in! I mean, do kids live in the building?"

I didn't see any kids, but that doesn't mean there weren't any actually living in the apartments that weren't being used for the "*performances*."

"It definitely felt weird. Invasive," I mumbled.

Linc shook his head as he ran his teeth along his bottom lip. His eyes flicked over to me. "I think it was kind of meant to," he said, lost in thought for a moment, then looked at me. "I'm sorry, Pip. I didn't know . . ."

I shook my head. "No, hey, it's fine. I knew it was gonna be weird—that avant-garde, experimental shit always is." And that was true. *But* that *was* . . .

A residual shiver ran down my spine, but luckily a breeze passed, and I don't think Linc noticed. I didn't want him to feel bad.

I mean, I didn't really know what to expect from this thing tonight, but *that* certainly wasn't it—and it was clear it wasn't what the boys were expecting either.

Lingering awkwardly for a few more seconds, Linc finally said, "Should we go to Queenie's?"

Ugh. Mr. Harris was supposed to meet us there after to talk about the show, but . . . *Ugh.*

"Oh, hell yeah," Ellis said. "I have questions."

Ellis started walking in the direction of Queenie's, and Linc took my hand, his eyes checking mine.

I did my best to give him a closed-mouth smile and walked beside him. I had no clue what I'd say to Mr. Harris, but maybe Linc and Ellis would be talkative enough that I could just nod and squint—pretend to be engaged.

LINC

Why am I so nervous?

Maybe it was Ellis's nonstop tangent, but I think Paige seemed okay. She was picking at the last of her grilled cheese. She even ate the crusts—*so she can't be* that *upset, right?*

Fuck, I felt bad.

Mr. Harris—*Jeremy*—had told us it was better to go into the show as blind as possible, but there probably should have been *some* warning.

"It was irresponsible," Ellis said, shaking his head. "I mean, content aside, it just seemed unprofessional. A QR code? *Zero* disclaimers or warnings? Honestly, there was no consideration given to the audience *or* the actors—"

My eyes widened as I saw Jeremy walking through the door. Ellis's eyebrows pinched as he turned around. After a second, he tossed up a casual wave in Jeremy's direction, before he turned back toward us, and his mouth pulled up.

I felt Paige's leg move beside me and then a small shuffle, followed by Ellis wincing. "Behave," she said quietly, and I cleared my throat.

As Jeremy got to the table, his eyes met mine first, then drifted toward Paige and Ellis. "Hey, guys. How's it going?" He shrugged off his coat and took the empty seat next to Ellis, pulling it off to the side a bit before he sat down.

No one said anything, at first, but I felt like it *should be* me, since I was pretty sure Ellis was about to . . . *Ellis.*

Luckily, Carrie came over and helped us stall for a second longer by taking Jeremy's drink order.

I didn't know how to field this. I certainly didn't like the play. But I also don't think I hated it as much as Paige and Ellis did.

Most of the time—with movies—I was able to find *something* I liked about it. The way it was shot, a cool visual effect, the writing, a character—*something.*

I just had to figure out what that was before Jeremy asked me. He'd only ever been supportive of my ideas and it felt shitty to not reciprocate.

After another silent beat, Jeremy chuckled. "All right, I'm sensing some negative opinions."

"No," I said, quickly realizing I didn't have a game plan past that word, but Ellis twisted to face Jeremy.

And *goddammit.* The way his posture straightened, the small tick to the back of his jaw. Earlier suspicions were confirmed. Ellis was about to . . . *Ellis.*

"What exactly is the purpose of producing something like that?" he asked, his tone cool, casual—exactly how he always started. Like a lawyer in a courtroom.

Jeremy's body language remained easy, leaning back slightly in his chair. He tilted his chin to the side, and his brown hair fell over his brow as he shrugged. "I mean, you know as well as I do, the only way to create anything new is from experimenting. Reality TV, puppets on-stage—they all started with an idea that was outside the box."

Ellis's eyes squinted but not in an angry way. He seemed to consider what Jeremy was saying. "Right. But shouldn't that come from the subject matter, not the setting?"

Jeremy shrugged. "Not necessarily. And the audience was made fully aware of the setting before they stepped in the building."

Ellis was about to say something, but Paige sat up. "I think what he means—" she said, then stopped, chewing on her lip. Her eyes flicked to Ellis, across from us, and she squeezed my hand a bit under the table as she said, "Just that . . . as the audience, we didn't *know* the space. Like, there was one apartment on the first level—where the couple came in—and I actually second-guessed whether or not we were supposed to be in there."

"Yes! See, but that's good!" Jeremy said. "The piece was meant to feel like something you shouldn't be watching. It wasn't meant to be *comfortable* by any means."

"You *wanted* people to be uncomfortable?" Ellis either didn't try, or was *unable* to fix his face.

Jeremy chuckled. "Not all discomfort is bad. In fact, uncomfortable, raw scenes in movies and TV are what make people feel connected or *seen* through the characters."

Ellis huffed and looked at the table. I glanced for a moment at Paige, who was thankfully two steps ahead of me, ready to break the tension. "I don't know," she said with an easy smile but I could feel her grip on my hand tighten. "I think it was just over my head. Obviously, I'm not a director." Her blue eyes widened for a moment, seemingly nervous as they met our teacher's eyes.

Jeremy smiled warmly. "That's okay. You belong in front of the camera." A brief silence passed, but I couldn't help but notice Ellis's gaze still transfixed on the table in front of him.

Then Jeremy turned his attention to me. "What did you think about it, Linc?"

I swallowed, still unsure of how I was going to handle this. Paige kept my hand under the table, and my eyes flicked over at her—just a quick peek—and I took a breath, then said, "I think I understood what you were going for with the . . . intimacy of the setting," I said carefully. "But to me, it felt more like a film than a play, and I think *that* felt kind of weird."

Jeremy's mouth ticked up at the corner. "Interesting. Can you elaborate?"

Paige gave my hand a squeeze, anchoring my courage. I was just *trying* to not piss off my mentor, while still giving honest feedback. I shifted in my seat, then said, "I don't know. I just know that film sets are a little more integrated. Everyone is working in one space once the film is shooting. But live theater is all about separation, backstage, onstage—watching the landscape. So, *Stories* felt like something we were supposed to be watching through a screen, but . . . we weren't."

Jeremy nodded with a smirk, and I added, "But definitely interesting," I half-lied.

Honestly, I just kind of wanted to wrap up the conversation as quickly as possible. I didn't like that I felt a weird need to almost mediate the conversation.

Ellis still looked annoyed, Paige looked nervous, and I was still uncomfortable.

Jeremy nodded after a second. "Well, it was very mature content. It might be something you find more interesting in the future. You're all so talented and smart sometimes I forget you're only eighteen."

"*I'm* still seventeen," Ellis said, quietly, his eyes pulling up from the table to look at Jeremy, and Paige's hand tightened in mine under the table.

I could tell by the tone Ellis was making an underhanded point. That he was *technically* underage, which I'm sure meant *technically,* Jeremy had broken some kind of rule—*law*—by Ellis's attendance at the show.

I didn't know if such a law existed, but there was no doubt in my mind that Ellis did.

God, this was uncomfortable. Jeremy's eyes lifted to Ellis. Other than a small flare to his nostrils, he seemed mostly unbothered, but then said, "C'mon, man. Casper Cinema puts out way more disturbing shit than that."

Holy shit, this is awkward.

Ellis snorted but then looked at me. I begged him with my eyes not to push it—*just let it go*—and the charge to his stare muted a bit.

He sighed. "Whatever. Guess it just wasn't my thing," he said in my direction, and I dipped my chin with a silent *thank you,* but I got the idea that he'd bitch and moan about this for at least the rest of the night.

Whatever. As long as it wasn't while we were still with our teacher. The *only* teacher at Providence who'd ever even *tried* to get me professional work. *Paige too.* And current opinions aside, Ellis knew that.

Carrie came back over and took in the quiet nature of the table, the empty plates. "You guys need anything else?"

I looked at Paige, who was looking at Ellis—who was pouting between sideways glances at Jeremy.

When no one said anything, Jeremy said, "No, I'll just take the check. You can put it all on my tab."

CHAPTER 36
LINC

We're driving.

It was her idea to drive together to The Window—as long as we didn't take her car.

I didn't understand it, but as I had already proven to myself this morning—*when I lost my fucking mind and kissed her in the kitchen*—I couldn't resist the temptation of . . . *her.*

I never had a fucking chance.

Just to hear her humming along to the song on the radio is a goddamn dream. Her citrus and cinnamon smell wafting between the open windows. From the corner of my eye, I can see wisps of her blue hair, catching the wind.

It's almost enough to believe things are the way they used to be.

My hands tighten around the steering wheel, and one glance down at the ink up my arms reminds me.

That's "the dream" talking, dumbass.

The pretty, quiet sound of her singing has kept my pulsing anxiety at bay. Even for as little sleep as I usually get—*two hours total* in the last forty-eight hours has me feeling a little delirious.

Not to mention the ongoing loop playing through my mind of our kiss in the kitchen—mere *hours* after beating my dick into her underwear.

So, so fucked.

I already washed them, but that's not the point. And *that's* just the physical stuff.

She thought . . . *God, it fucking decimated me. Learning she thought I left because I was . . .* disgusted *by her? For years—she thought I left because* she *did something wrong?*

It makes me hate myself even more—another thing I didn't know was possible.

I barely remember that time. *I just know . . . it needed to happen. I had to go away after what I did to her.*

A fact I suspect she's still denying. If she wasn't, she would have pushed me away immediately in the kitchen. And she certainly wouldn't have gotten in the car and let me drive her somewhere.

Never underestimate the power of denial.

"Huh?" she says from the passenger seat, pulling her chin over to me.

Guess I said that out loud. If she'd heard me, she would have recognized the quote from *American Beauty.*

I shake my head, muttering, "I'm gonna have a smoke." Shifting my weight, I pull the pack out of my back pocket. After I light it up, my eyes flick over to her.

There's no eye roll, no scowl, not even a dramatic sound of disapproval. She simply closes her eyes, and leans her head back against the seat. My eyes watch as the sun catches her skin through the windows, casting small shadows over her collar bone.

Her chest seems tense but it rises and falls while her full rosy lips still sing along with the music. I pull off the freeway, allowing my chin to twist and see her hair billowing in tousled, silver-blue waves over her shoulder.

I wish we could . . . go somewhere. On one of our drives.

Or if wishes are a thing, I wish she'd let me film her all day. Just watch her.

Living, breathing, beautiful.

I can watch it even after she leaves.

My nose pulls in a sharp inhale. *I won't, though.*

Even now, I have an entire box of home movies I took from our old house back in Venice. Countless hours that I have yet to brave actually watching, *terrified* they'll destroy the miniscule amount of progress I've made in the last five years.

But I guess that's shot to shit.

Flicking some ash out the window, I ask, "So other than drinking your weight in tequila, what'd you guys d-do last night?" The question is mostly an attempt to put my thoughts on a fucking leash.

She sighs. "That's it, really. It ended up being a sob fest over Gram."

Oh my God. I haven't even acknowledged—

I am such *an asshole.* But saying *sorry* in this scenario seems fucking dumb too. *Sorry,* is what you say to strangers.

Clearing my throat, I awkwardly start to tell her, "I-uh . . . I went to Venice last weekend."

Her inhale is audible, but she doesn't say anything right away. In fact, she doesn't say anything for a few long seconds, and I have a moment where I wonder if she doesn't understand that I went back to *her* house, but then she says, "I saw you found your mug."

My eyebrows hitch and my chin twists, just slightly, still keeping my eyes on the road. "Wh-Where did you find it?"

My eyes drift over to see hers, watching me, and my chest jumps with surprise. I can feel her eyes studying me. Like an ant crawling along the designs on my arms, an imaginary, feather-light touch of her thumb on my eyebrow. I can feel it all with her stare, and my body shifts.

Finally, she says, "In the hammock . . . just beside the lemon tree."

That's *why I didn't hear it break.*

But I don't know what to say to that. It makes me look creepy *and* weird on multiple levels. And the fact that she's talking to me—*staying under the same roof*—I still can't believe it.

But then I get that feeling again. The old, warm, familiar one—something resembling comfort as the words, *"Never weird,"* roll through my mind.

My heart rate picks up and I try my hardest to give her any bit of honesty I can. I visualize the words, think of the signs, then start, "I went back last week. On the anniversary." I take a breath, swallow, and she doesn't rush me.

Her hand moves closer and my body tenses. A strange reflex quickly has me tossing the cigarette out the window, coughing out the exhale.

"I'm sorry—" she says quickly.

"N-No—" I croak, but give a quick shake of my head. "No, if you want to—it just . . . surprised me."

How this girl *willingly* wanted to touch me was a fucking *treasure*. I could study it for the rest of my life and never understand it. And I don't deserve it. But I won't deny it.

Not while she's here. *I fucking can't.*

She still doesn't move her hand back, and her words from earlier—*"I thought you were disgusted by me"*—beat into the back of my brain.

Timidly, I reach my hand over, fingers shaking, and I take her hand, then pull it over toward me. I hover it over my knee, then flick my eyes over to hers.

I know she was about to do it anyway, but I still wait for permission. *Careful.*

After another second she lowers her hand to my knee, holding it gently, and my heart pounds, feeling like it's about to soar through the fucking windshield.

This is how it used to be. I remember.

When we were driving.

I used to keep one hand on the wheel and one hand on hers, which would leisurely hold my knee. She'd lie her head on my shoulder and sing to whatever song we were listening to—

God, the countless memories of that *exact* position—that *exact* feeling—it hits me with just the light contact of her hand on me.

Keeping me still. Here.

It's the exact opposite of the feeling I've gotten any time I've had to make physical contact with anyone in the last seven years. Not just the contact, but the *idea* of it—the anticipation of touch—usually sends me into some sort of spiral.

I clear my throat after another moment, refocusing, then my

eyes glance down to my knee, seeing she's taken off the flannel she was wearing, and my eyes widen.

I dart them back up to the road, remembering *I'm fucking driving,* but I can't shake the visual.

Her wrists are covered. Completely.

The lace wrist cuffs, the bracelets. I see a dangling penny charm on the one I recognize. *The rest are new,* I think.

But it's what they're *hiding* that's scratching at the back of my brain.

Her voice reels me back in, she's singing dreamily to some Norah Jones song, her hand on my knee, but she doesn't put her head on my shoulder.

You're lucky she hasn't called the cops on you—be fucking grateful, dipshit.

And *that's* my problem.

I'm so goddamn selfish with her. I always want *more.* More than I should.

I shake my head again, wanting to hold onto the lightness of this moment. Her hand on me, her voice in my ear.

Finally, I say, "I—uh—I stole lemons off the tree."

Her hand on my knee squeezes and my gaze flicks over to her, seeing her eyes are closed.

Another moment passes, and her mouth pulls up at the corners as her eyelids slowly peel back open. The sun from the windshield finds the sparkle in her eye—*the indigo glitter I'm addicted to*—just as she . . . laughs.

A *real* laugh. And it just knocks me out of orbit. It's the most beautiful goddamn sound I've heard in years.

My favorite voice. My favorite song. Her laugh.

This and the sparkle in her eye. *I want to keep both.*

I feel like the longer I'm in her presence the longer this list will become.

Her laughter settles a bit and she quietly says, "I saw," then looks over at me.

God, how will I go back to life without her?

Even now, it doesn't feel like it *used to be.* But it feels . . . better. Like I remember the *idea* of a life where . . . weird things weren't so weird. Not with her.

It was never weird.

The remainder of our ride was spent pretending. A delusion I was all-too-okay playing along with given the circumstances. But the tether to reality snapped back when I noticed her wrists again.

She put her flannel back on just before we started our walk to The Window from the parking lot. And my eyes are currently hyper focused on the forcefield she's built around her wrists.

It's where my eyes are now, waiting in Beck's office.

Distantly, I'm aware of Jackson and Paige talking, but I'm not paying attention.

All my mind can focus on is what's underneath the lace coverings.

Would she let me see?

No. And don't fucking ask.

". . . I have a team installing more cameras too," I faintly hear

Jackson say, and I blink back to now, realizing they've been having a full-blown conversation this whole time, while I've been trying to manifest X-ray vision.

"Do you take vacations, Jackson?" Paige asks.

My gaze drifts up to him. His silver eyes soften a bit, a film of amusement lifting them, as he says, "I've been told I have a hard time relaxing."

Paige fights a smile, and fuck me, do I want it. But she works it out and evens her expression. "'Cause of the stick?"

He lifts his chin up, pointing his face toward the ceiling for a second, like he's either fighting off a laugh or summoning patience—*maybe both*—before he lowers his chin again, "Yes. The stick."

I have no clue what they're talking about. But the conversation halts just as I hear the door open and close behind us.

Jackson's shoulders pull back as he stands to the side of a big desk in front of us, just as a man says, "Ah, hello." His voice curls with what sounds like practiced remorse.

He rounds the chair Paige is sitting in, straightening his pin-stripe jacket. "Blue, I was hoping to see you again. I'm sorry that it's like this," he says with a soft tone.

My fists tighten. I have to suppress the urge to rip his styled blond hair right off his head.

I'm sure you're really sorry, now, *asshole.*

Suddenly, he looks my way, like he heard my silent seething. "And you must be Cook. It's nice to meet you. I'm Beck Davis," he says, extending his hand to me as he crosses behind his desk.

Fuck me.

The discomfort that twists on Linc's face as he accepts Beck's handshake is palpable, and I shift uncomfortably.

Not Linc. "Cook." The new, gay security guard.

My eyes roll, but I keep them on the ceiling to hide it just as Beck takes a seat on the other side of the desk, his fingers slightly bent with the tips pressed lightly together. "I won't waste either of your time. I appreciate you coming out today.

"I want to start out by saying that this was a first for The Window. In our ten years of operation, I can tell you this is not a problem we've had before." Other than a glance of confirmation to Jackson, he directs nearly that entire part to Linc. But I don't have too much time to think about it before his eyes move to me.

"Blue, I am sincerely sorry for what happened. I feel terrible. Especially after it was me who assured you that you would be safe."

Linc's hands clench on his lap, and I notice a penny he's fiddling with in his right hand.

I wish we could go back to the car. That last twenty-minutes or so of the ride felt like . . .

We were driving away.

Jackson clears his throat, demanding my attention. "It will never happen again. Security will be present at all Veranda events going forward."

Beck nods. "Yes. We had been working on some plans to increase our security as the club's popularity continues to grow, and this made it all the more clear that it needs to be top priority."

Linc sits up a bit, his fists working to loosen themselves by fidgeting. The back of his jaw pulses, before he says, "How well do you know the men from that room?" His voice is tight but commanding, and my back straightens a bit.

Beck's chin dips, his lips tilting as he nods. "Yes, well, this is why I wanted you both to come in. It was clear from the footage that you . . . know each other?"

My eyebrows pinch, and I fight the urge to rub my head. The hangover headache has been coming in waves, but this meeting is only making it worse. And trying to remember who knows what isn't helping.

I don't really know why it matters that I know Linc, but I'm not willing to give Beck any more information. Not *real* information, anyway.

Using Linc's lie, I shrug. "He's my brother's boyfriend."

From the corner of my eye, I can see Linc shift his weight and our gazes meet. His mouth is flattened, his jaw tense, and I have to pull my lips into my mouth to hide my smirk.

I turn my attention to Beck, whose eyebrows lift, studying Linc. His dark blue eyes fill with confusion as he takes him in, and I have to actively work to even my expression.

It's fucking dumb—people's preconceived notions of what a certain kind of person is *supposed* to look like—or act like, for that matter. Even in a city like LA—*as a club owner*—Beck's expression reads—*"he doesn't* look *gay."*

I had seen it our whole lives with Ellis.

People often assumed I was his girlfriend when we were out in public without Linc. Classmates at school always joked about how he was the straightest gay guy they'd ever met, just because he wasn't outwardly hitting on guys all the time, or making bitchy comments.

He saved all that for us, I guess.

"I see," Beck finally says. "Well, Cook, to answer your question, I've worked with Tariel before. His company assisted with some location scouting for a movie I produced a few months ago."

Of course. Everyone in this goddamn town has a toe in show-business.

"What's the movie?" Linc asks, evenly enough to give the idea of casualness. His body is tight, though, his eyes determined.

Beck smirks. "Still in post-production, unfortunately, and the details are hush-hush till it's announced publicly."

A laugh snorts through my nose, but I pull my lips into my mouth.

Whoops.

"Which leads me to my last point," Beck finally says, ignoring my rudeness with a sigh as he directs his attention solely toward me. "We have already filed a report with the police, and we're preparing to press charges of our own, but I wanted to let you know that you have The Window's full support with any legal matters *you* would like to take as well."

The way he said *support* settled strangely in my mind. Like it meant something else. Was he offering to *pay* for legal fees, should I choose to press charges?

No, that couldn't be it. And I didn't want that anyway. I just wanted to slip back into the background, like a gust of wind merging back into its pattern.

Where it would blow, on the other hand, was anyone's guess.

I stay quiet, slowly trying to process exactly what he's offering. Beck looks back and forth between Linc and me, then stands, rounding the corner of his desk and planting himself at the spot closest to my chair.

The blues in our eyes meet again, and I take a deep breath as he grimaces. "I'd understand if you never wanted to come back here after today," he says, sincerely, shifting my stomach. "But I hope you'll consider staying at The Window. We can revisit your contract, and bump up your hourly rate. And despite the extra security measures we'll be taking, I certainly wouldn't expect you to ever work a Veranda event again. My business partners and I have big plans to make the club a more theatrical experience in the new year—perhaps we can utilize that voice of yours—add some singing performances to the rotation?"

Linc clears his throat. "*If* she decides to come back, our schedules will be the same," he states. It's not a question—and his eyes narrow up at Beck.

Well, well, well . . .

A resounding, *there he is,* rings silently through me, tilting the corner of my mouth up. It's also the first time I take notice of how his voice has been steady—no stutter—with anything he's said to Beck.

But then there's the skin about to break over his knuckles, and I fix my face as Beck simply smiles at Linc. "I don't see why that would be a problem. That way you can walk her to her car every night too. I'm sure her brother would appreciate that."

I ignore the strange tilt in energy with his last comment and instead take inventory. A single *close-call* in the Veranda has granted me: *immunity* from the Veranda, a raise, a singing opportunity, a personal bodyguard in the way of Lincoln Morrow— Cook—and ten thousand dollars sitting in my trunk an hour away that *no one* has mentioned yet.

There's no way.

My eyes are stuck on Beck, noticing again how his clothing only seems to crease in what looks like manufactured lines to outline his physique. Which is fine, I guess. I mean, it doesn't hold a candle to the inked up grizzly bear sitting next to me.

I can fully feel the tension rolling off Linc and wafting over to me from my peripherals, preparing myself to react quickly if things . . . turn.

Fidgeting in my seat, an equal balance of confusion and tension continues to build, just as Beck says, "Well, anyway, please take the weekend to think about it. We'll give you leave-pay until then. And you've already received your tip from the Veranda, correct?"

He tosses it out there so casually that I have to do a double take to him. There's something in his eyes that's lifted. It's barely noticeable, but since I'm pretty sure I'm not blinking at all, *I* notice it.

Tip?

He's referring to the *thousands* I *took* off the man's lap as a *tip?*

A tip?!

The word tip is starting to sound weird in my head.

His offerings dangle out in front of me.

The raise, the "promotion," the tip.

It confirms my earlier thought. When Jackson was calling me incessantly. He knows they fucked up.

"We support you."

But then I remember Jackson's apology. *And* what Beck had said to me in the Veranda—the unexpected humility—a seemingly genuine appreciation for what I brought to the table.

A table he left you to be eaten alive on, though, I remind myself.

The sound of Beck opening and closing the drawer to his desk brings me back to now. As he walks back around the corner of the desk, he hands me a business card. "It's my lawyer's card. If you decide to move forward with anything, give her a call. She's . . ." He chuckles, and somehow, I just *know* instantly that he's likely bent his lawyer over this very desk. *Confirmed,* when he finishes with, "She's a firecracker. She'll help you with anything you need."

Linc takes the card, somehow managing a tense grab, rather than the *snatch* his claw-like hand would suggest, and shoves it in his pocket, then stands.

Ope. Guess we're leaving.

No arguments here, though. Beck said I could take a few days, and I definitely need it. Get my bearings.

Make a plan.

Still, there was one thing I wanted to do before I left. "Is Rio here?" I ask.

Jackson takes a step forward, his voice it's normal, even tone. "She's teaching a class out in the valley. Won't be here till call time."

My mouth slopes down. *If* I decide to leave The Window—*maybe even leave California*—I'll still have to go back to Gram's before I leave. Maybe I can text Rio and invite her out to Venice or something.

We start toward the door again as Beck reaches out and gently touches my elbow. "Blue."

The reflex I've kept idle snaps to attention. I feel it before it even happens, Linc is turning around, but there's just enough hesitation that I'm able to grab his hand in mine. Catching it down by my side, I stop him from possibly hitting a very, *very* rich fucking man as I meet his eyes.

This behavior is hot, but not right now.

Fuck.

Why did I think that?

His mouth turns up in the smallest way and *fuck me*, does it do something to me.

*I wish it would just keep going—keep pulling up—*but it confirms our telekinesis is at least partially still alive and kicking.

And goddammit. I can't even be happy about it because he caught a spicy thought. *In front of other people.*

I quickly turn to Beck, forcing a polite smile. "Thank you, Mr.

Davis. I know you're a—a busy man," I say, though the tightness in my jaw cranks a notch. "I appreciate your apology, and I'll think about the offer."

I just want to get out of here.

Beck's smile pulls. "Still my best investment," he says with a wink that flicks at my irritation, but I swallow it and tighten my smile in a way that feels so unnatural it hurts.

His eyes flick down to my hand, still holding Linc's, which I guess is kind of strange.

Fuck it, what do I care? I don't explain it.

And I drop the smile before I turn and walk through the door, hand-in-hand with my *brother's boyfriend.*

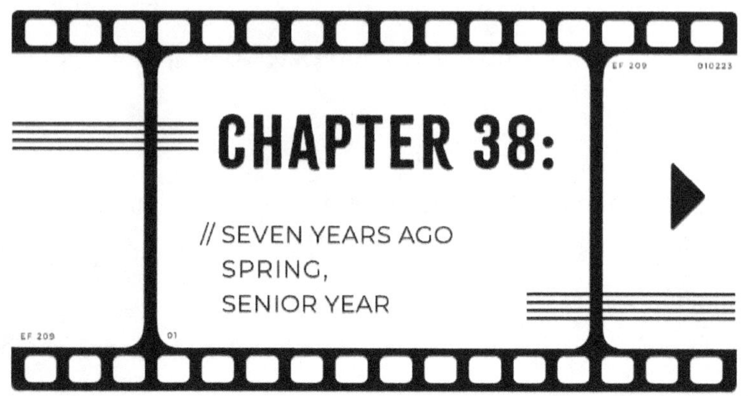

PAIGE

"It's fucking *weird*," Linc groaned, and I breathed a laugh, resting my chin on his chest.

"Your mom has been single for almost a decade and works eighty hours a week. She deserves to have a little fun," I said, sitting up.

He laid flat on his back, staring aimlessly up at the ceiling like he was looking at different routes on a map, and I had to suck my lips into my mouth to keep from smiling.

Christine had the night off, so Linc, Maisie, and I made chili, and about halfway through dinner, Christine announced that she'd been seeing someone since Christmas—almost four months ago. A doctor from the hospital.

And Linc had been a *fidget Bridgette* ever since. "Hey," I said quietly, and he looked over at me. I pushed a dark wave off his forehead, then said, "At least it's someone she met at work, ya know? It's not like she's been sneaking around—taking time away from you guys to actively go out and meet someone."

He sat quietly for a second, then shook his head. "No," he said through a sigh. "I mean, even if she were, I would understand. *God knows* she deserves someone good after my dad. But I just . . . I don't know—how do you *know* whether or not someone's good? How do we *know* this guy isn't a complete dickhead—or *worse* than the sperm donor?"

My eyebrows hitched. This was a bit deeper of a conversation than I was ready for, but I shrugged. "Instinct, I guess. Either that, or they prove themselves trustworthy."

He huffed, "Helpful, Pip," and I had to keep fighting the urge to smile.

It really is fucking cute—him being protective over his mom. But I took the moment to lighten the mood—mess with him a little. It's what we did when life was life-ing.

I smirked. "You're just pouting because your mom is a grown-ass woman with a sex life now—a hard fact you've gotten to ignore until this very moment," I teased.

He scoffed. "Ugh. You are *the worst.* Kick me while I'm down, why don't ya?" He shoved his face into his pillow.

I chuckled, nuzzling myself into his self-smothering. He playfully pushed away from me—*and it began.* We might as well have heard the *ding, ding, ding* of the match start.

I dove into him, but he grabbed both of my wrists and held me back. In an instant, he swiped my feet out from under me, and I flailed to the mattress with a yelp.

"Damn you, and your two-a-days!" I cursed, and he laughed as he caught both of my wrists with one hand, freeing up his other one, and immediately started to tickle my sides.

I howled with laughter, my cheeks aching. I couldn't breathe—"Stop, stop, stop!" I laughed, and his fingers halted, but his hand stayed on my stomach.

He was straddling my waist while his other hands still held my wrists. His dark hair fell forward a bit, hugging his hazel stare gleaming down at me, as the playful energy shifted.

Neither one of us said anything, but I pinned my lip between my teeth, our eyes passing a silent exchange. The same one that's lingered between us since we started dating six months ago.

We still hadn't gone further than over-the-clothes touching— but we kissed *and touched* like it had become one of our basic human needs.

And I mean, wasn't it?

But there was . . . *something* keeping us from going further.

Truthfully, our very infrequent alone time played a huge part in that. If we weren't at school or some rehearsal, or working— Linc was usually watching Maisie, or we had plans with Ellis. Gram and I were also pretty sure our house was falling apart, room by room.

There was just . . . *a lot going on.* And *right now,* we couldn't do too much . . . Maisie *and* Christine were home.

But the mischief in Linc's eyes only seemed to grow as he lightly brushed his fingers over my belly button.

There was a gap between my leggings and my cropped black

tank top, and his fingers slowly kept traveling north. My breath caught when he reached just below my ribs.

He stopped and his gaze sunk into mine. A silent question. *Yes or no?*

After just an inhale, my chin dipped with a nod, my lips trembling as his mouth closed over mine, licking and nibbling before his tongue brushed over my teeth—*God, the way this boy worshiped my mouth*—it was fucking divine.

His hands still tightly held my wrists as he resumed his movement below my shirt. Our noses brushed as he kept kissing me and his hand finally reached my breast, cupping it roughly, as he groaned. "God, fuck," he hissed, and my hips pulsed up on instinct. It was the only way I could reach him without the use of my hands.

I could feel his cock straining under his pants, pressed hard against me. He hummed low against my lips, as his fingers closed around my nipple, tweaking it just a bit, and I gasped before he caught my lips with his again.

He kissed back toward my ear and whispered, "Gonna have to be quiet," his voice low and hoarse as he flattened his finger and rubbed the pebbled, tightening flesh at an agonizingly delicious cadence.

"Ohh," I whimpered, then bit my lip, breathing heavily.

A small grunt pushed against my temple as he started to massage my whole tit and my mouth fell open on a silent gasp.

"Fuck, Pip. You look so pretty like this." His hoarse whisper brushed along my neck as he kissed along my jaw. I started to pant as he still diligently teased my nipple with his fingers, then rumbled, "So *fucking pretty* when I'm touching you."

If I looked anything like I felt, I imagined it to be an open flame flickering—*trying* not to blow away. My skin was burning, his touch an explosive mist. And *fuck*—his *mouth*—whether it was pressing against mine or muttering dirty thoughts.

Like he just couldn't help it . . .

I'm fucking addicted.

His hazel eyes peered down at me, my body thrumming with anticipation of his next move. He surprised me when his hand finally let go of my wrists, and I immediately raked my fingers through his hair and pulled his mouth to mine.

As our tongues tangled and stroked, I lost myself to the sensation of his mouth—a mouth I'd known nearly my whole life. Blowing bubbles in the creek, sharing water bottles and hot chocolates—popsicles.

This *is how we should be using our mouths,* I thought, then suddenly wondered if maybe that was at least part of the reason we were . . . *savoring* it all. *Taking it slow.*

We were both definitely enjoying the physical addition to our relationship, but it was also still new. The first *new* thing either one of us had really gotten to learn about each other in a long time.

And I was fucking into it.

The discovery, the teasing.

He moaned quietly into my mouth just as he started to play with my other nipple, but a sudden knock at the door stopped us dead in our tracks.

I sat up quickly, pulled down my shirt, and ran my fingers through my hair. Linc chuckled as he rolled off of me, though there was more of a grunt to it than usual. He adjusted himself as best he could, but grabbed a small pillow and put it over his lap before he mumbled, "Come in."

Maisie wanted us to all watch *Back to the Future* together, and since the Morrows didn't all get much family time, of course we obliged.

"I think Marty McFly was my first crush," I processed out loud, turning down "Cat and Mouse" by The Red Jumpsuit Apparatus. I kept my hand on Linc's knee as he drove, and he took the final drag off his cigarette with a small chuckle.

"Really?" His eyebrows raised, darting his gaze to me and then back out toward the road. "That's so different than . . . Wolverine," he said with a smile.

I pulled my lips into my mouth, nodding. "Yeah, but Marty's kind of a pioneer badass—skateboarding on the back of cars— *the tardiness.* And the guitar?" I made a *phew* sound and Linc laughed. A beat passed and I asked, "How about you?"

He flicked his cigarette out the window and held my hand on his lap, but then pulled it up to his mouth, kissing a small trail from my index knuckle to my thumb, watching the road.

I absently wondered if he even noticed he was doing it—if he'd heard my question—but my head leaned against the headrest, just enjoying the view.

God, he was hot. And mine.

We came to a stoplight and he shrugged. "I was always a fan of the girl who starred in all of *my* movies."

I snorted. "Come on," I said with a laugh.

"Okay, okay," he laughed, thinking for a second. "Ty in *Clueless*."

My eyes widened. "Brittany Murphy as the quirky tomboy in a *chick flick?!*"

He laughed. "I'm literally *surrounded by women!* What do you expect . . . *woman?!*"

We both laughed, but it was cut off after a few seconds at the sound of Linc's phone ringing.

He dug through his back pocket as we pulled onto my street, and he glanced down at the screen, eyebrows pinching.

"Who is it?" I asked.

He pulled into the driveway and said, "Jeremy."

Mr. Harris? When did they exchange numbers?

The film festival had come and gone. Linc didn't win . . .

So . . . I had no fucking clue why our teacher would be calling him on a Friday night, but he flicked his eyes to me and my lips pulled back with a shrug.

Just as we pulled into my driveway, Linc picked up the phone. "Hello?"

LINC

"Hey, Linc. Sorry to bother you, but I just got word from one of the directors of the festival. He said they're going to do a screening of the finalist's shorts for some agents and other directors tomorrow down in Old Town. Just wanted to see if maybe you guys wanted to make the trip down there?"

"Oh, shit," slipped out, my eyes widening as I looked over at Paige and her eyebrows lifted.

Her lips puckered and then opened with a silent, "What?" and I shrugged.

"Uh—I'm with Paige right now, but I think she has to work tomorrow."

She nodded, confirming. In my head, I was pretty sure Ellis *could* go, but he was still not the biggest Jeremy fan after the play last month, and I didn't really feel like fielding *that* for an entire day.

Keeping my eyes with Paige, I said, "I—uh—I'll talk with Paige and give you a call back."

"Okay," Jeremy said, through the phone. "Even if just one of you is available, it'll look good to anyone that's interested."

I nodded. "Yeah. I understand, I'll give you a call back in a few."

"Sounds good," he said.

I hung up and filled in Paige, and she confirmed again that she was working tomorrow. And I knew that, I just . . . I wanted her to go too.

"When did you give Mr. Harris your number?" she asked, curiously.

I shrugged. I hadn't really thought about it. "Back when we started shooting for *Moon*." *Does she think it's weird?*

I watched her carefully, but nothing about her face or body language read as something alarming, mostly processing, but then she smiled. "Well . . . " she added, "You *should* be there. It's your movie afterall. We were just the puppets." She lifts my arms, in a goofy way—like she's playing with a marionette.

My mouth pulled up—*Goddamn, she is so fucking cute.*

I quickly pulled her onto my lap from the passenger's seat. She situated each of her legs on the sides of my hips and cradled my jaw.

"Go. Make us look good," she said, her eyes glistening from the moonlight shining in through the windshield.

"What will I do without the moon, though?" I teased, running my hand up the small curve of her ass, up her back.

Everywhere she'd let me.

She giggled and leaned down, taking my lips, kissing me senseless, whisper singing between our mouths.

"I'll be, I'll be
Waiting for you
That's what you don't see
My love, I'm waiting for you
I'll be, I'll be"

After calling Jeremy back, he'd offered to drive us down to Old Town together—which was great from a financial standpoint.

We were only about twenty minutes away, and despite my small bout of anxiety about how awkward it would be to take a day trip with my teacher—it had actually been pretty fun.

But it shouldn't have surprised me—despite Jeremy's oddball theater ventures, we had a lot in common—one of them obviously being a love of film.

"Have you watched Jean-Marc Vallée's stuff?"

Jeremy nodded. "Yes, but I'm a little surprised you have, though I guess I shouldn't be. He's one of my favorite directors," he said inquisitively.

I kept the pride in my chest, but felt my lips curl up.

After losing the film festival—*well, not losing, but not winning either.* Third place won me a letter in the mail and an advertising spot for the movie in the production company's magazine. A piece of literature I was wholeheartedly certain was being used for toilet paper somewhere.

But all of that aside, I wanted to redeem myself with Jeremy, I guess. Not that I had any control over that with the screening today, but impressing him this way was something.

"Vallée likes the tight shots," Jeremy said, knowingly.

I smiled, nodding. "Yeah, I mean, clearly, he likes using his handhelds, and with the angles he finds, it's almost as if the lens is just another set of eyes in the room. The silent POV. Fucking brilliant."

"Definitely," Jeremy agreed. And just as the conversation settled, my nerves kicked up again as I saw the signs for the venue of where the screening was happening, and my heart rate increased as I took in all the cars.

"Decent turnout," Jeremy said, and I worked to even out my expression. This looked like a *pretty big* fucking turnout to me.

There were no free parking spots I could see, as my eyes drifted around the building, looking for the closest smoking area around the sea of cars.

I saw one off to the side of the entrance.

"Do you mind if I hop out and run to the bathroom real quick?" I asked him, hoping the lie was smooth.

"Of course not," Jeremy said, still scanning the parking lot. "I'll meet you inside."

With a nod, I unbuckled my seatbelt, muttering, "Cool, thanks," then opened the door and slid out, heading straight toward the pole marked SMOKING AREA, already reaching for my pack.

As soon as I lit one, I pulled out my phone, feeling my pulse still racing.

I wish Paige was here.

And as soon as the phone was free from my pocket, I saw a text from the beauty I was just thinking of—

Pip: I'm regretting not marking your
head with a "Property of Paige" stamp.
Tell the other hoes (actresses) to beat it.
Please and thank you.

I felt my lips pulling up as I took a drag of my cigarette, texting her back with the other hand.

Me: So weird.
Brittany Murphy circa 1995 is here.

My smile grew, knowing the scrunched face she would make in response. The blue color in her eyes would darken, weaving a comeback.

WITHOUT THE MOON

Pip: AS IF! I'm on my way.

I smiled again. It was just what I needed. She was *always* just what I needed. And I really wished she *was* on her way.

> **Me:** Wish you were here.
> Love you.

Pip: Love you too.
Kick ass, take names, come home.

I took another breath, another drag.

I can do this. I mean, really, all I have to do is sit there, I thought.

To my knowledge, directors weren't being expected to talk after their films—*just mingle.*

Ugh. I smoked my cigarette down to the filter before finally going inside to meet Jeremy.

It was a strange feeling. Being in a room full of people, watching something I created with my two best friends—and neither one of them were here.

My mouth sloped in the safety of the dark theater. At least Jeremy was here, sitting next to me, as the final minutes of *Without the Moon* played.

And if I had ever denied it—*which I hadn't*—it was so fucking clear in the way this movie turned out that Paige, was in fact, my muse. Every shot worshiped her.

The sustained, intimate shots held a yearning in the camera lens I could see just from watching it. I couldn't be sure if it was the big screen or the fact that I wished so badly she was here, but the sight was fucking breathtaking.

Paige and Ellis's final kiss awarded us a few contented sighs.

But it was the stillness in the theater after the final shots—the lapping waves on the rocks, glistening from the moonlight above just as the credits started to roll.

Whispers and then . . . applause.

A lot of it.

After the screening ended, there was a schmooze fest—one lacking booze or weed or anything to make it more entertaining. But there was a pretty impressive food spread, so I camped out by *that* table.

Jeremy had gone to the bathroom, and I definitely needed his help if I was expected to really talk to anyone.

A man walked up to the buffet table as I popped a shrimp in my mouth. A beat passed, and I could feel him looking over at me in my peripherals, so I turned my chin and looked back over at him.

With a plate in his hand, he gave a quick smile. He looked a bit older—older than Jeremy, for sure, given that he had a healthy dose of gray hair, more wrinkles around his mouth—a small scar on his upper lip.

He took a step in my direction, then said, "Hey, you're Lincoln Morrow, right? The kid who did the moon movie?"

I nodded awkwardly, my eyebrows pinching just as he shook his head. "Sorry," he said, quickly putting down his plate. "I'm

Dylan Mirth. I've known Jeremy for a long time. He had told me to keep a lookout for your film today. It was fucking great, man."

I smiled, dipping my chin graciously, then extended my hand—*a power move as Ellis had said, being the first one to initiate the handshake*—and Dylan reached out too. "Nice to meet you," I said.

He went on and on about how impressed he was that I shot everything myself and the praise was lifting my confidence. "And your leading lady—" he said with an impressed shake of his head. "She was outstanding."

Now *that* I could talk about. I nodded. "Yeah. She's amazing. She does a lot of theater. Beautiful singing voice, obviously as you saw in the film."

Jeremy joined us at that moment, and I was grateful for the help. Dylan seemed nice enough but part of the reason I liked doing the behind the scenes shit was because it was just that. *Meant to be unseen.*

After they caught up for a minute, Dylan looked back over to me. "Do you think she would be interested in reading some sides for a movie I'm shooting down here in a couple of months? It's an indie project, so it's nothing major, but I think she'd be perfect for one of the leads."

Jeremy nodded, with an enlightened, "Ahh," just before he looked over at me, "I've read the script. It's good. Dark. Paige could definitely sink her teeth into it."

It felt weird to answer for her, but I nodded, knowing she'd want me to say yes to any interest the industry was throwing her way.

"Yeah, of course," I said quickly, realizing I still hadn't responded. "I'm sure she'd love to. I can write down her email, so you can send her the sides."

"Perfect," Dylan said. "It'll be some time this week. And Jeremy is helping me with some of the camera work, so there will be at least one familiar face."

I nodded, chewing my lip. I didn't know how Paige would feel about that. I knew she wasn't as bothered by Jeremy as Ellis was, but I don't think she'd find his presence *comforting* by any means. *But maybe if she worked with him, got to know him a little better . . .*

Dylan cut off my thought as he asked me about the lighting effects and sound editing, which looped Jeremy into the conversation.

We stayed for about another hour. I gave out my contact information to a few smaller studio heads that were interested in my camera work—so, it would appear that it was definitely worth it to come.

But at a certain point I made eye contact with Jeremy, and saw the exact same expression staring back at me in the way of his tired brown eyes and grimaced mouth. *"Can we get the hell out of here?"*

I nodded emphatically, and he chuckled. We stopped by the small production team who had organized the event on our way out, thanking them—*bullshit, bullshit*—then headed back out toward the car.

Instinctively, I dug my hand through my pocket to grab my cigarettes, pulling them out before I remembered.

I'm in front of a teacher.

Jeremy's eyes peered over at me and he rustled back the longer brown strands of hair off his forehead. "Can I bum one?"

My eyes widened. I wasn't exactly expecting him to scold me—he'd proved more than once that he didn't really give a shit about the *authority thing* teachers were supposed to carry—but it still surprised me.

I extended the pack out to him so he could take one.

He picked one out with a sigh and held it under his nose. "*Oof*," he said and I breathed a laugh.

"When did you quit?" I asked, lighting mine and then handing him the lighter.

He chuckled, and took it, then lit his. "This is my last one."

I laughed again just as I pulled my phone out of my pocket. I wanted to let Paige know we were about to leave, since I had full intentions of going over and kissing her until we fell asleep after we got home, but my heart dropped when I saw I already had a message from her.

Pip: Gram fell.
When you get back to Venice,
can you meet me at the hospital?

CHAPTER 39
PAIGE

We chose the denial route on the ride back from The Window too. Truthfully, I had pretty much wanted to get back to the car from the second we left it.

The safety of another drive.

I let all the shit that just happened at The Window fly . . . well— out the fucking windows, which stayed open through our drive back to Ellis's house.

I put my hand on Linc's knee halfway through the ride. He didn't close his hand on top of mine, but when I went to take it away—when I thought maybe he didn't want my hand there— he grabbed it and placed it back on his knee.

"I could never think that about you." I had to keep letting the words resound through my head. Remind myself that the flinching, wincing, and tension that came along with physical contact wasn't for the reasons I thought.

My mind replayed the raw, anguish in his voice, and it cut through me—working hard to slash through the years I'd spent believing something different.

I think the connection—my hand—helped both of us, eventually. My thoughts settled and blended with the music, and after a while his shoulders relaxed. His breathing evened out, his posture slouched a bit.

And then it was . . . so good. So right.

Our escape.

But it couldn't last forever.

That's the caveat to escape. There isn't a single place we can run away to, where *this* won't be our reality. I have the realization as we pull into the driveway.

Just as the big gray cube comes into view from behind the massive gate, Linc pulls the car through the threshold and parks. I turn down the volume knob, softening Fall Out Boy's "Centuries," and twist my body toward him.

I'm not ready to go in yet. I can see the batmobile is also parked in the driveway, so that must mean Ellis is back from his meeting with Wade, and I just . . . need a second.

Linc doesn't turn the car off, but with the engine in park, he timidly shifts toward me too. I keep my hand on his knee, holding the contact as I search for the easiest thing to talk about at the moment.

Start with easy, then work our way back.

Careful.

I clear my throat, my voice still quiet as I say, "That tip Beck was talking about?"

The deep brown color in Linc's eyes only has a sprinkling of green, but it catches the light in a way that makes my fingers pulse on his knee. He jerks, and I mutter, "Sorry—" shaking my head as I start to pull my hand away, but he intercepts it by slotting his hand over mine. *Keeping it there.*

I gasp at the warmth of his hand, a little clammy, but as I peek up, I see him smirking, and he quietly mumbles, "Tickled."

My own lips inch up my cheeks. *That feels good too.*

Not *everything* needs to be doom and gloom.

Not yet, anyway.

I take a breath, then hesitantly meet his gaze again. "It was ten thousand dollars."

Linc's eyes bulge and his mouth nearly drops.

My thoughts exactly.

Eyebrows flinching, I add, "And it wasn't . . . a *tip*, really. I-I took it. It was on Sharktooth's lap when they were . . . holding me down," Linc's eyes light with anger, but his dark eyebrows pinch downward, and I clarify who Sharktooth is—"Tariel."

A tension bunches in his shoulders, and I don't miss the tick of his jaw as the muscles in his neck strain.

I squeeze his knee, but when the tension stays, I use my voice, "Linc, I'm okay. It's okay," I tell him quietly and his eyes blink back at me.

He's always been so protective. Of me, Maisie, his mom, Ellis— anyone he cared about. But this . . .

God, it breaks my heart.

It's like the anger I felt watching Gram be sick. The helpless feeling.

It's okay, I tell him, again, silently. Tears bite the back of my eyes, but I swallow hard, fighting them off.

He takes another breath, and I see him nodding, silently telling me he's okay. *Maybe he just needs a minute?*

I go with that, giving myself a few seconds to breathe too.

I just can't understand it. This . . . *man.*

The boy I knew—*now, a man*—is truly *convinced* he assaulted me seven years ago. But even now, he's sitting here with murder in his eyes—ready to carry out the deed against men who *almost* hurt me.

It doesn't make any fucking sense.

Why doesn't he remember what I remember?

I take a breath, and pull back my shoulders—feeling a physical threat in my throat—one that aches to mention the subject I've been warned to avoid—just as I see the rest of the tension drop from Linc's shoulders.

Careful. Start easy.

I refocus. After another beat, I turn the attention back to our distraction—*The Window*—telling him, "I mean, it's fucking weird, right? Like, *Beck knows* that *I know* what happened. And *I know* that *he knows* what happened because he watched the tapes. So if everyone is aware . . . *why* be weird about it and refer to that money as a *tip?*"

Linc nods and the corner of his mouth quirks—an *almost* smirk.

I'm not sure if it was my very scattered, inarticulate observations about how everything just went down, or something else that gave him a blip of amusement, but it drops quickly.

After a breath, he shrugs and slowly speaks. "I don't know. But the whole thing seemed . . . off. We need to look into the police report. I imagine *if* they made one—that money would be considered evidence."

An absent nod tilts my chin as I'm momentarily hypnotized by the sound of his voice. It's the longest sentence I've heard him string together and the sound warms my chest.

But I take in his words, eventually, nodding. He makes a good point, but—"You don't think they actually filed a police report?"

Linc shrugs again. He takes a second, his eyes move back and forth a couple of times, then he says, "I don't know. We should talk to Ellis. I should—call Desmond." His speech trips, just a bit, and I wonder if it's because he wishes we could just stay out here too.

Stay out here and pretend.

In the driveway. An imaginary road trip.

When I don't say anything, he continues to stare back at me. Not impatiently—not even with the creases of discomfort I've come to know on his face in this new reality.

He's watching me with . . . *care. Fascination.* It's an interesting combination of soft and protective, and it fills me with the same emotions.

"Can we listen to one more song?" I ask.

Linc's throat bobs and his hand tightens around mine on his knee. His eyes float down and the same flicker from earlier lights in my chest.

I can tell what he's thinking by the drop in his expression, the fine lines in his face creasing.

"I won't play that one . . ." I reassure him.

Not yet, I think. *It's not the right moment.*

Or maybe it is. But I'm not ready to listen to it yet either.

After another second, he nods, and I take a breath of relief. *One more song.*

"No, that's sketchy as *fuck*," Ellis mutters, grabbing a water bottle from the fridge and letting the door drop close, then whines, "*Goddammit*, why did I make myself agree to a dry night?"

I snort a laugh. *I guess his hangover has lingered too.*

Linc and I are sitting in the living room—him on the chair, me on the couch—as Ellis makes his way back toward us, and sits next to me.

I had just gotten done explaining what Beck offered me— *should* I decide to stay at The Window.

"Did they mention anything about you guys knowing each other?" Ellis asks.

Linc looks over at me, his eyebrow cocking in a way that makes my mouth tilt up. *Right.* I've now contributed to this little covert operation.

I pin my lip between my teeth with a shrug. "When they asked, I told them he was my brother's boyfriend."

Ellis snorts and Linc looks just as unamused as the first time it happened, but then he takes a breath and says, "T-Tell him about the tip."

I can see Linc's wheels turning. I'm not sure if it's all this nonsense about The Window or the mountain of other, more important things we have hanging between us, but focusing on this stupid club's scandal feels like as good of a distraction as any.

I quickly explain the whole thing to Ellis and before I've even finished, he stands.

"Ten *thousand* dollars?! You took *10K,* and they—" He shakes his head. "No. This is fucked. We've definitely gotta talk to Desmond. He's working with his charity in Bali right now, so I'll have to wait till he calls. Has service . . ." His hands clasp the back of the couch, his chin dropping, shaking the blond waves tousled on the top of his head.

Ugh. I should have known better. My distraction had all the makings of something to give Ellis a riot. *A lot of things do.*

It comes with the territory of caring about shit as hard as he does. *And I love that about him.*

Gram did too. She always used to tell me, "A woman who feels is never broken, she's just listening."

Pronouns aside, I never felt that to be more true than with Ellis Casper. Always listening . . .

The thought of Gram slumps my shoulders. I've barely heard her today, and the thought pulls an ache through my chest. My body shifts in an attempt to hide the swell as my eyes flick up to my right, still seeing Ellis, worrying his bottom lip between his teeth.

The sight pushes me to stand, rounding the couch, before I gently pull on his shoulder, then wrap my arms around him. "It's okay," I tell him. "No one got hurt."

He nods, hugging me back. "I know," he says, quietly, and while my face is pretty much buried in his chest, I can *feel* Linc's eyes on me—his stare like a pencil outlining my figure.

Ellis clears his throat. "I just hate the idea of what *could have* happened. I . . ." When he trails off, I pull back slightly, but still hold his shoulders. He releases a heavy exhale and steps back from me. "I don't think you should go back there, Paige. I know it's not my place, and . . . what they're offering you *sounds* good." He leans a little closer, his voice a bit quieter. "But you're worth more. You know that. And whatever they're promising you comes with expectations. Even if they're not saying it."

Funny. I remember having a similar thought in the Veranda.

And I know he's right. Ten thousand dollars is the most money I've *ever* had. If I break my lease in Hollywood, budget, and get another job quickly, it may be enough money to at least *start* making the repairs on Gram's house.

It feels right. And maybe that's what *all* of this has been.

The great and powerful Buffy, working some cosmic shift to set something in motion and finally get us to actually move on with our lives in real ways.

A plan.

No more Window. Back to Venice. Clean up the house. Clean up me.

But then there's him . . .

Just as my eyes start to wander back over to Linc, Ellis's sigh stops me. "Did Beck talk to you about anything Desmond mentioned?" he asks, looking in Linc's direction.

And now that I have a reason to look at Linc, I do, and see that he's again, watching me. Chills run down my spine under his attentive gaze before he finally blinks, then clears his throat. "N-No. Didn't mention anything."

Ellis blows out a breath. "Yeah, see, *that's* fucking weird." He swipes a palm down his face and then shakes his head. "And you haven't really had any interaction with anyone aside from Jackson and Paige?"

Linc's chest lifts with an inhale. "And Rio." Ellis's eyebrows pinch before Linc clarifies, "The o-one I've been using sign language with."

Now *my* eyebrows lift. *He's been using sign language?*

I feel my mouth pull up at the corners. Now that he says it, it makes sense. Rio isn't exactly warm and fuzzy. I mean, she *is*, but she makes you earn it. And to my knowledge, she doesn't really know the guards. Just Jackson.

She likes Linc—Cook. He's using sign language.

I drift off into thought, wondering if *he remembers* when we were little—our ASL lessons with Gram.

Ellis clears his throat and I can feel him looking back over at me, breaking my mental musings as he says, "You've been at The Window for a year . . . is there anyone you can think of that might be helpful? Someone Linc can make a point to talk with next time he's there—see if they have any information?"

Buffy bless, I'm the worst person for this, seeing as I barely remember *my* club name—but then I remember—"Selene." Ellis's eyebrows pinch, and I quickly explain, "She found your address for me. And she knew I was working the Veranda—which is weird 'cause as far as I know, they try to keep the events discreet. I think they're worried we'll kill each other, or something."

Ellis's eyes widen. "She *found* our *address*? Our *real* address?!" His eyes flick over to Linc and my gaze follows. "How the fuck did that happen?"

Linc's eyes look wide, surprised, and Ellis looks back at me—*tennis match conversations, and all*—just before he shakes his head again.

Another beat passes and he sighs, "All right, well, Linc I definitely think you should try to talk to this girl, see what she knows." He glances over toward the kitchen, his eyes peeking at the clock on the oven, then groans, "I've gotta start to go through some of the shit Wade found, but I'll grab you guys if Desmond calls. I imagine it won't be till tomorrow at the earliest."

The abrupt change in subject makes my chest jump, and I quickly tell him, "Well—I—uh . . ." *Dammit.* I shake my head, trying again, "I'm probably going to pack up. Uh—I should go back to my apartment and take care of the lease."

Ellis's eyes squint down toward me, then dart over to Linc, and my gaze follows, seeing he's standing.

When did that happen?

The twist of Ellis's chin as he turns his face back toward me pulls my attention back to him, and he says, "Where will you go?"

I shrug, feeling awkward suddenly, but tell him, "I was thinking I'd . . . go back to Gram's."

His mouth stretches into a soft smile. "I like that plan," he says sweetly, making me want to hug him again. "But there's really no rush. It's already dark. Why don't you stay tonight, at least? Or—however long you want. We can help you grab the rest of your shit from the apartment when you're ready."

I look over at Linc, who is . . . *unnervingly* quiet.

And that's saying something because he has the silent broody-thing *down fucking pat.*

Ellis sighs, "Anyway, like I said, I've really gotta try to work through some of this. See if it's even worth it to have Wade keep looking."

"What'd he find?" I ask a little too eagerly, clinging to distraction.

Ellis shrugs. "I don't know. Some old roster of names from years ago. A couple of videos." A heavy sigh pushes past his lips glancing up at the ceiling. "Three soft shell tacos and cheesy roll-up says it's a dead end," he mutters, then lowers his chin, looking back over at Linc.

Linc's tense stance eases just a bit as he meets our friend's eyes. The smallest smirk surfaces—the same one I've seen peek out a couple of times—and my insides do a small flip. Another beat passes, and Linc says, "Taco bets never end well for you."

Ellis snorts a laugh. "This is true," he says, starting off toward his hallway, then adds over his shoulder, "Maybe you guys should watch a movie or something," and I can hear the smile in his voice. The lofty way he delivered the salutation.

Daring us to . . . *watch a movie.*

CHAPTER 40
LINC

"Maybe you guys should watch a movie."

The suggestion lingers in the air, running alongside all the other information Paige and Ellis just talked about—but the fact sticking to the front of my mind is that Paige is planning to leave.

Which of course was always going to happen—*needs to happen*—but I'm not ready yet.

Her wide blue eyes finally leave Ellis's exit route and drift back over to me. We stand for a few seconds, just staring. Talking may still be a struggle, but staring at her is easy. *Always has been.*

The blue waves of her hair are billowing around her pretty face. The icy color of the strands look brighter against the oversized dark blue flannel she's still wearing.

My eyes drift to her wrists again—the bracelets and lace peeking out from the bottom of the sleeve.

A flash of *raw cuts along her skin, her small wrists bound with blood running down her arm,* hits me suddenly and I wince.

"I guess I should—" she starts to say, but I cut her off.

"Do you w-wanna watch a movie?" I blurt out, still tensing from the vision.

But disturbing images aside, I'm not ready for her to leave yet. The room. The house. I just want to be near her for as long as I can.

As long as I can, I reaffirm silently.

She doesn't say anything for a few seconds, but then her mouth lifts—*almost* a smile. A moment passes before she says, "Sure."

Okay. So. I panicked.

Paige went to the kitchen to make us each a drink—apparently she wasn't partaking in a dry night like Ellis, and I *sure as fuck* needed a drink. Especially since the movie I picked is over *three hours* long.

Yep. In a brain spasm, I found the first movie title I recognized—*one I knew she liked*—and clicked on it.

And that movie is fucking *Titanic.*

But she smiled when it started to play, so . . . it was worth it.

I remind myself of this *again,* as I'm acutely aware of any movement she makes on the other side of the couch. I can't be certain how far into the movie we are, because I've pretty much been watching her from the corner of my eye since we started it. I've even found a backup route to look at her if I feel like I'm being too obvious.

The big windows to the night sky are on the other side of me, so even when I turn my face away, I can still see her just behind me in the reflection of the window, the moon in front of me.

My eyes bulge when I see her face turn toward mine in the reflection. "Are you okay?" she asks quietly and my chin whips back over in her direction.

Did she notice me watching her?

Jesus. Not creepy at all.

But she doesn't look freaked out—in fact, she's closer than she was before and the realization starts a fierce rush through my veins.

Before—she was fully on the right-most cushion and now she's sitting on the cushion directly next to me.

Thankfully, I had the foresight to keep one hand in my pocket.

I take a breath as I fiddle the penny between my fingers, trying to reel myself back in. I've long since finished my drink, but the urge to get up and make another one is strong.

But God, fuck, her smell. It captures me in its cloud once again. The spice to her scent is extra strong, making me wonder if she put on some of that cinnamon chapstick she used to wear.

Her lips.

That's definitely the wrong thing to be thinking about, but of course, my eyes fucking linger on her plump rosy lips. My thumb runs over the penny in my pocket—dissatisfied with the bumpy outline of Abraham. My fingers twitch with a need to reach out and cradle the soft skin along her jaw, brush her bottom lip with my thumb—maybe even run the pad along her lower row of teeth.

Feel her.

But her soft smile steals my eyes from the more carnal thoughts when she says, "It's about to be the best part."

I blink, my mind zooms back out—away from her lips.

The movie. She's talking about the movie.

Reluctantly, I pull my eyes from her, and aim them up at the screen instead. The tension I've been holding releases a bit, loosening my shoulders, as I see what part of the movie she's talking about. My lips twitch and then stretch up my cheeks.

The third class party. Where Jack attends a dinner in first class, then invites Rose to the "real party" below deck.

It was *our favorite part.*

Paige and I saw this when we were young, but we always recognized that if we had been on the Titanic, we likely would have been down in third class. And their parties were infinitely *cooler. Pissed Ellis right the fuck off.*

An amused huff pushes through my nose. I focus on the screen, allowing myself to get used to her proximity, the familiarity of the movie, and slowly, I feel myself settling in.

We're watching Titanic. That's it.

And if we've made it to *this* part of the movie, then we're at least an hour into it.

A pang strikes in my chest, and my fists tighten at my sides. *It's a good thing,* I remind myself. Just two more hours. I'm already dancing with disaster just like Kate and Leo on the screen.

I sigh heavily, watching. I've been playing too heavily with my delusions—reckless territory. I know *well and good* that I won't be ready for her to leave two hours from now, when the movie ends. I won't be ready tomorrow, two days—*two years.*

I wasn't ready to leave her the first time.

The thought twists in my stomach, and my weight shifts. Paige fidgets a bit too, and my brain becomes hyper-aware of how easily I can feel her weight adjusting on the cushion next to me.

She's *so fucking close* and I'm literally trying to trick my brain—*pretend* that I have anchors holding my arms. But nothing can make it past the fucking *need* I have to pull her into me—onto my lap.

Hold her so tight she embeds herself into the emptiness her absence left. My key.

She's in a slightly curled position next to me on the couch. *It would take almost nothing to . . .*

Holy fuck. I think I'm hallucinating.

I must be. Because without warning, Paige is climbing onto my lap. A knee on each side, facing me. Images of her in this exact position zip through my mind. *In the front seat of my truck. Backstage. In her bed. In mine.*

"Wh-What are you doing?"

Her mouth tilts, modestly. "You keep . . . looking. I thought I'd make it easier." Her frosty blue waves are pulled to one shoulder, displaying the gorgeous column of her neck—my own experience knows of the hidden trove of freckles behind her ear.

But then what she said fully registers. *"You keep looking."*

She noticed. I mean, I'm sure it was pretty goddamn obvious—my eyes had a backup route, for fuck's sake.

"Do you want me to move?" she asks.

God, no. My hands latch onto her hips and a grunt pushes past my lips at the contact. *Goddamn,* she feels so fucking good. So warm.

"I'll take that as a no," she says with a small smirk and *God, I want to kiss her. How is it possible that our kiss in the kitchen was just this morning?*

The memory has a strange duality of feeling far *and* near. *Her full lips took mine. Her warm mouth met and matched my greedy need with every lick and bite.*

My already hardening dick becomes rock solid. I can feel it below my pants and suddenly, I'm aware she can likely feel it too since she's on my lap.

Fuck. Fuck, fuck, fuck.

Other than a deep inhale, she doesn't seem to draw any attention to it, and her blue eyes have me captive, staring down at me.

The night sky out the window and the television are the only light in the room, giving her various blue hues a soft glow. "Will you talk to me?" she asks, barely above a whisper.

There's a quiet desperation to her tone that I wasn't expecting—a sadness—like I've been keeping something from her.

My subconscious barks a humorless laugh at its own stupid thought, and my eyebrows pinch, trying to think of how to respond, but then she says, "Ellis told me I have to be careful. And I want to be, I don't wanna—" she stops herself again, shaking her head.

Ellis told her to be careful?

Of course he did. And he should. He knows what I did. Why he's left us alone together at all is fucking bizarre, but if I had to guess I'm sure it's because Paige told him she could handle it. *Handle me.*

And there was a time when I believed that to be true.

I swallow hard, outlining the words in my head, then say, "Th-There's nothing to talk about. Nothing that will change what happened."

Paige's eyebrows slope and her head shakes. "Will you tell me what you remember?"

"God—" I croak out, using my grip on her waist to lift her off of me and put her down beside me as gently as I can. As soon as I let go of her I scrub my hands up and down my face.

Her question still lingers in the air as my eyes finally peek out from behind my hands, her gaze waiting. Determined. I shake my head and my eyes fall to the floor again. "Pip, please don't make me say it."

The featherlight touch of her fingers on my shoulder makes me jerk and push to stand, suddenly, pacing away—farther from her, but she follows.

"Stop!" I bark and she does, but the hurt expression on her face nearly kills me. "I'm sor—I'm sorry."

"Stop," she says back, but unlike my desperate plea, there's an unmistakable command to her voice, and my eyes snap to hers. Her gaze is lit with a fury I've only seen once and it straightens my spine. She walks toward me, slowly. "Stop apologizing and tell me what you remember," she says, her jaw clenched.

I breathe heavily, trying to let some oxygen keep me here. Breathing the air *here*. But this conversation is set to completely annihilate me, and I can feel it in my spotty vision.

It's a specific pain—one I wouldn't wish on anyone. Having

to *convince* someone you love—*the person you hurt*—that you hurt them. After everything else, it's an agony I'm unprepared for.

I shake my head, looking at the words in my mind, hating myself as I find a concise way to give her what she's asking for.

When I see the words, my stomach rolls, and my voice punches out, "I s-snapped. I held you down, tore off your underwear, and then—" I gag. I haven't eaten much today, so luckily it's a dry heave because to puke in front of her after spewing *that shit* would really rub salt in the wound.

"No, Linc," she says quickly. Quietly. She reaches out toward me, but she doesn't touch me. It's probably a good thing, but I also find myself yearning for her to close the distance.

My eyes flick to the purple lace peeking out from beneath the flannel at her wrists.

And just like that, she lifts her hand, and places it lightly on my shoulder.

Like she's back in my head.

Not that I'm sure she ever left.

I don't wince or flinch. I *feel.* I feel *her.*

She says, "You're missing some parts. I . . ." She shakes her head and a sickly color takes over her face. She glances down at the floor, then looks back up at me.

My eyes search hers. She has that look I recognize. The one where she wants me to read her mind—but I can't. I fucking can't figure it out right now, and it only loosens the reins on my meager bit of control.

Finally, she clears her throat, but her voice still cracks as she says, "I have a copy of it. On a flash drive."

My heart drops. *Air, gone.* My eyes blink rapidly.

She's seen it?

She has it?

She's watched it?

The questions crash with the wave of visions that rush forward of screams and moans—tears and pain. Holding her down. Hurting her.

I'm sorry. I'm sorry. I'm so fucking sorry.

Blackness creeps in from the edges of my vision.

Paige, go! Go!

Did I say that out loud?

I think I tell her to run. I hope I tell her to run.

Because suddenly, I feel a cold, familiar darkness cloud my vision.

Ellis was right.

There was nothing like seeing the lights go out in someone's eyes. Eyes you knew better than your own.

I pushed too far.

I was sure he had no desire to watch the despicable eleven minutes on the flash drive, but I thought bringing forth its existence would somehow get him to see—understand—that I've never blamed him. I've shamefully watched the eleven minutes myself a couple of times—in my darkest hours.

Gram always said, "I don't think the darkest hours are always bad—some are just ominous. But the unknown has its own discovery. And wandering around in the dark means you're searching. Moving. As long as you keep going . . ."

The memory of her words bring me back to now. *Going,* I think. More specifically, *driving.*

I don't think *running away* is what Gram had in mind when she was encouraging me to *keep going*—but I had to go.

And *I'm not "running away,"* I remind myself. *Technically,* I did tell them I was going to go back to Gram's—and *that's* where I'm going. *Driving.*

I turn the music up a bit, releasing a breath.

Truthfully, I have every intention of following up with the men of my past, but I . . . pushed too hard.

And now I have to give Linc some space. Just . . . some time to recover. *Not forever,* I remind myself.

I clear my throat in an attempt to shove the thought away, then flick on my windshield wiper as a light sprinkling of rain falls from the early morning clouds.

I turn up the music—some Slipknot song is playing—but I'm not paying attention. I just need something to drown out the constant fucking replay that's been thrumming through me since it all happened a few hours ago.

It's all still so vivid—so raw—I feel like I can nearly reach out and touch the memory. *Like it's just on the other side of the windshield with the rain . . .*

At the mention of the flash drive, the first thing I noticed was Linc's eyes. His blinking pattern. It wasn't excessive or even rapid, but it seemed . . . pointed, somehow?

Then suddenly, an anguished roar tore out of him—the noise was so deep and rough that I felt it in my own chest as he choked out an unintelligible noise.

The wide space of the house felt bigger all of the sudden, as I saw his eyes turn nearly black—unrecognizable.

The snarl on his face sent a chill through my bones—even his stance became a taller, more looming presence, and I felt my heart cowering.

But I locked my knees, trying to push the shake from my voice as I said, "Linc," quietly, trying to get him back. Come back. *I begged for it silently, I begged him with my eyes, but the big tattooed man—the boy who wouldn't even arm-wrestle me in first grade because he didn't want to hurt me—was staring at me with endless, unhinged . . . confusion.*

I put some distance between us, rushing toward the kitchen.

I wasn't afraid of him. I wasn't. But Linc wasn't present, and I had no idea how to get him back.

I could tell he was disoriented because his steps were uneven. His face looked ready for murder, and his muscles were all contracting, but his coordination was sluggish.

His eyes were so far away, so dark.

Suddenly, Ellis barrelled in from his hallway and immediately took notice of my wide eyes, my tense stance. It was all the hesitation needed for Linc to grab him, and shove him into the wall, his hands fisting Ellis's shirt.

Ellis grunted at the impact, his own biceps bulged as he locked a grip around Linc's wrist. "Grab some ice!" he gritted out through clenched teeth.

I listened, quickly running to the fridge and yanking open the freezer, grabbing as many ice cubes as I could.

Cradling the ice in my hands, I rushed over to them. "Run it along his neck—put one in his fist if you can," Ellis panted, then barked, "Linc!" trying to get him to snap out of it. He pushed our friend away, trying to make room for me to run the ice anywhere I could. I dropped a few of the cubes, my hands shaking, but after a few fumbles, I managed to push the slippery ice along the back of Linc's neck—like Ellis said.

Linc hissed, and my fingertips could feel the heat from his skin—the flesh was bright red.

God, Linc. I'm so sorry.

The right side of the car dips, and I gasp as the cabin rattles and my eyes dart down to Cheeto—in her to-go container on the passenger's seat. And she is *pissed.*

Join the club.

We pass the canals, but the lingering memory of last night keeps my muscles tightened. *My mind fucking racing.*

And *that's* why I had to leave. I'm *too* hungry for answers right now. Since the moment I ran into him a few nights ago—*since I found out the real reason he left*—I've been counting on our longstanding connection to help repair us. But the problem is, I think our connection—*the reemergence of* me—is only making this guilt he's carrying around that much more painful. Overwhelming.

I'm a trigger. To *him.* The boy I'm slowly dying without.

And I'm sure Shakespeare would just have a fucking field day with this—but what the fuck?

I mean, Ellis said it himself, Linc hadn't had an episode like this in years—and it's no coincidence that it happened now. When I brought up the thing I wasn't supposed to bring up.

Fuck me. And look at that! It ended exactly the way Ellis warned me it would. *A disaster.*

One that broke my heart to see . . .

The ice seemed to help.

It helped bring some level of awareness back, because I could visibly see Linc's grip loosen on Ellis.

Ellis nodded, his own muscles releasing a bit as I continued to run some ice over Linc's neck, I dragged a cube to the collar line of the gray T-shirt he was wearing.

When the ice melted, I used the cool touch of my hands on his neck. I wasn't able to get any ice into his clenched fists, but his hands slowly released Ellis entirely.

Linc stood and stared at Ellis for long seconds—maybe even minutes—his eyes blinking almost like he was trying to get rid of a flash in his vision.

"It's okay, man. It's okay," Ellis said, quietly.

Slowly—so fucking slowly—I could see the green and brown flooding back into Linc's eyes. The flush on his neck and chest dissipated, but the color immediately rushed up to his cheeks.

He swallowed hard and his chin slowly turned to me.

"Oh my God," he croaked.

"Linc—" Ellis said.

"Oh my God, fuck—" Linc's hoarse voice ripped through my chest, his eyes wide.

"Hey," I said, quickly. "It's okay. Nothing—" I stopped, realizing I was saying this phrase for the second time today. "Nothing bad happened."

Bad had already happened.

Linc's breathing was still ragged, his hazel eyes were extra green— a sign of discomfort, I had noticed when we were kids.

I cleared my throat and slid my hand down his arm. He hadn't noticed I was still touching him, but the movement shifted his eyes.

I could feel him still shaking, still partially stuck wherever he just was—but he was trying so hard to shake it off—to seem okay. I recognized that feeling instantly. And it crushed me more.

Stopping at a red light, my foot hits the brake harder than I mean to.

Throwing a soccer-mom-arm over Cheeto's container, I skid to a stop. My fingers immediately dig through my hair, pushing back the unruly blue waves as I glance around.

Main Street.

It's early, and there aren't many people out, but my eyes peek about halfway down the block—seeing someone putting the sandwich board out front of Queenie's.

I could work there again . . .

The paychecks were nothing compared to The Window, but . . . *maybe as a side hustle?*

I shake my head. Too close to *before.*

It's already going to be . . . *rough,* staying at Gram's.

Our house.

And I'll still have to break my lease at the Hollywood apartment. But in my hasty exit from the Game Cube in the mountain, my body decided *here* first.

Drop off my stuff. Spend some time there. See if I can even make it the night—*make it through the door*—before I throw away my tuna can in the city.

That's my plan. If I can . . . *handle* being back home for a night or two, when I'm ready to get the rest of my shit out of the Hollywood apartment, I'll call the boys.

Just a breather, I tell myself again.

Fuck. Why does it feel like I'm trying to convince myself?

"Leaving was the right thing to do," I whine out loud.

The heavy weight of . . . everything *sat between us.*

But movement slowed. Ellis clapped Linc's shoulder gently, his chin lowering, trying to meet Linc's eyes.

I think Ellis asked him something, but the sound was garbled as a new flutter of awareness found me.

This trauma was different from mine. The awful experience we shared seemed to have manifested differently for both of us.

I know mine had taken on different forms throughout the years, but never anything like this.

At first, you could see mine. In my hollow eyes, my defeated, broken posture, my wrists . . .

It was obvious. But like anything else—with practice—I learned to hide those things. For Gram. And for me too, probably.

But the time and space between us had been given all the fear from a single experience, and sculpted itself into a mountain determined *to crumble down on top of us.*

Bury us.

Which was exactly what would happen if I stayed.

The avalanche of my need *to deconstruct what happened to us— to understand what happened to* him*—was too deep.*

It was clear in the following hour Linc spent agonizing over the episode. He sat on the couch, and I sat next to him while I explained what happened, keeping my hand on his knee the whole time.

And he held my hand. His grip tightened and loosened.

"I'm so sorry, Pip," he said over and over again. Same to Ellis. And each apology felt like another twist in my chest.

But really, no one got hurt—so, in the grand scheme of things, it could have been so much worse.

Worse was what would happen if I stayed and continued to poke and prod for information, for answers, he wasn't ready to give me.

Ellis watched with sad eyes as his friend blinked with devastation—the adrenaline crash—and I could feel the exhaustion in my own body.

Linc fell asleep.

And it's right when the ship started to sink on the TV.

It always sinks . . .

Just as I have the thought, my heart nearly capsizes . . . I pull onto our street.

So far so good . . .

I mean, the whole, *being alert while driving thing* seems to be a hard-fucking-pass, but at least I made it to our road.

And I can't be sure if it's my delirium, or the unfolding of last night still lingering in my mind—but the old beach shanty doesn't seem as daunting.

I'm still scared. Nervous.

The idea of walking through the house still sounds terrifying, but . . . the thought of being in my old room . . . well, it doesn't sound *bad.*

So, that's good.

God, I'm fucking *tired.*

I pull into the driveway slowly, my eyes dragging up to the dirty, pale yellow house.

"*This is right,*" I hear in my head.

I'm unsure if *I'm* telling myself or if it's Gram, but a warm comfort fills my chest with a deep inhale.

I look down at Cheeto.

Her big gray eyes stare up at me through the small, clear container. "Here goes nothin'."

Linc's breathing evened out and Ellis finally stopped the sounds of disaster on the TV screen with the remote, but I almost preferred it.

The silence was painful, it filled with the memories of Linc's rumbled nonsense.

I shook my head again, and then, slowly, carefully, wiggled my hand out from Linc's and I swear to God, I felt my heart skip.

Not forever, I reminded myself.

Once my hand was free, I hunched over, elbows on my knees, cradling my face in my hands

I could feel *Ellis's admonishing stare. When I finally peeked through my fingers, I could nearly see the* "I told you so" *scolding me with his eyes as he stared down at me.*

But then he surprised me when he said, "Did he–uh . . ." he trailed off, his voice barely above a whisper. "He didn't hurt you, did he?"

"No!" I whisper-yelled, then lowered my voice further. "Jesus, Ellis—"

"Well, what am I supposed to think?"

"Stop," I cut him off and flicked my eyes down to Linc, slumped over on the couch, hiding his face.

The sight made me wince, but I was grateful to see he was still sleeping. Resting.

I looked back at Ellis. "You know he would never hurt me," I said quietly, my jaw clenching. "It was my fault. I brought up shit, I touched him, I—"

Ellis scoffed, rubbing the bridge between his eyes. He looked back over at Linc, then sighed. Another roll of agitation passed through him, but then he seemed to shake it off. "Look, it's late. Let's just . . . get some sleep."

The creak of the door to the mudroom pushing open brings me back to now.

But the heaviness in my chest lifts a bit as I open the back door, then quickly call out, "Hello?"

Why? Who knows? But I left the door unlocked for a fucking year, so any number of things could be in the house.

Raccoons, dead bodies . . . Alive *bodies.*

It's also unlikely any of those things will answer me. But the house is quiet. I don't hear anything through the paper-thin walls leading to the kitchen, and the random array of shit I left on the table is still there.

That's where Linc's mug was.

My eyebrows flinch, but I ignore the memories of *that* day, and instead think about my route. *Straight through the kitchen, hard left through the living room, up the stairs, first door on the right.*

I must look insane. My duffle bag is strapped over my shoulders, I'm holding a gecko in one hand—*in what is essentially a lunchbox*—and my pepper spray is clutched in the other hand.

Insanity or not, I take a breath, and then I take off.

I try to keep Cheeto out in front of me in an attempt to not scramble her, but each peripheral image I catch feels like it slices at some deep part of my chest.

The piano. Fuck.

The pictures up the staircase. No, no, no.

I practically tumble into my room, luckily keeping Cheeto up like she's the football of a winning touchdown.

She looks terrified.

Breathlessly, I tell her, "Sorry," then spend an absurd amount of time on the floor, panting. Watching Cheeto.

She's racing around, but I think if I pick her up, it'll just rattle her more—literally.

My limbs shake as I kick the door closed to release some aggression, growling a bit as my foot makes contact with the door. The loud *slam* feels almost as satisfying as a kick to the wall.

Almost.

When my breathing evens out a bit, my eyes start to drift around the room, noting it still looks the same.

A mess.

The light blue walls are still riddled with tapestries. I look at the dresser that used to hold pictures on top. I took them away long ago, but staring at the empty shelf right now feels . . . off.

They're not gone anymore.

I told Gram to get rid of the pictures—of *everything* except the music box—but I'm sure she didn't. I'm sure if I looked for them, they'd be hidden somewhere in this house . . .

My eyes fall to my duffle bag, remembering my urge to let her cardigan experience the yard. The lemons.

I can't bring it to the tree right now because the rest of the house is a haunted graveyard, but maybe it'd like to see my room again.

Take a nap in my bed.

I pick up the heavy bag and drop it on the bed. After I unzip it, I dump everything out on the comforter.

I left in such a hurry that I literally rolled everything up in a ball and threw it in the bag.

I weave my way through the clothing, untangling the big beige sweater, when my eyes absently scan the pile.

Looking . . .

I lift a few flannels and T-shirts, a couple of thongs, but . . .

The longer I search the heap of clothing, the brighter the heat becomes in my chest.

I don't see them. I've held onto them for eight years at this point and . . . I don't see them.

Something like victory—hope—maybe a new breed of something I've never felt blooms deep inside of me.

The well. My deep sacred place.

And I can't help the dirty smirk that curls my lips.

He *is* still here.

And he took my fucking underwear.

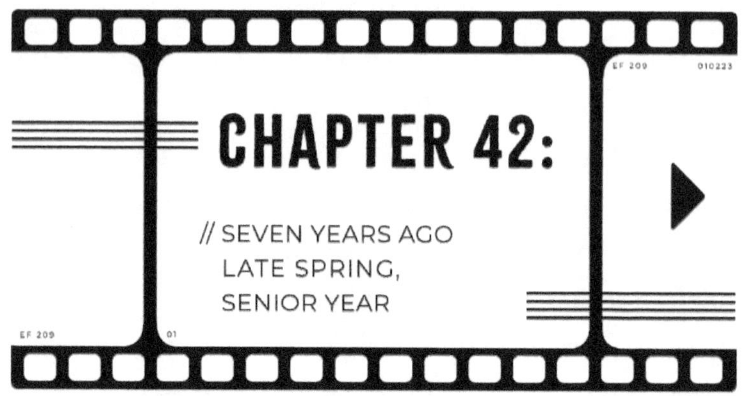

PAIGE

"I need a beanie, Paigey May!" Gram announced, hobbling into my room.

"Hey!" I said from the bed—a little harsher than I meant to—pushing myself off the mattress. I took a breath, looking at my sweet grandma.

Her fall a few weeks ago had me in drill sergeant mode. She was still *supposed* to be on bed rest—and I swear to Buffy, it was like trying to trap a hummingbird.

It happened the day Linc went to San Diego with Mr. Harris. I came home from my shift at Queenie's to find her on the floor in the kitchen, crying and groaning in pain.

I shook my head to clear away the memory, and instead watched as she started to try and reach up to the shelf in my closet. Her light gray hair was tied up in a wily bun, her cozy cardigan hugging her crescent posture.

When she pulled on a sweatshirt, a bunch of other ones came tumbling to the floor, and I walked toward her. "What'd I tell you about unnecessary movement, woman?" I muttered, trying to sound more playful, but I linked my arm through hers, and tried to slowly start walking her back to her bedroom.

"And why do you need a beanie?" I finally asked with a small laugh. It was the end of April—a far cry from the small bit of chilly weather we'd occasionally get in the winter months. "Are you too cold in your room?" I asked.

She gently pulled from my arm, and stepped away. "I'm fine, Paigey. I hurt my back—I'm not in damn traction!" This time, it was *her* turn to take on a harsher tone, making me swallow the lump in my throat.

Gram was an independent woman in every sense of the word. She was moving slower, her back was still recovering, but she was okay. And I knew better than anyone that she *could* take care of herself.

"I'm sorry," I said, honestly. "I just don't want you to get hurt again." I leaned my forehead to hers. "I need you, ya know?"

Her face softened immediately and she held my cheek before her arms stretched around my back, holding me tight. "You're sweet to worry about me, baby. But I'm doing just fine." She released me and backed up with a mischievous smile, the one that made my own lips pull up. "Plus, I've gotta stretch," she said. "Practice my dance moves for tonight." I snorted a laugh, and she added, "Elly-boy said I could DJ tonight."

I laughed again, with a nod. *The beanie made a little more sense now.* Still, I took Gram's arm with mine and slowly started walking her back toward the door, across the hall. "Even more reason to rest up."

When I tried to back out of Providence's prom, we had decided—well, Ellis *decided—that we were having an anti-prom here at the house instead.*

As we got back to Gram's room, I casually tried to edge her toward the bed, a silent suggestion to take her bed rest fucking seriously.

She shooed me away with a small chuckle. "If I take a nap, will you get off my hunch?"

We both laughed this time, and it felt good. I'd always appreciated her ability to laugh at herself—to be silly, even in scary moments . . . *even when we were waiting for the ambulance to get here that night.*

She was on the floor, writhing in pain, and she said, "If one of those fellas looks like a young Eastwood, you make sure he's *the one checking things out, if you know what I mean."*

I huffed a laugh. I still had yet to confirm whether or not she meant *Clint* Eastwood.

But more importantly, if she *was* in fact going to DJ our silly get-together tonight, then she really did need to get some rest.

"If you *actually* nap and don't just take a weed gummy, we'll talk," I told her, my mouth tilting with playful challenge.

She rolled her eyes, and I stood idly as she climbed into bed, her body flinching as she lifted her legs.

She yelped and I immediately held my hand out to her. She grabbed it, puffing out an exhale as her soft small palm tightened in mine.

Shit. "Are you okay?"

She nodded, her teeth clenching. "Muscle spasm."

God, it was *so fucking hard* to see her in pain. *I hated it,* but I kept holding her hand until it must have passed, and her grip loosened. I turned on the heating pad, and just a moment later, her body relaxed into the mattress. "Just twenty minutes with the heat," I reminded her.

She nodded. "Right. Don't wanna overcook."

A small laugh—mostly a sigh—escaped me. I could tell her quip was half-hearted. As I got back to her door, I lingered, then asked, "What color beanie do you want, Lemon Lady?"

She smiled, the same one that made *me* smile, then she said, "Yellow."

The house looked . . . Well, it looked like an over-decorated gym—at least it did last time I was downstairs. But Ellis was supposedly still *"setting up,"* so it was anyone's guess as to what movie clichés I'd be walking into.

It seemed like a lot of fuss for what was essentially no different than a regular Friday night. But I also couldn't deny that *trying* to have fun tonight sounded good. *Necessary.*

I'd have backup with Linc, Ellis, and Maisie—and thankfully, Gram had *miraculously* spent the day in bed. Granted, it was only because she was crocheting a fucking lemon beanie, but . . . she still rested.

Using the mirror on the back of my bedroom door, I carefully practiced the fading technique with my bronze color eyeshadow, going for a natural smokey eye.

Well, unnaturally, natural.

As I finished my other eye, I released a heavy breath, then added just a little bit of mascara, brightening the blue in my irises, and I used a small bit of highlighter under my eyes to hide the dark circles.

My chin lifted and my mouth pinched at the corner.

I was getting better at the makeup thing.

Maybe that would help with my *lack* of outfit options.

The night Gram fell—*the ambulance ride, the hospital stay*—it took a decent chunk out of our meager savings. Not to mention the follow-up appointments that would continue to add up. So, money for a prom dress was out of the question.

Of course, I would never mention anything about it to Gram, and I didn't tell the boys either. All I told them was I didn't want to go to Providence's prom because I didn't want to leave Gram alone.

Which was also true.

But the money didn't matter, I told myself. I mean, truly all that *mattered* was that Gram got the care she needed, and that she was okay.

I could always make more money.

In fact, I already was. Queenie was letting me keep my Tuesday night gigs through the summer, and had started giving me a cut of the cover charges. *And* I just snagged one of the lead roles for a new indie movie shooting down in San Diego in a few weeks.

I guess Linc had met the director, Dylan, with Mr. Harris at the screening down there a few weeks ago. I only had to send Dylan one audition side before Pauper Productions sent me a written offer last week.

The pay was actually pretty decent for a small-budget movie, and even *better* than that—Mr. Harris was able to get Linc a grip position on set. So, at least we would be there together.

The reminder that Linc would be there had a way of calming my anxiety about the whole thing.

I just wanted to do a good job—make a good impression. But film wasn't my forte, *despite* what my hot-director boyfriend might have thought.

Still, the promise of incoming funds lifted my chest, and I shook out the waves of my long, blond hair.

Crossing over to my closet, I looked where I had hung my options for tonight. I was still trying to decide if I should wear the blue dress Linc liked from my voice recital last year, or lean into the anti-prom vibe and wear my tight purple dress and rainbow fishnets.

A knock at the door made me jump, my eyebrows pinching. But after only a second, my mouth twitched as I felt it—*the sensation of eyes on me*—even through the closed door.

"Come in," I said, fighting my smirk.

Turning, I saw Linc popping his head in, his smile boyish and melting me down to goo. With a small dip of his chin, he said, "Hey!"

"Hi," I laughed. "Care to venture the rest of the way into the room, or are you trying something out?"

He snorted, "No—uh," he stopped, giving his head a small shake. "I—uh—I got you something."

"Buffy bless, you are terrible at this!" I heard Ellis calling all the way from downstairs.

What the hell is going on?

I walked over to Linc *lurking* in the doorway—and as soon as I cleared the view of the dresser, my mouth fell open.

He was holding a dark blue strapless dress with a neckline of crystal-looking stars along the bust. My eyes traveled the rest of the way down, seeing a soft tulle material for the skirt, also dotted with crystals.

It's so beautiful. My throat suddenly clogged with emotion, and my eyes shot up to him. But then I wasn't looking at the dress. A tingle stirred low in my belly. *Hot damn,* Linc looked fucking gorgeous.

His dark waves of hair were styled, but in the messy way that made my fingers ball up—*feeling grabby*—but his eyes were hypnotizing, a fierce mixture of greens and browns, gold flickering. And his toned body was all wrapped in a slate gray button-up and black slacks.

The urge to whistle was strong, but luckily, my mouth was still hanging open. I finally shook my head, then looked back at the Starry Night dress he was holding.

"Do you like it?" he finally asked.

My smile stretched, nodding, as I grabbed the material of his shirt and pulled him into the room.

"Wanna know how much?" I smirked just before I threw my arms around him, kissing him hard and pulling him into me. His lips met mine with matching enthusiasm, plunging his tongue into my mouth.

I nibbled and licked his bottom lip just as his hoarse chuckle pushed between our lips. "It's a selfish present, really," he mumbled, but paused to take my lips again, then whispered, *"I'm* the one who gets to look at you all night."

Oof. I was two seconds away from climbing him like a damn tree. But the reminder that we were in a house *full* of people stopped me. That, *and* the idea of what his face would look like when I put the dress *on* was enough for me to give him one more peck and pull away. He whined and my toes curled into the floor as I giggled.

He handed me the dress, but then pulled me back into him— "Oh, come on, can't I help you get into it?"

"Hoo-hoo! Thatta boy!" I suddenly heard Gram howling from just outside the door, and Linc quickly stepped back, bumping into the wall and tripping, before catching himself.

Gram's head peeked in. *Whoops. Guess we didn't close the door.*

A small rosy tint caught Linc's cheeks, and he looked down at the floor, chuckling awkwardly. "Sorry, Darlene."

Damn, I loved him. So fucking cute. I loved that he could be a bossy dirty-talker one minute, and a bashful bumbling goober the next.

Gram patted his shoulder with another laugh as she passed. "Nothing to be sorry about." She looked at the dress I was holding and her eyes brightened. "Can I help you finish getting ready, Paigey?"

I didn't have much to do other than put on the dress, maybe some lipstick—but I accepted the offer with a small nod and a smile. She looked like she wasn't limping as much. *That felt good to see too.*

Linc gave me another shaky-knee-worthy grin, then said, "I'm gonna go see if Ellis needs any help."

I reached out for his hand. "Thank you, again, for my dress."

He gave me an ever-so chaste kiss on my knuckle, a kiss that did not match the devious glint in his eyes, and then he walked away.

I watched him from just inside the door and as he reached the stairs, his eyes met mine with a promising smirk. *I'll help you* out *of it later.*

My shoulders jerked with a small huff of laughter, giving him my own silent message back—*You better.*

LINC

I swiped my palm down my face, sitting at the kitchen table. "What are you making?" I asked Ellis—who was in a full-blown tux, standing at the counter, and mixing some shit together in a bowl.

"Lemonade," he said simply, but then proceeded to free-pour a bottle of vodka into the bowl.

I pushed to stand, taking three quick steps toward him. "Jesus, dude—" I scoffed, my hand stopping him from pouring more. "Darlene's on painkillers right now, *Maisie's* here."

With an easy smile, he mocked, "*Duuude,* I already got the okay from Darlene—who agrees that a prom without booze is basically a baby shower."

I couldn't respond. *What the fuck did that even mean?* After another beat, Ellis shook his head, then gave my cheek a playful smack, "You've really gotta lighten up, man. You *and* Paige-Monster."

I frowned, irritated, but trying not to be.

I knew Ellis was just trying to make this a fun night. *And God knows we could use it.* But I also knew there was only so much fun Paige *could* have right now.

I had never seen her more distraught than when I met her at the hospital. Jeremy dropped me off as soon as we got back to town, but visiting hours were over. So Paige came out and sat with me in the waiting room while the nurses reset some of Darlene's IVs.

She cried and cried and fucking cried. And I couldn't do anything but hold her. I sat with her while the doctors talked to her. It was all good news—the fall wasn't from any underlying illness, her back would heal with proper rest.

She kept herself together while the doctor finished, but as soon as he walked away, she cried some more.

I just wanted her to enjoy herself tonight. *One* worry-free night.

"Ta-dah!" Ellis half-sang, then said, "I present Spiked Angel juice."

"Like *Buffy*!" I heard Maisie squeal, as she ran down the steps. She'd insisted on being part of "girl time," and as I met her in the living room, I couldn't help but laugh at her *varying* shades of purple.

Her sundress was more of a lavender, swinging with each of the last three steps, and she flung a violet sequined boa over her shoulder. "Can I have some Spiked Angel juice?" she asked, her big brown eyes widening.

I shot a look at Ellis, and he conveniently looked toward the back door where *no one* stood.

Rolling my eyes, I shook my head, then looked back at Maisie. "No Spiked Angel juice for you yet. It's *spiked* 'cause it has bad stuff in it. And you're just a wee Loaf, remember?"

She made a noise that sounded somewhere between a groan and a giggle, but still gave me a hug. I knew secretly—*deep, deep down*—she loved the nickname. Her face smushed into my torso before she looked up at me, her smile inching up to meet her light brown eyes. "Paigey looks like glittery midnight."

My smile stretched further—*certain* that Maisie's evaluation was a perfect description of the girl upstairs.

My girl.

Paige never came out and said it, but I knew money was tight right now, and Ellis agreed she deserved to feel like the beautiful badass that she was for a night, so we split the cost of the dress—*though, like the solid buddy he is, he let me take the credit.*

The sound of him dunking his cup into the bowl brought me back to now, and I looked over, watching him take a sip. His eyebrows flinched. "Strong," he coughed, then his lips smacked. "Tart."

Maisie and I both laughed, as I felt my shoulders relax.

Maybe Ellis was right. Everyone was crashing here, so we didn't have to worry about driving. And if Paige wanted to have some of his Spiked Angel juice—*I* could make sure Darlene was okay for the night.

Whatever she needed.

Just as the thought passed, Darlene started to walk down the steps in a simple, light green dress, with a knit hat that looked like . . . a *lemon*, but her eyes intermittently peeked behind her.

My eyes followed, and I saw black heels step onto the highest stair. My mouth ticked up at the soft click from the shoes, but it was nearly drowned out by the creaking from the steps.

It would have been funny, if I weren't *totally and completely blown the fuck away*, the second Paige came fully into view.

My weight wobbled as I took her in. The dress looked fucking incredible—*no surprise there*—but her hair is what caught my attention.

It was wild and teased with . . . *dark blue streaks.*

Suddenly, I felt a small hand push into my back. I assumed it was Maisie, but I couldn't confirm it before my feet staggered to meet Paige at the foot of the steps.

Her smile was practically glowing, like moonlight meeting the stars on the neckline of her dress—*Glittery midnight indeed,* I thought to myself.

Another beat passed before she huffed a small laugh, her eyes squinting. "Are we in *She's All That* right now?"

I shrugged, telling her, "I think it happened accidentally." But just as the words left my mouth—*fucking Ellis* started playing "Kiss Me" by Sixpence None the Richer, on his phone from the kitchen.

"Guh!" Darlene made a noise that jerked both of our chins in her direction, but we quickly saw that it was just a "*swooning*" moment. I chuckled, shaking my head.

When I looked back at Paige, she was giggling but her eyes sparkled—everything about her was shining—and I leaned into the moment.

Holding out my arm, I offered it to her. She smiled and playfully hooked her hand right above my elbow. "Such a gentleman," she said, but then her smile tilted, teasingly. "The *last* step is a real doozy."

Darlene chuckled, and so did I.

Such a brat.

This is better, I told myself. *Again.*

Only an hour into our prom at home, I was able to safely say this was way more fun than some cruise Providence Academy organized around the marina—340 bucks a ticket. Black tie. *Such bullshit.*

But this was more our style anyway. Maisie and Darlene made a bunch of snacks, Ellis convinced Paige to have one of his Spiked Angel drinks, and now they were blasting music and dancing—*well, more like jumping*—around the living room with Maisie.

Per usual, I was filming it, watching them all twirl each other—Ellis basically having to limbo to make it under Maisie's arm.

"Put your back into it, Ellis!" Maisie ordered, and Ellis laughed. Paige did too, clapping and bending at the waist—the soft tutu-looking material of her dress swaying.

Some Spice Girls song started as soon as I lowered my phone, and stopped recording. Just as I felt an elbow nudge into me. "Hiya, Lincles."

I snorted a laugh, looking over. But my smile fell when I saw Darlene's posture a bit more curled. "Do you need the heating pad?"

Paige told me she brought it down *just in case.*

She waved me off, shaking her head. "No, no. Jeez Louise, you kids are the most careful teenagers I've ever met. A little pain is just a reminder that we lived a little harder."

I smiled, but it was a sad one. Darlene was a wacky pool of knowledge and wisdom, but I was old enough to know that it all came from *a lot* of pain. Losing her daughter, her husband. And the world didn't stop and wait for her to recover from those things. Through all of that hardship, she was raising Paige.

She took my arm, bringing me back to now as she said, "That's quite a dress."

I smiled, looking over at Paige and Maisie doing a choreographed dance—while Ellis shook his head off to the side.

"You will never be the sixth Spice Girl!" he yelled, just as Paige tackled him.

"Take it back!" She growled, her dress fanning out as she took Ellis down to the couch.

Then Maisie jumped in with, "We can all be Spice Girls! Everyone calm down!"

I laughed and so did Darlene, as the fight from the three of them faded into noise. Darlene squeezed my arm as she said, "I'm so happy you all have each other."

There was a different tone to her voice—*dreamy but somehow serious*—it wasn't how she usually sounded, and I looked back over to her, meeting her stormy blue eyes. "A friendship like the three of yours . . . it's just nice to know you'll always take care of each other."

My chin dipped in a small nod, but I couldn't shake the serious pull to her voice, the tension in her hand around my arm. *Where was this coming from? Was this because she fell?*

My hand clasped over hers. "You *know* I'll always take care of her," I said, quietly, unsure of what else to say.

But I felt like that's where this was going. It made sense that a mortality scare would make someone a little more sentimental or worried, but she gave me a sweet smile, and looked up at me. A small sigh mixed with a tiny laugh escaped her before she shook her head. "Don't be so old-fashioned, Lincoln. I would never expect you to *always* take care of her." She leaned her head on my bicep, then added, "Love, partnership—I think it's all about *taking turns* holding the light in the dark pockets of life. Sometimes she'll hold it, sometimes you—hell, maybe you'll both lose it at a certain point. But as long as you both always remember you have it—*that it's there*—you'll find your way back. And you know our girl can take care of herself for a bit if she has to."

I liked and disliked everything she was saying. When Paige and I started dating, both my mom and Darlene were ecstatic. But, while we were both teenagers with a decent amount of responsibility, our parents never let us forget that we were young and had a lot of life ahead of us—that things could change. And I hated the very thought.

But she also seemed so sure that Paige and I were tethered,

guided by a light that only existed between the two of us. Something that *couldn't* vanish completely.

More importantly, it also felt like she was looking for reassurance of sorts, that Paige would be okay when she was gone—"*Our girl can take care of herself for a bit if she has to.*"

I gave Darlene an assuring squeeze on her hand with a small nod. I was certain she'd never have to worry about Paige being alone—not while I was here, but—"Of course she'll be okay," I said, then leaned down, saying a bit quieter, "You raised her."

Everything about Darlene . . . lifted. *Her eyes, her smile, her shoulders.* "I raised her." The pride in her voice filled in my own chest, as she stared at Paige like she was her life's greatest achievement.

In the distracted moment, I looked over at the piano, an idea surfacing just as I glanced at the big purple armchair we had moved to make room for the dance floor.

My eyes flicked to Darlene. "Think you could play a song if I moved the chair over there? Put the heating pad on it?"

Darlene's shoulders straightened even more, her eyes gleaming as she stared over at her piano in the corner of the room like an old friend. It swelled an ache through my chest, but she squeezed my arm again, her eyes a glittering sea as she said, "Now *that's* a party!"

"Linc," Paige said, holding onto me. "I think I'm going to be drunk forever."

I laughed, shaking my head as I pulled her forehead to me, kissing it, and then twisted toward her nightstand to grab the water bottle I brought upstairs.

I handed it to her. "No, baby. It'll wear off, but water will help."

"*Holy* water," she half-sang quietly, wiggling her shoulders with a little giggle, followed by a hiccup.

I laughed again. "Right. Drink the holy water."

Ellis created a monster with the Buffy-themed mixed drink—not just with the name, but the concoction was boozy *as fuck*—and I couldn't be sure how many Paige actually had. She'd told me anywhere from *none* to *all of them*.

Anti-prom came to an early close after Darlene played the piano. She pushed it—*playing a* few *songs*—and then willingly admitted she needed to go rest.

But it was worth it. The small bit of time Paige and Darlene spent by the piano was a joy unmatched. And Paige seemed to keep her inebriation at bay until Maisie fell asleep on the couch about an hour ago.

A quiet gasp, pulled my focus back to Paige as she put her water bottle back on the nightstand, then asked, "So, do you think Ellis ditched us for dick?"

I laughed, but she wasn't wrong, necessarily. Ellis ended up calling a car about twenty minutes ago, and since he was planning on staying here tonight, I guess that would be the assumption.

I shrugged. "I don't know. He hasn't mentioned anyone to me." Though, Ellis didn't really talk about that stuff with me.

The subject was seemingly dropped when Paige adjusted her weight, wobbling as she sat in a high-kneel position before I reached out and held her hips, steadying her.

Her hands clasped over mine, and it burrowed my fingers deeper into the soft material of her skirt. My eyes pulled up to meet hers and I felt the corner of my mouth tick up.

The glassy tint to her gaze looked like rippling water, while her blond and indigo hair cascaded in chaotic waves over her shoulders. The night sky fanned beneath her in her dress. *Shining,* I thought. She was the moon *and* the sea.

My eyes fell to the neckline of her dress, and I leaned forward, kissing her lightly on her collarbone.

"I'll need to find somewhere else to wear this," she said quietly, and I pulled back a bit. Her eyes glanced down at the dress. "It's too nice for just the living room."

Just then, I felt her hands tighten on mine. She quickly shot out of bed, and bolted toward the door—just before I heard her vomit from the bathroom.

Aw, Pip. She wasn't ready for Casper pours.

I followed behind her, preparing to help her through it. I opened the door to see my moon and sea . . . on the floor—hugging the porcelain goddess.

CHAPTER 43
LINC

I wake suddenly with a gasp, my eyes bulging as the blurriness clears.

Not in my room. I'm not in my room.

Quickly sitting up, my heart jackhammers through my chest, but as soon as I'm upright, I'm able to register the dim living room.

I'm at the house.

Ugh. My head feels like a fucking sandbag. A sound from the back of my throat rumbles as my toes wiggle in my socks. *I never sleep in socks. I never sleep on the* couch.

A shiver runs down my spine as my eyes pull over to the windows, seeing that it's morning. I catch the faint outline of my reflection in the glass and suddenly, everything from last night hits me all at once.

We were watching a movie. I watched her *in the reflection of the windows, she caught me, sat on my lap, asked me to tell her what I remembered, and then—*

Fuck!

My legs wobble as I push off the couch, heading toward the hallway that leads to her room. Using the heel of my palm, I rub my eye, shifting and rolling my shoulders to work out some of the knots from sleeping like a fucking bat.

But as I reach the hallway, I see the door is . . . open.

And I feel it immediately. *The void of* her.

After the last few steps, I push the door open the rest of the way, confirming what I already know. The room is empty. *Fuck.*

I rub the back of my head, massaging the tension at the base of my neck as I try to sort through the madness—*the episode. Did I say something?*

A zap of tension hits my shoulders with the possibilities of *what* I could have said, as my hand absently moves to my throat, my scruff scratching the tips of my fingers. *I haven't shaved in a few days . . .*

But the thought leaves as fast as it comes, my mind wandering—*I think last time I blacked out, my throat hurt more.*

But she left. So I must have said something. I was in-and-out when she explained everything to Ellis, but I remember before we all sat down, she had said nothing *bad* happened.

My mind rewinds as far as it can go. It takes a few seconds, but then a cold, hard feeling solidifies in my chest.

"I have a copy of it. On a flash drive."

My eyes slam shut, stumbling toward the counter and grabbing on, my hands shaking.

Fuck.

A copy? Fuck me. The idea of her *seeing* that . . .

A roll of nausea passes through my stomach, my head shaking—*but the fact remains*—and the longer it sits in my mind, something darker lands in the pit of my despair.

"It's okay. I'll help you."

God-fucking-dammit. The voice feels like nails pulling through my skull. *I'm pretty sure I heard it last night too. Before I snapped.*

I push it away, but in its wake, a heaviness settles deep in the walls of my chest. The tension racking my body loosens. I'm so . . . *fucking tired.*

The urge to disappear is strong. *Just* disappear. I'll keep going with the whole *life* thing—I just want an existence that doesn't need to be fucking managed—*tamed*—by other people.

I stand quietly, weighing the two disappearing acts in my mind. The temptation to *physically* leave bobs in one corner, while the unstable darkness—the hollow path to temporary numbness sits right on the edge of my awareness—taunting me with another brief escape like last night.

My chin tilts in a way where Ellis's hallway focuses my vision, tightening my awareness the longer I look at it. He's seen me through everything in this broken part of my life.

Last night included.

Something I'm sure he has *opinions* about—and they're probably all valid. But I'm so tired of him cleaning up my mess, making excuses—*managing* me.

I know it's all out of love. He's my brother in every sense of the word. But it's all because he refuses to believe the truth. If he did, he would have never continued to let me live here.

The delusion is ending, I think to myself.

Ellis and I were able to shove away the memory of the last time I went too far. With time, the event disappeared and it became easier to . . . *pretend.*

A fallacy I've clung to. Because it's the only way I've been able to peel myself out of bed for the last five years.

Since I . . . saw Ellis again.

Searching for *that* memory right now seems too risky, so I don't . . . and instead, I take a breath.

Something needs to change.

This didn't happen by accident. This isn't a coincidence.

This is a reckoning. Something always tips the scales, and the great equalizer comes to collect.

Without Paige around, Ellis will keep pretending, and I'll keep letting him because—*fuck,* it feels good to act like it never happened.

But it never lasts. The truth always finds me. If the memories don't, the bad ideas do. *Trespassing, kissing Paige—stealing her underwear.*

A heavy sigh pushes past my lips. There's no escaping this. How's that old saying go—"Wherever you go, there you are."

Destination fucked.

Now that I've seen her again, it's clear that every bit of love and obsession I've always had for her is still roaring with life— and it feels *so fucking good.*

Just to feel *that kind* of adrenaline—that deep unstoppable desire. *Alive.*

But all of it runs alongside the other shit. The other *mountain of bullshit* that has intensified since I saw her again. The guilt and despair—*pure fucking anguish.*

"Trying to reconcile too many things at once is a recipe for disaster. Prioritize." The therapy talk finds me, and helps at the moment. It keeps my mind from drifting.

Prioritize.

Paige said she was going back to Darlene's.

I'll try Venice first.

I need to make sure she's okay. If she left because of something I said when I was spiraling in a blackout, I can't allow another seven years to pass letting her believe anything other than the fact that I love her.

I hurt her *and* I love her.

I catch my reflection in the mirror by the entry hall. My nearly black hair is a disheveled mess, my gray T-shirt sufficiently pulled and wrinkled. My scruff is almost to beard territory, and the dark circles under my eyes are making my irises equal parts dark green, brown . . . lost.

So fucking lost.

Who is *this person?*

It's not the first time I've asked myself that question, but Paige's return has shifted the tone to a demand.

My mouth flattens and I start toward the door, shoving my feet into my boots, and grabbing my keys off the small table. I think I have a shirt in the car I can change into. I can't give myself time to back out—the drive alone will be hard enough.

But I can't let it end this way. Not this time.

I see the old blue Cabrio as I pull up to the driveway at the end of the cul-de-sac. Only about a week since my last trespassing tango.

Driving here was less awful than I thought. Just like a few nights ago when Ellis had texted me, telling me Paige was at the house, there was this heaviness that sat in my gut, but my lungs felt wide open.

I can't explain it, only that the idea of seeing her in *any sort of way* feels like the air is easier to breathe. The thought of her soft blue hair between my fingers steadies my heart to a nearly sedated pace. *Her smell.*

But I definitely can't touch her.

Not this time.

This isn't about that, I remind myself. Putting the car in park, I nervously fiddle with the change in my pocket. I match my jingling to some song playing—but I'm not listening.

A few seconds pass before I finally turn off the car. I take another breath, then push off the seat and open the door, closing it with a little more force than necessary.

My limbs start to shake instinctively as nostalgia seeps the air. Closer to the ocean, the citrus—even the breeze feels specific. Warm.

September in LA is like most seasons here—*temperate*—but I *met her* in September, and everything about this time of year reminds me of that one early-fall day where a pretty blond girl challenged me to an arm-wrestling match.

A smirk pulls up and tilts my lips at the memory, steadying my adrenaline.

My steps are slow, but driving toward my route. I open and close the fence, pausing, only because I think for a moment, I might puke, but then the citrus smell from the lemon tree sweeps through my nose.

Be a man and face her, you fucking pussy.

I wince. The words find me with a mix of voices—all low and deep—one even seems to have the resonance of my asshole father, and it tightens my muscles.

And then it hits me.

I'm no fucking better than him. I'm worse.

No, I didn't have a family to support, but I abandoned Paige. I hurt her.

I didn't want to, but I did it.

The blow is hard. Fuzzy memories aside, I always remember trying to do everything I could to be the opposite of him.

But hurting and leaving? Both *his* moves.

In an instant, anger snatches my despair with an iron grip.

I'm going to fix that.

My eyes narrow up the steps to the door. If there's one thing I can do . . . I can try my fucking hardest to look her in the eye, tell her everything I remember—*give her* any *answers I can*—and then let her decide what she wants to do with it.

My trek through the house was slow, keeping my eyes on my feet. When Paige wasn't downstairs—when I called out her name and she didn't answer me, I got worried. I rushed up to her room, but timidly pushed through her door—unsure of what state I would find her in.

It could have been anything—rage, despair, vengeance.

But she's just . . . sleeping.

She looks so small . . . curled up on the bed.

A sharp inhale inflates my chest as I notice the sweater she's wearing. *It was Darlene's.*

Cheeto is in a smaller container on her nightstand, next to her bed, alert and blinking at me.

She knows about the panties, I remind myself.

I mouth a silent "Sorry" then pinch my eyebrows.

Fucking Christ. Apologizing to a gecko.

My eyes drift back to Paige—her back is to me, but I can see her shoulders rising gently, thankfully, seeing as she hasn't moved at all since I came in here.

A tension builds in my neck. *The door was unlocked, for fuck's sake. Anyone could come in here!*

But then I see her toes wiggling at the foot of the bed, and for some reason the movement seems too calculated to be subconscious—too anxiously deliberate.

She's awake.

But she still hasn't moved. She hasn't turned over or gotten up. *But she knows I'm here.*

She knows I'm watching her. I stand for a few long seconds, unsure of what to do, when I start to hear a faint melody in my mind.

I'll be, I'll be

Waiting for you

That's what you don't see

I hear it—but only in my head. *She* is in front of me . . .

My love, I'm waiting for you

I'll be, I'll be

Before I realize what I'm doing, I'm unlacing my boots, clearing my throat.

She finally turns over, and the icy blue waves of her hair tumble in front of her face. As she brushes them away, her eyes meet mine with a soft invitation. It lingers in her expression for a second longer before her eyebrow lifts with a challenge. *Upping it to a dare.*

I take a deep breath. I visualize myself lying next to her. And then I do.

CHAPTER 44
PAIGE

I don't move. I don't say anything.

Neither does he.

Finally, I blink a couple of times, allowing my mind to fully wake up.

I heard him call my name downstairs—it filtered through my dream. We were driving.

It still *feels like I'm dreaming. Driving.*

But my hand isn't on his knee. My head isn't on his shoulder. He's not touching me, but his smell is within reach, so I take that.

God, I want him to touch me—I want him to touch me so badly that my skin ripples and peaks with goosebumps just looking at him.

The urge to close the distance between us is so fierce, I feel a breath away from shedding my fucking skin.

Shedding his *skin.*

But I tighten my fists around the pillow case, keeping the protective layer for now—*not by much*—just the small bit of self-control that's holding me back from reaching out to him.

He may be *here*—but I pushed him too hard last night. I can't do it again.

It's the reason I left.

But I would never send him away. Stuck in my daze, I finally ask, "What are you doing here?"

His eyes drift down to the comforter like maybe he thinks I'm asking him what he's doing *in the bed.* For a moment, I think he's about to get up, and my fingers twitch to reach out and stop him—but he simply says, "*You're* here."

The response is low and gravelly, and reels my eyes deeper into his. Like my irises are growing arms and *feeling* for everything he isn't—everything he *can't* seem to tell me.

What isn't he telling me?

I scoot toward him a little, moving away from *that* question. But as our bodies inch closer, the haunted forest in his gaze meets the violent sea of my own, and I feel the collision deep in my chest.

He's here because I'm *here, but he's not saying anything.* Our gazes still hold with our cheeks on the pillows, and after a few more seconds of silence, I rasp, "Please talk to me."

His eyes float away from mine for a second, and I instinctively lean in. I don't touch him, but the restraint makes my eyes well up.

I don't . . . I don't know how to *be* right now. With *him.* And I've always known how to *be* with him.

My throat tightens, but the pain staring back through his eyes is what breaks me. *The fear.*

The boy I've known my entire life is *scared. Fucking terrified*— and I know it's because he believes I'm in danger right now.

He thinks he's *dangerous.*

A sob escapes me at the thought, and his face blurs behind my tears. "Linc, this is . . . this is—*killing me.*" I barely make it through the sentence before another cry breaks free.

The anguished lines on his face, the fact that we're within reach, but we're not talking, not touching—*this isn't us.*

This isn't us.

This isn't fucking us.

This is why *I left.*

My sobs bellow, my heart throbs, and my mind throws a fucking riot. *It's so unfair. It's so fucking unfair that this happened at all. And if our shared horror wasn't bad enough, the following aftermath is so hopelessly daunting that it feels like we'll be caught in the Rubik's cube of this trauma for-fucking-ever.*

Stuck.

But I'm suddenly surrounded by the smell of woods. Ocean. *His arms.* "*Fuck*, Pip," he grits out, but my fists ball the fabric of his shirt, my fingertips digging into his back as he whispers, "I'm so fucking sorry."

I want to crush the apology in my fist, grind it into the fabric of his shirt still clutched in my hands. I don't *want* to talk right now. His hands suddenly shove through my hair, twisting, knotting, grabbing—and all I can think is . . . *more.*

Give me *more.*

"Oh God, please keep touching me." My voice is nothing but breathy desperation and I don't even care.

I don't fucking care.

Because *touch me* he does. My arms, my neck. The rough pads of his fingers hesitate as he reaches my collar bone, his eyes meeting mine.

I see the silent question and I nod frantically. Keeping my eye contact firm, I tell him, "Anywhere."

I've never meant anything more in my life, and I think he can see it. His gaze catches the permission like a shooting star. With only a second more hesitation, he buries his face into the side of my hair and runs his fingertips over my heaving chest, panting—*feeling me.*

"*This*," he *damn near* growls as he curls the tips of his fingers into my chest, his nose skimming the shell of my ear like he's marking me, and I match the movement.

Fucking mine.

We claim each other—*re*claim. His hand leaves my chest, but only to slide to my lower back, and the fist in my hair releases to explore.

God, his hands. His smell. Him.

But suddenly, his muscles tense, and I realize then that his hand is just breaching the curve of my ass. "Shit," he mutters, moving to pull his hand away, but I snatch it back immediately.

I snarl—*feeling goddamn feral*—before I plant his hand back at the base of my spine, the contact making a small *smack* that tightens my core. But I put his hand *right* where it was before I saw his intrusive thoughts take hold.

My fingers take his chin, my breath panting. "I told you anywhere, and I meant anywhere."

Our noses brush, and his eyes don't darken, so much the color . . . *shades*—like a cloud just pulled over them, filtering the greens and browns—but then I see the faintest gold flecks pulsing to life.

I'm not sure where my bossy-little-bitch persona is coming from, but it seems to be effective because he slowly resumes his movement. His palm covers my ass, and I lean into his neck, running the tip of my nose along his scruff.

Suddenly, I feel a *buzz* coming from his back pocket—*his phone.*

He ignores it, and I'm *sure as fuck* not willing to share one of his hands if I don't have to—not while we're riding out one more delusional, delicious wave.

His hands drag over my body in the most hypnotizing cadence, like my limbs have caught their own personal current.

When his hands move to my lower back again, it's different. His fingers slip under the cardigan, under my shirt, branding my bare skin, and a breathy moan escapes me.

We're pressed together so tightly now that I feel his cock—long and hard as a fucking rock between us. Another needy whimper escapes me as I slide my leg over his, practically dry humping him.

What is happening? What am I doing?

But I'm only met with his hungry rumble before he tugs my hair so that I'm looking up at him.

"You like it when I touch you," he rasps.

It's not a question, but there's curiosity to his tone, rough wonderment in his voice.

But *my face* must look mystified. A true and proper—*yeah-huh.*

Oh God, this is a bad idea. So bad. But all I can do is dip my chin in the slightest nod.

My brain is melting like butter as the fingers I've only felt in phantom touches for the last seven years *feel* every part of me—a desperate *reverence* setting my skin ablaze.

The mix of colors in his eyes smolder with matching heat. He keeps one hand in my hair, a slight tension in his fingers that keeps my chin tilted up, but he moves his other hand from my lower back up to my cheek.

His thumb runs along my bottom lip with awe-filled eyes, and my hips instinctively rock against his—but there's too many layers. Too much between us.

Still, our hips grind, and the friction makes me gasp. In fact, the room fills with a mix of heavy panting, greedy fingers, and desperately stifled moans.

"Fuck, Pip—" he grunts, then pins his bottom lip with his teeth.

Something inside of me snaps. In an instant, I'm sitting up, pulling off the cardigan, yanking off my shirt—*whoops, no bra*—and I pull my leggings off, all in seemingly *one* distressed movement.

Bared desperation, I suppose.

But then I'm sitting—in a high kneel position—directly in front of him on the bed. The silvery-blue strands of my hair fall over my shoulder, brushing against my nipple, and I try to catch my breath.

Linc sits up quickly too, his eyes wide and gleaming—taking me in—wearing nothing but a light blue thong.

This should feel weird. This *is* weird. But . . .

His eyes manage to drag themselves up from my nakedness, his voice gravelly as he says, "Never."

A shiver runs down my spine at his voice, and I breathe in his confirmation, my heart settling as he slowly moves toward me, but then his eyes drift down to my wrists, covered in lace and bracelets.

Oh, shit.

After a second, his gaze shoots back up to mine, and it's a *knowing* look. I think he's noticed the wrist decor already, and I'm certain he knows what they're hiding, but . . . it's on the "do not discuss" list.

And fuck—I don't want his focus on that right now either.

I shift my hands back—just behind the back of my thighs, begging him with my eyes. *Just stay. Stay with me.*

He holds the tension in his stare for another second. I can see the disturbed curiosity in his gaze, still edging behind me, but he quickly pulls his eyes back up to me.

My wrists seem forgotten as he moves a bit closer. I can nearly taste the heady desire pouring out of him. His fingers clench and release at his sides, but just as he reaches a high kneel before *me*, his head hangs. "I don't deserve this, Paige."

God, the hit hurts. It does. *And* he called me Paige.

But my instincts tell me I *can't* lean into his despair. I can't *feed* into this delusion he's been spinning for nearly a decade.

And still, every second he stares at me—*so slowly*—the fine lines in his face start to fade. His eyes move to my ear, they linger there.

After a moment, my mouth lifts. *The freckles.* Typically, I suppose it would be a major blow—to be buck naked in front of a guy and have him fixated on some freckles behind your ear.

But it's not. *Not with him.* And I can see something stirring to life in his gaze. Like a light pulsing in the depths of a cave.

I take what he said—*about him not deserving this*—and I swallow it. *I'll take* his unworthiness. I'll take it if I can keep a piece of him.

I just want *now*, with him. *This* comfort. *This* safety. *Just* feel *each other again.* And I can see he wants that too. He's just . . . fighting it.

"I'm begging you, Linc." My pride flayed the moment I cried, demanding he touch me—*long before that, probably*—and I don't fucking care.

If I need to strip myself down to nothing to show him I'm not scared, if I need to crawl and beg on my fucking knees for him to *accept* my consent—*well, I'm fucking doing it!*

And while he still doesn't touch me, his eyes are another story. They're . . . *intense.* But not in a bad way. Almost like he's darkening the outline of my figure. Shading the various dips and lines of my muscles—the curve of my hips. He *draws* all of me with the timid drift of his piercing eyes before they drop to my thong.

Which reminds me . . .

A newer memory fuels my objective. I keep my eyes with Linc's, but then take his hand, and slowly move it to my lower back. *His safety spot.*

A breathy whimper pushes past my lips, but it's his hoarse groan that tightens the coil twisting deep in my stomach.

"I can't, Pip. I'll—" he chokes out before his teeth grind. My hand finds the back of his jaw again.

"You'll what?" I ask, it's not meant to be a challenge, I'm genuinely asking.

But he doesn't respond with anything but a sharp inhale. And despite his words, he pulls me a bit closer, brushing my peaked nipples against the fabric of his shirt.

Our mouths are only an inch apart, and the rumble in his throat as he rubs and kneads his fingertips into my back is fucking divine.

Drunk and desperate, I whisper over his ear, "I know you took my underwear."

A buzz surrounds us and his fingers halt their movement, but he doesn't pull away. When his eyes slam shut, I instinctively clasp my hands around the back of his neck—nearly hearing the *sizzle* as my hands touch his skin.

He doesn't flinch at my touch, but the victory is short lived as I notice heat spread up his cheeks.

Shit. I wasn't telling him that to make him feel bad.

Tilting my chin, a barely-there, "Hey," squeaks from my throat, trying to get him to open his eyes. I gently run my thumb over on the coarse hair of his jaw.

It's longer than a few days ago when I did this.

When he carried me to bed.

My thumb massages the tension, and eventually, he opens his eyes. I can see the shame weighing down his eyelids and it lights that same furious match inside me.

But I use it. *I use the flame for us,* telling him, "I like that you took them."

The gold in the center of his eyes breaks off like embers,

spreading through the mix of dark greens and browns like fire-flies. His expression starts to turn as the gravity between us pulls. "Y-You do?" he asks.

The hiccup in his voice makes my heart skip, but I use it, I add it to the flame, and I nod.

Keep him talking. Touching. Here.

He leans into me, inching me to move back, but then I recognize he's lowering me down to the mattress. His clothed body presses against my naked one, but he doesn't lie on top of me.

Propping himself on his elbow beside me, he just . . . watches.

The heavy weight of his stare starts to feel overwhelming, and I take his free hand, keeping my eyes with his. When he doesn't stop me, I move it to my stomach, and gently place his hand just above my belly button.

My body intuitively squirms under his touch, but our gazes remain on our invisible tightrope.

Keep him talking.

The first thing I think to ask is if he recognized the underwear. But that seems like the worst fucking idea ever—so I move along.

His fingers twitch against my belly for a second, and I inhale sharply, then ask—"What'd you do with them?"

Linc's brows furrow, but this time it's from confusion.

Fucking hell.

My eyes float down to my thong—reminding him that before I was unabashedly lying here naked, we were having a *kind-of* conversation. Still naked.

Totally normal.

"I saw them the night I carried you to bed," he says, suddenly.

And *holy fuck*—the timbre to his voice has a resonance I haven't noticed yet. Rich, deep, *manly.*

A shiver runs down my spine as I hear his phone buzz again from his pocket, but I'm too captivated by his eyes, his voice. *I want him to talk again.*

Linc ignores the phone too, and after a second, he clears his throat. "I thought of you . . ." He stops and shakes his head, and I take his wrist, then start moving his fingers on my stomach again.

He looks up at me, and I nod with a silent, *keep going.*

He takes a breath, but then I see the light dwindling, the dark mass moving back in.

No. No, please.

He sits up and rubs his palms up and down his face. After a moment, he rakes his fingers through his hair and his eyes screw shut. I reach out to him, but then stop myself.

Instead, I grab my shirt and shove it back over my head.

I don't know what the fuck I was thinking.

Desperate times call for desperate girls, I guess, but just as the shirt is back on Linc grabs my hands and pins me back on the bed.

His fists tighten around my bracelets—my wrists—holding them over my head. His eyes look dark, but not like last night.

A beat passes, our noses bump. Keeping his voice low, he asks, "You want to know what I did?"

My eyes widen, but only because he—he sounded more like . . . like he *used to*—but the tendons stretching in his neck tell me he's anything but calm.

My body wiggles a bit, trying to adjust, but I meet his unyielding stare with my own dominant, "Yes."

There's this fleeting moment of confusion that flashes through his eyes, but it's gone before I have time to analyze it—I can barely breathe between his smell and his weight—*let alone* form a coherent thought.

There's one more sustained moment of eye contact where his eyes light with a wickedness I don't recognize.

His hands, holding me down. Him on top of me.

But it's like he's forcing that thought on me through his gaze—*using* our ability to connect without words to try and scare me off.

But all it does is *piss* me off. I'm two seconds away from baring my goddamn teeth at him, but instead I give him a message. A spoken one.

"I'm not fucking scared of you," I growl.

His chest inflates with a sharp inhale, his hands tighten around my wrists. Only another second passes before he seethes, "I beat my dick into your underwear, Paige. I thought of you, chained up and helpless beneath me, looking at me with everything I don't deserve from you anymore, and I fucking came more than I ever have in my goddamn life."

I tighten my face muscles to hide any sort of reaction. He's telling the truth. I can see that. But there's an edge to his voice, a cut to his eyes that still feels like he's *trying* to intimidate me.

This time I *do* bare my teeth, an anguished growl of frustration and anger—arousal and rage—it all whirlpools together and rains through me like a fucking storm.

I take a breath and then ignite. My hips bump up as I drop my elbows, catching him off guard, and freeing my hands. In a quick movement, I latch onto his torso, then climb and lock my arms around his left bicep, pinning the arm as I use all of my weight, and pure fucking fury to roll—pushing him to his back as I straddle his hips, and pin both his arms beside his head.

His eyes are wide, blinking up at me, brows furrowed with confusion. My fingers dig into his wrists, and our gazes stay locked.

He could retaliate—he's still stronger. If I were actually completing the self-defense move, I would have gotten the hell out of here, but I'm not.

Because I'm not defending myself.

My face lowers, closer to his, our noses grazing as I hoarsely whisper, "I'm in charge right now."

He gives me his eyes, I can see instantly. The memory pings a small glint in his gaze—*I've got him.*

I can't fight the smirk that tilts my lips as I loosen my grip on his wrists—but only to pick up his hands and plant them on my bare ass, only the string of the thong between my cheeks.

He grunts, but his fingers dig into my skin, his hips grinding up into me as a core-tingling groan rumbles in his throat.

I contain the flutter, the control, keeping his hands in place, his eyes in my trance. "Why would I be scared of you when you're the only person I've ever let touch me like this?"

His response is a tidal wave as his mouth crashes against mine, and my tongue dives into his mouth like a thirsty animal.

His hands lose all resistance and he kneads my ass, pulling and tugging the skin to the same rhythm that he sips on my lips.

My hands dig through his thick mess of hair, making it messier. Nothing—and I mean *fucking nothing* compares to my deep desire to give this boy—*man*—everything I can at this very moment.

Our mouths move ravenously—biting, licking. *Savoring.*

But just as his lips move to my cheek, my ear—*the freckles*—*my* phone starts to vibrate, rattling on the nightstand.

No one ever calls me. And someone's *been calling Linc.*

The thought manages to find us both, easing our lips, but not breaking free immediately.

Our kissing slows as my phone stops buzzing, and I press my mouth harder into his, not ready to end it yet. But then my phone starts to buzz again.

I groan just as Linc releases me, and I reluctantly pull away, rolling off him and looking over at my nightstand, the phone screen lighting up with Ellis's name.

It's what I suspected, but a wave of guilt sways heavily through my chest at the sight of his name. *Watching it ring.*

This is how I disappeared from him last time. Ignoring calls, texts. If he's been calling Linc too, I don't want him to think the same thing is happening again.

The call goes to voicemail, and I sit up, grabbing the phone off the nightstand. "It's Ellis," I mumble, my voice still raspy, the heightened feeling still buzzing through my veins. "I'm gonna call him back really quick, so he doesn't worry."

From the corner of my eye, I can see him do his old dance move—"the boner tuck," as Ellis affectionately named it.

My mouth tilts as I click Ellis's name, and put it on speaker. If we're about to be yelled at, I'm including Linc.

I *tried* to leave.

But then I also silently demanded he get into bed and touch me. Stripped myself down to nothing.

Ellis answers the phone. "Paige?" he asks with a deeper urgency to his voice than I'm used to.

"Y-Yeah. Hey, sorry. I—uh—I decided to head back to Venice—"

"Is Linc with you?" he cuts me off.

I nod, but realize he can't see me.

Linc clears his throat, then says, "Yeah, I'm here."

A heavy sigh pushes through the phone and it feels like a dead wind. The kind that sweeps through a space when someone's soul leaves their body—*but I have no idea why.*

"You guys need to come back here," he finally says, his voice still deep and serious, and the hair on the back of my neck lifts.

I shudder, already regretting it as I ask, "Why?"

My eyes hold Linc's, searching for any clue of what this could be about, but he looks confused too.

Ellis speaks up again. "Wade, he—uh ... he found something." His disturbed tone, the ambiguity—it all sends my heart rate into a fucking frenzy, and I swallow hard.

The flash drive.

It's where my mind instantly goes. A thousand other thoughts and questions blaze through my mind, but none of them make it to my mouth.

The quietness in the room, the silence from Ellis on the other end of the line—my eyes lock with Linc's, which are widening and drifting by the second. I take his hand in mine, and he blinks, his eyelids fluttering rapidly.

I watch for an indication that he's fully back, then give him the silent message—*stay with me.*

As if he hears it, he dips his chin in a jagged nod. After another beat, I take a breath, then ask Ellis, "What is it?" Linc's grip pulses around my hand, and I can feel Ellis's thoughts pushing and running into each other through the phone. My impatience gets the better of me—"Ellis!"

He clears his throat. "It's . . . it's a video of . . . you guys."

My heart drops at the confirmation.

It was always a fear—one that had also grown into a steep reality I wasn't brave enough to face.

The existence of this eleven-minute monstrosity has been something I've kept to myself. But there has always been the looming knowledge that it *could be* viewed by other people. I've just been too scared to even try and find it.

I kept it in my box.

My stomach turns at the reality. The dread. I have no words, and Linc doesn't seem to either.

"It's—" Ellis starts to say, but then it sounds like he gags, and my spine stiffens.

My mouth snarls. "Did you watch it?"

"What?! No!" he barks through the phone. "As soon as it started—as soon as I saw it was you guys, I turned it off—but . . ."

Buffy bless. What else could there possibly *be?*

Truthfully, my heart can't *take* anything else. It's already barely fucking flickering in the bottom of the well.

But suddenly, it's like Linc heard me slipping down—*falling*— and I'm suddenly surrounded again by his strong inked arms, holding me tightly to the wall of his chest. His heart races against my ear, and my fingers grapple for him—*anything* to ease the anxiety barrelling through me.

I take a breath. I breathe *him* in, just as Ellis says, "It's titled *Raw Footage.* And it's six *fucking* hours."

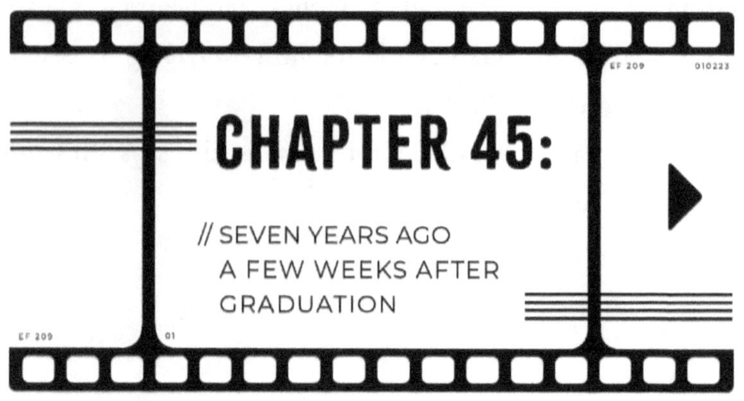

PAIGE

"You're thinking too much," Gram read from the script.

"You're thinking too much," I delivered my line back to her.

Her eyes squinted. "That's the only line for half the damn page. The two of you going back and forth saying 'you think too much.'"

I snorted, nodding. "Yeah, in the scene, my character is working with another girl on her Meisner technique."

"Ahh, Meisner. Brother of Kaiser," Gram said astutely, like a fact, and I cracked the hell up.

Buffy bless. "Wow. No." Another laugh pushed past my lips and I told her, "It's an acting technique."

Gram laughed. "Technique, shmecknique."

I shook my head. "You really are the world's greatest undiscovered rap talent, Lemon Lady."

She shrugged. "The world isn't ready for me." Her tea kettle whistled, and she stood carefully, walking over to it. "So, what time are you kids leaving tomorrow?"

"Early," I groaned. "My call-time is way earlier than Linc's—I have to be there by ten. I keep wondering if we should just leave tonight after Christine gets home."

"Where did this worry-wart mentality come from?" she chuckled. "Wait till the morning—better to drive in the daylight. And it's San Diego, not the moon." I nodded, agreeing. Then Gram said, "Have you heard from Ellis?"

My shoulders slumped. "He has shitty service, but he called a couple nights ago when he landed."

Ellis and his gap-year plans were going to make for a rough 358 days.

But who's counting?

He'd given us plenty of warning. It had always been his plan to literally *take off* after graduation. *Kerouac-ing* his ass around the world—which started at some elephant reservation in Thailand a few days ago. And while Linc and I both missed him like crazy, we also knew this was important to him. An adventure.

And he promised to bring us presents.

"I miss him," Gram said. "I'll need to make notes for our monthly meetings so I don't forget anything."

My eyes scrunched. "Meetings?"

She poured some honey into her mug, and I tried to *not* scrutinize the amount. She stopped pouring to stir, and I cringed inwardly, hoping she didn't notice.

"We get together once a month to talk about all of you," she clarified. Her tone was teasing, and it loosened my shoulders as a noise—something between a sigh and a laugh pushed past my lips.

Things had mostly gone back to normal since her fall a couple of months ago—except my silent inventory of all her habits.

Everything she ate, every bout of tiredness.

Since her back had fully healed, so had her habit of fluttering around nonstop, but the doctor wanted us to try and regulate her blood pressure, which was still higher than he liked to see.

All in moderation, as he said.

The word didn't exist in my head, apparently. But part of my *incessant moderation* came from the massive guilt I felt at the hospital.

The doctor had asked me about what she'd done that day—if she seemed "off," or anything—and I couldn't remember.

From what I *could* recall, she seemed fine. Maybe a little tired—she was napping in the hammock when I left for Queenie's.

So, I think at least part of my obsessive watching was because I felt like I'd missed something, and I didn't want to miss it again.

Plus, I was already anxious, knowing I was about to be out of town for a few days—without Ellis to tap in.

It would be fine, I reminded myself again, Gram could take care of herself. And it was only a few days. She was probably looking forward to getting a break from me, honestly.

My phone started buzzing from the table, and I smiled when I saw Linc's picture pop up.

His messy dark hair. A smirk so sexy it made my knees shake.

I answered, "Hi, you're on speaker with me and Gram."

"No dirty talk!" she called out.

Linc chuckled awkwardly, as he should, and I squinted my eyes in her direction as he said, "Uhh—"

A few quiet seconds passed, and when he didn't say anything else, I asked, "Everything okay?"

He cleared his throat. "Uhh—I mean, it's nothing major. I mean, it is, but I have a temporary solution. I just don't know how much you're gonna like it."

"You've sold it well. Go on," I quipped, making Gram breathe a small laugh.

I could hear the flick of a lighter through the phone, and the muted sound of his inhale just before he said, "The engine on the truck finally blew."

My eyes widened. "Holy shit. That's like . . ."

"Just over five thousand dollars," he said, and I caught the bitterness in his tone. "And that's *with* me doing some of the labor. Benny said he'd work with me on it, but the car's not even worth half of that."

My lips pulled in, flattening my mouth. We knew our days were numbered with his truck, but *damn*.

Linc cleared his throat. "Anyway, it's definitely not worth replacing it—but the bigger problem is, even if I did get it fixed, it won't be ready by tomorrow. It won't be ready by *next week*."

Right. *Shit*. We had our first professional jobs—*out of town*—and they started tomorrow morning.

"Okay. So, you have a questionable plan . . ." I prodded, hearing Linc take another drag.

"I talked to Jeremy. He was gonna leave tonight, but he said he'd wait till tomorrow and we could catch a ride with him in the morning. I'll just have to figure out the car when we get back." He said it all with an inching inflection—kind of like it was a question.

I pinned my bottom lip with my teeth.

He was right. I didn't love that plan.

He knew I was part Gremlin that early in the morning, but . . . there was something else buzzing my awareness, and I just couldn't quite figure out why.

Mr. Harris had gone above and beyond to help out Linc, and he'd used some of his connections to get me multiple opportunities this year. So other than his weird-ass play back in February, I had *zero* grounds to feel any sort of way about him other than grateful.

It was probably just my anxiety about leaving Gram, mixing with the constant current of my nerves. I'd pretty much been a chaotic stream of unease since I was offered the role last month.

"You guys can take the station wagon. I can walk to the library for a few days," Gram said.

"No," I said quickly—*too quickly*—but I shook my head. "No, it's okay. What time does he wanna leave, Linc?"

"I think five," he said, already sounding exhausted. "My mom should be off around three. I'll just ask her to drop me off, and Jeremy can pick us up at your house."

I nodded. That meant a couple hours of cuddle time before the trip. That would help. "Sounds good."

Linc took a breath, then said, "'Kay, cool. Love you, I'll see you then."

I said it back before I hung up.

Gram sipped her tea from her spot in front of the sink, staring at me.

My eyes squinted. "What?"

She shrugged. "You seem nervous. Got some big plans for this little getaway?"

There was no hiding her insinuation and I felt a heat spread up my cheeks. "Gram!" I gaped. Damn her strange spicy intuition. Her and Ellis were like sportscasters for lust.

And of course, I was nervous about that too.

Linc and I were ready to fucking burst. I was nearly certain that the second we were alone, in a locked hotel room, we'd skip right over all the bases we hadn't made it to yet, and pretty much . . . well, slide right home, I guess, to keep up with the baseball analogy.

But I wouldn't be talking about it with Gram. I cleared my throat. "I'm *nervous* because it's my first movie, and I wanna do well. And now I don't have the car ride to word vomit all my anxiety onto Linc," I whined the half-truth, then deadpanned. "He'll be so disappointed."

Gram's smile softened with another laugh. "Oh, baby," she sighed and walked over to me. I was still sitting at the table, and she cupped the back of my head, pulling me into her. "You always shine, Paigey May. And no one knows that better than the boy who will be helping behind the cameras. No matter what, you'll have each other. You can't underestimate the power of *back-up* out there in the big bad real world." She was essentially hugging my head, and I giggled as I nestled my nose into the soft yarn of her sweater, catching a few sniffs of her Irish breakfast tea and the honey.

A little whiff of courage.

"Thanks, Gram."

LINC

We slowly pulled up to the pale yellow cottage at the end of the cul-de-sac. *3:16 a.m.*

Ugh. It was gonna be a long day. I'd only gotten to sleep for a couple of hours before my mom got home. And I had less than no chance of getting any sleep once I was next to Paige.

Mom yawned from the driver's seat as she pulled into the driveway. Her brown hair was piled in a knot on top of her head, but she smiled over at me.

"Thanks for the ride. Sorry, I know you've had a long day."

She rustled her fingers through my hair, giving them a playful shake as she shook off another yawn. "Oh, kid. It feels good to help you out every once in a while. You're just . . ." Her eyes looked a little glassy. It was probably from her yawns, but I could see some kind of emotion peeking out of her exhaustion. "I'm just so proud of you. How'd you turn out so good?"

I snorted, but it was half-hearted. I knew she felt guilty for how much she had to work—how much she *missed* because she had to work. But I never resented her for it. All she was guilty of was surviving. *She* didn't abandon ship like my asshole father did.

"All right," she said. "Well, I know you'll be busy, but make sure you check in, okay?" I nodded as she leaned over, giving me a hug, and kissing my cheek. "Love you, baby boy."

"Love you too," I mumbled, hugging her back.

Jeremy seemed to think this job would lead to more camera work for me. If I could get something consistent, maybe I could start pulling in enough money that my mom *could* cut back at the hospital.

She finally released me, but gave me a small clap on my shoulder before she said, "Oh, and uh—don't forget to use protection, okay?"

It took me a second to realize what the hell she was talking about before my eyebrows flinched. *Ugh.*

Despite the fact that I'd used my key, pushing in through the mudroom in the middle of the night still felt sketchy as fuck.

I put my bag down and took off my shoes, then walked as quietly as I could through the kitchen, the living room, and up the stairs. But the floorboards under the steps were impossible to keep quiet.

I finally made it to Paige's room, and she was lying in her bed, stirring, but *holy fuck.*

She was only wearing a tank top and panties, while her golden hair fell in messy waves over her shoulder.

"Who needs an alarm system when your house basically screams 'someone's stepping on me'?" she said, smiling, her eyes still closed.

I wanted to laugh, but I was stuck on her bare legs, my curious eyes already roaming.

Finally one of her eyes peeled open. "Are you getting in, or what?"

I quickly slid into bed, right next to her, and she curled herself into me.

My arms wrapped around her, pulling her as close as possible, feeling that her hair was damp. The citrus to her scent had a zesty flare—freshly showered—and I breathed in deep.

I nearly moaned on my exhale, muttering, "You've got a lot of nerve inviting me over for a slumber party, and then ambushing me with a pantless Pip." My hands roamed every bit of her— her lower back, her belly, her shoulders.

"*Mmm*," she made a soft noise, burrowing her face in my chest. "And here I thought I was being considerate. Usually I sleep naked."

My heart picked up speed at the thought. If I had come in here and she had been naked my brain might have drained out of my ears.

Would she sleep naked at the hotel?

Her sleepy giggle cut off my stream of consciousness before she said, "They're not even sexy underwear."

I grunted, knowing just how *un-fucking-true* that was—*but how could I call her bluff if I didn't take a look?* My eyes peeked down, seeing white cotton panties with little bees on them, and my mouth ticked up at the corner.

So fucking cute.

"You're right. They're hideous. You should take them off," I said, pulling her into me and nibbling on her ear.

She giggled again, pressing a kiss to my jaw, then sighed deep.

After a few seconds, she said, "We really should get a little more sleep if we can. Need my beauty rest."

I chuckled. *She didn't need a damn thing,* but I knew she was nervous—and being tired would only make that worse.

Plus we'd already shared some dirty ideas of what our little getaway could entail. I fully intended on waking her up the way she told me I had in one of her dreams . . .

We had time. "Sleep well, baby. I'll wake you up in about an hour."

When I felt her breathing even, I looked down, seeing she had already fallen back asleep.

The first half of the ride passed by easily.

We had just stopped for gas, and I was having a cigarette over in the designated area while I waited for Paige to get out of the bathroom.

She pushed through the door a moment later, and her chin immediately turned over in my direction. Smiling, she started to walk over toward me.

My eyebrow cocked, catching two guys just behind her— checking her out—as they walked in the door she just came out of, and a smirk pinched my cheek.

Her steps slowed as she got closer, twisting her chin back behind her before she looked back at me again. A silent, *"What?"*

I shrugged as I took my last drag, then smashed it out, and

tossed it in the dispenser. "Seems like I'm not the only one who likes watching you."

She looked back at the door again, breathing a laugh and shaking her head as she glanced back at me.

The honey-colored strands of hair swept below her shoulders, over her black spaghetti-strapped tank top, and I pulled her into me, pressing a soft kiss to her lips as my hand slid into the back pocket of her jean shorts. "They can look all they want, but . . ."

"I'm yours," she said, rubbing her nose with mine.

I stifled the grunt that tried to break free by kissing her again, and murmured against her lips, "Fuck me, I can't wait till we wrap today."

She giggled, as she anchored a hand through my hair. "We haven't even started."

Just as an impatient growl pushed past my lips, Jeremy suddenly said, "Hey, guys, sorry to interrupt, but we should get back on the road."

Paige and I detached from each other. I didn't even see where he came from, but I saw now that he was carrying a tray of coffees.

"I've stopped here before on my way to Riverside," he explained. "The guys who run the coffee cart inside are from Cuba and the shit is delicious."

"Oh, hell yeah," Paige said, graciously taking one. "Thank you so much, Mr. Harris. You're likely saving someone's life by giving me caffeine."

I laughed, taking one of the other cups. "And that person is likely me—so, thanks." I lifted the cup appreciatively.

Jeremy chuckled, "Happy to help," and we all headed back to the car.

Twenty minutes after we'd gotten back on the road, I turned back to look at Paige, smiling when I saw her staring out the window.

Despite finishing her coffee in about three gulps, she still looked like she could fall asleep at any minute. In her tiredness, her eyes had taken on a darker denim color, but her lips tilted up her cheek when she met my gaze.

I mouthed, "Love you," and she did too before I turned forward again. My throat worked to swallow before I asked Jeremy, "How much longer till we get there?" But an abrupt bout of heaviness suddenly swayed my head.

What the fuck?

Whoa. I was hit with a sudden, intense bout of exhaustion. *Fucking drowsy.* Blinking, my eyebrows pinched.

Am I about to pass out?

I shifted my eyes to look at Jeremy, gripping the side of the door as I saw him glance at the sign we were passing. "We're about forty-five minutes away . . ." he said something else, but it started to sound tunneled. " . . . some sleep if you need to . . ."

I could barely nod my response before my head leaned back into the seat.

Still, my brows furrowed. *We'd just had coffee. Why was I so tired if we just had . . .*

I couldn't finish the thought before I fell asleep.

CHAPTER 46
LINC

I would never consider myself lucky.

Not in this life.

But I *have* been given years of not having to face her. And the universe even gave me some extra days. Gave me a *new* small taste of her. I got to kiss her twice. She let me touch her—"Anywhere."

Fuck me, I wish that moment would have just taken me for good. Taken me to the sky and left me on the moon.

I've imagined it so vividly, over and over on our drive back to the mountain—to Ellis.

Her touch—my hands on her—I was soaring. All it would have taken was flying a bit higher. I could have settled in and watched her from the moon forever. I'd live up there, not bothering anyone, watching the world like a movie with Paige on a constant reel.

But the shitty reality is, the world's movie is a fucking disaster film.

And I could never help her from up there.

Not that it matters. It's just a daydream. One I've conjured in various ways through the years—being in a place where I can see everyone, but I'm not *in* the room. No one's looking at me, worrying about me, watching me.

As the big gate to the driveway opens, I pull in. Fiona Apple's "Limp" plays quietly through the speakers as Paige's hand stays on my knee—even after I've parked the car.

We didn't taint the drive by talking or debating about what we were driving into—we just . . . took an hour-long drive. Her hand on my knee. Her head on my shoulder.

I thought about turning around multiple times.

Stopping this.

But that same feeling—the one I had before I left to go to her in Venice just a few hours ago, was starting to settle back into my bones.

Still, I can't deny her closeness. *Her.*

I lean my cheek onto the top of her head, burrowing my nose just a bit in the soft blue strands of her hair.

Somehow—even after she crashed back into my life—I got to live on with the delusion for a little longer.

But just as I thought earlier—*it was about to end.*

She sighs, whispering, "It's gonna be okay," squeezing my knee, and I slot my hand over hers, holding it as I breathe her in again. The lemon scent is strong and I feel it tighten in my chest—somehow trying to lock it away.

Keep it.

I won't tell her that *I know* it's not going to be okay. I wouldn't blame her if she finally called the cops on me after this . . . I mean—*six hours?!*

I've been warding the thought off since I heard it, but a roll of nausea twists in my gut just as she sits up, saying, "Linc," and I immediately miss her weight on my shoulder. Her eyes meet mine in this soft way—reminding me of that day my dad left. The day we took a road trip in her driveway.

She squeezes my knee again, regaining my attention, pulling me back to now, and I blink.

She sighs. "This is going to be . . ." she shakes her head. "Well, it's gonna be fucking awful. But let's just go in. Talk to Ellis. After he tells us everything he knows—*we* will watch what he found."

My eyes widen, ready to shove myself out of the car, and dive off the cliff.

She wants to fucking watch it?! Together?!

I shake my head, as my eyes clamp shut. No way. *No fucking way.* My mind crawls back to the inky corner it was in earlier—when Ellis first called.

I've seen a video of it. I've seen what I did to her. But I've only seen ten minutes, or so . . . I can't watch that *for* six hours.

Something else thrums through my veins, though, something darker. Colder. Remembering she's seen it too.

She has a copy.

My eyes squeeze tighter shut as another stab of anguish threatens to bleed me out—but I hear, "Linc," and my eyes shoot open.

Paige's gentle voice forces my focus back to the car, back to her in front of me. Her full rosy lips are frowning, as she holds my gaze like she's holding my hand, then says, "This could be proof."

I feel a smaller pinch in my chest at the hope I hear in her voice with the word *proof*. Because she's right. Whatever nightmare exists with that footage *is* proof. It's a *deplorably long confirmation* that I hurt her—violated her for a torturous amount of time.

But she refuses to believe it.

And sadly, there's still a part of me—a small sliver that just . . . *can't believe it either*. Then again, I wouldn't have believed myself capable of hurting her in *any* capacity.

But I see the determination staring back at me in the way of fierce blue eyes, her hand still in mine on my knee.

And just like this morning, I find myself accepting my fate.

If this is what she wants, then it's what I'll do. It will likely kill me—*hell, maybe she'll kill me*—but it'd be a fitting end to a fucking tragedy.

Ellis did us all a solid by pouring each of us a drink—but it's straight bourbon this time. I'm not sure what it is about the beverage choice that adds to my unease, but it does.

My eyes have been hyper-focused on the amber liquid in the glass since we sat down in the living room . . .

A while ago. I think.

Something stops me from reaching out and taking mine off the coffee table. *The color is just too . . .*

Ellis clears his throat, knocking me from my wandering thoughts. I move my hand to my pocket, jingling the change a bit before I hold onto one of the coins.

He finally says, "The video was attached to one of the names on that old roster Wade found." His eyes shift to Paige as he says, "The ones somehow connected to that website with the weird symbol."

I have no idea what that means. Paige seems to though, as she asks, "Have you found the password yet?"

Ellis shakes his head. "No, but the account that the video was sent to appears to have a few aliases attached to it—Thomas Run, Dylan Mirth, Gregory Marquis." He looks at his notes, then at me and asks, "You recognize any of those names?"

I can feel my mind backfiring—*trying* to think so quickly and so hard that all my thoughts shoot off like a bottle rocket and my throat clogs.

"Dylan Mirth. He was—" Paige says quietly, but stops and looks over at me, her eyes becoming cautious. "He was the director of that movie I got cast in right after graduation. The one . . ." she trails off for a second, as her gaze lifts and she finishes, "we were on our way to shoot."

A cold wind blows through my chest, seemingly out of nowhere.

I stand abruptly as the thought practically cuts through my skull. The confusion and overwhelm swirl and mass in the center of my chest.

Bending at the waist, I hold my weight on my thighs, wobbling with a bout of dizziness. Suddenly, I feel a small soft hand on my lower back, making me gasp. "Breathe," Paige orders quietly, and I do.

Or try to anyway.

I shake my head, blinking through the spots in my vision as she hands me a water bottle, keeping the other hand on my back with a steady balance of gentle and firm.

I take the water, gulping it down, as she asks Ellis, "What else have you found?"

Ellis's eyes take on a color I've never seen—*well, maybe once*—but I swerve away from the thought.

The water and Paige's hand are helping my heart rate settle, my lungs find some air, but I'm by no means calm, and the hunter green worry in my friend's eyes isn't helping.

They meet mine for a sustained moment before he shakes his head. "A few more videos. But it's nothing more than disturbing footage without any information. I wish I had more for you guys, but this was like—one of the first things I found—I . . ." He shakes his head in a way I recognize. A nagging thought he just can't shake.

I clear my throat. "What?"

He rubs the back of his neck. His chin tilts down for a moment before he swipes something off the coffee table, stands, and walks toward me. *Us.*

His eyes drift down to Paige for a second and seem to linger on her hand still holding steady on my back.

His mouth ticks up in the corner the smallest bit, but if I had blinked, I would have missed it.

His expression immediately returns to the graveness it's had since we got home. He sighs again, and finally shrugs. "I really don't know anything yet, man. I'm sorry. But as soon as I saw this, I had to . . . stop—for a second," he says jaggedly, a small twitch in his shoulder as he hands me a flash drive. "I'm having Wade work on finding any and all copies that exist, but it'll help the more information I can—" his voice cuts off as my stomach twists further. Shaking his head, he adds, "I don't know what the fuck this is, but something tells me what happened to you guys . . . is just the tip of the iceberg."

The word *iceberg* meets the stiff coldness tightening in my spine—the far away feeling calls to me, luring me to the dark edges of my awareness to escape, but then Paige takes my hand, clasping it over the flash drive still in my palm.

Her eyes are dark and cloudy—hiding *something* I can't help but feel through every part of me.

"After he tells us everything he knows—we will watch what he found."

Her words from the car find me now, and I hate them even more than I did then.

But it's different. I suddenly feel . . . *unsure* of what I'm about to watch. What *we're* about to watch.

I've never understood why I did it. Truthfully, I tried with everything in me to never think about it at all.

But there's a video to prove it.

My desire, my need, my obsession with her was unhealthy—is unhealthy—and it reached a breaking point.

I tried to . . . fix it. Fix me. But I was too weak for that too.

Paige's hand tethers me, though, squeezing in mine as she wraps her other arm around Ellis. "Thank you," she whispers, I think, but I can't really hear.

Sound is becoming tunnelly, but it's not the same fight-or-flight as last night. *No, this feels like . . . I'm already crashing.*

I think Ellis says something else to her, but the blood whooshing through my ears is making me squeeze her hand tight. *Tighter.* I think I'm subconsciously trying to break the small device between the clammy hold of our palms.

"Too tight," Paige says, quietly, and I release immediately, blinking back to now, as she seemingly finishes her conversation with Ellis.

Ellis looks over at me, then mutters, "Come and get me if you need anything. I'm gonna work through some of the other contacts . . . look for any . . . *consistencies.*" His teeth run along his bottom lip, a silent warning to me that he's about to ask me something I don't want to answer. But he's Ellis, so he does it anyway. "Did Harris introduce you to this Dylan person?"

The precarious state of my mind feels like it's only capable of sweeping my memory at the moment, but I shake my head. "I-I don't think so. I mean, th-they knew each other. I-I think?"

I really can't remember. And not being able to access memories right now—when Paige and I are about to watch the biggest black hole of my existence—has me feeling like I'm a moment away from that residency on the moon.

"Okay," Ellis says, with a nod of his chin. "That's fine, man. Good." Then he looks at Paige. "Remember, take breaks if you need to."

I can see it. The *management.* He's telling *her* because *she* won't be the one to blackout.

But strangely I'm not worried about that kind of episode right now. *Right now*, the far away feeling has dissipated, and in its place is the sunken feeling. *Too deep.*

The one you feel in the movie when the iceberg inevitably comes into view.

Just as Ellis leaves, Paige looks up at me. The muscles in her face are tight. Her muted, denim-colored eyes have a light glaze, clearly working to hold back tears as she asks, "Ready?"

I swallow hard, my grip on her hand tightening. I don't nod or say anything, I just start to walk toward her room. She carries her laptop.

My blinks slow down.

Sinking, sinking, sinking.

Seeing the iceberg in my mind again, just as we reach her doorway, my last thought is—*the ship always sinks.*

EF 209
010223
RAW FOOTAGE
// 2014-06-06
EF 209
01

00:54:06

PAIGE

"Paige . . ."

I heard a voice. It was distantly familiar, but tunnely. And I didn't feel ready to be awake yet.

"Paige, you've gotta wake up." This time, I registered the voice was Linc's, and his tone was . . . *something*.

Not normal. He called me Paige.

Fuck. I was cold.

My eyelids felt like rusty old garage doors as they creaked open into slits, my vision blurry until I blinked a few times.

The second my eyes focused, my lungs deflated. Realization hit my drowsy mind in slow, devastating, crashing waves.

First was the sight of Linc. He sat three feet away from me on a couch I didn't recognize, in a hazy room I couldn't place. Hands pulled over his head and shackled to a pole behind him. My body squirmed at the sight, quickly realizing I was chained in the same position, but . . .

I had been stripped of all my clothes. Completely bare in nothing but my fucking honeybee underwear.

Fuck. Fuck, fuck, fuck.

A whimper ached in my dry throat and my eyes scrunched when I felt the sound stifled by something over my mouth.

Stripped, bound, and gagged.

My pulse exploded and I writhed against the restraints.

But *fuck.* I was dizzy. So cold.

We had to have been drugged. This wasn't a normal bout of grogginess. It felt like my brain had been wrapped in some sort of poison-laced cotton.

"Pip." Linc's ragged, hoarse voice hesitantly pulled my gaze up.

His hazel eyes were dark and bloodshot, wide with worry, but he kept them on my face, and I tried to hold that small bit of respect tight—hide it in a place deep inside myself.

My eyes drifted down to my nudity, and I made another pathetic, muffled noise as the panic reignited. My body was still so sluggish but my thoughts were taking off like the goddamn Roadrunner.

Linc started to pull and twist on his chains, and I did too, but after just a few seconds, my body slumped. Immediately depleted.

I could barely feel my hands. They were handcuffed, but whoever put us here fucking *MacGyver'd* us to the poles by weaving a figure eight with additional chains around our hands too.

My shoulders jumped as Linc growled through a myriad of curses before his exhaustion finally won out and his shoulders sagged.

Unable to move, unable to speak, I tried to think of the last thing I remembered . . .

I was in the back seat. Linc smiled back at me from up front.

Mr. Harris.

Oh, God.

Had we been abducted at some rest stop? Did they kill Mr. Harris and take us? *Where was he?*

Everything from serial killers to sex-trade plowed through my brain and I again found myself uselessly struggling against the chains.

But I suddenly took in the room and a hollow gasp filled my chest.

There were cameras—professional lights with modifiers stationed around what appeared to be a living room.

A film set.

Using what little energy I could gather, I pulled against the cuffs on my wrists to help hoist my legs up in front of me—at least attempting to cover myself from the camera lens—noticing then that my ankles were also chained together.

Fuck.

My overwhelmed grunt pushed against the gag as my feet pressed into the cushion, curling my body as much as I could. It was wildly uncomfortable with my arms up and over my head but I didn't care. The whole naked, gagged, and chained to a pole thing was pretty fucking uncomfortable anyway.

My eyes fell to the couch we were on, noticing the copper tinge to the edges of the beige cushions. It looked old, beat up, as did the armchair next to the couch, and the brown shag area rug sprawled out before us. It looked like the space had been staged to be a basement.

The cold, hard stone sitting in my chest collected more dread as my mind slowly rolled it all together.

Quick bursts of air puffed past my nose, over the material covering my mouth, cheeks, and chin. I could feel my bare chest heaving just as I heard Linc say, "Pip," again.

His voice cut through my panic and my eyebrows flinched.

Goddammit.

Still, I felt his silent plea for me to look at him, so I did, and the look on his face nearly wrecked me.

This was . . . fucking humiliating.

And I could see it in his eyes. The pity. The knowing.

Knowing that there was a reason I was naked and he was not. An awareness that while we were both being held against our will, our positions were not the same.

Linc would do everything he could to protect me. I knew he would. But for the briefest moment, he let his steady, stoic mask slip and I knew. I *knew* that knowing, helpless look would haunt me forever.

And just like that, he blinked it away. His face hardened just as the green in his eyes flared. His eyebrows suddenly hitched at the faint sound of four beeps that were coming from the front corner of the room.

He twisted, craning his neck toward the sound, but I kept my face on him.

Whoever this was would make themselves known soon enough, and I couldn't help but cling to *this* moment, *these* seconds.

There had been a few times in my life where I'd felt some sort of great shift in my being. Up until now, I had been lucky enough that most of those things had been good shifts.

But not this. This shift was sharp and itchy, and *holy fuck* did I feel it.

I watched Linc's eyebrows pinch as the sound of the door opening and closing came and went, and his eyes lifted, lightening just a bit as I heard . . .

Footsteps.

One, two, three . . .

And I was wrong.

This was the look I would never forget.

That small light in Linc's eyes had twisted with each step that got closer, the color slowly draining from his face. The harsh light of reality settled into his features, step by fucking step, and I ached to reach out and hold him—to *be held* by him.

The second I felt the shadow looming over me. The moment I saw the boat shoes I'd seen *this fucking morning* when we got picked up, a burning, rageful fire smoldered in the pit of my stomach.

Motherfucker.

I wouldn't look at him. My chest was splitting open, branching between stark awareness and complete disbelief. Although, how I hadn't realized it before now was a testament to how fucking zonked I was.

We weren't abducted at some rest stop.

Some strangers didn't chain us up and strip me down.

We were tricked—*taken*—by our own fucking teacher.

LINC

My eyebrows slammed down on my eyes and my glare sharpened with every step he took toward us. Each one seemed to mark the deepening blow of reality.

"What the fuck?" hissed past my lips involuntarily as his eyes met mine.

I thought about it. I *had the thought* that he was behind this when we woke up and he wasn't here, but then I quickly refuted it.

I trusted him.

He was our teacher.

My friend.

Even now, that betrayal was tearing through me, leaving a destruction in its wake that I was certain I'd never recover from. As soon as he stepped into the room, as soon as I saw the expectant, casual look on his face, I knew he wasn't here to help us.

This was *his* goddamn doing.

Stupidly, there was some thread—some worn, frayed, barely-hanging-on piece of me that *hoped.*

For what, I didn't know. I just knew I couldn't let things play out in any of the crazy, vile ways I'd imagined since I woke up.

"Jeremy, what the fuck is this?" I asked again, pulling uselessly at my chains before making myself stop. My strength and energy were depleting by the second.

My eyes flicked to Paige, but only for a moment before I took a breath, attempting to even my tone through my clenched jaw. "Where are her clothes?"

Jeremy's eyes dipped down to Paige but I rattled my chains

against the pole and his gaze shot back to me. A snarl tugged at my mouth as my glare deepened.

Eyes up, motherfucker.

His smirk, the damn near twinkle in his dark brown eyes—it all ticked up my already racing pulse. After a second, he tilted his chin down, wandering over to a seat by one of the cameras—still saying nothing.

I hadn't really paid much attention to the cameras—other than the fact that they were here—but looking now, I could see there were two.

The job . . . it was . . . it was all a set up?

To do this?!

I had no idea what the fuck *this* was, but it was clearly fucking demented. Blinking heavily, I tried to keep my mind from spiraling, and studied the cameras again.

Both were on tripods. It looked like he'd also stationed a third one—a handheld—off to the side of the couch, closer to me. My eyes squinted as I saw a ghost icon at the corner of the camera face.

"This is . . . professional equipment," I rasped. I'm not sure what about that realization sent a new wave of unease through me, but it did.

Why did some creepy-ass dungeon have seven-figure recording equipment?

Jeremy cleared his throat and my eyes reluctantly pulled back to him. He sighed. "Look, guys. I know this all seems . . ." He trailed off, giving a quick peek around the room. "Well, I know this all seems a little dramatic but . . . the end product will be worth it."

"What the fuck?" My head shook. It felt like the words were scrambled. None of it made sense, but a very visceral panic bubbled deep in my gut.

"The level of discomfort you experience over the course of making the film will depend on you guys," he said, almost clinically. "But I have high hopes. Given your history. The rehearsal will probably take care of it."

My eyebrows scrunched. His words were barely able to find their way from my ears to my brain. *History?* "Rehearsal," was the word I said out loud, but it wasn't a question. I was processing.

He nodded, his eyes meeting mine. "The client has requested an intense scene. I'll be directing, so it's important we take some time to get comfortable with each other. Push some limits. Build some trust. Then we'll shoot."

"The *client? Shoot what?!*" I barked, shaking my head. I didn't understand. And something told me there was no possible way I *could* understand what was happening.

Jeremy didn't respond. His eyes started to pull back in Paige's direction, and another deep growl shook my throat. "Motherfucker! Keep your fucking eyes off her!"

The sound of Jeremy's small laugh twisted in my chest before he said, "How are we supposed to build trust if I can't look at her?"

I couldn't help the humorless snort through my nose. "*Build* trust?! Are you fucking serious?!" He continued to simply *stare*, his brown eyes and indifferent expression gave absolutely nothing away, and I shook my head, my frustration beginning to climb again. "You brought us here under false pretenses, drugged us, and then stripped my girlfriend down and gagged her." I grit out. "Chained us up."

I didn't think I needed any more reasons to be fucking livid, but the creep's eyes glittered. I couldn't be sure, but I think he liked that he was getting a reaction out of me, and it only made me more furious.

After a moment he shrugged. "Well, I happen to think Paige looks stunning like this." His eyes cut over to her and my eyes followed.

And goddamn, it hurt to see her like this. I had been trying to keep my eyes off of her. There was no way to look at her without seeing . . . *something.*

And while that *something* was a fucking masterpiece, she wasn't *willingly* showing me her body right now. My eyes fell to the monstrosity strapped to the bottom half of her pretty face— a thick gray cloth—and the stabby feeling in my chest twisted.

Her blue eyes were frozen glaciers. Cutting and sharp, but glistening with moisture. She was terrified. Exposed. But she was fighting like hell to keep the fight in her eyes. And I couldn't do a fucking thing. Not chained to this pole.

I took a breath. "What do we have to do to get her some clothes? Get that . . . *thing* off her face?"

I couldn't even begin to stomach the vague "rehearsal" plans he'd given us. *This "shoot."* But if Jeremy ended up leaving the room again, it'd be a lot easier to come up with a plan if she had the use of her voice.

Jeremy sighed. "Naked Paige is a requirement, I'm afraid." His voice was soft with apology, but had the remorse of telling me he was out of band-aids or something.

Not exposing my girlfriend.

I blinked rapidly, half-expecting another creature entirely to shed the skin of the man in front of me.

How is this possible?

When Jeremy remained—*not a body snatcher*—my anger relit, staring back at him as he finally said, "We might be able to negotiate the gag, though."

I tried to think past the burning rage running through me. I couldn't even bring myself to imagine what this negotiation would cost.

The room felt . . . *crooked.*

My head swayed and I shook it, trying to keep myself conscious.

Paige needs me.

I cleared my throat with a small shake of my head, trying to focus. Thoughts of anything other than survival and keeping the son of a bitch's hands off of Paige had to wait.

As he walked over to her, my spine lengthened. But when his hand reached out and cupped her jaw, I immediately lunged toward them. I couldn't even feel my arms, my hands—but the stampede of fury from seeing his thumb brush over her covered lips was sending me into a blinding rage.

Her muffled whimpers cut through me as I growled, "You son of a bitch! Don't fucking touch her!" thrashing wildly.

Jeremy peeked up at me. I was breathing like a rabid bull and my vision was narrowing but I could see this . . . almost *impressed* glint in his expression and a tightness gripped my throat. It was a similar look to ones he'd given me while working on my film project this year.

I swallowed the lump in my throat, and the thought—*that wasn't real.*

Paige used the distracted moment to jerk her face away from his fingers, and Jeremy chuckled. "I'm kind of surprised, Linc. You really don't like seeing your girl trussed up like the perfect little sex doll?"

My gaze shot to him with a glare. I wasn't about to dignify the perverted musing with a response. But he didn't wait for one. He took the couple of steps between us, putting himself in front of me, and then crouched down.

Without hesitation, I lifted my legs, shot them out, kicking him square in the chest, as hard as I could. I was so tired and weak that the effort only managed to knock him over, probably piss him off, but whatever.

It felt good.

He stood back up, straightening himself out with another pleased tilt to his lips. "Keep that fight. You're gonna need it."

In an instant, he climbed on top of me, straddling my lap and I bucked against him trying to knock him off.

What in the ever loving fuck?

I think his hands were holding over my wrists, but the lack of circulation was making it hard to tell. He pushed his body weight into me and Paige screamed from behind the gag, but his dark gaze held my eyes hostage. His weight, his hands, the chains.

I pressed myself far into the couch—putting as much distance between us as I could before his hands moved . . . cradling my jaw.

Seriously, what the fuck is this?

"It only seems fair that a *mouth* should pay for the freedom of another mouth, don't you think?"

I blinked rapidly, still trying to jerk and push away from his hold. But a prickling sensation tightened up my spine when what he said finally sunk in, and I saw his eyes on my lips. A hardness pressed into my groin.

I could nearly feel the thud in my chest from my heart bottoming-out.

Digging my heels into the floor, I pushed so hard I thought I might blow through the back of the couch.

The sounds of Paige's desperate, muffled screams filtered back through, while somewhere in that time, one of Jeremy's hands had moved to my hair. Running his fingers through it . . .

My glare shifted from one of his dark brown eyes to the other, but they looked nearly black, glittering.

I don't know this person.

It was . . . unsettling. I was so confused. *Fucking disturbed.* But the thing that came out of my mouth was, "Y-You're gay?"

Grinding his teeth, his jaw wiggled a bit and his eyes hardened. It looked like he was working to keep his expression even, and I inhaled deep.

Hm. Did I strike a nerve there, asshole?

The fingers digging through my hair said, *yes,* and I tucked the observation in my back pocket. After another second passed, he sighed. "My preferences are unimportant." His voice was tight, wrought with something distantly wounded, but he just as quickly blinked it away.

I again tried to pull my face away from his touch, but his fingers scraped into my scalp and twisted my hair at the roots. Not enough to really hurt, but with my arms numb and chained, his full weight on top of me, his fucking boner digging into my hip—I was *defenseless*.

My eyes shifted away from his. The fucker may have had me twisted and stuck in his web of perversion, but that didn't mean I had to look at him. "What do you want?" I finally mumbled.

Using the fingers still raked through my hair, he pulled my chin up. Like he'd somehow heard my silent defiance and decided to prove me wrong.

Watchful, slimy eyes stared down at me before I felt his grip on my hair loosen and then disappear. But not even a full second later, he was running his thumb along my lips.

My mouth immediately tried to sink its teeth into his hand, but he caught my chin with an easy swoop. Paige's stifled protests reignited as his eyes darkened further, lit like a black flame, as he used one of his hands to pry my jaw open.

I pushed as much as I pulled. It didn't even feel like I had fucking arms anymore and my struggle was useless. All it took was him pressing his knees into the couch cushion, dampening his weight on top of me, as his thumb pressed down on my tongue.

The invasion took me by surprise and my instinct to bite down was denied by his other hand, still tightly gripped around my jaw.

"Listen. It's nothing crazy," he said with a casualness that licked flames down my spine. "You're just going to kiss me. Convincingly."

Paige's ragged, muffled voice started screaming again just as his thumb started to slide further back—closer to my throat, and then slowly forward again, like he was petting my tongue, and bile rose up my throat.

Yes, puke. That'll get him off me.

But my body didn't cooperate. I had nothing in my stomach, so when he pushed his thumb a little too far back—hitting my gag reflex—it sent me into a dry-heaving, coughing fit.

And while he did ease his thumb back, he didn't take it away. Drool fell from the corners of my open mouth as he leaned into me and said, "Follow the directions, Linc," he said low, his voice strung with warning. "The boss already has eyes on us, and you don't want him involved." With the threat-laced words, he finally freed my mouth and I gasped in a hard breath, only to cough it back out a second later.

The boss?

My body convulsed between trying to breathe, while simultaneously choking on toxic coughs from the vomit that still wouldn't actually surface.

There was someone else? Someone *already* watching this shit?! *Who?*

The thoughts flew through seconds of me hacking, all the while I could see Paige thrashing and kicking beside me.

Jeremy's eyes flicked over to her, and after another choking breath, I worked to swallow. "W-Water," I croaked.

His mouth flattened, clearly irritated, not that I gave a shit. He opened his mouth like he was about to say something, but then decided differently and closed it. After another beat, with a huff, he pushed off of me.

My eyes shot to Paige but her eyes were staring daggers at Jeremy—two sharply cut sapphires firing in his direction as he crossed the room.

After rounding the armchair, he bent down to a small mini fridge I hadn't noticed before, and he grabbed two bottles of water.

Placing one down on a stool by one of the cameras, he brought the other one over to me, unscrewing the top. The *crack* of the seal on the bottle cap lifted my chest with some relief.

He held it up, offering it to me and *fucking hell* it was going to sting to drink from his disgusting hand.

But I needed to move this along. Paige was still silenced. I swallowed my pride and dropped my jaw, accepting the water.

Through measured sips, I tried to let each gulp fuel my fight.

He wanted me to . . . *kiss him.* I had no clue why, but that's the thing about madness—to understand it was to be it. So, I guess the silver-lining was that some of my sanity was still intact.

Another few sips . . .

One thing was for sure, I was less than useless as long as I was chained to this pole—completely at his mercy.

The gag is negotiable . . .

Maybe I could negotiate the chains too. And if I kept myself hydrated, maybe I could work my strength back up to . . .

What? Kill him?

It wouldn't be hard. Not mentally, anyway, seeing as I'd already envisioned myself doing it a hundred different ways since he walked in here.

As he pulled the bottle from my mouth, my chin hung forward, hauling in some deep breaths. Just as the slight coolness raced through my veins, Paige's bare thigh came into my line of sight.

My eyes pulled up to her. Her terrified gaze was darting back and forth between me and Jeremy, and my eyebrows scrunched with a desolate blink.

She needed water too.

Which would require getting the gag off.

01:13:46

LINC

My chin stayed toward Paige, away from my teacher while he *re-straddled my lap.*

Paige's suppressed sounds were barely audible, but I could see her helplessly draining her energy, trying to stop a situation my mind was working tirelessly to come to terms with.

I told myself, *It's fine.* I could endure some nauseating discomfort if it meant she could get the use of her voice again. If we could come up with a plan.

I can do this for her.

Nostrils flaring, I repeated it over and over again in my head as my eyes pulled up to Jeremy from under my eyebrows.

Sick fuck. I took a deep breath and kept my voice low as I said, "Chains too."

His head tilted, his eyes lifting curiously. The ease he looked at me with, chained and pinned below him, was unnerving as fuck. My body shifted as much as it could just as I cleared my throat, but my voice was still rough as I clarified, "If I do this. You take off the gag *and* chains. And give her water."

The whooshing in my ears became a fucking hurricane.

I didn't know how he'd react to the demand, but I had to try to *gain* as much as I could. Something told me the "favors" would cost more and more in a place like this.

There seemed to be rules in here, but they were to some twisted game where none of the spaces made sense, the prize and punishments were unknown and unwanted, and the gamemaker was a fucking lunatic.

The mad conductor of a crooked symphony.

Jeremy pulled in a deep breath then released an audible exhale. "Gag and water, yes. Chains . . . will be determined based on your performance."

My eyes squinted at his words. *Performance.*

I became aware again of the cameras.

"The boss has eyes on us already."

His body covered my view of both of the tripods stationed across from us, so I couldn't see if any of the rolling lights were on. But a drop of my eyes revealed the handheld camera next to us was off. *At least there's that.*

Nothing about it felt like a win, though. There was nothing victorious about my current situation. My mind was fighting the urge to just . . . shut down. It had been since I woke up and saw Paige naked but . . .

Forcing me to kiss him? *In front of her?*

Despite the man straddling my waist, my eyes needed the small bit of relief only she could bring. Lifting my gaze from the spot I'd been staring at on the couch, my eyes collided with hers.

They were wide, the blue even more bright against her tears and bloodshot stare, silently begging. *Begging me not to do this?*

Begging me to help her? I wasn't sure, but the desperation in her gaze was pooling heavily with unshed tears.

A frown pulled at my lips. I was caught in the violent winds of depravity. I didn't know *what* the right thing to do was. *I don't think right exists here.*

But there was no doubt his little choking stunt before was a power move—a warning.

Using the same thumb he'd used to violate my mouth, he pulled my chin toward him and I cringed, sending a small tingle up my otherwise numb arms.

"You ready?" he asked, and his gravelly tone grated just below my skin. Paige's body weakly writhed and Jeremy's eyes cut over to her. "You, behave."

My eyes flinched before they widened with complete fucking confusion, and the words slipped from between my clenched teeth before I could stop them. "Why are you doing this?"

I had convinced myself that his reasoning was unimportant. That since I was certain I couldn't understand it, it didn't matter.

But it did.

Of course it fucking mattered. I trusted him. She trusted me to trust him.

Jeremy sighed as his hand timidly moved to my hair again. I swallowed hard, letting him do it. Fighting it was useless, and getting his response was more important.

"Our films are very . . . exclusive," he explained, "The client requested Paige, but they gave me creative license to cast the male role." He continued to stare down at me, with this strange twisted peacefulness as he added, "And you get the immersive art thing. You *get it*."

That fucking play?! I most certainly did not get it.

I was just trying to be polite.

Impress him.

But not because I was seeking *this kind* of attention.

I just . . . I thought . . .

I thought he was . . .

I shook my head, despite his hold on my hair, with another grunt.

It didn't matter. It didn't matter what I thought. I *thought* a lot of things before this very moment. But this kind of thing, it's the thing that changes you in a chemical way.

Trust will be different now.

People will be different now.

If there even is a time after this. After he forces us to do whatever vile acts this client seems to have requested—certainly he's not just going to let us go.

I won't ask that question. Not right now.

"Look, Linc. This will be easier if you treat it as an exercise. Have you ever kissed a man before?"

I shook my head immediately, but my nostrils flared and his eyebrow cocked.

"Never?" he prods.

Ellis kissed me once on Halloween a few years ago. But it was mostly so that Spike and Angel could kiss. But it was a joke. It was Ellis. It wasn't . . . I don't know. It wasn't this.

I shook my head and he asked, "Okay, well what makes you uncomfortable about it?"

"I don't want to," I say through my teeth.

"But you've never tried it," he quips back.

What the fuck is this?

All the while Paige was still fucking naked and gagged a few feet away from me while we were playing psycho-babble MadLibs.

Then Jeremy says, "Sometimes, in a scene, it's about connecting to your motivation. Right, Paige?"

The way he looked at her, the way he was talking to her, had this condescension that was dragging down my spine like sludge. And I fucking hated seeing his dark pervy eyes roam her body.

A growl erupted from the back of my throat, my hips bucking, but the movement was barely noticeable with two hundred-something-pounds on top of me.

Still, it at least pulled his eyes back to me, and his sinister, conniving face sent a sweeping coldness through my veins.

Any remaining familiarity I saw in his face . . . drained away.

This wasn't the same person I'd known for two years—someone I looked up to or confided in. *That* person wasn't real and . . . I hated the final twist of that realization in my chest.

He lowered his face to mine, tugging my hair and tilting my chin up. It wasn't a hard grip, but just enough to silently remind me once again—*I didn't have a choice.*

His minty breath hit just below my nose and the nausea that had been stirring started to rise again. My eyes slammed shut. Suddenly, everything became too real, and I gulped in air through my mouth.

"Hey," his voice got closer. His fingers loosened in my hair, but still sifting, as his other hand moved to my shoulder. The rough feeling of his cheek as it bumped against mine made me wince before his mouth hovered right over my ear. "Relax. I've got you."

I stiffened, jolting like a Taser had been taken to my spine. He leaned in and my lips instinctively sucked into my mouth.

He gave a small squeeze to my cheeks, forcing my lips back out, but said, "What are the directions, Linc?"

I swallowed, glaring, then grinding out, "Kiss you."

He leaned down, into my space again, his mouth an inch from mine. "Kiss me how?"

God-fucking-damnit. How I hadn't snapped a tendon in my neck, or puked all over him was beyond me, but I had never wished *something* would happen more. *Something* that put me out of my fucking misery.

With flaring eyes, I finally mumbled, "Convincingly."

The only thing I could think of was that this was a power move. He'd stripped Paige down to nothing, and while he'd left me clothed for the moment, I was by no means exempt from whatever sick and depraved things he had planned.

He was close enough to my face that his smirk to my response was right below my eyes. I could see the pattern of the stubble on his cheeks, and the itch beneath my skin returned.

Stop. Get this over with.

But he made no move. He didn't lean in any closer. He was . . . waiting.

Fuck me.

I tilted my head to the ceiling, blinking once before lowering my chin and reluctantly looking at Paige.

I needed her.

Her eyes were wide, heartbroken, and *God* I just wanted to fucking hold her.

I wanted *her* mouth.

Her breath brushing my skin.

Her voice in my ear.

"Close your eyes," I told her, my voice a hoarse whisper. The man on my lap could hear me, obviously, but I didn't give a fuck. I didn't want her to see this.

She stoically kept the tears pooling at the corner of her eyes, scrunching them, as a breathy grunt pushed through her nose. After another second, she did as I told her, and closed her eyes.

I did too, keeping the image of her in my mind. But from a different night. Just a few days ago. *The moonlight spilling in through the windshield of my car, putting the softest sparkle in her light blue eyes.*

Her.

I could convincingly kiss her.

Keeping my eyes closed, I sunk into the splintered awareness of my mind, branching out and creating an alternate reality.

One where the mint smell, warmed and spiced to cinnamon, brightened to citrus. One where the rough, calloused hand cradling my jaw sanded and buffed to the soft, delicate fingers I woke up to yesterday.

I leaned in, still cringing as I lightly pressed my mouth to the lips in front of me.

PAIGE

I couldn't take it.

The taste of pennies filled my mouth. I must have bitten my cheek. My throat worked to swallow the blood—the only moisture in the desert of my mouth.

What had started as light pecking noises beside me, had grown to wet, heavy breaths—muffled by clasping mouths—a couple of soft groans too.

And they weren't coming from Linc. The noises were hungry and rattling through my stomach . . . it was *him.*

In my forced silence, I had decided *Mr. Harris* didn't exist. This man wasn't our *teacher,* and since I didn't know who this psycho was, I decided I'd simply refer to him as the Man.

The sounds ebbed and flowed, echoing like surround sound. Slurps and lips smacking. It went on for what felt like forever and with each minute that passed, my lungs deflated. Shriveled.

With my mouth covered, my eyes closed, and the despicable sounds filtering through my ears—sensory deprivation worked my pulse into an explosive frenzy.

I can't fucking take it.

"*Mmf.*"

God, the vile sound of the Man's stifled mewl makes me dry heave behind the gag. Unable to take the imaginings from behind my closed eyelids a second longer, I slowly opened my eyes, still keeping my gaze downward.

I don't want to see it. I just can't be . . . in the dark.

Being stripped of my clothes and silenced was dehumanizing enough.

I tried to tune out the sounds. My eyes traced the hilly threads of the dingy-looking couch. As my head hung heavily, I absently wondered, if I were given the chance—could I smother the Man with this couch cushion? If he miraculously *did* release my chains?

A heavy sigh pushed through my nose. *No.* Even under normal circumstances, I probably wasn't capable of that, but definitely not right now. Dehydrated, weak . . . I couldn't feel my hands, but my wrists were already cracked and bleeding from fighting against the chains.

My eyes honed in on a loose thread at the corner of the couch cushion, viscerally aware I *couldn't* just reach out and grab it, but wishing I could. Like maybe it was the secret way to unravel this moment.

Suddenly, the light sound of chains clinking instinctively pulled my eyes up, as the Man released a deep, sated groan, and my gaze became trapped—stuck like fly paper to the sight in front of me.

The Man—his hips grinding. Linc beneath him. His hairline sweaty, his skin flushed. His mouth. *Their* mouths. Tongues.

Each disturbing image blew through me so viciously, it felt like they'd been permanently lodged into the walls of my chest.

My insides turned further when I saw the strain in my boyfriend's neck, between his brows, and white-hot rage tore through me.

One of the Man's hands was shoved through Linc's hair—*hair meant for my fingers.* His mouth moved to Linc's neck, and my eyes dropped again, unable to watch the pleasure surfacing on the Man's face.

But that's when I saw . . . his other hand. The one that had originally been on Linc's shoulder, and my eyes bulged.

He was rubbing Linc's dick . . . over his pants.

My arms instinctively pulled, and the pain radiated in my wrists. Immediately, my eyes slammed shut again as a series of hoarse, muffled whimpers pushed against the gag.

Murder was my only thought.

My fingers twisted between the chains. I was mentally draining the life from the Man—strangling him with the chains or smothering him with the cushion—*feeling* his last breath leave his fucking body.

When this horror show started—*when I woke up naked*—a variety of sick acts played out in my head. I had started mentally preparing myself for what seemed to be an inevitable assault.

But I could have never predicted this.

With another blink down at the shitstain-colored couch, I let the tears I'd kept in my eyes fall. I felt the moisture soak into the material still covering my face, rubbing salt in the wound.

Linc was doing this to buy me back a basic freedom. A *baseline* privlege the Man had no fucking right to take away from me in the first place, and the fury boiled through me with a voracity that shook down to my marrow.

The tunneled sounds of the Man's assault finally slowed, and I breathed heavily through my nose, partially with relief, partially to reroute my rage.

With my arms still up and over, I shoved my face into my bare shoulder, wiping away any indication that I'd been crying.

Any sight of weakness.

My heart hurt so fucking much, but I used my anger to curb the pain. That is, until the Man quietly rasped, "Good boy. Got a little excited there, huh?"

Screwing my eyes tighter shut, my brain rejected the words.

Dead. I want him dead.

Buffy bless, I had never wished *more* to unhear something. Unsee something.

I waited for Linc's voice. I'd felt bad about opening my eyes, but I just . . .

I shook my head. I just wanted to be there for him, even though I knew that was impossible. Even though I knew he didn't want me to see it.

The guilt deepend at the sound of Linc's ragged breathing next to me, tightening in my own chest. His coughing and gagging clogged in *my* throat.

Do not cry.

"The deal," Linc's voice rumbled, cracking at the end.

Since my eyes were still closed, I couldn't tell if the Man was still . . . on top of him, or if he'd relieved Linc of that, at least. Though, something told me he was still continuing the torture.

After another second passed I felt weight lift from the couch, but Linc still hadn't given me clearance to open my eyes.

I wondered if he was still just trying to catch his breath, or if he was steadily swallowing vomit like I had been all night—*or however long we've been here, I have no fucking clue.*

Maybe he just . . . needed a minute.

He was just molested—*assaulted*—by a man he trusted.

Someone I'm pretty sure he had considered a friend, and my heart broke a little more.

Suddenly, I felt a presence in front of me, and my eyebrows sloped down. Hands circled behind my head and after a second, the pressure over my lips, cheeks, and chin lifted.

I sucked in a heavy breath, gasping, and *Jesus Christ,* the air that finally met my mouth suctioned any remaining moisture away.

Still, my eyes pulled over to Linc. His chin tilted down and his dark hair stuck out—thoroughly tugged—while he continued to take heavy breaths.

His wide eyes were pulsing with . . . humiliation? Shock? It looked like an equal bit of both.

I couldn't be sure, but my mouth flattened—new anger ablaze. I wanted to reach over and curl into his chest. I ached to take his lips and wipe away that disgusting memory. But more than anything, I wanted to tell him . . .

He forced you, Linc. It's not your fault.

From my peripherals, I saw an open water bottle appear in front of my face, and my chin reluctantly twisted away from Linc.

The Man stood in front of me, ready to feed me water like a fucking hammster, and *holy fuck* I wanted to deny it.

But I needed something to help combat the dizziness, the stress. I needed energy to fight back.

In my mind, I drank some of it and then spit the rest back out at the monster in front of me.

But I wouldn't do it. Linc's sacrifice would have been for nothing.

Begrudgingly, I opened my mouth and took the water. With nowhere to look but into the Man's beady, dark eyes, I couldn't help but notice that he looked at us—Linc and I . . . *differently.*

Despite the fact he had forced Linc to kiss him, I saw this . . . *fondness* that wasn't present in the passive, disinterested way he was staring down at me right now.

After a few more sips, the Man pulled the bottle away from me. I gasped, swallowed—tried not to puke it all back up.

Fingers quickly caught my chin, and returned my eyes to the Man, my jaw clenching.

His light brown hair was disheveled, and there was still a light flush to his cheeks that ground through me.

"What do you say?" he asked.

My eyes widened. If stares could kill, my eyes would have done the deed and were now chopping him into tiny pieces and burying them. Watering and tending to them so I could grow him and kill him again.

He wanted *gratitude?*

For fucking what?

He twisted my chin to look over at Linc, who had now turned back toward us, and was staring at the Man with a murderous flare in his eyes, just as the Man said, "Your boyfriend earned that for you. The least you can say is, 'thank you.'"

Bastard. I *was* grateful for Linc. But not for that. Not that I was ashamed of him, either. Not at all. *He didn't have a choice.* But being *grateful* for what the Man had just done to him felt like *appreciating* a terrorist act.

My chin remained captive. The pressure of his steady thumb kept my face toward Linc, and my breath shook as I inhaled. Linc's gaze finally met mine, and I nearly felt the thud behind my eyes and the squeeze to my heart.

They were so . . . green. Shredded like broken ancient moss. The sustained eye contact was enough to lift my chest a bit. It reminded me I was still naked, and I wondered at what point I had become numb to it. But every harrowing detail of the room—*of this reality*—stood still for just a second, retracted and blurred.

I gave Linc a silent message, one I hoped desperately he understood.

I'm sorry. I love you.

It looked like his eyes wanted to smile just a bit, and I sighed. I could tell the Man wasn't going to let me go until I followed his order so after my private, secret message to Linc, I said what I was ordered to say. "Thank you."

The Man's grip on my jaw tightened slightly. It didn't hurt, but his fingertips dug into my cheek as he said, "For the rest of rehearsal, you'll call him, 'Sir.' Understood?"

Of fucking course.

Linc muttered a curse as my teeth clenched under the Man's hold. *This guy is completely fucked*—probably had a list to the moon and back of psychological issues. And I was gathering that one of those issues might be women . . .

This was the difference I saw earlier. Where Linc's plight seemed to be from an attraction from the Man, my role seemed to be degradation.

"What do you say?" the Man prodded, still holding my chin.

"Jesus Christ, man. Enough," Linc all but groaned and I sucked in a deep breath.

I didn't want Linc to suffer anymore. I didn't want the asshole bruising my cheek to retaliate. I needed to cooperate until we could come up with a plan.

Don't do anything stupid.

Taking another breath, through my teeth I said, "Thank you, sir."

Linc's eyes fell to the couch again, shaking his head as the Man finally released my chin.

"The chains," Linc rasped, keeping his face down, almost as if he was trying to summon something. But if I had to guess, his mind was probably trying to wade through the aftershocks of his assault and exhaustion.

God, I wanted the chains off more than anything. I wanted to be in his arms.

Far fucking away from here.

The Man's chin tilted down to the floor. He stayed there for just a second before lifting his eyes back up. His gaze drifted back and forth between the two of us before landing on Linc. "Okay. You've earned it. But . . ." he paused, likely for dramatic effect—*creepy fucker*—and then added, "You should both know we are in a secure building. There's a key code to get through that first door you see behind me, and the door past that requires a fingerprint for access. Beyond that, there is armed security stationed at all exits. I'll be removing the chains, but not the handcuffs. Are we clear?"

A new wave of unease swelled in my throat as the information punched my brain like fists to a fucking boxing bag.

Key code. Fingerprints . . . armed security?

What the fuck was the point of chaining us up like animals if we were in a *secured building?*

Maybe he's lying.

Still, my nerves rose. Linc had said something earlier about the equipment. So, it seemed possible the Man was telling the truth. Clearly, there seemed to be quite a bit of money behind this crooked operation.

The Man stood in front of us still, expectantly, and I remembered he'd asked me a question. I nodded, jaggedly. I don't even remember the question but *whatever* will get me out of these chains.

He moved toward me, reaching into his pocket, pulling out a small brass key. As he stood over me, unweaving the excessive chains, my tired mind tried to gather all the information I could.

We were here to make some fucked up movie for a creep who . . . requested me. No idea how—but the male role wasn't a request. The Man chose Linc—but his motivation for kissing him doesn't seem relevant to any of this.

I'm only more confused.

Suddenly, one of my hands fell.

Oh my God.

I willed myself to move it. To pick it up and claw at his face— gouge one of his eyes out with my bare hand—but I couldn't move it. I couldn't even wiggle my fucking fingers.

"Oh, fuck." Linc's voice filtered through my frustration and my eyes pulled up to him, but he was staring down at my lap.

My eyes slid back to my hand, still unmoving, but I saw now that the skin on my wrist—the skin that had been beneath the metal cuff was cracked, raw, and bleeding down my forearm.

The Man finally picked it back up, securing the wrist once more, tightening the metal over the broken skin. I winced.

Still, there was some relief to not having my arms pulled up and over my head, and I suddenly realized I could tuck my legs tighter, better covering myself. So, I did, but I gracelessly had to use my knees to shift my arms, situating them to drape around my calves, and the cold chains to the handcuffs clinked against my shins.

The Man chuckled and my fingers twitched with the urge to clench my fists. "I'll get some ointment for your wrists, and get you guys some food. You're going to need your energy," he said, then looked at me. "I'm trusting you to stay put, okay?"

Yeah fucking right.

Still, I nodded like the robotic little sex puppet he wanted me to be—but then my eyebrows pinched, asking, "What about him?" My eyes drifted over to Linc, who still had his arms chained to the pole behind him.

The distant, vacant stare in his eyes seemed a little better, but still farther than I wanted.

A heavy sigh sounded from my side, involuntarily pulling my eyes back to the Man as he said, "He earned your relief. You'll have to earn his."

The threat left his mouth and lifted, orbiting around us, all-knowing and up where nothing could touch it and everything was possible.

Torture, rape, mutilation—a depraved rotation of all three.

I didn't want to find out whatever the fuck it meant, but one of the many things that remained unclear was . . .

"Are you going to kill us?"

The Man's eyebrows hitched before his features hardened again, almost impatiently. "Everyone will be fine as long as we deliver the film."

The film.

What the fuck is this? There were plenty of *legitimate* ways to make porn. And I couldn't be certain, having not been in the industry myself, but I was pretty sure all parties were *consensual.*

Maybe not . . .

The Man stared at me a moment longer, and I could see a silent warning. *Trusting me to stay put.*

Evil and *dumb.*

He backed away and started toward the door.

One, two, three . . .

Twelve steps before he opened the door and left. And not even a second after, a croaked sob pushed through my lips, as I scooted desperately over to Linc.

"Wait, Pip," he said, but I winced as the prickly-static feeling in my hands started to come back, spreading up my arms in the most intense pins-and-needles sensation I had ever felt.

"Fuck . . ." I whined, still shuffling toward him.

"Pip—" he rasped again, but I huddled against his chest and stuck my face in the crook of his neck, taking a big breath of him.

Silvers. Sea Salt. Woods.

My guy.

He leaned his cheek on the top of my head. "You were supposed to stay put," he said, pressing his lips into my hair.

"Fuck him," I huffed. My arms and hands were still zapping back to life as the circulation continued to find its way back.

The ache in my wrists throbbed, and since they were still cuffed, I couldn't wrap my arms around Linc the way I wanted to, so as my fingers regained their feeling, I twisted the thin material of his T-shirt.

My nipple brushed against the cotton material, and I fidgeted. After a second, Linc sighed. "I wish I could cover you." My chest softened at the sweet roughness in his voice. Our position didn't allow me to see his eyes at the moment, but I could *feel* them scanning the space for anything we could use to cover me. Our bodies slumped, though, seeing the only thing was the dirty shag carpet, partially positioned under the couch.

Pressing my face into his chest, I finally whispered, "I know." And I *did know*. He'd do anything for me.

He just suffered a molestation on my behalf.

I can't let that happen again.

A heaviness darkened around us. There were things to be said. *So much* to be said. But I didn't know how long it would be until the Man came back.

I also couldn't bring myself to leave Linc's side yet.

I wanted to kiss him. But I wasn't sure if he'd want that right now, so I just decided to stick close by, let the smell of him try to work through my exhausted and overwhelmed brain.

"What are we gonna do?" I breathed the words involuntarily, almost like the thought had quite literally escaped through my lips.

Linc's cheek still rested on my head. The room was quiet, save for our breathing and a random *clink* every few seconds from the chains still holding Linc's hands.

"Did you hear him say there's someone else?" he asked.

I shook my head, glancing around the room. Seeing the cameras again, I curled myself further into him.

I could feel his despair at not being able to cover me. It was in the slight lift to his shoulder, the tight inhale of his breath.

"It's okay," I told him.

It's not. But it's not okay for him either.

I could feel the silent, erratic scheming of both our thoughts, trying to figure out what the Man was going to make us do, while simultaneously trying to plan an escape from a locked-down room.

All the while trying to forget what just happened . . .

My tired brain felt like a runaway train hitting a dead end. After another beat, Linc's head lifted. "Maybe there's . . . something. Something in the room you can, I don't know—hide under one of the cushions—in the back, between them? Use it as a weapon?"

It was as good of a plan as any. Reluctantly, I pushed myself away from him, but only a second after I started to move, I heard him say, "Wait—"

I stopped. My fatigue, and the fact my body felt like I'd been beaten with a small, but very real bat, meant I hadn't moved very far.

Which made the return of shame to Linc's eyes even more apparent.

My heart sank, but I held his glassy, forest stare with mine.

His gaze was a combination of longing and uncertainty, shadowed with humiliation. I moved closer to him, inching my face forward—close enough I could brush my nose with his.

I swallowed, then quietly told him what I had wanted to say right after it happened. "He forced you, Linc. It's not your fault," I whispered between our mouths, then added, "I love you."

It wouldn't change what happened. But it was all true. And I hoped it did something for him to be sure that *I knew* he wanted no part of what the Man just did to him.

He hesitantly leaned in, timidly brushing his lips against mine, like he still wasn't quite sure. It wasn't like the kisses I'd come to know from him, but it was still all-consuming.

I pressed my mouth against his before my tongue slowly breached the seam of his lips, testing, but then he swallowed my tongue.

I followed his lead, giving him complete access.

Whatever he needs.

He sucked and bit, growling as his mouth suddenly became aggressive, pleading, greedy.

Take it back.

I felt the words through every move of his mouth against mine. I remembered my exact urge to do that very thing, and my only thought was—*it would be my fucking pleasure.*

My limbs were shaky, but determined, as I straddled his lap, pressing my naked body up against him. His soft groan was all I needed to lean forward and devour his mouth.

We didn't have time for this. But fucking hell, if we *died* like this I'm not sure either one of us would regret it.

Despite my nudity, and the hungry way our mouths were moving, this wasn't sexual. It was *untamed connection.*

Our pocket of moonlight glittering on dark and ominous waters.

My lips slowed when I was sure I had reached the deepest depths of his mouth. I ended the kiss by nibbling along his bottom lip, with the small licks trailing behind them, knowing it drove him crazy.

I was rewarded with his hoarse grunt pushing against my lips when we finally pulled apart. Even with my tits mere inches from his chin, he kept his eyes on my face—just as he had the whole time we'd been here.

"I love you," I told him again.

The smallest pinch pulled at the corner of his perfect lips before he rasped, "Till the end."

Buffy fucking bless, I really did love him. Our stupid, cheesy tagline—the one from our friendship oath. It refueled my fight.

We *had* to survive this.

We had to survive *past* this.

My eyes peeked around the room again. "How long do you think we've been here?"

He pushed out a heavy exhale, and I used one of my hands to hold his face, my thumb brushing his bottom lip. Leaning his cheek into my hand, he gave a small shake of his head. "I have no clue."

After a few seconds of us staring back and forth, his eyes shifted—*reluctant, but reminding*—and I sighed. He pressed a kiss to the tip of my thumb before I awkwardly scooted my way off of his lap—off in search of some makeshift weapon to hide in the cushion.

As I pushed to stand, I almost fell right back down. My knees were shaking, rattling the chains around my ankles, but now that I could feel my arms again, I pulled them up and crossed them over my breasts.

I fought through my wobbling steps over the scratchy threads of the shag carpet in front of the couch, my toes digging in, an attempt to sturdy my steps, while my eyes scanned the room.

The sound stage was dimly lit, but the area by the couch had a few umbrella lights. It illuminated the "set," which looked like the *Ninja Turtles'* living room and the cement walls solidified the cold, dank setting.

My eyes glanced behind the cameras, up at the softbox lights, the sound boom. If I could snap metal, I could crack the boom in half and stick that in the cushions.

A small laugh pushed past my lips. The idea that bludgeoning the Man with the sound boom would somehow make his death louder made me smirk.

But my mouth quickly fell as terror struck my spine like a whip.

Through the small rectangle window on the door, I saw the Man staring directly at me. He was just . . . *waiting* in a room that led to another door—the one that required fingerprints, I guess . . .

Linc's voice was suddenly alert. "Pip, what is it? Come back!"

I wanted to go back to him, but my feet were stuck and my eyes squinted back at the Man through the glass.

Had he even left?

The menacing glint to his dark brown eyes was an image I was certain would haunt my dreams for years to come. I swallowed hard.

No. The asshole hadn't left.

It was a set up.

He *knew* I wouldn't follow directions and surprise, surprise, he caught me.

Fuck.

My heart leapt into my throat as Linc barked, "Paige!" and the Man started toward the door—the one to the room we were in— and I panicked.

My chin dropped looking for something—anything.

I haven't found a weapon!

My eyes suddenly locked on one thing, not a weapon but—I did *something*. Just as the Man opened the door, I shoved one of the tripods over, crashing the camera down on the concrete floor.

Linc's shouts echoed with my ankle chains dragging along the smooth concrete as I staggered in the opposite direction of the Man.

He stalked toward me, but in just a few more steps, I was already at the other tripod, knocking the second camera over.

I watched as it fell, panting heavily, but everything seemed to slow down.

The *crack* to the body of the camera felt like a mallet to my chest, the small pieces of glass and other mechanical bits were my heart, breaking and falling as a paralyzing realization hit me.

What have I done?

Punishing fingers grabbed my waist as an immediate pinch hit my neck.

Fuck, fuck, fuck.

"Everyone will be fine as long as we deliver the film."

The edges of my vision faded as the sounds in the room swirled and combined. The muscles in my face were sluggish but I mumbled, "Pl-Please, don't hurt him."

Linc. No. I'm sorry.

It was my last thought before everything went black.

03:31:29

PAIGE

A heavy throb filled the darkness in my head, and my eyebrows flinched. It felt like my eyelids had been fused shut, and a dry noise ached in my throat.

Jolting suddenly, I realized something was . . . *in* my mouth.

Memories of where I was suddenly came flooding back in an instant, and horror took on a new, deplorable depth when my eyes shot open.

My cheek was resting on a lap while a tight grip held my jaw open. Salty, unwanted weight was resting in my mouth and I cried out around it, trying to squirm away.

It's . . . oh God, it's the Man's—I gagged.

"Shh," a voice slithered above me, and my spine stiffened.

Him.

My pulse detonated.

Oh my God, oh my God, oh my God.

No, no, no, no!

I tried to move again, and that's when I realized my hands were tucked under my chin, strapped tightly to my chest.

A garbled whimper escaped as I fidgeted more, but between

the restraints and his iron grip on my jaw, all I could do was shift my weight.

A whimper pushed through my nose when I noticed the fucker had taken the remaining bit of my clothing. The cotton material—*the small bit of dignity*—between my legs was gone. My body bucked, but my eyes bulged when my bare pussy brushed up against . . . something.

I could only move my eyes, so I lifted them to the outer corner of my vision, and cried when I saw my boyfriend's face, chin tilted down, eyes closed.

Mortification wove through my aching bones, realizing my bottom half was resting on Linc, and I could feel now that the denim fabric beneath me was bunched around his thighs.

The Man pulled his pants down.

Oh my God. I whimpered again, my jaw trembling through the hand holding it open.

Suddenly, the Man's other hand was casually petting my head, followed by another, "Shh." He waited a moment, then said, "You put yourself in this position, Paige."

My eyes slammed shut. I couldn't be here. I couldn't take the nonsensical rapist babble.

This can't be happening.

This was violating in a way my brain couldn't even comprehend. Shit like this existed in a world I didn't know. *Below freezing.*

"I told you the rehearsal period would be about building trust. Linc followed directions. He did what was asked of him. After what he did for you, you couldn't do the same?"

The cameras.

My eyes winced. I wanted to shut it all off.

With my head held captive on the Man's lap, pressure built behind my eyes. My lips stretched, my mouth full— all I could do was breathe through my nose and try not to vomit.

My tongue lifted slightly to swallow, and I cringed when it grazed the velvet-like appendage in my mouth, but I suddenly realized . . .

The Man isn't hard. And he didn't seem to be making an effort to . . . *arouse* himself either. His soft dick was quite literally just sitting in my mouth, and I cringed.

A light curtain of blond hair covered my eyes, giving me a momentary break from seeing anything. But it was short lived when he brushed it away, and then quickly took his hand back again . . . *like he didn't really want to touch me.*

My breath quickened just as he said, "The thing is, Paige, you can film a movie with anything. Even a camera phone."

Heart bottoming out, my eyes bulged. For the first time, I let my gaze pull up, seeing the Man's dark, insidious face holding a fucking phone over me. Filming me.

I screamed around the invasion in my mouth, the sound was muffled but loud, seeing as he was still prying my mouth open with his hand.

He gave a small, shallow thrust into my mouth and I gagged as the surge of nausea resurfaced. But I didn't fucking vomit. More garbled sounds of my objection fell on demented ears as I felt drool starting to pour from the corner of my mouth.

Oh my God, oh my—

"We're going to try this again," the Man said, capturing my

panic in the fist of his tone. "You told me once that you liked how *specific* I was with direction, so I'm going to be as thorough as possible this time."

His patronizing drawl paled in comparison to the physical assault he was forcing on me, but it still pissed me off. He was *fucking vile,* but I had no choice but to continue to listen to him. "This is your punishment, Paige. And you've set us back, so now the rehearsal is going to be more about preparation and less about easing your comfort level. I'm going to take my hand away and you're just going to take it in your mouth while we prepare for your scene."

Rot in hell, pig.

The words *prepare, rehearsal—comfort.* Words I'd known my whole life sounded foreign coming from him. But the thought didn't get farther than a prickly feeling before I became aware of his expectant eyes on me from above, the camera still hovering— all in my peripheral view from his lap.

So . . . as if it wasn't *totally fucking obvious,* I couldn't exactly respond.

As if hearing my silent seethe, he said, "I'm going to need an answer, Paige. You'll refer to me as 'Master.'"

Tears pooled in my eyes. *Degradation was my plight,* I suddenly remembered my own conclusion, and this confirmed it. I was supposed to call Linc "sir" and this fucker wanted me to answer him *with* his dick in my mouth.

An obvious and foul display of power.

If this wasn't the seventh circle of hell, I wasn't sure the place existed.

I never thought of myself as sheltered. I lived in a city, I went to art school—my parents were fucking dead. I understood that bad things happened.

But this is . . . proof, I thought.

Knowing bad things happened and *experiencing* them were entirely different entities. *Knowing* was a telescope, but *experiencing* was being caught on a fallen star while it tumbled into a black hole.

The Man cleared his throat, his bruising grip still on my jaw as he muttered, "If you can't do as you're told, just remember you're not the only warm mouth in here."

Bastard.

Fuck . . . no . . . Linc.

The weight under my hips began to shift and my racing pulse kicked up tenfold.

I could only see Linc if I angled my eyes up to the very corner. A shitty vantage point where I couldn't see *how* he was restrained, but he was stirring, and I could see *something* was holding him back. Upright.

I slammed my eyes shut and the pounding punishment in my head intensified. This *was* my fault. *My* stupid move. I couldn't let the Man do this to Linc.

Breathing heavily through my nose, more tears fell, adding to the puddle of drool on the Man's lap. But my throat worked to swallow as best I could before my croaked, unintelligible voice said, "Yes, Master," around him.

His satisfied sigh made me want to take it back instantly, but I kept my eyes on the dark, wiry hair around his belly button, imagining something similar was in his chest instead of a beating heart.

The fingers around my jaw finally released, but my body lurched when my lips naturally fell around him and I coughed.

"Suck until you get used to it," he said with zero emotion, almost bored, and my fingers dug into my palms still tucked under my chin—it was just about the only movement I could make.

That and I could . . . wiggle my toes. *On Linc.*

So I did that.

Using my big toe, I traced the letters to our promise on his thigh.

T-I-L-L

T-H-E

E-N-D

I did it over and over, closing my eyes as I . . . followed the directions. I played my part as the degraded little whore, mumbling my incoherent response and then . . . sucking, cringing, *proving* my obedience just as I heard, "Holy fuck! Paige!"

Linc's thunderous roar, his voice—the *thought* of him seeing this—all of it combined and catapulted me to the clouds.

I landed far away and sank into the soft cotton-like puff, using them like lily pads to hop along the night sky. Then I slipped into the crescent moon like a hammock.

Linc's growls and yells, the degrading scene—it was farther away. I didn't want to leave Linc, but I needed something to drown out the sound.

He'd understand.

On my stereo in the sky, I sifted through a playlist, and found a song I hated.

But I listened to it, in the curve of the moon. I sang it with hateful spits in my mind. I memorized it—backward like a broken turntable in a horror movie.

LINC

I could barely see through the crimson flashes blinding my vision.

But I didn't need to see any more.

I had seen enough.

More than fucking enough.

"Paige," I barked again, knowing she couldn't answer me.

After a second, I thought I heard her make a noise. It sounded like she said something, but I couldn't tell because . . .

God. *Fuck.* This was *so fucked.*

I couldn't move anything other than my head and forearms. The bastard had put thick straps over my legs, just over my knees, and a tight, thick band over my chest and shoulders. So, I could use my arms but I couldn't reach farther than *right fucking* in front of me.

I had already snarled, spit, and screamed for what felt like hours to get him to stop. The chilling nature of him sitting there, undisturbed and unbothered, only rattled my rage.

With my voice all but blown—the only sounds in the room were the ones from her mouth, and my ragged panting.

My weak muscles pulled against the restraints, but I couldn't take a full breath. As the moment became too horrendous, I was certain I was about to actually combust.

When that didn't happen, I croaked, "Jeremy." The name felt foreign on my tongue—as much of an unknown entity as the guy who was violating my girlfriend right fucking next to me, and something inside me broke. "Please, stop this. Please. I'll do anything."

And I fucking meant it. We were in a lawless room and I meant it with every breath. I couldn't take this. I couldn't . . . *watch* this.

I dared a look at Jeremy's face, hoping I saw something—*anything* merciful, but that's when I saw the phone he was holding steadily over her. Was he . . .

"Are you fucking filming this?!" My voice was strained, barely audible from screaming. Pulling and shifting, I fought again against the belt around me when I suddenly felt a . . . *softness* brush against the tip of my dick.

My head whipped down to my lap and the thud of dread landed in my stomach.

I'd been too distracted by all the other despicable happenings that I hadn't noticed . . . The most private part of Paige was completely bare and lined up with my dick. I choked on my breath. "Wh-What—"

"She cost the production a lot of money and time," Jeremy cut me off. "She knows what she did, right, Paige?"

I blinked, forgetting for just a moment that there were *so many* things shaking my limbs.

The position he'd put us in, the position he'd put *her* in.

I couldn't bring myself to look down at her on his lap again. I knew it made me weak, but just a second of the image when I first woke up took ten years off my life.

A muffled mumble came from Paige and my eyebrows pinched. She *was* saying something . . .

"Let her fucking talk, you sick fuck!" I roared hoarsely, my voice reviving the slightest bit.

"Fine," he seethed. He put the phone down and then grabbed a fistful of her hair, yanking her mouth off of him. She coughed and spit, gasping to catch her breath.

"Pip—" I rasped, but any remaining sound got caught in my throat seeing her teary blue eyes, muted and . . . blank.

"Pip . . ." I whispered again.

Fuck.

I recognized the vacancy in her stare. I imagined I had a similar expression before when he made me kiss him, but this was . . . *so much worse.*

Worse than anything, I couldn't protect her. I couldn't haul her up in my arms and take her away. I couldn't try to fight him off. *Fuck,* I couldn't even hold her hand through it.

"Tell him," the voice next to me said, as Paige still hauled in heavy breaths, her cheek resting on his thigh.

After another gulp, her shaky voice said, "This is my punishment for . . . b-breaking the cameras," she whispered breathlessly. Jeremy's grip on her hair tightened before she grit out, "Sir."

My back froze. I had never heard her sound so . . . scared, so broken, so . . . *not like her.* And with nowhere to send my rage, I grit out, "I'll do it."

Paige's eyes widened. It was almost as if something had landed back in her pupils and she shook her head.

Jeremy looked at me, his eyebrows lifting. "You'd take *this* punishment for her?"

The very idea made me gag. But watching this was killing me. Sputtering through some coughs, I swallowed hard before giving a jagged nod.

Jeremy looked intrigued, but then he sighed and after another moment, he pulled Paige back into him. Her mouth *onto* him. And my soul crushed further through the concrete floor.

"Tempting as that is, I'm afraid you have other work to do. She needs to be prepped."

"What . . . I—" I stopped. There was no word—no combination of words that would explain what was happening right now.

"You said she's a virgin, right?"

I shook my head. "I never told you that," I seethed. *Never.*

"Yes you did. On our way to San Diego. Said you were dying to, but that she wanted to wait," he said with an ease that daggered into my stomach.

My eyebrows scrunched and I tried to place the memory. But my mind couldn't make it past the horror happening actively in front of me.

I would have never told him that, I assured myself. It wasn't even true. Yes, I was dying to have sex with Paige, but I didn't mind waiting . . .

And I certainly never wanted something like this.

A hiss from Jeremy's teeth knocked me back to now as he said, "Though, she's pretty good at this. You *sure* she's never done it before?"

Holy fuck.

I *would* kill him one day.

One day, motherfucker. I'll chop off your dick and feed it to you.

Unable to respond, I blinked at the dark spots in my vision as he said, "I'm going to pleasure you with my hand. Get you hard."

Paige made a noise and I cringed as my chin tilted up to the ceiling. *This was too fucking much.* I felt like I was going to pass out. When I lowered my chin all I could say was, "Have at it, asshole. There's no way I'll get hard."

Maybe I was feeling just a bit numb, but *that* was fucking true. Forget the fact I'd been drugged and had zero stamina just sitting here, but I had never been more disgusted in my entire life.

Jeremy let out a soft grunt, his hand brushing through Paige's hair. He kept his eyes down on her as he said, "Well, I'm up for the challenge. Plus, she has to do *this* until we make *that* happen."

Fucking Christ. The smell of the room soured.

There was no way. There was *no fucking way* this was happening.

"Maybe it will help that *your* job is to touch Paige," he said.

My heart drained through my feet as Paige squirmed a bit, and the movement caused her pussy to brush up against me again. The instinctive tingle from the contact evaporated into the black hole of this room as my mind tried to swallow one nauseating demand after the other.

He'd touch me, while I touched her, while she did . . . that.

A train of abuse. A crooked recycling sign. The most vile thing.

My eyes scrunched shut. I needed to move this along. Paige was already suffering, but . . . I couldn't . . .

"I won't touch her. Not when she can't tell me if it's . . . if it's okay." The words scraped past my lips, my eyes staring down at my lap. Down where our bodies almost connected.

Maybe I was stalling. I knew in a different time, in a different place—galaxies away from this one—Paige would let me touch her.

She already had in some ways, and it's all I wanted to do. I wanted to worship every inch of her beautiful body.

But not like this.

Never like this.

"Ah," Jeremy gasped, pulling Paige off of him. Reminding me I had to get my fucking shit together.

She coughed, and the sound felt like a sandstorm blowing through my chest as a deep command came from my side. "Give him permission, Paige."

Her body was trembling now. So was mine. Not just from rage, but because I was still fighting against the strap holding me back, the horrendous reality coursing through me.

"Y-You can touch me, s-sir," Paige said quietly, just above a whisper.

Chest caving, my eyes scrunched at the sound of her voice. Her words. "Pip, please . . ."

I dared a glance at her, and my spine stiffened. There was this hardened look in her eyes that shook me to my core. She still lay on her side, her cheeks wet, her lips swollen, but she clenched her jaw through a swallow, a mindless glare staring straight ahead at our captor's stomach.

Her lips shook as she said, "P-Please touch me, sir. I w-want you to."

My heart was turning to dust. I could still see she wasn't all there. And I didn't blame her. I didn't want to be here either. I wanted to be wherever she was.

She'd told me once that sometimes when she was acting, she had to go to this other place inside herself. *To become someone else.* Find the connection between herself and the character.

In this case, that connection was likely survival. I couldn't be sure if that's what was happening, but aside from the obvious assault she was enduring, it was the only reason I could think of for why she'd be going along with this.

"That's good, Paige," the voice next to me said, before carefully moving her mouth back to him.

My eyes slammed shut. *Holy fuck.* I had to pretend too. But I wasn't a fucking actor. And this went beyond the spectrum of performance.

The "film" hadn't even fucking started yet.

And my "role" seemed to be a dominant asshole who enjoyed assaulting and degrading women. A predator.

Eyes pulling to the man next to me, I looked at the living, breathing version of the part I was playing.

Ideas moved to shadows in my mind, they darkened, adjusted to the cooler temperature, and settled into the shade.

Maybe sinking into this role, this *task,* would be enough that I could find her, meet her—*wherever she was.* Maybe I'd been there already.

The *snick* of a bottle cap echoed through my mind, but I was wandering, searching. Looking for her, looking for the strength to do this. *To survive this.* Not just with our lives, but our minds.

A goopy, warm fist suddenly wrapped around my dick, making me jolt, and I hissed through my teeth. A small noise from Paige made me twitch in his hand, and I cringed inwardly.

"Oh, I think he likes hearing you, Paige."

I shook my head. "N-No, I—" I stopped.

I pulled my lips into my mouth to keep myself from saying anything. Nothing I had to say right now was what my *part* in this completely fucked film we were *preparing* for would say. And if Paige was trying to escape this way, I wanted to give that to her.

The hand holding my flaccid length started to slowly move up and down. Warm, languid movements that had me digging my heels into the floor.

"Hold out your hand," the voice next to me said.

My eyes were screwed shut, but I held out my hand as much as I could when I heard Paige gasp.

The grip on my cock disappeared for a moment and took my hand instead. I released a breath I didn't realize I was holding.

My eyes peeled open to see him lifting Paige's upper body just a bit, which I could see now was being held by a similar belt-like restraint, but it kept her cuffed wrists just under her chin.

Her full, rosy lips were wet, same as her chin, and the side of her cheek lying on his lap. I wished so badly I could reach a little farther to wipe it all away.

The hand holding mine pulled it in front of her face as he said, "Suck."

Her wide, bleak, distant eyes peered up at me. Dark indigo pools asked silently if it was okay, and it felt like kerosene to the burn in my chest.

Given what I was about to do to her, it seemed obvious she could do whatever she had to do to me, but I nodded. I couldn't speak.

Her lips were shaking as she drew my fingers into her mouth. The familiar, soft feeling of her tongue shot involuntary warmth through my veins as she sucked my middle and ring fingers.

I blinked slowly, my throat bobbing, silent disgust rolled through me for any small wave of pleasure that came at her forced contact.

The voice next to me said something else, but I was doing my best to tune it out. It filtered back in when he said, "Tell her what a good job she's doing, Linc."

My molars ground painfully. "Good job," I said, through clenched teeth.

He snorted. "Okay, we'll have to work on the praise talk," he sighed through a chuckle. His other hand took her chin, and pulled her mouth off my fingers. "What do you say, Paige?"

Her big blue eyes were tear soaked and bloodshot as she timidly stared up at me, swallowing. "Thank you, sir."

He gently twisted her face to look at him, and brushed some of her hair off of her face. "You really are being so good."

So epically fucked. Slowly, mercilessly, he put her back into her position on his lap. I shut my eyes. I couldn't watch him resume the punishment.

And I have to get hard.

It was gonna be fucking impossible.

"She got your fingers wet, Linc," the voice next to me said, resuming his steady hand around my lifeless dick.

Just fucking kill me.

My hand shook as I reached out. The angle was weird with her on her side, but it was the least of my worries.

I was going to touch her *there*. For the first time.

Like *this*.

My eyes scrunched as I nestled my hand between her legs, not quite at the apex, but I just rested my hand there for a second.

Flashes of our childhood—*innocent times*—rolled through my mind in slow, painful ways, breaking my heart as the heat from my hand burned between her thighs.

She jolted at the touch with a small whimper, and my fingers dug into her soft skin.

This was degrading her on unspeakable levels. Being . . . *used* at both ends. Whatever roles we were playing—*I don't give a fuck.* I needed her to know *my* touch wasn't the same as his. *It isn't.*

My hand gently rubbed. "I've only ever wanted to love you here." My voice was nothing more than a gravelly whisper. But I hoped she could hear the sincerity, feel it in my hand.

I suddenly became aware of her light breaths. Her mouth must have been free and my eyes cut over to her. She wasn't staring straight ahead—her eyes were angled toward me, her gaze gripping mine.

There was this harrowing awareness that flit through her expression, but it just as quickly dissipated, and the shield resumed.

She swallowed, then rasped, "We're just playing parts, sir."

My fingers clenched harder on her thigh. I knew she was doing what she had to do—saying what she had to say—but the destruction through my chest was devastating.

The voice next to me said, "Good, Paige. You've earned a break while we get started."

Well, thank *all holy fuck* for that, at least. The smallest breath of relief loosened the muscles bunching in my shoulders. With her mouth free for the moment, I just had to cooperate. Get through this.

"We're just playing parts."

But the problem was, the only way I even had a *chance* of *rising to the occasion*—was through her.

Her body. Her warmth.

Her, her, her.

Suddenly, her thighs clenched around my hand, still resting between them, pulling my eyes back to her.

She wiggled her hips as much as she could, and my eyebrows pinched. It registered then, that she was trying to help me. Not only was she playing her part, but she was trying to help me play mine.

Her. The one being openly abused, was trying to make this easier on *me.* My teeth clenched. Borrowing some of the determination from her stare, I started to move my hand a little farther up her thigh. With unblinking eyes, I watched her face—watched for any indication I should stop.

With locked gazes, I felt us—*Linc and Paige*—zooming out, allowing *these people* to adjust and focus into this horror show.

This moment wasn't ours. It was *theirs. His.*

Just a puppet, I told myself. My fingers finally grazed her entrance, and she gasped as I ran my finger up and down her crease. The warm sensation got the better of me, and a breathy grunt pushed past my lips.

She wasn't wet, but she was so, *so* warm. So perfect.

Don't hurt her. The words echoed from deep within me.

"L-Lube," my voice shook out.

I pulled my hand from her, and held it out. I knew the bastard had some. He had already used it on me.

The moisture from her fingers was long gone due to the fact I was being a fucking pussy, and couldn't get my shit together.

"Most boys don't know what they're doing down there the first time—the girl almost never comes. But you just want to make sure she's stretched," he said.

God, I have to find a way to shut out his voice.

Still, he squirted some of the substance onto my fingertips. I rubbed them together, and again met Paige's glassy blue eyes as my hand resumed its place. Gently, I pressed into her—just a little bit—just to spread some of the lube.

But the wetness, the heat. *Her.* I felt fucking dizzy. "Oh, God," I moaned, but clenched my teeth.

My dick twitched and I hated myself even more.

Not me. Not me. Not me.

"Do I feel good, sir?" her voice was breathy. Like a practiced scene partner, she was guiding me back to the moment. *Our task.*

She sounded completely unlike Paige, but then I guess that was the point.

This wasn't us.

We are safe, down below.

She rocked her hips ever-so-slightly against my touch, and pushed my finger a little deeper, just past the knuckle. Pulling my lips into my mouth, I practically moaned, "You feel like heaven, Pip," and then cringed.

Not us. Not us. Not us.

But *Goddammit*, she did feel like heaven. Not that I was sure such a place even existed—*even less so after this*—but if it did, it felt like her. Warm, safe, cherished . . . *home.*

PAIGE

Linc's finger sank inside me and I bit my lip to stifle a small noise. His hands, his touch—they felt so good.

But he was breaking. I could see it.

His wide hazel eyes looked completely shattered as he moved his finger in and out of me—cringing his way through it.

It's the circumstance, I'd told myself. I knew that. But something about seeing him so uncomfortable touching me was giving me such a hollow feeling of dejection, the shame started to rattle my resolve.

We just have to get through this.

Play our parts.

Survive.

Then, therapy.

Fucking lots of it.

But for now, I had to be strong. I had to help Linc in whatever way I could. It might have been *my* body being violated, but I knew the boy currently touching me tenderly, lovingly, wouldn't be doing this if he had any other choice.

He'd made that clear earlier when he offered to take my place for my "punishment." And I had felt the same way when the Man had forced Linc to kiss him.

I think something about surviving our own pain seemed easier than witnessing each other's. Which is why, when the Man moved his hand to Linc's lap and started stroking him again, I tensed.

Linc's breath was raking through his teeth, his hand between my legs pausing as his own molestation began, but he ground out, "Are you okay?"

I nodded, unable to give him a verbal answer.

Using my obedient sex-bot voice seemed to be going well with Professor Pervert. I had been trying to use it to sink into this depraved scene he was forcing us to participate in, but Linc made it too . . . *real.*

I'm just . . . not that good of an actress, I guess.

Not with him. *And this isn't fucking acting.*

I found it strange I had to keep reminding myself of that. Somewhere in the abuse I'd just endured, I had accepted this was happening.

But just like all things, the reality of that acceptance was heavy and tasted sour.

I took a breath, and focused on Linc's touch, the gentleness of his finger.

"I only ever wanted to love you here."

In a far-from-tender moment, it was a beautiful thing to say. And I knew it was true.

Even like this. Even in this room. *His* touch was love.

Suddenly, Linc added another finger and it brushed inside me in a way that made me tremble. The lube he was using had some sort of warming agent and that, coupled with the knowledge it was *his* hand, was helping me relax.

There was still hesitancy to his touch, and my hips moved against him. I wanted to give him reassurance it was okay.

The pitch-black area of life we found ourselves in was confusing and vile for a multitude of reasons. One of them being that we *were* attracted to each other.

We *loved* each other. I had wanted him to touch me like this so many times—but this . . .

He added his thumb to the mix, circling my clit, and I gasped, "Ohh," as my fingernails dug into my palms again.

It felt . . . good. And the shame in that alone nearly swallowed me whole.

But *fuck,* after what had felt like hours of degrading contact, to feel something soft—*reverent, even*—felt like a power paddle to my soul.

"You feel like heaven, Pip."

I pushed myself into his touch, deepening his fingers. It stung a little, but the connection was worth it. It felt like we were doing something behind the curtain of this disgusting scene. Something that only existed in the intimate contact of him inside me.

The Man surprised me when he didn't pull my mouth back to him, but instead sat me up on Linc. The shackles around my ankles provided enough give I could straddle him, but my eyes shot down, aware that my face was probably a mess.

I could feel drool on my chin and cheeks.

Dirty.

Linc slid his fingers out of me and a small, embarrassing whine escaped at the loss. His restraints only allowed him a small bit of movement, so he placed his hands on my hips, his fingers digging in.

My eyes locked with his as he rasped, "Kiss me."

I leaned down, giving him my lips—lips I couldn't believe he wanted. But he sunk into my mouth like a sanctuary. His tongue moved in slow, savoring movements along mine.

Tears bit the back of my eyes as our mouths moved together, breathing in each other's strength. I was nearly certain the true horror of this night was just getting started, but the relief of being in front of him, kissing him—I gave everything I *had* to him.

"Keep touching her, Linc," the Man said, interrupting our moment.

But it isn't our moment.

Linc's kiss was a bandage, just like mine had been when the Man kissed him. An attempt to reclaim each other. And there was something reassuring about that. That in the darkness, we were still finding a way to comfort each other.

We'll get through this.

The Man's hand snaked between us, resuming his hold on Linc's cock, and I gasped. "I'm giving you a second chance," the Man said, his voice quiet, but authoritative, just beside us. "I've stopped your punishment early. Don't make me regret it."

I knew better than to ask why, and I wanted to do anything in my power to avoid it from resuming.

But the Man is touching Linc . . .

I kept my eyes on my boyfriend's face as his hand tensed at

my entrance. I could see the small beads of sweat at his temples. The agony etched between his brows fell to his eyes—which had been stripped of any brown and were a flaring, intense green.

I could see it all. Being touched like this right in front of me, being forced to touch me while it happened—*it was killing him.*

He definitely had the more difficult job right now, but I had no clue how to help him.

I wouldn't let my eyes drop to his cock. Not unless I had to, and not without his permission. But since the Man's arm was visible, I was able to see the . . . *pace* he was touching Linc.

I adjusted myself—it was difficult to keep my balance on Linc's lap with my arms strapped to my chest, but his other hand was still on my waist, steadying me.

Once I readjusted, our eyes locked again, a collision of wild, terrified brokenness. But together.

Till the end.

I saw the message sink into his stare too, and I took a breath. "Trust me, sir?"

His eyebrows pinched. Still disturbed by the "sir" bit, as was I, but he nodded, "'Course I do."

I nodded too, leaning down to kiss him again. I used his mouth to strengthen my nerve, and then rolled my hips into his touch, slowly working myself on his fingers. I kept it slow, trying to match my own rhythm to that of the Man's hand, and Linc responded.

His lips pressed harder against mine, but another hand invaded—*the Man*—pulling Linc's chin.

"Enough," he simply said, and then dragged Linc's face to his, literally *stealing* his lips from me. Linc fought as much as he could. His fingers from one hand dug into my thigh, while the ones moving inside me halted.

I should have known this was too good to be true.

And that was saying something, seeing as *good* still wasn't fucking great.

As Linc tightened his lips, the Man held his nape, and pulled back slightly. "Come on, Linc. Didn't you tell me two guys turned her on?"

Scum. Fucking filth.

His manipulation didn't even have finesse for how deranged he seemed to be. He was even further down the rabbit hole if he thought for *one fucking second* I was buying Linc had told him *any* of this.

Me being a virgin—or anything *about my sexual experience. Fantasies.*

I don't know how he knows any of that, but it wasn't because *Linc* told him.

It all boiled just below my skin, but then I saw the Man's lips were about to connect with Linc's, and instantly, I channeled into my role. "M-Master?" My voice came out shaky, not from fear but rage, as I met the Man's eyes.

Dark, glittering madness stared back at me. I noticed he had stopped touching Linc for the moment and I took a relieved breath. Linc's fingers were still inside me, but just barely, just resting there—*connected*—and I found myself grateful.

Except I had no plan. I just wanted to stop the Man from kissing Linc, but I didn't have another suggestion, and the Man looked impatient staring back at me. "If you can't be good, Paige, we can find a way to occupy your mouth."

Linc shook his head and without warning his fingers plunged farther inside me, as he slammed his face into the Man's, kissing him like he could kill him that way.

His fingers moved more aggressively, no doubt needing the contact, and I tried to give it to him. Strange as it felt to rock into his hand while this was happening, that's what I did. All I could do was let him know I was here.

Suddenly his thumb reentered with a featherlight touch on my clit, and a whimper punched out of me at the small swirl low in my stomach.

Jesus. This was so . . . *fucked.*

Was I so weak that the depravity of this room had found a way to seep into my pores already? Were my lungs already polluting my brain with the sick fumes?

How I felt any pleasure at all was beyond me, and I cringed. But Linc must have felt my walls tightening, because he did it again, and I slammed my eyes shut, choking on my breath, "S-S—"

So good? Stop?

Both felt wrong. All of this felt wrong. *Why was my body reacting this way?*

Maybe my sex-bot doppelganger was returning. I hoped that was it. Otherwise I feared that something was shifting in me, something I didn't want moved to a dark and ominous corner.

And oh, God. I didn't want Linc to think watching this was turning me on, but his fingers were fucking demanding. "S-Sir, I—" I gasped.

I thought the use of the name would make him slow down, but Linc's fingers moved ruthlessly. He'd found my spot, and now he was crooking his fingers and moving them along it with a hypnotic cadence.

I sucked my lips into my mouth, reopening my eyes when I heard the Man say, "See, she's already purring."

"Fuck—" I bit down on my cheek to keep myself from saying *fuck you* to the man who had no problem sticking his wet noodle dick in my mouth.

"No more kissing," the Man said. "Just watch each other." His hand moved back between us, back on Linc. I could tell when he made contact because Linc winced, but again moved his fingers inside me.

His stare was such a mix of things—but I could barely register anything over the intense rage, and I gasped. Something . . . something was gone. And for the first time tonight, I was worried we wouldn't be able to get it back.

LINC

My vision had tunneled. All I could see was the long, winding, dark path we had to lead and I tried to lose myself to the sensations.

The sight. Her blue eyes, wide, the rosy tint to her cheeks—the way she was pinning her lip to keep herself quiet while I slid my fingers in and out of her.

The sounds. Or maybe I should say the *restraint* of her sounds. She'd make a small squeak, or a breathy sigh every few seconds and each time, I'd imagined what the finished noise would sound like. It was like they only existed for us, and each imagining swelled the arousal stirring.

But *God, fuck.* Her plush warm walls, the way they were tightening around my fingers—*the feel* of her getting wet. I underestimated the . . . effect it would have on me.

My dick was half mast just from feeling her, hearing her—knowing I was making her feel good in a room where good went to die.

"That's power, Linc," the voice next to me said just over my ear, and I winced.

Tune it out.

He was taking my silent, and what I could only imagine was a worshiping expression, and warping them to fit whatever fucked narrative we were playing out for him.

I shook my head, refocusing on her, but that became more difficult when he leaned toward her, using his free hand to pull her chin to look at him. "You're being so good for him, Paige," he said, tracing his thumb along her lips before pushing the tip of it inside her mouth.

Her throat worked to swallow but she kept it in her mouth, and I used my fingers to brush the spot inside her that made her tremble. Her eyes shot back to me, gasping as much as she could, wobbling, since she couldn't really hold herself up with the belt around her.

"She'd be better if she could use her hands," I grumbled, but my eyes widened. *That sounded wrong . . .*

The voice next to me chuckled, confirming my fear, but then he said, "Can I remove the belt, Paige? Will you still behave?"

With his thumb still in her mouth, she waited a beat, then nodded, and his hand tightened on her chin. "Answer."

"Yes, Master," she garbled.

He took his hand from me, and I gasped with relief as he stood. There was no time for us to make silent plans or promises, just a sustained gaze between Paige and me. As Jeremy moved behind her, he twisted what appeared to be a key to unlock the belt, but she still had handcuffs on.

My face scrunched, scrutinizing her wrists. They were so raw and torn—bloody. Mine were banged up too, but I hadn't been cuffed since we woke back up—just strapped.

I hadn't noticed he'd pulled up a chair behind her. "Let's reward her obedience, shall we?"

I hated it. All of it. His smirk. His position right behind her. He'd pulled his sweatpants up, but that didn't mean anything. What I hated most of all was the insinuation that we were some-how doing this together.

Unable to say anything that *my role* would say, I ground my teeth together as his arms snaked around her naked torso, his hands roaming her stomach.

She leaned into me, away from him, and it pushed her pussy back against my hand. She gasped as she raised her arms up and over me so that the chain to her cuffs were behind my head, on the back of the couch, her arms caging me in.

"Keep touching her, Linc, or I'll have to take over," he said from behind her, his big slimy hands touching her—inches away from my face—and when his fingers tweaked her nipple, a predatory wave pummeled through me.

I used my one hand to grab her hip, pulling her closer, as I teased her entrance with the other. Dipping my finger inside, I leaned into her, sucking her nipple into my mouth, nibbling, growling, "Mine," through clenched teeth, with a sudden rush of voracity.

I'm not sure what it was—maybe it was him touching her right in front of me, the threat of him *"taking over."* Maybe it was the countless ways he'd violated us both, or maybe I was just reaching some sort of carnal breaking point, but possession took over.

I moved my finger in and out of her with a liveliness I couldn't muster before, and she gasped, "Yes, sir. Yours."

Buffy fucking bless. She was meeting me on this hill of depravity. Even if we died here.

Till the end.

Jeremy had moved closer, his hand pulled around Paige—*between us and freshly lubed*—he started moving up and down on me again. I groaned, sucking Paige's nipple into my mouth.

God, she tasted even better than I imagined.

A surprise came when I felt another large hand reaching around Paige to hold my jaw, pushing my face deeper, settling between her tits.

And *holy fuck.* The smell of her. Even the musky scent of the room clinging to her body couldn't hide the spicy citrus combination that lit me the fuck up.

I couldn't be sure if it was my face burying in her skin, or if it was easier to lose myself to sensation because I couldn't see him. Maybe it was my swell of fight that had reignited some adrenaline, but I started to . . . respond.

My dick hardened in the hand moving up and down on it, and my hips gave uneven, involuntary thrusts as my thumb found her clit again.

"That's it," the voice rumbled from behind her like a cloak of perversion over her back.

Tune it out.

His grip on my chin made it difficult, but I pulled my eyes up to her. Another zap of arousal shot through me when I saw she was already looking down at me

With her chained hands still on each side of my head, she moved one to my nape and tugged, tilting my chin up, which resulted in Jeremy's other hand, the one that had been holding my face, falling.

She smirked.

Just like she was mine. I was hers.

I returned it with a weak pinch at the corner of my lips, enjoying her quiet defiance until—

Slap.

Her body jolted, falling forward a bit as her pussy clenched on my fingers, but I was trying to figure out what happened.

"That was a warning, Paige," the voice said. "Next time it'll be a belt."

My nostrils flared. He fucking *spanked her?!*

I wished I could snap through *this* belt and use it to beat *him* unrecognizable.

More unrecognizable.

"Sorry, Master," she mumbled, her body still tightened from the strike. My fingers moved along her, inside her. It was the only thing I could fucking do, and she swiveled her hips into my touch.

Her blue eyes met mine, tears teetering on the edges, just as the hand on my length picked up speed.

I choked on my breath, unprepared, but my free hand moved from her hip to her ass—fingers stretching as far as it could, anyway—and I rubbed where the skin was still warm from his slap.

She moved with my hand, and my grip on her ass tightened, still rubbing.

"Thank you, sir," she said quietly, pressing a small kiss to my neck, but pulling back immediately, probably remembering that he said no more kissing.

But fuck it felt good. Almost normal.

And he seemed to let it slide.

But my mind was in shambles as I shook my head, the unrelenting fist he had around my cock—a hold that had my thumb again finding Paige's clit and circling it. She bit down on her lip.

We kept at it. I wasn't sure what the finish line was here—if this "preparation" was about getting me hard, it had surprisingly happened—*she* made it happen.

But it didn't matter. None of this made sense. And I felt myself succumbing to the madness—almost like I needed to tie a rope around my waist, so as not to lose myself in the abyss of it all.

Abyss sounded like . . . relief. It sounded . . . *fucking easier.*

She felt incredible and I loved her, and if this was the only way I could show her right now, *fuck me* if I wasn't going to give it to her.

Groaning as the pleasure heightened, the wet warmth squeezing my cock was matching the rhythm that she was rocking into my hand. She rolled her hips into my touch with a moan, and we both suddenly gasped.

Our eyes widened together.

We both fucking felt it.

The tiny pulses around my fingers, her walls quivering.

My eyes came to fucking life. "A-Are you gonna come?"

She released a sharp breath. Her eyes screwed shut, but her mouth dropped as she whimpered, and I felt the clench on my fingers again.

I leaned forward and drew her nipple into my mouth, teasing it with my teeth as her body bowed, and her eyes reopened.

My lips curled up, still flicking the pebbled flesh with my tongue, as her blue eyes blazed down at me. The rope—*the tether*—I'd been keeping myself on was slipping.

Another small noise she tried to pin between her teeth escaped before she breathed out, "D-Do you want me to come, sir?"

Fucking Christ. She sounded more like herself that time, and it swelled my erection into its tight warmth. A fist I was fully thrusting into, imagining it was her.

It was her as far as I was concerned.

The sound of *her* voice returning knocked any remaining

sense I still had out of my fucking ears, and I choked out, "Yes." I was lost, spinning, landing in a world where this was some sexy little game we were playing. "God, yes. Please, Paige. Please come for me," I growled out.

"Linc, I—" she gasped.

04:46:58

PAIGE

A tornado of feathers danced through the lowest part of my stomach, swirling and flying while a flurry of stars burst through my chest.

The cry that tore out of me was cut off by Linc pushing on my lower back, crashing my face to his, and catching the sound with his mouth. My hips moved harder into his fingers, his warmth. I moaned around his tongue as the tendrils of pleasure hit low in my belly.

God, it felt amazing. *So good. So much better than any orgasm I've ever given myself.* Like my soul was riding a wave that rose high enough to splash the moon.

Tears streamed down my face at the trickling pleasure, the heat spreading just below my skin.

Linc stroked me through the release, his finger moving possessively over my clit, spurring a couple of small convulsions in my core with each caress of his finger.

Alive. Wanted. So, so good.

He groaned into my mouth and I tugged on his lip. Our mouths slowed and I gave him a small lick. The undertow of my arousal settled as he sighed against my lips, and a sudden, stark awareness blew through me.

Heat pulled up my neck, and lit my already flushed cheeks on fire. The absolute horror hit me like lightning. "Oh my God," I cried.

Euphoria crashing, the sound of my chains *clinked* as I pulled my hands back over Linc's head, rattling my disgust, and I shoved my face in my palms.

Oh my God. Did I seriously just . . . *come? Here? Like this?*

I'm sick. My earlier worry about this place infecting me was confirmed, and the vast hit from high to low spread like wildfire through my veins.

I couldn't catch my breath—desperate to flush the humiliation—but my mind was clogged and my heart was sputtering.

I distantly registered Linc saying my name.

But I can't look at him.

Not because I blamed him. He was just doing what the horny little doll riding his hand was begging him to do. I couldn't look at him because . . .

He was *Linc.*

And I'd *just* . . .

My head shook. *What was I thinking . . .*

I wasn't. Feeling the Man take his hand away, out from between us—*reminding me* he'd been molesting my boyfriend—I choked on a gag.

I'd had the Man's dick in my mouth earlier.

Sick. Disgusting. You're *disgusting.*

"Pip," Linc said again, and his tone was hard enough that I peeked out from behind my fingers and looked at him.

Worriment aside, his tender eyes had gotten a bit of their chestnut hue back, and I wished I could somehow bury myself in the soft earthy color of his stare.

I felt so *fucking* gross. I *wanted* to be underground.

A lot had been done to me—*to both of us*—but this was the first thing that made me feel like . . .

Like I *was* the role I was playing.

I could see Linc studying my humiliation, before an agonized film glazed over his eyes. His throat bobbed just before his voice, gravelly and hoarse, said, "Baby, I wanted you to feel good. *I* wanted it. Okay? I'm sorry. It's my fault." His eyes were wide, sincere—emanating guilt.

I felt *fucking terrible*—and still strangely good, which made me feel worse—but some stupid part of me found a small glimmer of warmth at his use of the word "baby" in this moment, and it spread through my chest just before I felt a finger on my chin.

The Man. But he was staring over at Linc. "Don't lie to her. She wouldn't have been able to come if some part of her wasn't turned on by this. I told you, girls almost never finish the first time." My nostrils flared and he turned to look down at me. "It seems Paige has a little bit of a freaky side. But that will be helpful with the shoot."

Speaking of shoot, if I had anything at all I'd aim it right between his fucking eyes.

But my mouth dropped, unable to hide my horror. I quickly pulled my lips into my mouth.

Linc snarled, "No, dickwad. Unlike you, I don't need a map

to find a clit."

The Man huffed a laugh, but there wasn't any humor to it. In an instant, I was being hauled off Linc's lap. He thrashed, roaring, "No, fuck! Paige!"

Before I could steady my footing, the Man swiftly twisted the chain between my cuffs on my wrists and pinned my hands over my tits, then clutched my upper half tightly against him. My back to his front. His hot rancid breath scratched my ear as he gritted out, "Never cared much for pussy, but multiple orgasms are pretty fascinating."

My vision became spotty. A couple of flashes of Mr. Harris—*my teacher*—popped through my memory, his voice now meeting other things he'd said to me—like a car backfiring over and over.

"You belong in front of the camera."

"So talented."

Slamming my eyes shut, I screamed, kicked, pulled—*lost my fucking mind* as *the very same man* tried to drag his free hand down my hip.

Linc was yelling a myriad of hoarse, furious threats, but the Man's grip over my chest only tightened as his probing, invasive fingers found the wetness of my arousal between my legs.

The one Linc had given me.

"No, please," I cried. "Please, please, please!"

"Fucking bastard! I'll fucking kill you!" Linc growled.

The Man used his strength, his weight, and his fucking madness to wrestle my weak and used body down to the shag carpet. *Right at Linc's feet.*

I fought with everything I had. I snapped my teeth when his

hand got close enough to my neck, but with his full weight pressed on top of me, I didn't have a chance.

He growled, "We'll see. I might get lost . . ."

His other hand snaked back between my legs, closer to my asshole, and I screamed, using every bit of strength I had to buck him off of me.

His eyes met mine, and everything stopped. For a moment—*every bit of anger I'd been holding back, every bit of anguish I'd swallowed down*—came rushing forth to join my fight.

In a rageful growl, I hawked every bit of moisture in my mouth—*spitting in the motherfucker's face.*

The hand between my legs disappeared, but I had no time to be grateful because a resounding *smack,* whipped my face to the side. A sharp pain pulsed through my cheek, radiating to my skull, and setting my brain on fire.

I felt tears run from my eyes, but the cry was soundless, and the room did that thing again. Sound became tunnely. I could hear Linc yelling, but the words felt . . .

Far away.

My chin was still facing Linc's feet. His denim-covered calves. Through my daze, I was able to register that the Man wasn't touching me for the moment, but the realization came with the sound of a soft beep.

Had this actually been a dream? Was an alarm finally waking me up?

But the weight lifted off me, confirming I was still in a living nightmare.

Suddenly, the sound felt like it quite literally dropped back into the room, and I was able to recognize the noise was . . . a watch beeping. And when my body caught up to my brain—*the Man wasn't on top of me anymore*—I gulped in a big breath, sitting up and scurrying away, back to Linc.

"Pip, fuck . . . your cheek," he rasped, still stuck to his spot on the couch.

Right. The pain was still there, but I felt it pulse as I took in the purplish-red welt on his biceps. The strap from the leather had nearly broken skin.

He'd been fighting to save me. Keep the Man from touching me.

I curled into him, hiding as much as I could.

It doesn't count. He barely touched me. It doesn't count.

With my face tucked into Linc's side, I couldn't see the Man, so much as *feel* him standing in front of us. "Our geography lesson will have to wait. I just got the warning we've got to start if we have any hope of making the deadline. Replacing the equipment cost us time."

Feeling the pointed words, I didn't have to see him to know that comment was directed toward me, but I do open my eyes and look over to the other side of the room.

New cameras.

Scumbag. All of that "punishment" for something he had replacements for.

They look the same as the old ones.

Have they been rolling the whole time?

The Man said, "Here," tossing something from his pocket over toward me, and it landed on the shag area rug—a silver key, glistening in the threads. "Take off his restraints," he mumbled as he started checking something on the camera.

My shaky limbs wobbled to pick up the key, a tiny treasure that would give Linc *some* of his freedom back.

As I moved to free the first lock on his legs, he whispered, "Did he . . ."

Still looking at the lock, my eyes widened. *Right.* Given that Linc was essentially strapped to the couch, he couldn't see once the Man got me to the floor.

I quickly shook my head. It was only a half-lie.

It didn't count, I told myself again. Plus, I think if I told Linc, it would . . . *escalate* things once his restraints were off.

We just need to get out of here.

Clearing my throat, I peeked over to the Man, asking, "This film . . ." I swallowed the lump in my throat, then continued, "Once it's done. You'll release us?"

The Man didn't even bother to look up from the camera as he said, "That's the plan."

It wasn't a *yes,* and I sure as fuck didn't trust it, but it was clearly the only answer he was going to give me.

I twisted the key in the second lock, hearing the *click,* and the moment Linc's arms were free, he pulled me into him, holding me tight. *So, so tight.*

His warmth, the soft feeling of his clothes brushing against my naked body.

God, I just want to stay here.

"I love you. I'm sorry." His hushed apology nestled into my hair, his hand gripping the back of my head and holding me to him.

I still had to take off his leg restraints . . . pull his pants up . . . but he was crushing me into his chest and I couldn't deny him. There was some part of me that needed those words. His embrace.

"Let's move this along, guys. I've already gotten a warning," the Man said over my shoulder and my chest deflated.

Is that what the beeping was?

He kept alluding to someone else, but we hadn't actually *seen* anyone else. Not that I was willing to challenge it.

Survive, rang through my mind, and I started to pull back as Linc muttered, "Fucking bastard," just before I met his eyes again, and I tried to use our silent path of communication.

We just have to get through the film.

He said he'd let us go.

I saw the back of his jaw tick, and I felt my own nerves spike. I still wasn't sure if I believed it myself, but I started to work on the multiple locks to Linc's leg restraints.

It seemed like a huge risk for the Man to release us after this. I mean, the nature of a film was its permanence. Why release us when we can go to the cops? And *somewhere* there would be hard evidence in the form of a video.

I was nearly certain Jeremy Harris wasn't his real name, but everyone at Providence knew what he looked like.

Though, I think one of the things Linc liked about the Man was that he didn't seem driven by money—or at least that's what he told Linc. And since we'd already established that whatever the fuck this was had some impressive financing behind it, maybe whoever he was working with was someone with money. Power.

Two things Linc and I did not have.

It doesn't matter, I told myself again. *Survival* was all that mattered. We'd get past this, and one day, we'd take this moment back. *Every degrading piece of filth we endured in this room will be ours again one day*, I promised myself—I hoped, prayed to Buffy, or anyone who would listen.

As soon as Linc's legs were free, he pulled up his pants and pushed himself to stand, wobbling, but he locked his knees and seethed at the Man currently adjusting the camera on the tripod.

"Linc," I said quietly, warning.

"I'd listen to your girl," the Man said quickly after. "I've been instructed to perform the scene myself if you give me any trouble. I mean, unless you'd *rather* shoot it?" He challenged Linc with a cock of his eyebrow.

I immediately yanked Linc back down to the couch, but he growled out, "You sick fuck! I'll kill you for this one day! You hear me? You're fucking dead!"

In a few steps, the Man was grabbing Linc's shoulder, and hoisting him back off the couch. I screamed, "Stop! Don't!" but it all fell into the maddening noise of this room.

The sound of the lights, the cameras, the depravity.

My chains between my wrists and ankles clanked as I moved toward them—not even bothering to try and cover my nakedness. I hadn't been for a while.

What the fuck was the point?

The Man didn't hit him, but he was holding him by the shirt, and his voice was disturbingly low and calm as he said, "I think I've been pretty lenient so far. I mean, shit—all you have to do is perform a hot sex scene with your girlfriend. You know I'll make it look good, so, *man the fuck up* and just do it."

Linc's face mirrored the horrified confusion of my own.

Not that there was any doubt, but the Man's small outburst just now was confirmation his mental capacity was so crooked, he didn't *see a problem* with *forcing* sexual acts on two people who happened to be attracted to each other.

"You got hard when you were kissing me earlier, and when I was touching you. Maybe you're just more into guys than you thought." The Man's voice crawled to Linc's face. I could physically see Linc working to swallow, and I felt the roll in my own stomach.

And it lurched the words, "M-Master. P-Please. He'll cooperate. I-I will too. P-Please," I stuttered in sudden panic. I suddenly needed the Man's hands off my boyfriend. For some reason, it felt more dangerous than his threat to stand-in for Linc in the film just before.

Dark beady eyes, the color of rotten tree bark, met mine and Linc shoved off of him—*away from him*—but the Man's cold gaze traveled down my body. A silent reminder that he'd overpowered me, stripped me down—*watched me come.*

I cringed thinking about mere moments ago, when he had me pinned down on the floor—*his grimy fucking hands.* But the thought fell away just as Linc moved back to the couch, and pulled me into him, covering me as much as he could.

My body curled into his side as the Man took the couple of steps toward the couch and his hand reached into his pocket.

I took a moment to breathe in Linc, soak in any bit of comfort I could, but I gasped when I saw what the Man pulled out of his pocket.

He presented the only bit of clothing I started this deranged experience with, and extended them out toward us.

Linc swiped the underwear out of his hand, and the Man smirked. "Let's get started."

05:04:59

LINC

I knew we'd reached a point of no return when I started to grow used to the nausea twisting in my stomach.

But there was a numbness settling in I didn't want to get too comfortable with.

"Chain her to the pole," Jeremy had said . . . some time ago, but I felt myself zoning out, until . . .

Tick, tick, tick . . .

My eyes snapped up to see Jeremy was still back behind the camera. "We need to hurry this along. The timer is your final warning after a direction. One minute."

My body jerked, dropping the key to the floor. I quickly bent to swipe it back up. He didn't need to say the silent threat, I'd heard it the first time, and I think it was the final shove into my muted state.

"I've been told to perform the scene myself if you give me any trouble."
I can't let that happen.

Paige's big blue eyes stared up at me. "It's okay," she said quietly. "As long as it's you. It's okay."

I could tell she was trying so hard to be strong, to not let me see how much this was killing her. It didn't matter how well she hid it because I felt the agony running through my own veins.

"Paige, lie on your stomach," Jeremy said from the corner. Her eyes shot a glare in his direction for only a second before they swept back up to mine. With a dip of her chin, she gave me the same message as before, silently.

As long as it's you.

I nodded, and she slowly turned, lying on her stomach and extending her hands over her head, toward the pole beside the couch.

He had let me take off her ankle chains, and she was able to put the underwear back on, but he also told her not to get used to them, and my teeth ground as I saw her cute, cotton-covered butt beneath me. I moved to *follow my direction.*

I have to stop stewing about the inevitable.

We were overpowered. We were no match for a mad man with drugs, chains, and a *fucking fingerprint entry room.* Not to mention, it was clear that insubordination—an attempt at escape—was met with even *more* deplorable acts.

We just have to do this and deal with everything else after.

I wanted to believe we'd be okay, I *wanted* to believe we'd find our way back to where we were after this—*we had to.*

But it made me think of what Darlene had said at anti-prom. *About taking turns holding the light, losing it . . .*

There is no light here.

Not even the moon herself could give it to us right now.

As I unlocked the handcuffs, Paige whimpered, and I held her wrist, my eyebrows scrunching. My thumb moved over what appeared to be a clear bandage on her wounds.

In the midst of the madness, I hadn't realized. He must have done that after she broke the cameras.

I couldn't find gratitude, but I *did* wonder why he took the time to clean them up . . .

I caught movement out of the corner of my eye, and saw him turning on the handheld stationed by the couch.

Right. For the camera, I thought. *The cuts don't look as gruesome with the bandages, and they're clear so he won't have to edit them out.*

I'm assuming he'll have to edit this.

God, it all just added to the rock sitting in my gut.

I rubbed her wrist, pressed my lips to the bandage, then looked down at her again. She was looking unwaveringly up at me too. *It's okay.*

I pulled the chain around the pole, *wishing it was his fucking neck,* and I fit the cuff back in the groove, but tried to leave it loose.

"Nice try," Jeremy said, then eyed the restraint with an expectant tilt of his head. I glared at him as I closed it.

One day, asshole.

I sat there like a jackass after my direction was complete and Jeremy stood behind the camera.

After a few seconds, he finally said, "Do you need some assistance with putting some wind beneath the sails again?"

"Fuck you!" I snarled.

But *fuck.* Forgot about that.

I had to get hard.

I had to get hard, or *he* would rape Paige.

"Use me," Paige said quietly and my eyes shot down to her. Her eyes were peeking back over her shoulder, then looked over to Jeremy. "Master, can I change my position? T-To kneel?" There was a tightness to her voice, similar to the way she was talking when we woke up with her on his lap. *When he . . .*

I shook my head, wincing at the memory as a cranking noise brought my attention back to the room.

Fuck, I was spacing off, and I needed to keep my shit together. Not now.

Tick, tick, tick . . .

"You have a minute before I get involved," Jeremy said.

Paige scurried up to her knees, and looked back at me again. "Stand up, take off your pants."

I blinked, shaking my head, but followed the order with the same urgency. I moved so fast, it wasn't until I was pantless and standing in front of her that I realized her plan.

She was eye level with my dick. Only the thin layer of my briefs covered me, and her eyes widened.

I guess . . . now that I think about it, she didn't look at it earlier. Not once through that whole "preparation" part.

I could see her lips shaking, and all I could think was . . .

No. Please, no. Not like this.

"C-Can I just—" I shook my head. God, *fuck.* "Can I touch you instead?"

It would work. It had to. And there was some tiny, shriveled up piece of me that was clinging—*fighting*—to *keep* as much as we could.

In accepting this shitty circumstance, I found myself only willing to do things to each other that were absolutely necessary for survival.

And I think I could save this.

She nodded quickly, her eyes flicking toward Jeremy. I saw the lube on the floor and quickly swiped it up, coating my shaking fingers.

With the *ticking* sound behind me, my heart was about to pound through my chest as I shoved my hand in her underwear with zero finesse.

She gasped and I cringed. "S-Sorry," I mumbled, but she shook her head.

"What do you need from me?" she asked, and my eyes sunk into hers.

Just you. Just the promise that you won't hate me.

She seemed to understand and some part of me settled at the feeling of *her* in my hand again, cupping her heat as my fingers started to slide through her slit.

With her in a high kneel, I kneeled in front of her and started moving my fingers.

Her wrists stayed on the arm of the couch as her forehead fell to the crook of my neck, trying to give me *something* to kickstart my erection.

Her.

And it worked. *Slowly.* Her smell, the feel of her warmth on my fingers—my cock stirred as she breathed into my neck. "That feels so good," she whispered and my dick twitched.

Buffy fucking bless. My fucking girl. And for once, I was grateful for my unstoppable attraction to her. That it was managing to override this horrific bullshit.

And though she wasn't wet, there was a breathiness to her voice that made me think what she said wasn't a total lie.

I hoped. I made her feel good before. Maybe I could again.

I tried to focus on small ugly victories. I felt less worried about Jeremy having to "take over" but I don't think I was ever *actually concerned* about that.

I knew I could have sex with Paige. *Of course* I could. *She's the girl of my dreams* and in my mind, we'd done it thousands of times already.

But that's just it. *Those* were all in my mind. A fantasy. *For us.*

Neither one of us had actually had sex, and we were going to do it now in the most indecent of ways.

"Are you hard, Linc?" Jeremy asked.

His voice didn't help and my teeth clenched just as the timer went off.

My movement halted as I saw him with the handheld camera. He walked over to us, and said, "You can keep touching her while I explain the scene."

PAIGE

It didn't matter how many times the Man told us what we were doing. How many times we practiced the small bit of shitty *"dialogue."*

We were both shaking, shivering balls of nerves as Linc got to his mark. He was entering the scene to me already chained and naked. Panties on. *To start.*

"We can play with any appropriate *creative choices,"* the Man had said, but the general synopsis was, *"A boy on the verge of manhood, finds his best friend's sister down in their basement, chained—as one always is—and decides to play with her, take her by force."*

This was likely the numbness I was harvesting, but I found myself thinking . . . *for something that seemed to be catered to some creep's specific tastes, the storyline seemed pretty flat.*

Definitely the numbness, I thought again.

My fists balled, clinking the chains around the pole as my hands moved slightly, thinking about my one and only concern at the moment.

Linc.

Not that I was any better off, but everything I had to do was a *reaction* to him.

And doing this—no matter how many times I told Linc it was okay—*this* was going to destroy him.

I saw it in his eyes when he left me on the couch to stand out of frame

*Our silent promise passed between our gazes—*till the end.

We just have to make it till the fucking end.

But I'd be lying if I said I wasn't worried about the execution. *Him holding me down while I cry and fight him off.*

It's going to destroy him, the thought gnawed through my brain again, as the Man said. "Standby."

My dialogue was all reactive—an assortment of *"Nos"* and *"Please, don'ts"*—a real *"use your imagination"* approach.

Part of me wondered if the Man was being *deliberately* vague, just to be a dick about the fact that once—*another fucking lifetime ago*—I'd told him I liked how specific his directing style was.

But I lay as naked as I had been all night and took a breath. *I have to try and lead the scene as much as I can. For Linc.* He wasn't given much *"dialogue"* either, but he had the harder job to do.

We're just playing a sick and twisted version of make-believe, I told myself—same thing as I told him earlier. *We just have to pretend.*

I closed my eyes, just as the Man said, "Action" and from behind my closed eyelids, the tears already started and my mind searched for him.

I love you. We'll get through this.

Linc sighed, but there was no way to know if it was a telekinetic response, or the defeated horror of starting this.

I heard his steps come closer, and my muscles tensed. I could *feel* him looking at me.

"Pip," I imagined him saying in my mind, with one of his heart-throb smiles, but out loud, he said, "Well, well . . . someone left you all ready for me."

Linc's deep hoarse voice sounded like he'd aged twenty years and I cringed. The tone had more control than I anticipated, and I wondered if he was trying to lean into the role.

He should. It's the only way we'll get through this, I reminded myself. If this was just a . . . game. *We are playing a game.*

I stirred as Linc got closer—*as directed*—wiggling my ass a bit—I could only pray the movement helped Linc keep his ever-fleeting hard-on.

But suddenly there was no movement.

I was supposed to keep my eyes closed until he touched my face. My eyebrows flinched, and just as I was about to open my eyes, I heard . . .

Tick, tick, tick . . .

I heard feet shuffle and the steps resumed. I felt him getting closer, his looming height over me just as I felt a knuckle brush over my cheek.

I opened my eyes and widened them—trying to meet him like any other scene partner—trying to find the urge to be scared of Linc, towering over me—but I couldn't . . . I *couldn't.*

Ten years without an ounce of stage fright—and it hits me now?!

"Cut," I heard the Man say with a grunt. "I have given you guys more than enough chances. This is the final warning. Get the shot, or Linc and I will switch. *Or* I can call for assistance and Linc and I will shoot it together."

Linc's glare was deep and dark. I thought he might manifest something—*conjure* a phoenix to rise up from the floor, or a meteor to crash in this very spot.

"Take it from where you touch her face," the Man said, monotone and digging into every ache in my body.

Linc turned back toward me. His shoulders dropped a bit, the hard lines of his face softened as his eyes drifted the length of my body again.

There was something foreboding in his stare, something I didn't understand—maybe he didn't either. But he sighed and took the step or two so he was directly over me.

"Close your eyes, Pip. As much as you can, okay?"

I nodded, but I had no intention of leaving him alone through this. Not if I could help it.

But since the scene started with me *asleep*, with one more lingering stare up at my best friend, I held the reassurance that it was him above me as I closed my eyes.

"Action," the Man said.

I *woke up*, startled, gasping, pretending to notice the chains. "What's happening?" I glanced down, acting like it was the first time I was noticing my nudity, and I yelped, squirming.

The familiar calloused pads of Linc's fingers met my back and traveled down. The tickle in my spine followed the path of his hand.

My next line, "No! No."

Linc's touch fueled my fight for a second, and I started writhing. Screaming and crying. It was my own battle cry. I hoped he could feel it. *I'm unleashing for us, Linc.*

For *us*.

His limbs shook as he barely used any strength to fight against me, so I bucked and flailed harder.

I needed to give him something to react to.

I had to help him. He stood to move, and I kicked out my legs behind me. Not hard, but just enough to make him stumble back a foot or two.

My eyes shot back to his.

We'd wrestled before—it was always playing, but we'd done

it. Our eyes connected and for a breeze of a moment, we reminded each other.

I love you.

It only lasted a second before Linc lunged toward me.

"Spank her." The direction came out calm, cool. "Spank her and then pull the panties off."

I pulled on my restraints to lift my ass, doing whatever I could to help make the scene *look* more violent than it was. In addition to that, I wanted to do anything I could to possibly help Linc hold an erection long enough to do this.

A hand connected with my ass and I yelped, doing my best to ignore the tingle that came with the contact.

So confusing. I'm so tired.

Just get through this.

Hesitant, trembling fingers met the waist of my panties, pulling them down my legs.

Slowly, gently.

"I need more, Paige. You look a little too peaceful right now." The Man was barely visible behind the bright lights he'd added to combat the shadows in the shot.

There was something ironic about that, but my fatigue and endless fight to survive this kept me from following the thought.

I used the simmering rage that had been building inside me to tighten my muscles and squirm beneath Linc. "No, no! Please, don't do this. Please."

Unbelievable. Terrible.

I was worried about Linc's ability to commit to the moment, but at least he was delivering on the stupid bits of dialogue. I sounded as believable as someone rustling a wrapper through a phone receiver.

The Man appeared through the bright mass with the handheld, and I averted my gaze away from him—the camera—luckily, that's what I should have been doing while he was filming.

"Lose your shirt, Linc. Start fingering her, and give us the next line," the Man said, from behind the camera.

And the specificity of his directorial style returns . . .

I mean, *fuck.* He was practically *feeding* us the blocking and dialogue, frame-by-frame—with a handheld.

Was he . . . trying to make this look *natural?*

The thought turned my stomach, but I rejected it. There was no amount of editing this guy could do that would make this look like anything other than what it was.

Linc's warm goopy fingers found my entrance and I shifted my weight to make it look like my arms were pulling, but I intentionally pushed my hips back on his fingers, expelling a breathy gasp from me.

"No," I whimpered weakly, but it sounded like . . . *not no.* I was, again, giving the worst performance of my life. Sucking my lips into my mouth, I shook my head.

"The line, Linc," the Man said over us and I squirmed again, trying to move myself against Linc's hand in a sneaky way when suddenly . . .

Tick, tick, tick . . .

Linc's fingers moved with new life, pushing into me and stroking me the way he had earlier. My toes curled. *Fuck, I really am sick.*

Trying to understand the multiple bouts of arousal this whole event had included would be something I had to deal with one day, but today wouldn't be it.

Today, I had to lean into whatever made *this* more bearable. And his touch made it more bearable when he leaned over my ear and grit through his teeth. "Such a pretty little whore. You've been teasing me for years, and someone finally left you here, helpless and waiting."

The Man ordered him to spank me again and he did, followed by, "Now take yourself out. Keep touching her."

It isn't us. It isn't him. This isn't real.

I pretended to fight against Linc but his movement between my legs somehow managed to keep a tenderness. The digits never let me forget he loved me. That he cherished my body. And I could feel his heartbreak pushing inside of me every time his fingers thrusted.

It's okay, it's okay, it's—

"Stroke yourself. Next line," the Man said.

My eyes slammed shut as the sounds of the room started to feel . . . *drippy* despite the fact there was no running water.

Tears streamed nonstop down my face as I weakly tried to fight against Linc, crying harder when it felt too difficult to do that.

I wasn't acting. I wasn't pretending.

I was *failing.*

I was *crying.*

But not because Linc was touching me.

That was my only peace.

It was everything around his touch that was crushing my soul. Linc leaned over and kissed my tears before I heard the voice I'd come to dread saying, "Lick them."

Lick my fucking tears.

Linc did it, but then he rubbed his nose on my cheek after. A silent unnecessary apology.

I love you.

I noticed his other hand moving up and down on himself, trying to summon some blood flow to his cock.

Undoubtedly trying to hurry this along.

I wanted that too.

I wanted this to be over.

"Fight, Paige," the Man said. "He's about to take you, and you were left here defenseless. Give it to me."

Fuck you! Fuck you, fuck you, fuck you!

I moved. But not for him. I fought like it could somehow claw us out of this room. Dig us out from six feet under ground. I fought for *Linc*, who was pumping his fingers in and out of me, jerking himself to complete a despicable demand.

We'll take it back, I reminded myself again.

Linc coated my pussy with lube, and a peek behind me revealed he'd used it on himself too.

But my eyes bulged as I finally saw . . . *him.*

I hadn't looked at his cock the whole night, and for a moment— *a split second* of not paying attention—I broke my own rule.

His erection was long and thick, impressive by any means, and I instantly wished I could replace his hand with mine. *Touch him like he's touching me.*

His eyes were unwaveringly on my face as he stroked himself, touched me, and everything slowed for just a second. An *actualizing* moment that made my blood run cold.

We are about to have sex. A fact I'd been aware of for a while now, but it was actually sinking in. Linc was about to be inside me.

We were having sex for the first time. On camera. In front of our teacher. To be delivered to a client—or so the Man said—*but who the fuck knows.*

Like music with no melody. It's all just . . . noise.

Linc's hand moved harder, bringing me back to now, scissoring his fingers and stretching me—*prepping me*—and my body adjusted to the small ache.

He was being gentle, and I was trying to compensate by working my hips against him—to *look* like I was struggling.

Sinking back into the scene—I felt further away as I blinked through my wet and heavy lashes. The weight on the cushions behind me dipped, and I glanced back at Linc again, seeing his legs shake as he positioned himself between my legs.

His dark hazel eyes were shattered. A forest burnt to ash. His messy dark hair was pushed and shoved in every direction. It would take *movie fucking magic* to edit that out.

I was sure I looked destroyed too, but at least that fit with the role I was playing.

I tried to give Linc one of our silent messages—*it's okay, as long as it's you, till the end*—but they all swirled away down the emotional drain between our gazes.

The Man said, "You look good, Linc. Flex your muscles, a bit."

Fucking pig.

Tune it out.

Linc's eyes glared sideways, not directly at the Man since he was filming us, and we needed to hurry this the fuck along.

But the far-off floatiness of my mind had me saying, "You *do* look good."

Linc's gaze shot back to mine and locked.

A small recharge lit in his eyes, resuscitating mine.

Listen to me. Not him.

A glint pinged in the corner of his gaze with my silent message and his chin dipped.

"All right, turn up the fight, Paige. Once she starts, Linc, that's your cue."

Fucked. So fucked.

Linc's growl from behind me revved up my heart. I armored my chest and put everything I had into this last bit. Sprinting toward a fiery-gate finish line—or maybe diving off the plank.

I suddenly felt his hands gripping my hips from behind and hauling them up, shoving my face toward the corner of the back of the cushion.

It all happened so fast and jaggedly, I couldn't quite catch up. But the confusion only lasted a second before Linc's head fell just beside my temple, burying his face between mine and the back of the couch, as a sharp sob hit my ear.

Linc. No.

I twisted my chin and shoved my face against his instantly wet cheek. Our tears mixed as our faces pressed in the small hidden cave of our own creation.

I don't think I'd ever seen him cry before. Not when his dad left, not when he busted up his chin skateboarding. The only time I thought I'd seen him get close was the time Maisie wandered off to their neighbor's house and he thought he'd lost her.

But just like he'd always been—*stoic, dependable, steady*—he quickly reeled the emotion back, kissing my jaw with trembling lips before he sat back up. Still, he kept his fingers in my hair, keeping my head down.

My heart stuttered as my mind found his thought path and figured out what he was doing. *Maybe I had dipped down to my safe, sacred place and he told me,* but I *felt* what he was doing. And my tears streamed harder at the silent intent. It wouldn't last, but I understood.

He was trying to position me so that when he *first* entered me, when he pushed inside—*we* were keeping whatever came with it.

He was suddenly over me again and his ragged, choked sobs pushed into my ear. "I love you, Paige. I'm sorry."

"Wipe the tears, Linc. Go," the Man directed and my teeth clenched.

Nothing made me more furious. Not even when I woke up with his fucking dick in my mouth.

He was forcing Linc to take my virginity. He was forcing me to take Linc's. It was unspeakable conditions, and Linc's emotions deserved some fucking space.

But the thought dampened immediately. Why I expected any sort of compassion from this guy was beyond me. But it made me feel a little bit better to know that while this room was shifting things within me, darkening my soul in irreversible ways, at least there was still a tenderness, a warmth between Linc and me.

A complete contrast to the Man. In my mind, I'd killed him in multiple violent ways, all at once. Resurrected him, and then hung him by his balls, burning him alive from some perverted mount.

Linc's growl tore through me, rushing me back to reality as his fingers bruised my hips, and then I felt him . . . *everywhere.*

Anywhere he didn't claim inside me before, was fully inhabited when his hot, slippery length slowly pushed into me. The slow pressure forced a long, breathy whine to escape, but I pushed my face into the cushion, knowing that's what he wanted.

I wanted his eyes, but I stayed put.

We'll take it back.

The sharp pain, the infamous tear—it didn't hurt.

It *howled.*

The sensation, the fullness, *him*—the feeling whooshed through me like a wolf's song to the moon. The feeling was so intense, I gasped into the fabric darkness. "Ohh . . ."

Linc groaned a long, drawn out "Fuuck," his fingers digging, and I welcomed the bite as I hid another moan.

He'd fingered me long enough and used enough lube that the pain was minimal. The feeling of him inside me, coupled with the solitude of the cushion was enough to forget for just a second this moment wasn't ours.

But I need his eyes. I twisted my chin to look back at him, his broken stare watching me, *"taking me by force"*—*forced* himself.

But he only kept the contact for a second before he pushed my face back into the cushion.

And I knew it was to hide me. Doing anything he could to make this less horrible. I knew that. *But it still hurt.*

The feeling of his hand behind my head, pushing down, pushing into me.

He confirmed my theory, though, when he leaned down over me, whispering, "Stay down," continuing to thrust.

"Stay in character, Linc," the Man barked, then added, "Another spank. Then give us the line," and Linc's movements halted, his grip on my hips tightening as he just stilled inside me.

I could feel him softening. I could feel it in his fingers too—his fight was fleeing.

I wiggled my hips a bit and it rattled my chains. The ache in my wrists was just like the rest of this night—they hurt, but after enough time, it was all just one massive pain. One I was sure would stay with me forever.

With us.

I turned to meet his eyes again. I loved him for trying to help hide me, but the damage had been done. And he deserved connection too.

I hoped he felt it inside me. I squeezed the weak muscles of my inner walls, tightening around his cock. He hissed, "Fuck," then thrusted instinctively, but I nodded.

Yes. Feel me, Linc.

No one will ever see that, I found myself thinking. *Just like his fingers inside me.* He thrust in and out of me slowly, reverently, and I felt a tingle deep down.

In *our* space.

I moved with him, but jerked my arms and shook my head, trying to make it look like I was fighting.

But I wasn't. I was hiding. With him inside me.

It's you and me, Linc.

Till the end.

LINC

Every thrust felt like nirvana *and* like I was falling deeper and deeper into an endless grave.

Jeremy's orders had become white noise in the room. *"Spank her. Now the line."*

And like the twisted circus monkey this night had forced me to become, I did.

Slap. "That's it. Take it you filthy fucking tease."

"No, again. Harder. Rougher."

I cringed, but then she did that thing again—where she pulsed around me, and *God-fucking-damnit.*

A desperate, hoarse groan pushed past my lips with her silent permission to follow the direction, but my hips moved harder at her pull, and the friction decimated me while simultaneously sending me to the fucking stars.

"Oh, *fuck*—" I grunted. "Fuck, Pip."

"Stay in character, Linc. Last warning."

My eyes slammed shut, bottling all of my anger and keeping it sealed. It would age well. It'd carry the bitter taste of this room, the dizzying smell of this act, and the rage of my bleeding fucking heart.

I did it again, spanking her hard enough that she yelped and my chest flinched, but I grit out. "That's it. Take it, you filthy fucking tease."

"Lift her up a bit. Make sure her face catches the light."

Good fucking Christ. I needed this to end.

Not because she didn't feel good.

She felt fucking incredible. Her tight warmth pulled me in and my cock thrusted deeper inside.

She felt like every bit of beauty I always thought she would.

I lifted her up, and Jeremy said, "Grab her tits. And Paige, I need more noise, still fighting but give me some hot whiney sounds."

Fuck me, this is so fucking terrible.

But we'd found a rhythm where our bodies connected. The back of her hips ground into me, and I used the opportunity to fist some of her knotted blond hair in my hand, and twist her face toward me, still thrusting.

Her blue eyes were hooded, but there was a flickering sparkle in the corner as our gazes collided. Pulling her lips into her mouth, she released some breathy whimpers. Mewls. A heavy moan as I angled my hips to move deeper.

And the sounds were . . . *definitely hot.* Each one moved my hips faster. Harder. Her eyebrows flinched, and I immediately stopped.

"No, stay in it," I heard Jeremy say. "Keep going, Paige. That's very good. Linc, when she really starts to get going, I want you to shove her panties in her mouth and finish."

A gasp hollowed my chest—nearly knocking the wind out of me. Just like everything else about this shitshow, my brain felt like it was in a crazy long race of trying to catch up to any sort of rational thought.

I suddenly noticed my mouth was hanging open as the words, "I'm not coming inside her," finally breached my lips, *breaking character,* but I didn't give a shit. Never claimed to be an actor, and never wanted to be.

"Yes, you will. Don't forget, you have an understudy who is ready to go." He paused to look down at the camera, rubbing his dick over his jeans before he looked back up at me. "You really should do more in front of the camera."

My mind took off like a broken sprinkler, misfiring and sputtering in every direction.

Accepting the fact this guy wasn't who I thought he was, was difficult enough—but the creepy display of attraction while I was doing . . . *this* was bizarre by the most perverse proportions.

"It's okay," Paige said quietly, returning me to the present, and my eyes widened, just before she said, "I trust you."

Remembering the newest demand, my stomach rolled, but strangely, my mouth actually ticked in the corner like it tried to smile.

The feelings *felt* contradictory, but they happened.

I always hoped she knew I had never been with anyone else. I thought it was clear in the way I only ever had eyes for her, but this *proved* she knew it.

And I knew she'd never been with anyone either, but . . .

She could get pregnant.

I shook my head, and decided to take hold of her resolve.

We'll deal with it if we have to.

We just have to get out of here.

When she saw the idea settle, she closed her eyes for a second before her chest lifted. I took the opportunity to squeeze her tits. It was part of the direction, and maybe it would help with her noises.

My instincts proved to be right when she moaned loudly, shoving her face into my neck as she worked her hips back and against me. "*Mmm*," she moaned, trailing the tip of her nose along my jaw.

I moaned too, squeezing her and pinching her nipples, kissing her cheek, her tears—*I licked them*—but because *I* wanted to this time.

I swear, I'd take all of her sadness if I could.

"Say, 'you like that,' Linc."

My fingers tightened in Paige's hair and I rubbed my nose with hers, then delivered the line and her breathy whimper brushed my cheek.

I couldn't tell if she was acting like it felt good, or if it actually felt good.

I wanted to reach around her torso and rub my thumb along her clit like before. I wanted to watch her mouth drop and her breath get snatched by a feeling *I* gave her.

But I didn't. *This wasn't our moment.*

Jeremy gave me more filth to say.

Take it.

That's right.

Look at you.

All it took was chaining you up and taking you myself.

Paige had worked herself into a screaming, moaning mess—and the physical reaction it was giving me was drawing some sharp, confusing lines in my mind.

"Panties, Linc," Jeremy said, and his voice sounded . . . *salacious.* It disturbed me to no end that this seemed to be turning him on.

But we are almost there.

Almost through the worst of it.

Still inside her, I bent down and grabbed the underwear, but emotion clogged my throat for an extra half-second.

Deflating everything.

My mind shuffled through all the times she might have been wearing these. Innocent times.

Watching a movie, a hike at the creek, singing in the passenger's seat of her car with her hand on my knee.

Tears bit the back of my eyes the longer I stared at the fabric clutched in my hand until I felt *her.* Again.

The internal squeeze that helped not only bring me back, but also revived my ever-precarious hard-on.

Every bit of my arousal right now was only because of her. She was fueling it, driving it—and if I was capable of blasting off, it would only be because she lit the fuse.

I reminded myself of that as she screamed again and I stuffed the panties in her mouth, muffling her.

"Bring it home, Linc. Now."

Paige whimpered, cried—all muffled from the fabric stuffed in her mouth. She writhed and squirmed but pushed back into me, deepening my cock inside her and I moaned again. My front draped over her back, our bare, slick, skin—covered in dirt, sweat, and a lifetime of tears.

I held her tightly to me as the euphoria built. She met me thrust for thrust, clinking her chains around the pole.

It's almost over.

I burrowed my face in the back of her hair and moved my hips harder, deeper—I couldn't fucking see straight. All I could do was pound toward the end point.

The lemon smell of her hair filled me as she screamed and cried, fighting against me.

But she has to. We have to.

Her tight, wet, warmth squeezed around me as her muffled screams filled the room. Confusion caught the wave of my orgasm, but arousal overpowered it and my dick shot off like a rocket.

A guttural roar exploded past my mouth.

Fuck, so good. So, so, so fucking *good.*

I'm coming. She was screaming and crying, trying to get away and I was *fucking coming.*

Hard. So hard.

What the—?

I came for what felt like a minute straight, my hips unable to stop, but tears followed. *Sobs.* I was crying into Paige's hair and spilling inside her at the same time.

And what a humiliating sight that must have been.

But I couldn't stop. The emotion erupted like a volcano—into her, on top of her. I sucked my lips into my mouth and twisted my face away from the camera, praying I didn't just blow it.

God, please, no. I can't. I'm barely fucking breathing.

"Linc, baby," I heard Paige's barely audible, broken voice beneath me. She must have gotten rid of the underwear—I barely shoved them in her mouth.

I heard Jeremy's throat clear, and a static-like feeling itched up my spine. I couldn't hear anything past the blood rushing between my ears.

"I think I can work with this," he said, the sound still garbled, but I was only half-listening anyway. "You guys should get some rest."

I didn't say anything to him as I heard him walk away. I wanted to get out of here, but I couldn't fucking move. And more than anything, the promise of him leaving sounded too good right now.

To be honest, I felt a second away from losing consciousness. *Adrenaline crash.*

I heard him put something down next to us. My eyes slid to the floor to see water bottles.

His steps got further away, and while I wanted answers, I couldn't pull out of Paige yet. I couldn't fucking move.

Shock, maybe.

Keeping myself huddled over her, my teary eyes blinked down to see her face pressed into the cushion, her body shaking with silent sobs.

I did that. I made her cry.

I shook my head. No. *It was okay.*

It was okay, it was just . . . a lot.

Too much. But it's over.

I thought so, anyway. *God,* I hoped so.

He said as long as we delivered the film, he'd let us go.

Just as I heard the beeps to the door, my gaze shot up and I inhaled sharply when I saw Jeremy looking back at me.

I could only imagine the wreckage of my expression, but I tightened everything, including my hold around Paige. My teeth ground and I sharpened my eyes, giving him a message.

One day, motherfucker.

I didn't have a specific threat, just that if this was it—if this whole thing was over and he got what he wanted. If he let us go, I'd be back for him.

But I didn't say any of it out loud. I didn't need him to retaliate. I needed to be more prepared—but something told me he got the message.

My muscles tensed and a chill swept down my spine at his expression across the room. I couldn't be sure, but it looked like he was meeting my silent threat with his own wordless promise—one that felt like it was telling me, *This isn't over.*

EPILOGUE
PAIGE

Wiping my eyes does nothing. The tears are endless.

Six hours, three minutes, and twelve seconds of footage.

It seemed longer while we were there, I remember now, and yet, when Ellis called and told us the video was six hours long—I couldn't believe it. Only the last half hour was spent filming the eleven-minute *edited* film I've held onto for seven years.

It's amazingly tragic what your mind is capable of blocking out after *years* of shoving it down.

I wanted to watch this because I knew it would prove Linc's innocence, but . . . it showed me *I* forgot a lot too. I forgot *so* much. I can't be sure if it happened quickly or slowly, but clearly I forgot how long it went on, and I can't remember anything past where the footage ended.

Just him, holding me.

A shiver runs down my spine as the footage continues to play through my mind. I forgot about the glaringly obvious attraction the Man had for Linc.

I forgot about the deep shame spiral I fell into multiple times after—trolling the internet for forums of people who had climaxed during an assault.

Thanks to a counselor at the free clinic, I learned it actually happens more than people think. It's just not information survivors are exactly eager to share so the statistics aren't very reliable.

Not that I ever believed Linc assaulted me—but the footage made it all the more obvious that absolutely nothing about what happened to *us* was consensual.

The only thing I always remembered was that Linc didn't actually hurt me.

But the hollow depravity of that room—*the hours of degradation*—had all settled into a gray mass in my brain.

Even now, staring at the blank laptop screen, neither one of us are moving. The footage ended minutes ago, I think, and I feel *stuck* in that mass.

We've been sitting, hand-in-hand since the four-hour mark. But I haven't been able to look at him.

Not since the part of the footage where I broke the cameras.

It was the first and only thing we skipped through a bit, but otherwise, we watched. I followed his lead. It was almost like he was afraid to stop it. Like he only had the strength to start it once.

Or maybe I'm projecting my own shit, but that's why *I* didn't stop it.

Linc's stillness next to me keeps me from looking at him. The rage is pulsing off of him in palpable, heavy waves.

The last time I peeked over at him—a few hours ago—he barely looked like he was breathing. Almost like he didn't recognize what we were watching at all.

But even that emotion feels . . . *stale,* so I decide to stay quiet. Give us each some time to process everything.

For years, all I had was an eleven-minute movie *I knew* was curated. Watching this now, I'm pretty sure the Man even took audio clips from the raw footage at certain parts to dub over us.

But with no witnesses and *no fucking clue* where Linc went, I was too scared to look for the Man without him.

The most heartbreaking thing of all, though, is somewhere in all of that time, I forgot how tenderly Linc looked at me through it all. How much affection he *tried* to show me inside that barbed-wire situation.

And Buffy bless, what a difference remembering that *would have made to me seven years ago.*

Somehow, in his absence, I'd forgotten all of that and the event was steamrolled by the disgust that passed across his face.

Watching the footage—*watching what actually happened—*allowed me to see the disgust was with himself. *And the Man.*

It makes me want to tell him, "I went to Chicago."

Ope. So, I do, I guess.

Linc doesn't say anything, but that doesn't surprise me. After a second, I clear my throat. "After you left, I was a mess . . . I still used to go to your house. Watch Maisie."

His hand tightens in mine, shaking, but I keep my eyes on the comforter, clean and white, dotting with wet spots from my tears. My lips shake, but I continue, "She told me she talked to you one day. That you were living near *Wiggly* Stadium in Chicago. So, I went. Ready to kill you."

I huff a breath but it can't quite find any humor. I really did have every intention of showing up and kicking his ass for leaving me.

I was so, so mad at him.

I swallow, pushing forward. "Even though I thought you left because of me, I went—I took a bus, and I shelter-hopped for two weeks. Walking everywhere—showing anyone and everyone your picture—asking if they'd seen you . . ."

I don't need to finish the story.

Clearly, I never found him.

But after watching this, I just need him to know I looked for him. I *never* blamed him. I didn't want to stop looking for him at all, but Gram's health took a turn . . .

When he still doesn't say anything, I ask, "Were you ever in Chicago?"

His pressure in my hand has been tight and steady for a while, but suddenly his quietness no longer feels like processing.

It feels like . . . the ring in your head from blunt force.

It's that thought that finally pulls my eyes over to him, gasping when I see that his pupils are blown. His eyes nearly look black.

"Linc?" His name comes out as a gasp, but I'm suddenly terrified.

While there is plenty to be disturbed about after watching that, *I* mostly feel relieved. This *proves* Linc didn't actually assault me. Maybe we can go to the police now.

But he looks . . . murderous. Unhinged.

"Linc," I say again, my heart picking up speed.

His eyes snap to mine for only a second and I choke on my breath. It's all it takes for me to see . . . he's already gone.

Lights out.

Before I can even exhale, he's standing and plowing toward the bedroom door.

"Hey, no—wait!" I call after him, but he's already popped the door open and halfway down the hall by the time my shaking knees make it to the doorway.

I start after him, but he's already walking down the entryway.

"Ellis!" I call out, then hiss when I stub my toe on this *fucking floor* that has craters in it.

Distantly, I hear keys jingling.

No.

"Linc, wait!" I cry out, just as the front door closes.

By the time I catch up, he's already tearing out the driveway.

I run back inside and grab my keys off the counter just as Ellis comes running out. "What happened?"

Still moving toward the door, he follows me. "He left. We just finished. We were right. He was forced to do it. I thought we were just . . . taking a second, but when I looked up, he . . ."

My voice trails off as we reach my Cabrio, Ellis hops in the passenger seat, and we both quickly buckle up as he says, "Did he take his phone?"

I shake my head with a shrug. "I don't know. I think so." I tried to remember if I saw him take it out of his pocket when we got back from Venice.

I zip down the mountain, as Ellis says, "I installed an app on his phone with GPS."

My eyebrows pinch, but I keep my eyes on the winding gravel path. After another moment, I finally ask, "Why?"

My fists tighten on the steering wheel, twisting as I await his response. Another second passes before he sighs. "There were a few times—a few years ago when he would . . . he'd wander off at night, wake up somewhere. It hasn't happened since he first moved in, but he asked me to put the app on his phone just in case."

Jesus. The thought twists in my chest. I've had my own share of strange behavior over the years, but . . . I never did *that.* "Where did you find him?"

"He's heading toward the 101," Ellis says and I get over a lane, ready to make a turn. I glance around to get my bearings. Another moment passes before he says, "The couple times it happened, it wasn't far from the house. On the porch more often than not." I hear him take a breath like he's about to say something, but then he stops. A beat later, he clears his throat. "I watched some of the other tapes. I saw . . . I saw Harris."

I swallow, nodding, unable to do anything but watch the road. I won't feel okay until we get to Linc.

I can't let him disappear again.

Why is he running?

I know this is overwhelming, but . . . I just can't understand what's happening. It still feels like I'm fucking missing something.

Keeping my eyes on the road, my foot steady on the gas, weaving through cars, Ellis speaks again, "Paige, I . . . I need to tell you something,"

My heart rate spikes, my eyes widening by the second just as I slam on the breaks at a red light.

"Shit!" he yells at the same time I yell, "What is it?"

This is *not* the time to test my patience, but the color draining from Ellis's face tells me what he's about to say is difficult. *He's not purposefully withholding,* and I take a breath, trying to calm myself down.

"I didn't tell you everything," he says. "About when Linc and I reconnected."

Yeah, no shit, I think to myself, but I'm impatient enough to *keep* it to myself as he explains, "Desmond got a call five years ago from the cops in Falmouth County—up in Maine. Some neighbors called about a possible trespassing situation."

My eyebrows pinch, but no words surface. I try to give Ellis the time—patience. Swallowing hard, I merge the car onto the freeway when he finally says, "Linc . . . he was at the property. And he was . . ."

I am about to goddamn lose it.

He must feel it, and he finally rushes out with, "*He* was there too. Harris . . . was there too."

Blank. My mind is blank.

Much like the movie we were forced to make—*in that room*—my mind isn't *able* to put it all together, despite everything right in front of me.

Like I'm tossing puzzle pieces as if they're confetti.

How? Why?!

My mind feels like it's being sucked through a tunnel as we fly down the highway, and my throat swells.

"Look," Ellis says quickly. "I don't *know* anything. Linc has been adamant that Harris was . . . helping him through a rough time. That I was gone, you guys had broken up, and he leaned on Harris. But he . . . " His voice breaks, then croaks, "*God*, Paige, he could barely fucking talk when I first saw him. And after those videos? Seeing what that fucker did—"

"Stop!" I practically scream, cutting him off, but if he keeps talking I'm going to drive us off the bridge we're crossing over.

My eyes blink in measured beats as my foot instinctively presses harder on the gas. Outwardly, I don't react at all—other than the stone-like expression I've had since Ellis's reveal. All of the emotion is stuck—*clogged* in my eyes, my brain, my *fucking* heart—*I just need to get to him.*

I need to get to him now more than ever.

Because suddenly, I *know*. How I hadn't even considered it before shows how much I really did suppress that night. Those six hours.

But everything I thought I knew about the fucked up workings of the world—every inch of skin I thought I'd grown to protect myself flays and blows away like feathers in the wind. *It burns.*

Because like a proper horror show, the finale is the most heart-wrenching part.

My eyes fill, and I try to blink away the tears, but they're furious and streaming—they can't be stopped.

"Rage. Rage against the dying of the light."

I've never felt so close to blowing away, but *I hear her.* Rallying my spirit. Holding me up. I'm thankful to have Ellis, but I need *her* right now. I need *Linc* right now.

Because despite Ellis's disclaimer about whatever bullshit Linc has told him. I can also see that he knows better. Anything we told ourselves would be a denial of the truth.

The truth was . . .

Linc didn't leave me.

Linc didn't *leave*.

The Man fucking kept him.

TO BE CONTINUED . . .

ACKNOWLEDGMENTS

As always, I'll start with my main squeeze, Drew Moyer. I'm always so grateful that while he isn't exactly interested in joining our feral waters in the romance genre, he always gives me love and support through my agonizing writing process—agonizing in a fun way, though, right?

A huge thank you to my beta readers: Jasmine, Anna, Brit, Allie, Amber, and Annica—you ladies signed on to read my longest and most daunting manuscript yet, and I can't thank you enough for your feedback and friendship.

Thank you to Julie, my editor and friend. I'm always so thankful for our brainstorming chats, and the cheese, of course. And a big, momentous thanks to Anto and Jessi. Anto, thank you for designing a cover I absolutely love, along with the chapter headings and some logos (one of which still has yet to be unveiled!) And Jessi, thank you for powering through my layout in the midst of becoming a new mommy! I appreciate you ladies so much.

I also want to thank Brit for being an awesome PA and trying to help me navigate author life. I've loved sharing this process with you, and can't thank you enough for your help.

To the Bookstagram community, I am eternally grateful for the love and support you show for me and my books. Y'all are truly incredible for supporting indie authors the way you do, and I'm not sure I'd be able to publish books if it weren't for you guys.

Till the end, friends!

www.ingramcontent.com/pod-product-compliance
Lightning Source LLC
Chambersburg PA
CBHW020512110726
47899CB00004B/1083